The Mysteries of the Mountain

DR C A BUCKLEY

Award Winning Writer

ISBN: 978-1-965679-55-5 (sc)
ISBN: 978-1-965679-56-2 (e)

Rev. date: 11/19/2024

CONTENTS

CHAPTER 1

The Fallen Man

The Mountain fell. There was uproar in Maheragh, the village at the foot of Patrick's sacred western reek. The news raged through the tiny hamlet that Danny Pat, known as the Mountain, had fallen to his death from the edge of the pilgrim path onto rocks deep below. The tragedy caused consternation in the surrounding countryside where he had been revered. An accident no doubt or something more sinister people speculated. He knew that mountain like the back of his hand, would he have missed his footing on a path he travelled a thousand times to tend his sheep or pray on the mountain top? But he was old maybe he had a seizure or a heart attack others speculated? But surely he was as hardy as a mountain goat and as healthy as a highland snipe and his head injury was so severe it couldn't be caused by a fall? The mining company wanted to mine a gold deposit on the old man's grazing section of the mountainside. He refused to let them on his land. Did they plot this "accident"? Whatever the cause of his death everyone mourned Danny. They remembered him as a servant of the area, getting the post office and the pilgrims' hostel, and organizing effective protests when the council wanted to the pull down the saint's statue at the base of the climb. Many hill folk now demanded retribution for this mountain guardian's murder, if murder it was.

Even as the tragic news filtered out, his son Red Jim was bent with shock and grief by the body. Red, a tall sturdy specimen of mountain manhood like his dad with foxy hair muscular arms and a ruddy complexion, was inconsolable. Bridie his sister, a mature girl with a pleasant once beautiful face and a form going slightly to fat from her sedimentary life as a postmistress, was even more distraught. As they waited for the ambulance crew, she wailed and wrung her hands. Eventually she threw herself on the body and had to be dragged off when the stretcher bearers came to take the corpse away. She was comforted by his other son, Davey, a slight and more effeminate version of Jim, his face also pale with shock. Though he and his father hadn't been close he also felt deeply his father's sudden bloody demise.

The eldest son's sweetheart, Noreen Mackie-O'Donoghue, a handsome young woman with curly auburn hair and charming freckles who owned a section of the mountain pasture further down from Danny Pat's plot, knelt by Jim's side, her arm around his shoulders comforting him: "this is terrible Jim dear, I'm broken hearted for you, your gentle father that everyone loved, what is the world coming to? God help us, how could this have happened? I'm with you in this terrible tragedy Jim dear, if there is anything I can do just tell me, if it would help you I'd gladly take Danny Pat's place down there on rocks". "Noreen darling I'm glad you're with me I..I need you now..need you", Jim answered in a broken voice, "I can't bear seeing him there his head all bloody and beaten.. what will I do? What will I do? "We'll all be lost without your dad", Noreen said, looking at the larger implications of the scene, "he was always a tower of strength for everyone". Just then the parish priest Father Manus arrived to give Danny the last rites and they all moved aside to make way for him.

CHAPTER 2

Jim's Resolution

Father had been on the mountain ministering to the people on the great annual July pilgrimage. He was preparing a homily for a later pilgrimage group as he descended for his lunch. It was to be about all people having a mountain to climb and a high place to reach. He wanted to show that that was part of God's creation and evolutionary plan; man was to evolve to be the eventual divine element in creation. Otherwise why did he create us in his image and gradually recreate us in Christ when we tended to revert to the slime, the regressive way of sinners and unbelievers? The words of the Messiah, father Manus had been playing it on his DVD player, kept echoing in his mind: "get thee up into the high mountain and the glory of the lord will shine upon thee". That's what we needed he thought today too to climb above the lowlands of the soul to the mountain peak of God, represented by Patrick's mountain and example, the glory that was our human evolutionary destiny. He had been thinking of this and the ongoing tragedy of man, due to free will, his constant making of the wrong choices, his falling away from his high place in God's plan, for Genesis is not history but a parable for all time we are all Adam and Eve. As he paused to jot down some of these thoughts, sitting on a rock by the edge of the pilgrim way, for some reason he looked down and saw the broken figure of an actual man who had fallen from the mountain path into the valley abyss at its side. Down there among the rocks a fallen man! It was as if the biblical story had come to life. Goodness gracious, he thought, down there among the rocks a man who is injured gravely maybe. Oh no! Could it be the mountain himself Danny Pat Sugrue, looks like him? Clearly he'd had a terrible fall from a great height, terrible. Tentatively the priest climbed down, watching every step for the valley's side was steep and rocky, to bring Danny the saving sacrament of anointing which he always carried with him. Several times he almost fell himself as he descended to Danny and a small group of his family gathered around him in tears. Now almost in tears too, for Danny had been a great friend of his, father anointed the bloody head with the holy oils and said the prescribed prayers for the dead, this is one way the church had ordained to bring all back to final salvation a reversal of the fall, he thought continuing his earlier train of thought even amid this sordid scene.

After saying the prayers for Danny's noble soul, echoed by his mourning family standing around, the aged priest stood repeating soulful lamentations like a broken gramophone record, the tragic reality of the event was suddenly brought home to him forcefully: "awful tragedy, awful tragedy yes such a good man, awful tragedy yes, such a good soul yes, this is a catastrophe for the village indeed, indeed a great tragedy, a great tragedy for all people of the mountain, of the mountain yes". Slightly doting he'd a habit of rambling on and repeating himself which the people, given his age, had tended to readily forgive. He also at times went off in vague theological tangents, though some said there was method to his madness when he was mad as the poet said.

After the prayers, which had been a consolation to the mourning group around the body they all waited in stunned disbelief for the doctor to come and stretcher paramedics to take Danny Pat's corpse to an ambulance at the mountain's base. It would take him to a hospital mortuary in the nearby town. No vehicle could drive up the rocky mountain path or reach the valley rocks among which he lay. Curious climbers and pilgrims gathered to watch the tragic events unfold. Some offered help but in fact all they could do was stand and stare, for no aspect of the "crime scene", if crime it was, could be interfered with before the authorities arrived.

At length the local guard Pat Joe Murphy and Dr Denis Moriarty the local GP arrived. Nothing could be done for Danny, likely he had been dead for an hour or so, the doctor concluded. No one had seen him sooner for the steep rocky incline where he lay was shielded from sight by mountain scrub. The guard sealed off the site for future investigation. Foul play was possible though he was of the opinion that it was most likely a tragic accident. There would have to be a post mortem of course, the guard noted. Indeed they should identify the cause of this tragedy as quickly as possible lest it sully the reputation of the mountain community which had never before seen a tragic event like this. They would need the evidence of forensic and medical experts before reaching any conclusions as to the cause of Danny Pat's tragic fall and death, the guard asserted.

Finally the paramedics arrived and Jim, Bridie and Davey accompanied the body down the mountain, and to the hospital mortuary in the nearby town. Next day, after the post mortem, it was to be taken to the church to await the funeral mass and burial afterwards, the details of which Jim had arranged with the priest. The sun had gone down over the western shore and shadows were creeping up over the holy hillside by the time Jim left the hospital chapel, prayers for the dead having been recited and a large number of people having shuffled past the remains, murmuring "we're sorry for you trouble" to the family lined up on the seats by the wall. The rosary had been recited by members of the family some in broken voices and wiping away tears as they intoned the consoling mantra prayers.

A day later the body was transferred to the church where an even larger assemblage filed past the coffin and offered their condolences to the family seated together in the front pews. As usual Community solidarity and prayer was the best antidote to the snake poison of evil, thank goodness for the church the priest said for it brought communal spiritual blessing to the diseased and comfort to those mourning him, the old priest said in the homily, but the perpretators of this evil deed must also be brought to justice. Like in the killing of Abel, one of the first fruits of man's fall, the blood of Danny Pat was crying out from the earth for God's justice.

The subsequent funeral procession to the cemetery was a large affair; people came from far and near to mourn and pay their respect to Danny at the graveside. A group of neighbours with various musical instruments struck up two traditional hornpipes, "the snipe among the rushes" and "the sheep among the clover", and they sang

"The Men of the West" before the grave was covered. Danny had been part of that traditional group and had played with them at venues from Miltown-Malbay to Moher. Some of the family was reluctant to leave the site. Bridie could scarcely be dragged away; he's in a better place some said, but she didn't find that much consolation, wailing "yes but I won't have him anymore".

Jim headed home with an aching heart after the repast arranged for the mourners in the nearby Hillside Rest pub had been consumed. There Jim scarcely touched a bite, his heart was too sore. After going in the door of his little apartment in the village, he sat on an old settee for a long time, head bowed. Lilly, Danny's collie bitch, lay by the fireside whining intermittently. Since the death she had been roaming the mountain barking for her master and she was desultory in her eating, growing thin and ever more distraught day by day; she and Danny had been together on the mountain for many years since he got her as pup from a neighbour who bred and trained sheepdogs, dogs like her were as vital to the mountain as pilgrims to its slopes. She had been part of the family when they were growing up, Jim reflected, time after time she rounded up the sheep with them. She was gentler and more human than the mine's thug fixer the Masher O'Leary, the most likely perpetrator of this crime, Jim thought. Who's the brute and who's made in God's image Jim asked himself?

As he spoke soothing words to Lily, stroking her affectionately and thinking God made no mistake in creating this beautiful gentle animal, his mind was racing. The guards are useless he thought, sitting behind desks in the barracks, drinking endless cup of coffee and filing out endless forms to pass the time; I suppose there wasn't much they could do anyway, the case was beyond their local scope. We'll have to do something about this crime ourselves, he concluded after much thought, don't you think so Lily he said? He forgot she was just an animal though to his father and the children she'd never been just an animal. Now she seemed to understand his grief, gazing at him fondly with large soft limpid eyes. The two of us will bear this and fix it together he thought, though we may need some outside help also.

So when he finally came to his senses he also came to a firm resolution. He picked up the phone and called his second cousin Inspector Donnie Deverly of the Dublin police, a famed detective who had retired recently and now specialized in solving private cases. In the time since his father's death Jim's grief had gradually been replaced by rising bitterness and anger. This was no accident he felt in his heart, a fall wouldn't have battered his head so badly; someone did it in malice of forethought. Someone pushed him over the edge into the abyss and hit him again and again as he lay helpless. What a callous crime, what callous fiends are we dealing with? When inspector Deverly finds that person who did this foul deed to my father I'll tear the fiend to pieces with my bare hands, he vowed, God forgive me. At that he broke down again and Lily whined louder, resting her paws on his feet. She won't long survive this he figured. Sure enough she died shortly afterwards; they buried her by the house and put up a tiny wooden cross in her memory.

That night Jim took some time to drift into a painful sleep, he'd a nightmare of a large black panther tearing his dad to pieces. Then the ghost of his beloved mother, who had died ten years previously of cancer, appeared to him, her face full of pain. "You'll see justice done for my beloved Danny won't you Jimmy dear", she said. She held out hands to him from some faraway golden shore of the saintly dead, for a saintly woman she had been, saying prayers with them every night and climbing the mountain with them every July. She had been a gentle mother, baking homemade sultana scones, cooking nourishing stews from vegetables and potatoes grown in their own garden in the little field beside the house, and stewing spring lamb fresh from their hill pasture. She had loved them all and sewed their clothes and sent them off to school with shining faces. Danny had done his best to fill her shoes when she was gone but now he too was wrenched from them leaving a total void in the family's life.

Jim woke up drenched in sweat and cursed the world, even the lord that had allowed her to die and Danny's foul killing to take place that even troubled her in her place of rest. His one consolation was that Danny was now by her side again. But everything was empty and meaningless for their son. All that was left for him it seemed was grief and pain, alleviated only by the prospect of justice being done. He got up and drank a glass of local poteen to help him sleep.

He was about to go to sleep again when he was jerked fully awake by Lilly barking loudly and rushing to the door; she sensed some intruder outside bent on mischief. There was a sudden crash and a shower of splintered glass. When he went to investigate he found the kitchen window had been shattered by a stone with a message wrapped around it, "be wise sell out or suffer a worst fate than your father". This was too much. But far from frightening him into submission it just accentuated the rage in his heart and his determination to resist such intimidation and get those who were doing it. When I find out who is behind this which he suspected had also something to do with his father's death, they are the ones who will suffer, he resolved.

Unable to go back to sleep he decided to go to see Noreen, a little down the valley. She was in bed and when he knocked and came out in a dressing gown with a startled face to open for him. "Jim dear, what brings you out this late, has something happened", "she said, her sheepdog Missy barking by her side at the stranger, and her adopted nephew Paidi in his pyjamas trailing behind her wiping the sleep from his eyes. He was her brother's son. She had adopted the boy when her brother was killed in one of the terrible storms that afflicted the area; previously he had been separated from his wife and had been given the custody of the boy; when he died his ex wife had no interest in claiming the child.

Jim held Noreen close with a flood of tears but he felt better when they sat down to some tea and her homemade scones drenched with butter and blackberry jam. Then he sat down with his head on her lap and she stroked his head tenderly muttering words of comfort while she held Paidi with her other arm and Missy stretched at their feet. It would be a long night for them all.

CHAPTER 3

The Mighty Magnates Gather

A FEW DAYS LATER ON THE OTHER SIDE OF THE VILLAGE A DIFFERENT scenario enfolded. Miles Ramsbottom was entertaining some colleagues from the mining enterprise in his Celtic Tiger mansion by the bay. Many wondered how he got the planning for a house that stuck out like a sore thumb against the beautiful landscape previously dotted only by low traditional houses that fitted into the landscape like a glove on a countryman's calloused hand. Doubtless a few brown envelopes went astray before the construction of Miley's house of the vanities. He was a small spare man, he might have been an austere monk from his appearance, but he was dressed in an expensive well-cut suit and saw himself as a local somebody of note, a champion of industry and progress in a rural backwater of quaint and superstitious natives who climbed the so-called holy mountain every year as their ancestors had done from time immemorial. Trapped in a superstitious time warp they were, he felt. He had no time for that superstitious nonsense himself, one had to move on; the mountain was just a mass of rock and heather to him, it should serve not hinder the community's effort to progress into the 21st century, a century of science and enlightened rationalism that Ireland at last was awakening to, a new era of catching up with the rest of Europe. We have even shelved the neutrality that had kept our little island in peaceful tranquil isolation during the terrible imperial and ideological wars on the continent. Now the Republic will be just like everyone else in our troubled Europe, he thought with satisfaction.

He went to the counter of his spacious sitting room with its plush leather sofas to pour drinks for his distinguished guests. A grand company they were; they might have been a cross-section of the new global magnates that ruled the world through business and industry: Lars Willander a Danish businessman, Sven Haaland a Norwegian mining engineer, Sir Herbert Makepiece Grout an English geologist, a florid American investor, Samuel Lichenberg junior, an Irish secretary, Daniel Joseph Fleming the Forge (for his father had been a blacksmith he had drifted a long way from his roots) and a Scottish mining engineer, Hamesh Mackie McMackey the younger. The group was seated around a table with maps and plans for the future mine laid out in orderly fashion before them. These showed that the deposits of gold on the mountain were extensive and so potentially of enormous value if they could be got at. The big question that remained to be answered was how one could get one's hands on the loot.

"I Just got strange news gentlemen that might be relevant to our project", Miley observed as he dished out cocktails to his colleagues, "it seems Danny Pat Sugrue who owned the land on which our proposed mine is to be situated has just been buried, recently he was found dead on a hillside incline a few hundred yards north of his cottage. It is a great tragedy for all of us and the village of course he was a highly revered member of the community. But I hate to admit it now, one shouldn't speak ill of the dead, I won't really miss him. I worked for him once and it wasn't a pleasant experience. In his traditional mind set there was no room for my ambitious plans for this area; he laughed at me, 'Leave it be Miley little ambitious tycoon business boy, sure we got on fine up to now, we don't need your industries blackening the area, leave it be, leave the mountain in peace for us and the pilgrims who come here. Don't desecrate it with the vile blackening machinery of mindless industrial progress, God save us from all harm'. He couldn't see beyond his nose, the old throwback. But he was a good and noble man just the same, God rest his soul, (Miley crossed himself sententiously though he was not much of a believer really, he mainly believed in himself and the god of industry).

"Naturally we had nothing to do with his demise", he went on, "but it's fortuitous all the same, though we're not out of the woods yet in terms of access to the mine site. His eldest son may be as recalcitrant as he was, these country bumpkins can be very obstinate, don't know where their real future interests lie" he said this with more than a hint of angry frustration. Pride, egotism, anger and greed summed up Miley's usual moods. He couldn't abide any opposition to the progress of modern Ireland and the future industrial prosperity of the west as he saw it. "His other son and daughter are more pliable I think", he went on hopefully, "Red Jim is the one problem, a chip off the old block and just as obstinate an obstacle to much-needed acquisition of mine wealth for the progress of the area into the modern world".

Lars the chubby Danish developer sitting next to Miley spoke up in reply, his English a bit stilted, a worried look on his florid and neatly bearded countenance: "Miley we would be wanting no unpleasantness here from the local population, it would be well to keep everyone on our hands I would be thinking (the others nodded at this). That's the sensible policy I do be thinking. I love Ireland myself and its great landscape and lore, my family often come on holiday to this grand scenic area with its welcoming people and sacred lore. Our own country is lowland low and drably atheistic by comparison. But if this is isn't a clean project best we get out while we can, we have other alternatives such as the uranium deposit in Tanzania, it might cause less flack, and the natives there are more pliable and more easily persuaded, though also a grand and noble people". Sven, the engineer, echoed this sentiment, but more in favour of the mine. He presented a series of charts and prospectives showing how the proposed mine had to and did conform to Irish EU and international environmental laws and it also obeyed the UN's directives on respecting and preserving heritage sites. "Since all norms are going to be followed", he observed "the people should be content, we are not marauders, but if they still have reservations I agree we should shelve the project, there is as you mentioned the mine in Tanzania as an alternative".

Miley winced at even a hint of this latter prospect as he sat at the head of the table. He badly needed this local Irish project, not some foreign pie in which he would have no finger. He needed this development, his array of unfinished house from the disastrous Celtic Tiger recession had left him deep in debt, and now another possible recession loomed with the war in Ukraine and the prospect of galloping inflation, an Ireland possibly on the cusp of another economic downturn, mired in a possible EU recession. We're no longer our own masters he thought and maybe it was inevitable that all the warring European ideological power struggles and economic booms and bursts we avoided during our peaceful period of neutrality were creeping in here now. The last thing he wanted was for the mining project to be shelved. He needed a hedge against the increasing difficult times and he meant to get it by hook or by crook. He wouldn't admit as much to his distinguished colleagues, doyens of global economics with fingers in many different pies internationally the magnates who really ruled the world and a good thing too Miley thought, he was a fan of globalization. But he was worried they would drop this project and flee to greener pastures, the world was their oyster, they would run for cover at the slightest hint of bad media publicity or local organized environmental demonstrations. Carpe Diem was Miley's motto, seize the opportunity. He had his own mountain of ambition to climb and by shrewd business he meant to get to the top using whatever means possible.

It was irrelevant to the others that he Miley was flirting with the disaster of being bankrupt, only his more hidden nefarious business of drug dealing kept him afloat, he wanted to drop that and pursue more legitimate pathways. He was fearful that his nefarious activities might land him in trouble with the law, though he had always been able to fix the local law with some strategic bribes.

"Lars, be assured, there is no need to worry ", he said softly, seeking to allay their fears "I can handle the local part of it, I was born and reared here and know the local set. They can be persuaded, a few brown envelopes here and there will help, all in the quiet of course. We can win with a combination of the carrot and the stick. I've got many projects through that way in the past. Be at ease gentlemen, these country people may be a bit behind the times in their thinking but they know where their bread is buttered in the long run. If they see long-term monetary advantage and employment in this they'll row in with us. The key is the village meeting a few weeks from now, if we set that up to our advantage and create a majority to back us, we'll be Ok. I'll prepare the groundwork". Partially assured the group turned to the project's technicalities.

After they had left for their hotels in Westport and an evening meal, Miley sent for his fixer, Jasper the Masher O'Leary. He was called the masher because he was known for his bullying activities when a boy. He'd force the younger boys to give him some of their pocket money or their school lunches. He was always a thug and now he was Ramsbottom's human rotweiller some would say. He came into Miley back kitchen his face red from climbing down from the pilgrim path in the summer heat. He had grown into a burly man with a broad slightly crooked face, a slight Limp from a fall on the mountain and shifty eyes. He seemed the typical villain of fiction but actually he had mellowed quite a lot in recent times.

"Did you do as I asked at Jim's?" Miley inquired anxiously. "Yes", he said simply with a hint of a grin, "all will be well boss, have no fear, I've fixed everything up for you. I can assure you, boss, that nothing illegal was done, I had no part in any wrongdoing. I revere the Mountain", Miley didn't believe the latter statement, the Masher revered nothing and was revered by no one.

"Jasper, I have a small job for you", Miley said. "I want you to continue to gently scare off some of those environmental idiots coming here to oppose the mine. But no rough stuff. I know that you are always careful in all you do for me, and I'm glad all of our doings is above board, legal and non-violent, make sure it is. Go home and rest, it's been a hard day and I may need you tomorrow to do another little task for me, speak to your local friends or some from further afield and get them to attend the upcoming parish meeting on the mine and vote for it if there is a vote, they should make a majority. I want to leave nothing to chance, but again all must be above board and as inconspicuous as possible, softly softly is our approach".

Miley wanted to talk to him further but they were interrupted by the entrance of Miley's son, Terry. The father was a little angry with his son. He thought the latter was indulging too much in religious and philosophical reflections centred on the mountain and the saint at its top that he revered as a godly local inhabitant still; "sure he's still with us in spirit" Terry would say, "I believe that and the hoards of people who come here know it and are wise".

I'll soon cure him of that, Miley said silently. He'd get him to knuckle down to the more scientific, hard-headed practical and more lucrative processes of the family businesses and the secular European trust of modern Ireland. Religion and quaint customs often got in the way of that, one couldn't live or rise in the world on airy-fairy dreams. Miley was trying to instill in his son a more practical bent, yet it was vain effort, counterproductive. The more he pressed him to be rational and practical, to quit his day-dreaming the more his son seemed to go in the opposite direction; children always do so. Ah, the teenage years and their rebellion! There was one way to deal with that, he reckoned, threaten to cut down his generous allowances; he loved the high life and impressing his female admirers, and spending his father's money freely without promoting his father's enterprises. That would have to change and Miley meant to change it.

It was in this cantankerous mood that the latter went up to bed. There already was Ava his wife, a tall aged beauty of the Cavendish-Bedford family that was once the aristocracy of the area; she had bank-rolled many of Miley's projects, old money. She was of fragile health, extremely neurotic and a hypochondriac. Miley wanted to send her to Switzerland for special treatment he had tried every local mind quack to no avail. Most of the time she managed to get along reasonable well, but occasionally she became difficult to manage. She would be either silent and impossible to reach or ranting and raving; it was another reason he wanted money from the mine, to give her the treatment abroad that he felt she required. People are a mass of contradictions. At the moment she was going through one of her periods of good mental health, many could discern nothing unusual about her behaviour, it was that of a dutiful wife and mother. She said softly, as he undressed and climbed into bed, seeing he was flustered: "Miles is everything all right dear, I heard Terry coming in, he seemed drunk or high as usual, you should be firmer with that boy and get him to straighten himself out, he's the laughing stock of the area as it is, though he is a good boy at heart, just teenage rebellion. I rebuke him but it goes over his head he thinks of me as just his mad sugar mother in many ways and I suppose so I am, he's all I have, he knows I wouldn't have the heart to criticize or harshly correct him, but he might listen to you".

"He might, we'll see. How is your health today dear", he asked worriedly.

"I had a few headaches, and I felt a touch of the flu might be coming on", she said fretfully, "I was feverish and listless all day. I took some of the tranquillizer pills Dr Moriarty gave me. After that I was a little better, don't worry about me I'll be fine as long as the world is fine around me, Louise will look after me. Miley dear I don't know how you put up with me, you are more than I deserve".

"No, Miley said, "you were always above me, I don't know how you still love me after all these years, you're great Ava dear". At this there was the sound of the door opening and Louise coming in. Louise was the little French maid-cum-nurse that they employed to care for Ava, it had been her day off. Immediately Ava was soothed by her presence.

"I have some business to attend to tomorrow but Louise will look after you" Mile said. "And don't worry your head about Terry, I'll talk to him in the morning about his drinking and irregular hours coming in at night, he going around now with a group that I fear do drugs". He knew very well that a major problem with Terry from his early years was the erratic behaviour of his mother. One day she'd over-indulge him another she'd treat him coldly. This left him confused and he preferred his friends to home.

Besides his mother's behavior, Terry thought as he mounted the stairs, he was tired of his father trying to get him to help with the family businesses. His real interests lay elsewhere, in literary, intellectual and spiritual pursuits free of care. He wanted an honest authentic life not his father's hard-headed ruthlessness injurious to the soul, his father's dog eat dog world he thought of as part of a modern globalist rat race in which the Rats were winning; this was not progress for Ireland but return to the savage. One of his favourite songs was that one by the Boomtown Rats with the lines:

"it's a rat trap baby and you've been caught". He intended to put a stop to it all, he'd done too much of his father's dirty work already. He'd do the dirt no more he'd wriggle out of the trap as his great mountain ancestors had done.

CHAPTER 4

Deacon Lofty Goes West

Two weeks later Jerry Lofty of The Cottage fame was driving to his ideal spot, Patrick's mountain. He was going to visit his friend, retired guard Jim Deverly, in the village at its base. The detective inspector had been called in by his cousin Red Jim Sugrue to investigate the circumstances surrounding his father's fall and death. Jim had suspicions that it was not an accident; he wanted those suspicions proved or allayed. Jerry was visiting the area anyway for a holiday, his wife Deirdre was giving a lecture in Galway on the need for a post postmodern departure in today's fraught world, a return to more traditional values such as the mountain represented, man climbing back up to his highest point of being and wisdom, a spiritual focus lost today, despite the progress made in so many other areas in bringing Ireland up to date. Jerry was delighted to go to that holy place for he loved mountains and especially the sacred reek of the west that he was convinced was one of the planet's rarest treasures, he felt it kept sane and holy not just the local people at its base but the whole country and the whole world.

In any case he always felt an urge to climb famous mountains. He climbed the reek every year on the prescribed Sunday in July. Why? He was not sure! Perhaps it was out of a deep unrecognized desire to rise above the mediocre plains of life. The mountain represented for him, a poet and church deacon, the world of the higher person within he felt we needed to develop above all, the vast cosmos of deeper faith and truth that was the soul of humankind and the heart of anyone with any soul at all. He felt that the curse of modern science and materialism was that it was a prison house whose walls and bars shielded us from the greater reality of a depthless cosmos within that needed to be nourished above all, the church's role; the true object of evolution was to bring us to our divine destiny. By neglected this most important truth Jerry thought we're producing superficial beings without soul, T S Eliot's hollow men. Jerry as a similar poet saw Patrick's mountain as a pilgrim way to reach the summit of the heart's desire and the riches at the soul's core, to find the glory impossible to gain in the lowlands of human mediocrity and the relentless getting and spending of the cold soul.

Jerry had always been a seeker after the heights of life in the clouds and many laughed at him as a hopeless romantic and a dreamer but without the dream that is the God within and around us in our grand country we are nothing, he'd reply to the doubters. He always felt he was approaching that peak of truth when he climbed this venerable holy mountain of the west where Patrick had reputedly spent 40 days in prayer and penance for the conversion of the people of Ireland to the true faith as he saw it. That is why Jerry was also a staunch believer, a deacon in his local church. So when the letter came from his friend, the former inspector of police in Dublin, to come and visit him and maybe aid him in the Sugrue case, they had collaborated as you might remember on the Diamond Cottage incident, he jumped at the chance to expand his horizons.

There was also a practical reason for his western pilgrimage. There had been a slight strain his relationship with his wife Deirdre; so they felt a few weeks apart would do them good. In any case Deirdre and their four children had gone to stay in the house of his aged aunt Kate, his old wise mentor from the Lofty homestead of old. She was bed-ridden now, and having lived alone since her husband's death, she needed some care and company. She abhorred the idea of going into a home. Jerry and Deirdre her nearest kin decided to put that off as long as possible, to take the care burden on their own shoulders.

But Kate was presently in respite home for a few weeks and Deirdre was just minding the house. So for the moment Jerry was at a loose end. His holidays were due anyway from the parish where he worked as a deacon, supplementing that income with his writings, so he happily set out on my pilgrimage to the West, for him always a land of his dreams. He had been married ten years and maybe it was the ten year itch that accounted for his partial rift with Deirdre. He wanted to explore new fields, stretch his horizons a little away from placid domesticity, not that he really felt his marriage was a burden. It was not something he ever regretted deep down, she was part of his soul but he felt that a change might do them both good.

He didn't want to be a prig, but he did try, in all humility, to live according to his calling, to strive to be a faithful married man, through thick and thin. When things got difficult he felt one must work hard to restore any love or harmony lost, get back to the first spark, another aspect of keeping alive the man within. A hopeless romantic he had always admired the chivalry code of the ancient knights, where honor and integrity was all. He didn't see why that could not be lived today too, inner honor and integrity and beauty in relationships. To live his life in humble integrity before God and men, to practice an honourable way of life, not because one had to, but because one believed that it was the best road to happiness, and to making a difference by one's short life here on earth.

So he reflected as the car purred westward. At the same time he knew that he was all too human, with the failings that entailed. But he also dared to believe that all could be transcended even today, like Irish ancestors did on the mountain of their greatest aspiration made concrete in the great yearly climb to the sacred summit of Mayo and Ireland and the whole world. It was done by the locals sometimes in bare feet and with a series of holy masses at the peak at eight O'clock. Jerry hoped the visit to the mountain might revive his flagging enthusiasm and beliefs, re-energize the Lofty ideals he'd always espoused enthusiastically.

And indeed when he came to the mist-clad mountain after a long journey from Kerry, he was mesmerized again by the green glory of this heart place, this fountain of peace. It was a fine July day when he saw the vista of that holy mountain stretch up into the beckoning clouds, with its alluring pyramid shape. It's strange how the pyramid shape has always denoted inner holiness and mystery, from Egypt to Ireland, he thought, as he drove on through soft evening mist. I suppose it's because the base is solidly set in the earth but the peak pierces the clouds, like the spires of churches, and towers of other holy temples; it is both earthbound and spiritually free in towering soul aspiration like the best people.

When he got there he saw that the village itself, at the base of the mountain, was a cluster of little quaint houses with a narrow road winding through. At its core was a post office cum grocery store, a pub, and some low traditional houses. But on the periphery more plastic modern town houses and apartments were spreading outwards like a rash. To his perhaps prejudiced over-romantic eye, they were like the new patches on old wine bags of the biblical reference, out of place. As was the estate of finished and large empty houses, and another array of half-finished houses that would probably never see habitation; here was the old Ireland and the ignominious remains of the Celtic Tiger in uneasy juxtaposition.

He stopped at the post office to inquire the way to Jim Sugrue's house, where his friend, the erstwhile Inspector Deverly, was staying and where a room was reserved for Jerry. The lady behind the counter, a fine mature woman, who, he guessed had once been one of the village beauties, greeted him cordially when he inquired, and was genuinely surprised.

"Ah, you'd be Jerry Lofty, I think, the famous Diamond Cottage man himself, God bless us; it's a privilege to have you with us, surely. I'm Jim's sister Bridie, I work here, but the shop is owned by Ava Ramsbottom, wife of the local developer. I surely can direct you to Jim's house for it was there I was born, at the foot of the mountain. Take the first turn right at the end of the village and it's the last house on that narrow road wandering towards the Reek. Welcome, again, and take care, you may not be familiar with our narrow roads; what a surprise indeed! The diamond cottage man, well, you're most welcome, the village will be agog at this new blow in, great, a celebrity among us, you'll be a nine-day wonder surely", she said shaking her head in surprise and delight.

"Thank you Bridie", he replied, "I'm sure the road is no different from the pot-holed ones of Ballymac where I now live, country roads are getting neglected again, I think; I suppose we poor country folk don't count much in the larger Dublin 4 via Brussels scheme of things. Well, thanks very much; I'll be on my way; maybe you could give me a bottle of good malt whiskey for my visiting friend, the ex-inspector of police (for he saw that there was also a little snug at the back, it was a sell-all, from the time when people didn't have cars and relied totally on the local shop for everything from a nail to an anchor).

As he drove on up the narrow road, suddenly he decided, the day was still young and he had started out early, to climb a little bit of the mountain at least. So when he came to the base, a little past Jim's house, he pulled into the new spacious car park, there were some useful new developments here at least. An old trader came up to him selling sticks for the climb, he bought one, though he had a stack of them at home already, the stack of mountain staves the children called them, sometimes using them to play swords or drive cattle alongside the local farmers.

CHAPTER 5

Discord in Hillside Rest

WHILE JERRY WAS PHILOSOPHIZING ON HIS BELOVED MOUNTAIN AND preparing to ascend its slopes, Billy Fleming and his half-sister Kate were doling out frothy pints of beer in the village pub under the pilgrim path; it was an old-style pub with the remnants of a snug, polished wooden benches and an old weathered oak bar. Pictures of local heroes of the war of Independence, and local Mayo GAA footballers past and present decked the walls, especially the ones about when Maheragh won the Galway junior championship. The bar was busy, full of those after descending from the strenuous hill climb and the Hillside Rest had become their immediate Mecca. Large pints of the black stuff were downed with much pleasure and smacking of lips and coffee or tea and ham sandwiches were doled out to the teetotallers by two pretty female students, decked in the black and amber colours of the local team, earning a few bob for the holidays.

Kate oversaw all this. She was a plump jolly woman, with large breasts bursting at the seams of her bodice, a wealth of black curly hair surrounding her broad pleasant face and twinkling eyes that made her very popular. She loved to gossip with the women who came into the bar and flirt gently with the younger men. She would lean out provocatively over the bar so that her opulent breasts were all too apparent. She would then laugh heartedly when they made some irreverent remark. As she'd say good-humorously to her female mates, using the parlance of the day, "if you've got it, flaunt it" and she'd laugh heartedly.

The only one who objected to her good humoured playfulness

was her burly mountain boyfriend Pat the Matt Delahunty; he was called the Matt after his father Matt the mighty mountain man, a beast of a man who could catch and toss a sheep for shearing like it was a child's toy. His son Pat was a similar tall hardy individual with a wealth of curly black hair going bald at the temples and a slightly truculent demeanour, but he had a heart of gold and was involved in every good cause in the area, as well as being a staunch church man, collecting at mass and carrying the canopy at the Eucharistic procession, and setting up drink stations on the way up on the occasion of the main summer mountain climb when untold thousands descended like a swarm of locusts on the tiny hamlet. A simple sheep farmer he owned some grazing on the hillside for sheep and some lower fields for cattle and goats, he sold the goat's milk to patrons in Westport, and made a small amount of delightful goat's cheese for himself and special patrons, notably the pub where its inclusion made the sandwiches popular. His drawback was that he was insanely jealous of Kate. They'd been going steady for years. He felt it was about time she stopped playing the field and settled down as his humble mountain bride and served the usual local role of homely wife and mother. He needed her there for he was lonely in his well-furnished cottage at base of the mountain since the death of his parents. Matt the elder had died when he was hit by a car on his way home from one of his notorious sprees. It broke his wife's heart and she died soon afterwards. Now Pat's house lacked a woman's touch. Though she loved the Matt dearly, Kate baulked at being his old-style doormat slave wife. She was reluctant to leave the excitement of the pub for the more staid life of a quiet sheep-farmer's wife. It didn't suit her happy-go-lucky lifestyle.

By contrast the other part owner of the bar, Billy Fleming, was a more sober, quiet person but as they say still waters run deep; he saw himself as deep thinker which is why he enrolled in the philosophy course at the university. He was a fair-haired blue-eyed boy of medium height with a frank open handsome face and a winning smile that attracted everybody to him, especially the young women who frequented the pub. But at the moment he was going with Molly Deverly, the daughter of the aforementioned retired Dublin superintendent of police. Billy had met Molly at

Galway University where they were both studying literature and philosophy, mainly the latter. He had enrolled in the philosophy course also because he thought of himself as a bit of an agnostic free thinker. He was also a bit of a philanderer underneath his staid outward appearance. Socially Molly was not his only iron in the fire, it was rumoured that he had got a local girl pregnant, and occasionally went to visit and support the resultant twins. People were inclined to overlook Billy's amorous adventure, saying sure the poor innocent boy was led astray, that Houghton girl had two other children out of wedlock by two different local boys; she's a slut, he's not to blame. Maybe Billy was led astray and maybe he wasn't, why should the woman be always blamed? It takes two to tango, the more modern feminists of the village were wont to say.

Billy's favourite philosopher was Nietzsche and he thought with the latter that God was dead, and so all things were allowed. One should put no obstacle before one's needs and desires, live it up was his motto; we only live once and then it's nothingness, no matter what you do in life its all the same in the end, darkness and emptiness so we must make the most of the little time we have in this world, and let nothing stop us fulfilling our desires to the full no matter how dark they are. He had a copy of "Thus Spoke Zarathustra" under the counter that he perused a quiet periods in the pub, since it was summer the university was closed, but he and Terry Ramsbottom were doing papers for and against atheistic philosophy. He was naturally on the atheistic side, he didn't think one should still abide by old morals or outdated religious ways of living, but Terry curiously unlike his father, was a champion of traditional faith and morals.

When he heard that Jerry Lofty was coming to the area, Billy resolved to have some philosophical debates with him, mainly to disprove the value of the rich Irish Christian tradition since Patrick Jerry was such as stickler for; it kept us backward and up in the clouds of airy-fairy theories Billy thought, he followed Dawkins, Harris and Hitchens and their atheistic arguments on the YouTube with relish. Kate frowned on such atheistic libertines and their rabid godless books. Though liberal in relation to women's rights she was at the same time a good committed Catholic and traditionalist at heart and she saw Billy's books and their authors as the serpents in Patrick's sacred mountain garden that must be guarded against with every means possible lest every modern Adam and Eve suffer the same fate as the original duo, exile from paradise in this world as well as the next, reversion of the body to a world of slime and the death of the soul forever. The Genesis story for her had perennial resonance, and she thought too many today like Billy succumbed without a murmur to the old vile deceiver of humankind and his human minions. When she said as much Billy smiled disarmingly in reply. It was hard to think anything bad of him. Younger than Kate he'd a fresh-faced innocent air about him and was generally liked. Kate loved him but didn't agree with him on the salutary faith and morals she thought so necessary for the great civilized order of Irish society since Patrick; we don't need to import foreign decadence via books like Nietzsche's was her motto, our own great spiritual heritage as embodied by the mountain should be more than good enough for us.

This particular day, a week after Danny Pat's fall, Kate was busy at the bar and Billy was in the corner consorting with some young men that Kate had never seen in the pub before, strangers from the city she guessed. It made her a little uneasy. She suspected possible drug-dealing in the quiet. Was it Billy's way of supplementing his income? She also suspected him of dipping into the till occasionally to fund his own habit? She upbraided herself for such suspicions he was not the sort one suspected of such things. Yet when he came back to the bar she decided to have it out with him, she didn't want their pub, The Hillside Rest, to get a reputation for anything unsavoury. It had always been a respectable village hostelry and she was determined to keep that way. Otherwise she felt her saintly parents Bob and Molly Fleming, and Billy's mother Grace Costello, Billy was her half-brother, might turn in their graves.

Her suspicions had been heightened by her finding a small envelope of some white powder under a seat when she was sweeping out the bar the night before. Being a moral traditionalist also at heart she abhorred the creeping of a drug culture into even the smallest village and town in Ireland and she bemoaned the fact that this was woefully ignored by media and government though it was, in her view the major threat to the health of our Irish youth of today. Maheragh could do without this like other inroads of so-called "progress", hellish enslavement in this world and the next was hardly "enlightenment". Billy had been drawn into the drug trade, even in a small way and there was evidence of that in the little sample she had found while cleaning the lounge area, then she resolved to nip it in the bud. Billy was too good and innocent a boy to be drawn into anything so seedy. She was his half-sister and she resolved to protect him and the reputation of the pub as a simple wholesome local hostelry. Her saintly mother and father God rest their souls, would turn in their graves if she turned a blind eye to any possible illegal activities in their old-world wholesome hostel.

"Billy dear, she said when he came back up to the bar, "Would you come into the back parlour for a moment, there's something I want to talk to you about".

"Wait until I finish serving these people", he said, he was serving vodkas and Red Bull to two young giggling girls in skimpy shorts and tops hyped up by the drinks and flirting outrageously with him, which he wasn't adverse to. As noted he was very popular with the women, something about his naive air appealed to them, and he was good looking in his frank humble clean-cut way.

When he finally dragged himself away from the girls and came into the back parlour Kate assailed him with her suspicions, though she felt guilty in doing so, possibly all this is just my imagination she thought, anyone could have dropped that envelope, every type visited the bar every day.

"Billy darling", she said she called everyone darling, it was part of her bar-room charm offensive, "What were you doing with those young men in the corner this morning, there was something about them that didn't look right, they were not local boys and certainly not pilgrims, are you into something you shouldn't? Look at this envelope I found in the same corner, how can you account for that, you know I want to keep this bar, that serves the pilgrims from the mountain, ultra respectable, any rumours of unlawful activities could ruin us and our trade and our saintly parents would turn in their graves."

"Kate, be at ease", he said laughing, but secretly he was annoyed, irritated, even angry not so much about the event as the fact that he had been found out, if she comes in the way of my little business I might have to deal harshly with her in the future, he thought and then he rebuked himself for being so mercenary.

"It was just a few packets of marijuana they wanted; it's a harmless weed now everyone is taking it, I get a small supply from Miley Ramsbottom" he said. "It helps to beef up our trade and it's quite harmless. I smoked a bit of it with Terry when we're out on a bash in Galway and got to like it, everyone does it nowadays and sure its legal in the States and Canada, it'll soon be legal here too, we're catching up with the rest of the world fast. But if you want me to stop selling it here I'll do so, I didn't think you would object, but I won't go against your wishes, we're in this pub together, and should agree on everything. That's what I want too. I don't want anything blatantly unlawful going on here, but even the guards turn a blind eye to marijuana smoking nowadays. Sure the local guard's son is my best client".

"Be that as it may Billy dear, this is a family pub and always has been. I don't want anything to sully the reputation of our little hostelry. We have enough business from the pilgrims anyway, and the passing tourists, you must stop this trade, I forbid it, it may be harmless to you but nothing illegal has every taken place in this pub, and it mustn't have its reputation sullied now, I won't let you drag our little pub through the mud, stop it I say or I may go to the guards and get it stopped that way", she'd suddenly got very angry at his blasé attitude shaking her fist at him. But then she calmed down and said quietly, "We don't need this sort of trade, Billy it's abominable. Sorry to be so adamant, I know you mean well, and you're a good boy, I believe in you and I trust you to let this trade go".

"Well Kate", he said taken aback by her vehement response and the mention of the guards alarmed him, "if that's what you want, I'll stop it immediately, you are my closest relative and partner in this enterprise, I respect your integrity and I'll do what you want, its harmless as far as I'm concerned but if it upsets you I'll drop it like a hot potato, OK, take my word for this, you know I can be trusted to keep my word, OK. I'm finished with it. You won't see me doing this anymore. Does that satisfy you dear partner?" He kissed her on the cheek.

"Yes, Billy darling", she said, "you have put my mind at ease, I think we can leave it at that, I'm happy it's settled", she kissed him on the cheek back and they went back into the bar both to them partly satisfied that the issue was at rest. But she resolved to keep an eye on Billy from in the future just the same to make sure he kept to his side of their agreement. It was a wise resolution.

CHAPTER 6

Jerry's Magic Mountain

WHEN JERRY REACHED THE BASE OF THE MOUNTAIN HE WENT INTO the Hillside Rest for some refreshments. Kate came up to him and when she found out who he was she was over the moon, ready to eat him alive as it were: "Sure we'll have to have a get together, just the two of us at a quiet time later, I want to pump you on your great adventures down south", she gushed, her breasts bobbing excitedly. He was saved from serious embarrassment by customers demanding Kate's attention; as he walked to the bar someone jostled him and whispered "don't get involved in local affairs you know nothing about", he looked around and the person was gone. Is everyone in this bloody place half mad, he thought?

Billy served Jerry and mentioned that he would like a philosophical chat with him at some stage. "I want to pick your brains for a philosophical thesis I'm writing in favour or atheism. What do you think of Nietzsche and the death of God and creating one's moral values beyond good and evil as traditionally understood, and power as the only real value we should live by?" Jerry said he didn't think much of that fascist gibberish, it was dangerous rubbish and echoed the Nazi creed that might is right, he preferred Chesterton or Dostoevsky or Tolkien or Kierkegaard whose views were saner. Nietzsche the old secularist fanatic did after all end up in a lunatic asylum trying to write an alternative bible, doing Satan's will, Jerry said bursting Billy's bubble; how arrogant can one man get. Jerry added that he hadn't time to discuss that now, yes they could meet at a later date, and gladly he'd debunk that self-centred madman, Billy's aristocratic Prussian. He said he loved a good philosophical discussion the more heated and one-sided it was the better. God may or may not be dead, he laughingly added, but Nietzsche certainly is.

There was a great hum of activity there at the base of the mountain near the pub when Jerry came out. People were meandering up and down the holy climb: pilgrims, tourists, sightseers, mountaineers in full gear, or at the other extreme women going up in high heel shoes, a miracle of balance, small children in their arms or trotting along beside them in shorts and floppy hats. He had a strange sensation that they were all angelic forms climbing up to heaven itself. And he was reminded of lines from an old poem he wrote about a previous climb:

> To climb a holy mountain's a pinnacle of human aspiration,
> On high to oversee panoramic vistas of timeless creation
> And receive a saint's rich legacy to a grand island nation.

He always associated mountains with the quest of the divinely inspired artist that he aspired to be. It became for him a symbol of the mountains we all climb in body soul and mind and heart, the rise to the sublime that is our deepest spiritual part, an effervescence like that of a golden sunset or starlight on the sea. It represented for him the deeper mysteries of life that humble our vainer human pretensions. Far from lowland existence, it seemed a fair high domain that took us beyond the level of lowland man, mired in godless worldly clay. This hill was as mystical as the Irish psyche had always been. As one poet had put it the Irish since Patrick had one foot in this world and one in the next and it's what has made them great. An ugly industrial heap of mine waste could hardly replica that soul greatness that is our unique heritage among the nations, all we have to enrich our new super state masters in Brussels and maybe convert them to putting something about God and traditional values in the secularist EU constitution.

People always said that Jerry was a hopeless romantic idealist and spiritual poet and they sometimes laughed at his airy fancies; at times he didn't live in this world at all, even Deverly said. All this criticism didn't deter him. Indeed he had continued to reach for a high cloudy destiny in his life and in his art. He wanted that art that came from deep in the heart and the soul, for he knew that was the only art that mattered and lasted. The poet uses words for that, the painter paint, the sculptor stone, but the end is always the same, as he had once written for a literary journal to embody the vision of purest truth and beauty that's always struggling for expression within the restless core of the human soul, our high and godly immortal part that he thought so neglected today in a glib, superficial and technologically and mechanistically anti-human un-authentic media world.

For him, as he looked up now at the pyramid point of the mountain, it seemed suddenly to embody our earth with all its beauty, where a greater heart and soul dwells. For his sense had always been that the perfection of man is possible only in a divinely ordered universe, man one with God who presides like a mountain over our frail existence, raising us up to glory from the worldly mediocrity of the lower clay soul. All else, he thought was just useless human pride, dust and ashes in the long run. The divinity present in the human soul must be sparked into life by vistas such as this, which raise us up to "more than we can be" as the song says.

This mountain, as he looked up at it on that fine summer day, gathering his courage to venture up its stony slopes, was a peak of mystery bathed in diamond June sunlight. He saw it as an emblem of the Irish soul and it's striving for oneness with the Spirit animating all creation and union with which makes Ireland whole.

And standing there, amid a bustle of excited voices bargaining with a man selling staves of local wood, Jerry remembered the guide they had when he first climbed, an old man going up in bare feet. The thrill of gathering at the base of the mountain was to him then like a preparation to restore his inner fountain of youthful idealism. To him those great ascending masses of rock, moss and heath, were shining with the glory and mystery of life, like the infinite depth of the human heart itself that no one could fully fathom except in a context such as this.

The old guide had put that well and Jerry had written it down. He said that our climbing was just part of a universal human experience of divine aspiring, but one here also uniquely Irish, for the universal is always rooted in the local. For Jerry too this part of the west of

Ireland was the most glorious place on earth, the heart of a people as old as the hills and wonderful with timeless wisdom. He knew progressive cynics would see it as another Irish tradition to be destroyed for an imported ideology of clay, lest we have anything unique to give the world. To Jerry, a poor ignorant believer, that seemed sadly blinkered. There was inner gold on the mountain and we ran after imported clay gold. There was soul gold in our great land and many now aped only the clay idol of money and imported soul emptiness. He had written a poem about that too:

> Our guide urged us
> To press on to the summit,
> Telling us, as a consolation,
> That there was no great
> Achievement in it,
> For billions of pilgrims
> Before us have trod,
> And still thread,
> The universal sacred mountain
> To the summit of God

As he looked at the cascades of purple heather and the golden clumps of furze and the placid groups of grazing sheep with little lambs gambolling among them he thought what a sight of grandeur and beauty. Should all that be trampled down by the hard noisy progress of money – making machines. No! To climb this mountain was our true wealth as individuals and a nation we were climbing to claim a priceless heritage.

Not that on that day, after his drive North, Jerry found the climb easy. In fact, eager to see Donie and Nelly, he only went up part of the way. He wanted to stretch his legs after the long drive and have an appetite for the plentiful grub he knew his friends would have ready for him. But maybe because he'd put on weight lately, too many snacks and fizzy drinks late at night while doing his writing, he chickened out early in the climb. Must be getting old, he thought. But maybe he just needed someone to support him and urge him on to reach the summit; it's difficult to climb on high on one's own.

And as he grew older it grew harder and more testing for body and soul, but the joy of even partial achievement, even just aiming at the summit was always worth the effort. It was like the climb of life he thought within, and wrote it down, fishing an old piece of paper and the stub of a pencil from his top pocket.

Being a literary man, the lecturer resurfaced in him always. He was reminded, when climbing, of Li Bai's **Ascent of Mountain Fuji in a Dream**, a work he loved, where the seer conceived the great tenets of Taoism above the paddy-fields of Japan. And of course Moses received the Ten Commandments on a mountain such as this, and he had gone down to the lowlands to find the people still seeking the fleshpots of Egypt, people do that in every age. This made Jerry reflect that civilizations can regress as well as progress; there is no necessary steady upward curve in human culture, despite the central endless progress myth of modernism. History shows human life is more a series of upward and downward spiritual and moral and cultural curves. Now we are going down rapidly, he felt, but one didn't have to go with the tide, as scripture said "let the dead bury their dead". Jerry felt deeply the loss of a more innocent Ireland in the present era. He was reminded of the lyrics of the great modern singer-song writer and fellow poet Don McClean in his masterpiece "American Pie" which bemoaned the loss of a more innocent America, and a more original creative art and music, "the day the music died". For Jerry the beginning of the erosion of a more authentic integral and innocent Ireland began with the divorce and the subsequent steady selling out of the vision of the founders of the nation and our great spiritual heritage since Patrick as embodied in the constitution of the fledgeling nation in its emergence from decades of repression by a super state. It was kind of ironic to him that after struggling for 400 years for a free independent nation we should now be gradually selling out all its traditional values, all that made us unique, and our hard- won freedom to rule our own affairs, to become the province of a super state once more a conglomerate that would turn our green glory to uniform European grey.

Certainly, his trip to the west was because of what he saw as a local manifestation of another regressive tendency creeping into our green idyll. Some greedy developers, it seemed, were seeking to destroy this mountain, and with it a huge slice of our rich Irish heritage, to make way for a gold mine and the mountain of poisonous waste it would leave behind. Maybe the efforts of the mining company here to mine the mountain out of its serene existence reflected a universal tendency in man nowadays to put all his effort into winning power and wealth even if it undermined his very soul, causing him, despite eras of stored wisdom among his people, to regress to the level of the beast, a level of total soulless self-centeredness and self-interest alone, of wealth and power as the true God, or rather the cruel perennial human idol of greedy emptiness, a reversal of the evolution of man to his free natural and divine destiny.

He consoled himself with the view that those who threatened the mountain were mainly interlopers, though some locals were in it with them. But most that inhabited the plains around here were full of the indestructible spirit of a race that had endured much with grace, from famine to exile to colonial oppression. Now they faced the new colonialism of ruthless global economics, one more imported obstacle difficult to defeat. But he had confidence that, as usual, a saving middle way could be found. For the people here, like those all over the island, were the finest imaginable. It was just sad that a rotten apple was being introduced into the barrel from the outside.

Donie in his letter had hinted at such a potential spreading vein of corruption in this scenic paradise. Something about a vein of gold that had been found on the side of the mountain, that a foreign-based mining company wanted to develop regardless of the mountain's sacred inherited glory; profit for global fat cats was the supreme and only real value. Jerry hoped this was not a sign of an Ireland being shaped amid the dust and smoke of a shattering heritage. He wanted to stop this tendency to sell our souls and all the glory that our forefathers had clung to, for vain gain and vapid desires. Maybe the mountain, and the movement to save it, was a symbol of a refusal to sell out the independent and unique nation our ancestors had forged with their lives in difficult times?

In any case he had to find out if the people would really tolerate the destruction of Paddy's Mountain for a mountain for gold? But of course he was also an interloper and the will of the people who live here was what mattered. They must balance employment gains against the colder consequences of a ruthless development. Donie and he would be helpless before the people's approaching choice.

This was not a matter of the sky falling down, or any such silly apocalyptic alarmism, though in its own way it was a matter of life or death. Things would go on even if the mine company got its pound of flesh, but it was a crucial struggle, nevertheless. Jerry felt it was a do or die effort to save the quality of life and the environment for ourselves and more so for our children, lest we leave them a devastated mountain and lock them forever in a lowland of despair, where money grabbing was the one absolute, and life was weighed down with the lead of useless passing economic tyrannies imported from abroad.

But maybe he shouldn't be shocked, he thought, about what was going on here. Always there is a serpent in the garden. Like that film of the same name, there is no "beach" of untroubled sand and paradise. There is no escape from our inner and outer darkness since the fall. We carry our inherited seed of latent inner corruption wherever we go. The key, always, is to strive to transcend that inner decay, to achieve the best that is also within us in pain and suffering, as the saint had done, and his humble country devotees had done here for 1500 years. Jerry bowed to them and their wisdom. For life's worldly greed and vanity passes but only the soul's upward strivings expresses its nobility despite the pain and suffering that always entails. So he philosophized, for doing so was one of his vices, or virtues, depending on your point of view.

When he descended from the mountain, Jerry went to seek Donie out to ascertain the cause of the trouble he was having in this particular western area, and see if he could help him solve the problem. Jerry was little prepared for the complexities he was to find. It turned out to be an extremely fraught few weeks. But then he was ready for a bit of excitement after the relatively dull life of Ballymac that was yet his present abode in another land of eternal beauty. He was ready for a new adventure in the mystic west with its mountains, bays and promise of peace for all our days. But Jerry got more than he bargained for in his pilgrimage to the mystic west of his waking dreams, the mystic land of the inner heart that figured also in so much of his poems. Yet as the wise man said, the dream is father to the integral human being and the west was always a land of dreams that the best always struggled to bring to life.

CHAPTER 7

At Home with Friends

It was growing dark when Jerry Lofty left the mountain slopes and retreated to the little farm house that Donie and Nelly Deverly had got from Jim Sugrue for their stay in Mayo. As noted Donie had come there to investigate a few strange occurrences that needed to be cleared up. A cousin of his, twice removed on his mother's side, Jim Sugrue had invited him to looking to the death of his father in strange circumstances. The shrewd and experienced garda superintendant of Dublin fame, now a commissioned private detective of note, even with the little he knew of the case shared Jim's qualms about the death.

As he pulled into the gravel yard of an old farmhouse Jerry saw that it was only a few hundred yards from the car park at the base of the sacred mountain. The farmhouse had been Danny Pat's home but now it was let out to tourists. Jerry immediately marvelled at the setting. No doubt the Surgue family kept sheep in the side of a mountain towering over the cottage, a frail living now. Their house was a long traditional dwelling extensively added to and modernized. It was low and sheltered for these windy parts, with a roof covered with slabs of slate mined from the local quarry, and with walls, three feet thick, of clay mortar and local granite stones. It had the usual small square windows covered by curtains of local lace and little thick shutters of restored sturdy local oak wood painted green.

He was admiring all this tastefully modernized tradition, when the intrepid Nelly came fluttering out the door. Doubtless her husband, his good friend, who was growing a little deaf in his old age, hadn't heard the car. Jerry was immediately enveloped in a large bosomy embrace, and he kissed the plump cheeks of his host and old friend with relish for he loved her dearly. Like her husband her frame had expanded since he saw her last, but no harm, she had become cuddlier and jollier as a result, her mischievous twinkling eyes full of affection and good nature. He thought of Shakespeare's lines said by Julius Caesar, "Let me have about me men who are fat and such as sleep at night". Nelly was a woman one could rely on totally, a woman whose heart was as big as the mountain, Jerry thought.

"Ah Jerry, welcome, or should I call you Deacon Jerry, or reverend, or such like", she said. "Where's the good woman herself and the children now I heard you've thrived in that god forsaken place down south, we expected a whole bawn of you. Donie is inside studying the case I hope it doesn't land him in more trouble and danger. Why can't he be quiet and just let thing be, like any other man? Only the other day someone threatened him when he was taking a stroll around the village. But there's no holding him when he gets onto a difficult case, the more difficult the better. When a juicy conundrum like this case arises, he's like a dog with a bone, shaking and knawing at it until it crumbles and he can gobble it up with a smile on his face. Come in bring your luggage, and whatever other traps you have. O, my word, it's good to see you, you old recluse, we were just talking about you, and how we miss you and Deirdre and the kids. By the way we have some bad news, Sally slipped on the way up the mountain and suffered a minor strain of one leg, she claimed she was pushed by some ill-looking shifty man, I doubt that, though she had just been telling someone of her father's reason for her coming to the area. Be that as it may come in, he's dying to meet you".

She led him into a large kitchen with an open fire and a back door leading into a garden with roses and trellised climbing plants all blooming and fragrant in the June twilight. Among this idyllic scene, the ex-guard was perched before a deal table, on a large wicker chair, with beer and sandwiches before him. Jerry noticed his rotund frame had grown even larger than when he saw him last. He heaved himself up from his chair and rumbled over to Jerry, grasping him in a fierce bear-like hug. No wonder thugs feared the old policeman, Jerry thought, even his embrace nearly squeezed one to death.

"How is our deacon now, not too hoity-toity religious for us, I hope", Donie said, launching into his perennial joking style. "Which reminds me of a joke about a parish priest visiting for the stations; he had an open umbrella for as usual it was raining and they wondered how to get it through the door; suddenly the priest closed it and opened it quickly inside the door again. Say what you like the man of the house said, they have the power, he thought it a miracle. I suppose we have to cow tow to you now Jerry now that you *have the power*".

At this Donie laughed uproariously as was his wont, humour was his other great quality, as it is of every sane and humane human being; evil people are so because they take themselves too seriously he felt. He led Jerry inside his arms around his shoulders, for he was affectionate homely man and a steadfast friend.

Once inside Jerry noticed a leaner younger man on the opposite side of the kitchen table loaded with goodies, a man with a ruddy outdoor face, a crop of foxy hair, and the air of a native of the place. This, he later learned, was Red Jim Sugrue, son of the man who had died in strange circumstances, and now owner of the house. He had summoned the ex-super to discover the cause of his father's death with which he was so obsessed he could hardly think of anything else, he had adored his dad he was a noble mountain man like Danny.

"Grand to see you two again", Jerry said, breaking into the stream of Nelly's speech that was rumbling on like a mountain torrent after heavy rain.

"I'm coming to give moral support in this case, Donie, you old demon, but it's about time I came to visit you anyway. I thought of you immediately I had a few weeks to kill. How are the girls, my emerald Sally and ruby Molly, the jewels of my heart in the old days, grand innocent pretty girls as I remember?"

"Well. But to tell you the truth", Nelly broke in, "they are no longer the young innocents of your remembering. You know with young girls, they grow up and enter those difficult teen years before you realize it, concerns with their figure and love life come to the fore. They're off with their boyfriends to Galway. There they're joining a gang of their girl friends coming from Dublin for the gig of some gorgeous boy band that seems to be the draw now; pretty boys that have the teenyboppers swooning. Sure we were the same when we were young. I remember when I was an adolescent girl how I adored Elvis and dreamed of him picking me out from the crowd and living with him in some secret hideaway in the heart of glorious Memphis; its extraordinary what young girls dream of, very idealistic like all of us were at that age, much of it due to the hormones raging in the blood no doubt", she said laughing.

"Yes, every age is both the same and different", Jerry said, "The young have their perennial crushes and idols, that's part of growing up. But they always try something different the one sin for them is to be clones of their parents."

"Yes, the young always rebel against what their parents try to ram down their throats", Nelly said, "That's how life moves on. Not that Donie and I were ever hard on the girls, always gave them their heads, we did".

"You were quite right", Jerry said, "for the young the faraway hills are always greener, and they must learn from their own mistakes in life, follow their own ideals, however wrong-headed they may be. I remember writing a poem about that once, as you know I still write, and about everything that strikes me. I seem to be very prolific, very boring I suppose for others when I keep referring to my poems, and quoting them, but it's my passion. I believe poetry was always meant to be oral and for the people, not just books published for a few "discerning" critics and stiff-necked academics".

"No", Donie interposed bravely, "we don't find your poems boring, not always anyway", he added with a grin, "You have a great gift, my boy, as long as you keep it to yourself", again he laughed, "maybe you'd give us a bit of that poem, if you remember it. I know all about teenage crushes, I went through them myself. Indeed, I met Nelly at a Rosemary Clooney gig, in a ballroom in Dublin; Clooney's soft crooning voice used to put me into a trance. But when I met Nelly, she was gorgeous then..(he paused and she gave him a glare).. and still is", he hastily added. "Meeting the great mate of my soul (this description seemed to soothe Nelly and she glowed), put a stop to my gallop I tell you, there was no one else for me from then on", he gave Nelly a kiss on the cheek and squeeze on the buttocks which made her jump, she took no offence she knew he was slightly tipsy.

"Nelly and myself met on the back of an ass" he said with another prolonged belly laugh; "we had no other way of getting home from one of the country dances we frequented, and a stubborn ass it was too as I remember, stopped several times along the way which happily gave us more time for cuddling and canoodling as the ass brayed in derision", at this he laughed again uproariously.

"Ah go away you old inveterate liar", she said to Donie returning the embrace, "take no notice of him Jerry, he made up that silly story about the donkey to embarrass me, the old codder, but things were simpler in those days, no cause for heads in the air, we were down to earth, before the age of plastic middle-class mores as a friend of mine describes the ethos now". She turned to me and said:

"Yes Jerry", "give us a taste of one of your modern poems, that one on Elvis, I'm sure its reflects my own crush on him, before I met Donie of course, thin as a rake Donie was then, look at the old devil now, but still as handsome an old cumugil as they come.", she said reflectively, giving him another great big kiss.

"Well, Jerry said, "let's go down memory lane, I think it goes like this:

> When Elvis sang in Tupelo,
> In glittering velvet tuxedo,
> The young girls screamed,
> And swooned, "We love you so".
> I was young and thin then
> And so were they, and so was he.
> He grew fat and died of drugs and booze,
> And they faded like flowers
> To dream of how they felt,
> When Elvis sang in Tupelo,
> In velvet tuxedo,
> And they screamed
> In youth's first idealistic glow
> "We love you so".

"Not too bad, not exactly a timeless masterpiece of art and thought either", Donie said with a grin, "at least it's simple, no big words, I hate writers who're too obscure, writing complicated tomes for university professors to decipher. We were wildcats in the Elvis days, dancing the night away in ballrooms of romance as wild as mountain goats at the time of rutting", he laughed loudly again and Nelly said "mind your language, remember you're talking to a man of the cloth, tone it down you old codger, keep your language civil, the stout you've been drinking all night has gone to your head, tone it down you old half-drunken rogue".

"Some even think the King is still alive", Jim, Donie's younger companion, the swarthy native, normally taciturn, butted in with his tupenny-hapenny worth to add to our coming-together revelry and reminiscences,

"My sister Bridie and I loved Elvis too, though we were more into Margo and Big Tom", he added. "They packed the ballrooms around here, 'flowers for Mama, just a simple bouquet'; and 'far, far away on my Donegal shore', or 'Tipperary so far away' - country and Irish you know, we'd tried to have the best of both world I suppose. The American dream and the Irish color, patriotism and romance. Sure it was a grand time then altogether in the ballrooms of romance as they called them then, dancing until four in the morning. No alcohol allowed in the parish halls, only minerals, but we didn't complain. Some liquored up in the pubs first, but the doormen could smell the drink and might bar you".

"You know", Nelly said, "about some still adoring Elvis, sure there was a story recently of the Galway girl who went to Memphis and stayed for days by his grave, said she'd stay there forever. The police had to arrest her and ship her home forcefully; I suppose she never married and remained faithful to him in her mind, clung to the dream, however absurd it seemed. The heart is very strange indeed at times, not much logic there".

"Yes, Jerry said, "and idealistic love is I suppose the only thing we cling to in crises in life. I remember hearing that during the 9/11 crisis in the States what those on the plane about to crash said on their mobile phones. "I love you", that was the main thing they wanted to say to those close to them. I don't want to bore you but I wrote a poem about that too, very short and to the point, like that poem of Cummings about the plums in the icebox: Baby I love you, mum I Love you, dad I love you, goodbye". There was no concern about stock and shares or such like then, only the most important thing that touches the core of the soul, love", he added, becoming the lecturer again for a moment, it's amazing how we fall into type at times.

"We're too dull now, as I suppose, we are to the girls anyway", Nelly added, "but you can't hold back the clock, it gets us all in the end" (yes, Jerry reflected quietly and only the things of the soul endure and defeat the tyranny of time).

As Jerry grew solemn, lapsing into nutty professor mode, Nelly broke the spell,

"Sit down there at the table with Donie and Jim, Jerry, and drink something and try some of my sandwiches and cakes. We've been talking about you all week"

"Ah yes Jerry old son, relax and enjoy yourself, it's no time to be solemn and preachy, we're not your congregation, just a bunch of old inveterate hedonistic sinners (he grunted with good cheer and belched from the good food), you are on holidays, enjoy yourself, let it all hang out, great to see you, old boy, here's to your health", he took a large swill of beer and grunted with satisfaction, and Jerry followed suit, beer dripping down the fancy white Aran sweater he had bought for the western trip. As he looked at Donie he thought of the cool analytic brain that resided under all that boisterousness, the sleuth par excellence hidden there.

Becoming more sober Donie said, "I was going to seed here, no one to drink a pint with or discuss this cantankerous case. Sit down and relax Jerry. Nelly will you get us another beer? Jerry will have a few more of the sandwiches and maybe a few of your homemade sweet cakes. Sit down now Jerry, boy, and tell us all about yourself and how things are going in Ballymac and the writing, and the family, and the parish work. I hear the place is famous now with all the progress it's made with your help".

Jerry filled him in on his rich, happy, and largely uneventful life in the aforesaid idyll, since they last met. When he had finished, Donie said,

"By the way this is Jim "the Red Sugrue", indicating the gaunt foxy haired young man by his side, "this is his house, and the strip of mountain above us. He lives in a flat in the village, and his father lived with him there until his sad recent demise, it was more modern and easier to heat in the winter. They rent this place to tourists, but he's given it to us for the time being while I'm on the case. We've set up a room for you and there's another for the girls and for Deirdre and the kids if they decide to come".

Jerry shook hands and noticed a kind of healing scar down one side of Red Jim's face; the scarred Celtic warrior, the Brian Boru of Clew, Jerry named him immediately, following his propensity for giving people poetic names. Here was another lusty warrior, he thought, fighting the new Viking invaders of his land. It seems he had he been attacked or something. Looking at him he thought of an old poem he'd learned when young, about rough but integral mountain men who sow high up in the hills, "And soon will reap, close to the gates of heaven".

Doubtless someone had tried to bring him closer to heaven by the look of things. That was not good! Apparently, he told Jerry, a gang of company thugs had attacked him one night, out of the blue, when he was up on the mountain caring for some sick lambs that had just been born in the cold of February. But he had a large knotted shepherd's stick with him and gave as good as he got, he was a sturdy chap grown strong from roaming the mountain with his lovely black and white collie bitch, Lilly two, a replacement for Lilly One who had followed Danny Pat into the grave. Not easily scared or put off this mountain man, Jerry thought, after all he had his father's fearless genes running in his veins, and the bony hardiness of generations of mountain men.

They sat under the mountain, supped stout, ate sandwiches and talked of the weather, crops and the price of sheep. Eventually the topic of the case came down. Donie was rearing to go. They didn't realize the pain awaiting them.

CHAPTER 8

The Testimony of Red Jim

The conversation flagged as they finished their beers and food, Nelly hovering around like a mother hen about to lay an egg, with various cackles of satisfaction when we tucked into her cakes with gusto. Jerry was hungry from the journey, ravenous in fact. At last they sat back with satisfaction over glasses of good Middleton malt whiskey and water, Jerry was reminded of another McClean line "good old boys drinking whiskey and rye", he hoped this wouldn't be the "day that I die". One noble man had died already they had to make sure others wouldn't follow, so to finish off the repast, they turned to the particulars of the case.

"Well Jerry", the ex-guard said, "I gave you a hint in my letter, Jim here has had some trouble lately. In fact he's buried his noble father, Danny Pat. The Mountain he was called by the locals, God rest his soul, a man I knew well when young. A kindly man he was that everyone loved and respected, a great man of the rural community in every way. He was constantly organizing local cultural events and playing local traditional music. What a crowd there was at the funeral, eh Jim!"

While he was speaking, as was his wont, Jerry thought of an old song he had heard when young about the death of a mother, who had lived down "the Old Bog Road":

> The neighbours said her waking,
> Was the finest ever seen;
> There were snowdrops and primroses
> Piled up beside her bed,

And Ferns church was crowded
When the funeral mass was said.

He imagined Danny Pat's funeral was bit like that, Jim confirmed his image.

"Wonderful funeral for my father, the Mountain himself, ever so many flower bouquets piled over the grave. A great father to us and the whole community he was; we miss him so much now; I'm at a loss to know what to do with myself now that he's not here; only for my work with the sheep I'd have gone crazy altogether", Red Jim said, growing lonesome all of a sudden and absentmindedly caressing the new little collie at his feet. Jerry could sense his great loss in the lines that had recently been etched on his ruddy face.

"Sure he was known everywhere from here to Croagh to Louisburg and even way back as far as Maam Cross", Jim added, "There he traded many a bawn of mountain sheep. But as you say the mountain was his special love. I remember when we were young we always climbed the reek on the correct Sunday, and he'd go up at six in the morning in bare feet, for the first mass on the summit at half past eight. That people are continuing this belief now and still find it infinitely life-giving despite the creeping secularism of today's world. To him it was the greatest argument against atheism, people voted with their feet for the faith".

"Look boys", he'd say when we asked about the peculiar bare feet part, "sure we have to do some penance for our sins, God help us, and please the holy saint. It's always been a tradition in our family from the year dot, and further back (he would laugh). And I hope you, Davey Joe, Jimmy Pat and Bridie that ye'll continue after I'm gone, sure after all it's our main role in life now, to please the man above and look after each other and the grand mountain land he left to us to look after. Sure without the man above and Paddy's mountain we'd have nothing at all".

"Sure, I little realized after we climbed last year that he wouldn't be with us this summer", Jim added, and at this he seemed even more overcome, the grief was still raw in him. We kept a respectful silence, giving him some space until he was able to recollect himself.

When he continued it was in a more bitter angry tone, tears welling up in his eyes:

"Fell from the north cliff they said, nonsense! He knew that mountain like the back of his hand, every inch of it. If you ask me it was because he wouldn't sign the deed giving them access to the mountain, and the gold they say is there, that they used bloody foul play to get what they wanted. They've tried to intimidate me in the same way, maybe kill me too, for if I was out of the way they'd have a free reign; Bridie and Davey are inclined to sell, but I beat them at their own game, I clobbered the thugs sent to intimidate me until they fled like rabbits (at this he rose up in his chair and expanded his chest in a proud defiant way).

"I won't rest until whoever is responsible is found out", he continued, "I tell you they'd better look out, those greedy fat cat outsiders congregating in the village and seeking to wreck the mountain under our very feet, like those bringing in the gas over our lands and wrecking everything, or like that awful destructive fracking project in Sligo. I feel my father won't rest easy in his grave until whoever is responsible for his fall is found and brought to the justice they deserve. That's why I called in Donie I know his reputation as the best."

At this the ex-guard glowed with pride, his large frame and large head, now covered with a frosty thatch, would have swelled even more if that was possible. He could never be accused of humility.

"Good, he said, "You were wise, I am the best, I never fail, I always get my man, but tell me about this part of the mountain and who owns it and why it's so important?".

"Well", he said, "the ownership is complicated. Our mother died long ago, from a tumour in the brain, a frail but wonderful woman, God rest her soul, we sorely missed her growing up, but Danny was mother and father to us, though an ancient aunt on our mother's side sometimes came to help until she became too gaga to do so. My dad left the house and the land around it to me, but part of the mountain the mining corporation is interested in is owned by Davey and Bridie. Davey is the eldest of the family. He wasn't interested in the farming, went away to Dublin to train as a teacher. Danny Pat left him the grazing rights on the other side of the mountain from the pilgrim's path, he lets it out. He's the principal in the local school now, and lives in a little flat near the school. There is a further complication in the will. If the mountain area is sold, a third part of the money must go to Bridie, my sister. She lives in a big house in the country; works in the Post Office to keep the wolf from the door. Her husband, Big Bill Sheehan, is from the other side of the mountain. He is, or was, a plumber, but he's out of work at the present due to illness. Biddy does part-time work but how they manage otherwise, I don't know, with three children to look out for, though one of them is grown up and has gone away to Australia, he sends money home; we'll all be living out there soon the way things are going, God help us!"

He paused and took a long draught of whiskey, and a big sup of stout, to calm his nerves and oil his narrative. Then he added;

"That puts further pressure on me to sell, seeing their need. I do the farming and I work part-time in the local farmer's co-op. I rent out the house here in the summer; it's too big for me as a single man living alone; I have more company in the village. We're all determined not to let the mining corporation get a hold of the land. They indulge in strip mining and would wreck the whole environment in my view, without being of much benefit to the area economically in the long run. If we let them wreck the mountain my father would turn in his grave. This is a holy mountain, and it's been part of our family for generations. I want to hold on to it like a leech for the sake of my grandchildren, and all the people around here who take so much pride in it as Patrick's mountain steeped in history and lore from when time began, God help us all!"

"Who are behind this mining scam then", Jerry asked, "is it local people or outsiders?"

"The company has an exploration office in Westport, and its global fat cats come here sometimes, but there's a local man very much involved too, Miley Ramsbottom, big shot around here, owns the Post office. Involved in all the housing developments during the boom, all those awful unfinished and unsalable houses you may have seen at the end of the village. He wants the mine so that his houses will be saleable again, to get him out of a hole he's in; awful pushy individual who thinks he's God almighty, come down in the world with the recession, but still thinks he owns us all. Then the local TD, John Joe Christie, is also pushing this, revenues for the government in the recession and all that and to make employment around here anyway respectable, most are on the dole at the moment, and the rest have had cuts in their take home pay. Another pushy type, I don't particularly like him, got the planning for the mining company, subject to our entrance permission, maybe he was slipped an envelope or two in my view, or a fat donation to the party coffers, instead of location, location, location, it was corruption, corruption, corruption; that's modern Ireland for you, the brown envelope and the uninhabited mansions", he added bitterly.

At this their discussion was interrupted by the crunch of a car pulling up in the gravel outside the house and a chorus of young voices approaching the door.

CHAPTER 9

The Complications of Youth

They were suddenly assailed by lots of shrill girl giggling and deeper boy voices blending raucously in a bawdy rugby song:

> "We'll drink a drink a drink
> To Lily the pink, the pink,
> The saviour of the human race"..

It was the girls and their consorts returning half-sloshed from the boy-band bash. They burst into the kitchen, laughing and singing, and then drew back a bit abashed when they saw the visitors. Jerry hardly recognized Molly and Sally. They had been transformed into young women since he saw them last, with all the paraphernalia of current youth fashion. Sally was wearing an extremely short tight mini-dress that hugged her Twiggy-type slim figure, with a skimpy top that revealed budding young breasts well, and her hair was cut short and all spiked up like a porpoise, with extremely black eyeshade and curious black spots on her cheeks and extremely long red fingernails like Dracula's moll ready to suck one's blood. Molly wore similar clothes but a little more subdued and her figure was fuller, more voluptuous some would say, like her mother; she had various curious tattoos all over her arms, silver rings in her nose and a rose on each of her boobs. Sally was a religious intellectual, Molly was a happy-go-lucky hedonist. Under all this style and makeup Jerry feared they were not the same girls he'd known in days gone by, as people mature the more permanent aspects of their personalities develop. Yet he praised them for going with the fashion, they were young, exploring new horizons was youth's mission he thought sententiously.

"Ah," he said, rising, and going to embrace them, ignoring the fact that in appearance they were far now from the little girls he had once loved like his own.

"Ah my ruby of Dublin and my emerald of Ireland, my two little gems of the wild", he said, giving them their old nicknames. They embraced though the girls drew back a little, no longer offering the full embrace that they once enjoyed.

Deverly also got up to look at them, and Nelly:

"Well Girls", she said, un-phased by the entrance racket, "how was the show, all the boy heart-throbs there, bowled you over did they?"

"Yes", Sally said, giggling, "they were gorgeous, I can't believe that Briany actually spoke to me, I was in tears. But mum, maybe you haven't met Terry Ramsbottom my fiancé".

She presented her boyfriend without a blink, though Deverly was looking a bit askance. He was a tall dark boy with piercing eyes that Jerry though a bit menacing, though it was maybe his prejudice. He had longish black hair, tied in a pony tail, with a silver ring in his nose and the same in one ear and cross tattoos all over his arms. Jerry thought of Shakespeare, "my bitter enemy become my greatest love", or words to that effect, he couldn't remember them exactly.

Later they were to learn that the bold Terry had a dubious reputation in the village, though some said he was curiously devout as well. When he was younger, he ran over an old harmless drunk who used to torment car drivers at night, lurching out into the road and such like. Terry was driving too fast and left him in vegetative state, a hit-and-run. His father got rid of the car to a scrap dealer in town, and he hot-footed it to Australia. But he came home later when the hue and cry had died down; the guards said the old drunk was always lurching onto the road in front of cars and Terry wasn't really to blame in any way. He hadn't done so well down under. Too soft to do any work, the local gossips said, brought up in the boom and had everything handed to him by his doting and neurotic mother, and so hardly likely to do any menial work abroad, where, like all emigrants, he was asked to start at the bottom of the ladder. He came quickly home to daddy who had him working in the office, mostly sitting doing nothing except ogling the busty secretary in between scoffing endless cups of coffee and iced donuts and reading Playboy on the sly. Yet despite all this unlike his father he was a great fan of the faith and a great lover of the mountain and its heritage; people are always a mass of contradictions. His mountain was thought.

Yet some said the father had him doing some of his dirty work, rumours of him being involved with drug dealers in Galway, and that was what kept their heads above water during the recession. This was hard to believe given his beliefs. Guards looked into it and nothing could be proved. Maybe Terry was also involved in Danny's death urged on by his father? Jerry thought, unfairly again. In any case he seemed not the type Deverly would have wished for his daughter, but then love is blind, if love there was in it. From the way they looked at each other Jerry thought it a real possibility, but maybe it was just a first crush, they could hardly keep their hands off each other. Sally was already wrapped up the mystery of boys and in real or imagined suffering and romance that went with that, as was the case with her sister.

Indeed Molly now also presented her beau to us with a gleam in her eyes, "Mum, dad, Jerry have you met Billy Fleming?" she said.

"Yes, Jerry said "I met him briefly in the bar earlier today".

Billy was a small shy looking fair-haired young lad with big innocent blue eyes, apparently the son of the local publican now diseased by whom he had been left an equal share in the pub with his half sister Kate. He had more respectable short hair, but wore scruffy torn jeans and a t-shirt with a large Bono visage printed on it, to look more up to date and a tattoo of a shamrock on his neck with My Irish Molly O printed under it. He worked behind the bar in the pub and was well liked as a kind of innocent abroad. Molly always had the better taste, Jerry thought, but who knows what's in the heart, and appearances can lie. Sally and Terry were hands all over each other and kisses and embraces, Molly and Billy were more subdued in their love expressions, for them holding hands was enough.

"How did you lot meet?" Deverly asked, waking up from his first shock,

"I didn't know you knew anyone around here Sal".

"Well we are in classes together in Galway University, these are my closest friends there", she said "when they came here I looked the boys up, we'd been keeping in contact anyway".

Another complication in this whole unholy mess Jerry thought. He shook hands with Terry. He staggered a little and his breath smelled of liquor, maybe drugs too Jerry thought, unfairly. The other boy seemed soberer, less hyped up.

When they had gone Nelly and Donie rounded on Sally, an embarrassing domestic scene, upbraiding her and mentioning the unsavoury reputation of the Ramsbottoms. They were unprepared for what came next. She burst into tears and rushed up to her room. It seems it was more serious than they thought.

"The teenage years, very difficult, you have it all before you, with your gang", Nelly said. Not a very comforting thought.

When things had settled down, Jim mentioned another case complication.

"Boys, he said, "we have to prepare. Miley Ramsbottom on behalf of the mining company has called a village meeting to support the mining project. If the people go with him we're in deep shit, pardon the expression", he said to me. "We have to spike their guns, get all our arguments and ammunition ready for this meeting. Do you have any suggestions? We have a further problem. Davy is leaning towards selling, he doesn't really like the teaching and sees a way out, a way to a more leisurely life, there are also rumours of some scandal he was involved in the school though nothing was proved, he was accused of interfering with one of the girl pupils, no truth in it of course, at least no proven truth. He wants out but he is also conscious of course of his responsibility to the community and the future of this scenic area and its holy site he feels his father might turn in his grave if he sold. But they might be able to persuade him, we must be able to step in first".

"Well", Deverly said, "I have some ideas but let's sleep on it we'll be able to think more clearly in the morning".

At the top of the stairs Jerry heard sobbing from Sally's room and

Nelly's soft soothing voice calming her down. Tomorrow, he thought all this will blow over, but it was a vain thought and tomorrow would only bring fresh headaches.

When they went to wake Sally in the morning it was difficult to do so. Apparently she had become depressed and taken some ecstasy drugs that were common among her friends, or maybe one of these slipped them into her drinks unawares after the boy band bash. Eventually the doctor came and they rushed her to the hospital where they pumped the offending opiates out of her system. But the incident made Donie and Nelly more repentant of ever coming to this place and becoming involved in the whole mine affair; "this will be the death of us all", Nelly said in one of her more despairing moments. This made Donie as determined as ever to clear up the mess as quickly as possible so life could get back to normal and they could hot foot it back to their comfortable modern estate house in the posh Dublin suburbs of Blackrock.

CHAPTER 10

The Passion of an Environmentalist

Jerry struggled out of bed at nine or so only to find that Deverly had already risen at six, which was his wont, from his police days, when, as he said one could think more clearly in the early hours. Jerry thought of an old rhyme we learned in school: "Early to bed and early to rise, Makes a man healthy and wealthy and wise". If that was the case he would be the poorest and most foolish of men he surmised. He grabbed come coffee and toast and some scrambled egg and bacon Nelly had prepared, and joined Donie on the terrace, all sorts of plans and maps laid out before him. Nelly was at his beck and call and had a large smile on her face; she was also the early bird that got the worm, she was scoffing jam donuts.

"Well, you old demon", Jerry said to Donie, "out with it, why are you smiling like a cat who had nabbed the fattest mouse? What scheme has been concocted in the night in that dark devious brain of yours?"

"Sit down, Jerry, he said, "relax, I've been thinking of a friend from the old days that I have in Westport, beautiful town that. A man named Tim Thornton. He helped the people with the gas pipeline protest to get their facts right. Knows all about mines and oil companies and that sort of thing, an ardent environmentalist like you Jerry. I think we should pay him a visit today, pick his brains on this, he'll give us the lowdown we need for the forthcoming meeting to scuttle Ramsbottom and his imported crew of slick expert marauders".

At this we were interrupted by Sally sneaking down the stairs.

"Hello our little lily of the valley", Jerry said reverting to his habit of giving the girls various poetic names. She gave him a withering look and marched straight out the door without a glance back or a reply. Suddenly he realized she didn't want to be treated like a little girl anymore, and she was right.

"Donie", he said, "you'd better start treating that girl as a young woman or you'll lose her the more you criticize her liaison with Terry the more she will be determined to see him".

"Yes", I realize that now, he replied, "we made a fatal mistake, but only because we love her and don't want to see her hurt. But our concern has had the opposite effect. That's adolescence, some phase, now she's off to cry on the shoulders of her boyfriend no doubt and maybe spill the beans on us and our plans, though unconsciously, I'm sure she'd never betray us consciously. I don't know what to do with her half the time, it's an awkward age, but that's my problem, you'll have it soon enough. Let's get on to the case. I've contacted Tim and he'll meet us for lunch in that nice pub and restaurant in the square, The Speckled Cow, at one o'clock",

"Combining business and pleasure as usual", Jerry quipped, "you old scheming rogue, well I'll look forward to that too".

"Nelly, Donie shouted, she was in the kitchen, "don't get any lunch for us we're off to Westport to hob-knob with the tourists and day trippers",

"Well, she answered, "Haven't ye the cheek, as if I was here to wait on ye hand and foot, you can get your own supper when ye come home, or are ye too helpless to do that?"

"No", Jerry said, "with Deirdre off on her post postmodernist lectures every day, I often have to cook for myself and the kids. Whatever about Donie, the old sleazebag, I'm the modern man after all, in spite of what Deirdre might say, equality in everything and a good thing too, not overdoing it of course", he added, with a mischievous grin.

She came out and clobbered him playfully with a tea towel.

As they started off Jerry looked up at the mountain; you'll be there after we are long gone, he thought, luring our children also to your peaks of peace. Already streams of pilgrims and sightseers were streaming up the reek, for spiritual profit or most just for momentary pleasure, which was fine too. He thought of the perennial challenge of the old daunting peak, and a piece of an old poem he had once composed about the purifying process of the tough prayerful ascent that assisted one to reach "the saint's fervent faith and the serenity of the blest".

There were no usual mists or soaking wet today on the hill top, they were getting off lightly. The climb had no cleansing penance that wise old saint had intended.

The drive to Westport was pleasant, along the bay road, with gorgeous views on either side of Clew Bay. It was a fine summer day, this summer had been unusually fine, and Jerry even composed a little poem in his head as they cruised into the little seaside town. For some reason, maybe the weather, the muse was strong in him and he felt moved to finish a composition with fulsome praise of the "Westport of welcoming blue eternal seas".

In the town they found Tim Thornton sitting at the bar in The Speckled Cow, a spacious gleaming modern bar geared for tourists. Tim had a glass of Galway Hooker, or some such modern brew, before him. He was a small thin man with a face like those old Celtic sculptures, a broad forehead tapering to a small chin, like an inverted pyramid, and sharp shrewd eyes, the eyes of a lawyer but also with the look of a humane man in them Jerry thought.

Jerry ordered some of the black stuff and a plate of mussels with thick sea-food chowder and crispy rolls. Donnie ordered a more substantial feed of double fish and chips with side salad and double toffee pudding to follow. No use arguing with him to be more abstemious, he was what he was and enjoyed it to the full. Jerry marvelled that he was still alive but he had the sturdy western constitution. His grandfather and father had come from near the reek, ate and drank copiously and smoked to their heart's content all their lives and all lived to ripe old ages, it was in the genes; having survived the famine and everything else they were as hard as nails, it was a case of the survival of the fittest.

After introductions and pleasantries, when they had settled down in the corner of the neat establishment, they explained their dilemma to Tim, and they were soon buoyed up by his advice.

"Sure I know all about that awful mining company, he said, "and I can give you a lot of ammunition to use against it. Indeed, I brought some with me."

He pulled out a large folder that he had by his chair, full of maps and photos of their nefarious activities in other unsuspecting native and un-spoilt lands far away. Apparently they were ruthless capitalist marauders who grabbed the spoils and moved on, leaving an unholy mess and an environmental hell behind them. He showed them mountains of slack in Nicaragua; left after the opencast mining they engaged in, seeping poison into water ways still after many years, unsightly sores blotting the landscape, leaving people around with cancers and other diseases from the effects of the carnage. They were shocked, but glad at the same time that they had some ammunition to wake people up to what was before them if they acceded to the mining project.

They rubbed their hands in glee, here was evidence that no one could ignore. But they were to learn that more than a few photos were needed to convince people in this dirty war. Their adversaries were prepared to get very dirty indeed.

CHAPTER 11

Tim gets Carried Away

AFTER THE MEAL THEY WENT TO TIM'S OFFICE TO MAKE ENLARGED copies of the material, and outlines of the planning the mine had obtained for Patrick's mountain, the prospects were fairly horrendous and they wanted everyone to know what horrors they might be committing themselves to. Tim explained further, and his passion about it surprised them, he got really worked up; he seemed to have a bee in his bonnet about most everyone when it came to this issue; there were real or imagined enemies everywhere if he could be believed.

"We want people's eyes wide open on this", he said. "No hard wisdom after the event. We must pull the wool away from people's eyes before it is too late and the laughing boys have absconded with the loot, simple bumpkins fooled again.

They have even gone on RTE with fine visions of their plans and the modernists and bland develop-minded gurus there, little up in the air girls with the latest hair does and make-up, living in some other world of Dublin 4 fairyland, who haven't a clue, rowed in with the mining company's propaganda with gusto. Good to get rid of anything authentically Irish anyway, especially if there was any "religion" involved. And what were they doing we learn now, slipping public money to their fair-haired boys under the counter, no accountability while they demand rigorous accountability of others such as the church". He paused to get his wind.

"Ah perhaps they're not as bad as that, really just sinners like us all", I said, thinking he was going a bit overboard and trying to reign him in.

"You don't know them and their global industrial masters in Dublin 4 or Europe", he went on unheedingly. "It is hard commercialism of the imported American dream that rules them in their glossy newness without thought of cultural roots of any kind. Just hard cynicism of IMF and EU controlled economics, and hard cold voices to match with ready glib solutions for every problem and arguments to justify any robbing of natives such as us. With some caveat or two to give the illusion of "fair mindedness", but ultimately you always knew what conclusion they are always going to reach on their programs, the liberal capitalist globalist one; and all of us paying their license fees too".

"Yes", Jerry said, "I suppose as a public broadcasting company they should be scrupulously fair; look what happened over that poor priest they maligned unfairly, just a few raps over the knuckles they got and they moved happily on. If that was the church there would be no end of it, and they themselves as corrupt as hell; look at all the brown envelopes stuffed with cash they gave under the counter to the presenter of the Late Late Show, taxpayers money for they are heavily subsidised. And look at the constant drip attacks on the church, it's one of the reasons our youth lack the faith they need for their happiness here and hereafter". He was about to air other bees in his own bonnet against the media and RTE in particular, but the environmentalist interrupted him with a new tirade:

"It left us in a bad light surely, that TV program on the mountain and the mine. Ramsbottom and Christie played the church card well, to work the Dublin 4 gang who rule us into a suitable feeding frenzy, hinted cleverly that it was all a medieval plot by the church to halt the march of progress, mayhem followed.

Said the mine was in more in keeping with a wealthy 'modern Ireland'. What was some obscure holy mountain to stand in the way of the progress of contemporary post-nationalist post-Christian EU Ireland? Get rid of this sacred cow, if needs be. At this the glib Dublin liberals snickered and licked their lips with glee.

These so-called woke 'progressives', in my view", Tim went on as we sat back like dazed lectured schoolboys being rapped over the knuckles, "are manipulated zombies of foreign interests and cultural imperialism that we were all succumbing to in the name of 'progress'. All that led us into the sink we are in now. No one was wise enough to say the emperor had no clothes when the banks were selling us down the drain; God knows what they'll lead us into now. No one dared stand in their way when they were pontificating on TV. They had the media in the palm of their hand. It was the primrose way to the bonfire of the vanities and the sleek so-called economic 'experts' led the way, no room for common sense".

Jerry and Donie listened, slightly embarrassed, their secret middle class mores meant they were not happy with shows of passion though maybe passion was what was needed in relation to this issue. He may have been over the top but passion was always what was needed in this area. He ploughed on.

"We are not going to sit idly by in this case. We are not going to be fooled or manipulated anymore by fat men in posh suits with smiling faces, concealing sleaze and devastation with fine words and devious greedy strategies invented by the think-tanks of their foreign masters. But the west is awake, they won't fool us again, we're done with the dictatorial rule of the fat cats, these sleazy Dublin 4 fuckers who care nothing for country life. Feck them I say, feck them, we'll beat them yet, get our own back on the greedy blood-suckers, feck the lot of them!"

He sat back banging the table, his face purple with passion; having vented his spleen and prejudice against the Dublin philistines, though Jerry was sure there were some ardent environmentalists there too, maybe more, great gentle people he had met during his time lecturing in a university in the heart of the great Capital city that always amazes him whenever he visited it, though he didn't take too kindly to all the grubby graffiti along the tram routes. It was a sad sign of the new Dublin, and the new nation.

Yet he knew that there were great environmentalists also among a great and sometimes fair-minded media too, though that fair-mindedness was evaporating fast, superficial imported woke ideology was gaining hand over fist, there was less originality now. Yet, like the presidency, the role of public broadcasting is to represent all the people, even the church which represents over 80% of the people still. It must be fair to all, not propagandists for liberalism or any "ism", but even-handed and giving everyone and equal say and an equal crack of the whip, impartial and even-handed, like the president, who is supposed to be a broad impartial and all-inclusive father to all, not a party fanatic or secret anti-church liberal as some threaten to be. We need an impartial father of all not another dictatorial ideologue. Jerry was sure most were trying to do this, though the targeting of that missionary priest who was defamed was worrying, making one think that impartiality was thrown out the window in some areas. Maybe Tim wasn't so off the mark in condemning new foreign masters at home via Brussels?

Indeed, in one area Jerry wholly agreed with Tim, his mention of "experts" on TV pontificating as know-alls. Jerry remembered them at the start of the recession, saying confidently on TV that the recession would be over in six months, and the average house would be worth a million in a few years, and all should invest. And he thought of Socrates. He came to the conclusion that he knew nothing, so he went and spoke to all the so-called wise men of his age. He came back from that enterprise convinced that he was the only wise man because he was that he was the only one who knew that he knew nothing. That reflects aspects of our age too, Jerry thought; we listen too much to fake experts and don't think enough for ourselves or seriously question what is being fed to us, whether by the media or any other areas of influence on our lives.

"The maps and photos are all right, we're very grateful to you Tim, and you have been following the case and know more about it than us", Deverly said, giving him some time to rest his case and calm himself for like all enthusiasts he got carried away at times and full of vehement views.

"But we want a good alternative plan also", Donie added, with the voice of reason written all over his face, "that will convince the people and the media and benefit the area and its traders financially. Money seems to be the bottom line in most issues nowadays culture or heritage seem to no longer cut as much ice as it used to. I listen to reports on radio and TV about local art or culture events and the last sentence of the report is always, it will bring in many millions for the area. That's more often than not the bottom line today whether we like it or not. Jerry, though you take the art and heritage approach, you're fooling yourself if you think art in itself is always the main concern of our new masters. Sadly, money seems to be the bottom line in much thinking today, it's the new god, that and total self-interest is a new version of what was always the main idol men worshipped instead of the true God. The first commandment is the first because it is the most important and the most broken; golden calf idols abound today too".

"So is there any lucrative incentive we can offer, any alternative source of wealth and employment that might save the mountain? As they say, if you we can't beat them, join them; and we must recognize that the area badly needs some form of development in these difficult times; the local people can't eat the mountain, or heritage", Jerry observed to Thornton.

"Yes, I have been thinking along the same lines. I suggest we draw up a plan for a small non-open-cast mine, owned and run by the community", he replied. "I think it could be done. Sink a shaft underground from the other side cover it with suitable environmental greenery. Just a small enterprise, and it would actually mean more local involvement and more lasting employment, the company would bring in mainly people from abroad, grab the loot and leave the area worse off in every way. There always is "another way", as a wise old Christian black woman once said to me on a bus in the Southern USA.

"Yes, we can do it our way. We can send the ore away for refinement, I say, and bring it back to make souvenirs related to the mountain. In that way the community would benefit double, like the old sugar factories, they benefitted farmer and industry alike, but some fat cat in Brussels decided to get rid of them and we went along like sheep...no real local voice of reason was heard, only an ideology ruthlessly imposed from afar. That is always the way with centralized super states, they lose touch with the people on the periphery; it's why all super states eventually collapse under their own bureaucracy. The EU won't last, but in the meantime it will do much harm to our independence and integrity".

Before he embarked on another hobby horse, I broke in:

"Tim, that sounds great, give people a better alternative; take the ground from under the feet of the so-called progressives, who see only one way, the big money and foreign control way.

With the company it would be a snatch and grab and it would benefit only the moguls of the company sitting in foreign countries and plundering the world for their benefit, far from the local hewers of wood and stone they largely despise".

"Yes", Tim said, I had unwittingly introduced a new rag to the bull, "Those fat moguls think they can rule the world by means of ruthless finance, they won't rule us, the greedy bastards. Feck them.. feck them again I say..the faceless fuckers...Sorry for the intemperate language man of the clothe but all this gets my goat, we need a new 1916 revolution to restore our long lost ideals".

By way of pouring oil on troubled waters Jerry introduced a film anecdote since he was also a bit of a film buff.

"Spot on there, Tim", He said, "you know that scene in the Titanic, where the US widow says to the poor boy asked to join the table of the wealthy first class lot; 'After dinner they will retire and engage in their plans to rule the world', or words to that effect. When the ship sank they were in the same boat as everyone else. Death knows no class distinction, nor does God, nor does our holy mountain.

With a smaller community co-op the gold vein would last for a very long time, benefit our children too, and all the profits, apart from the refining costs, would accrue to the people here in the Clew area".

"Draw up a prospectus for that too and we'll pick it up in a few Days", Deverly said, anxious to move on, and his ears burning from Tim's tirades, yet secretly pleased with what he said and what we had gained. He knew that Tim could go on forever about environmental issues and get more and more worked up; we had got as much as we would get from him on this and it was a lot.

"Tim, we appreciate this, I know you will be a real angel of mercy to us, and a devil to our opponents", Donie added, shaking his hand warmly as a way of ending the meeting,

"At least now we have something to work with, and I think it will work, the people are proud of their mountain, however much they are lured by vain promises of passing profit and the glib propaganda of the mining company reflected in the media and plush ads. Once we answer their qualms in relation to employment and development for the area, we'll be on the pig's back".

After this they parted in good spirits. Donie and Jerry on the way home were full of excitement and optimism, the glass was half full after all. Sadly they heard that Thornton had been assaulted in the street a few days later and was in hospital in Galway, they only hoped he'd recover before the village meeting.

CHAPTER 12

Children's arrival and Deirdre's lectures

WHEN THEY PULLED IN THE GATE OF THE COTTAGE A PLEASANT surprise awaited Jerry, the sound of chattering children's voices. Deirdre and the children had come unexpectedly; he was delighted for he had sorely missed his vivacious kids, even though he had been separated from them only for a few days. Deirdre had come to give some lectures at a Galway university's summer school on post postmodernism, whatever that was, and the kids were leaping out of their skins with excitement at the new rocky playground all around them, and at being united with Dad. They came shooting out and swarmed all over him, with hugs and kisses galore. Shouts of "Dad I did this and dad I did that, and look at this and look at that, and where can we go tomorrow, and Nelly wants to take us to Westport Zoo and the play area, and we might climb the mountain...".

The house will be bursting at the seams, he thought, but Nelly assured them that the two girls had gone off to stay with their local boyfriends a thing Donie and Nelly weren't wholly happy with but knew better than to make a scene and get their hackles up.

It was only after they had settled the kids that Jerry notices Jim in the corner, a gloomy look on his face.

"What's the matter, Jim", Jerry said, joining him in a drink.

"Bad news, I'm afraid", he said, "it seems that Davy has give in to pressure and agreed to sell out his part of the mountain to the mine company; it looks as if we're scuttled after all, sorry, I thought our pact not to sell was rock solid, must have got to him in some way, twisted his arm, he's soft and easily swayed, sorry!"

After all their grand plans and schemes, all the excitement and gains of the day had suddenly collapsed around their ears. They were in a deeper cesspit than before and it would it get even deeper.

Though surrounded by hyper kids, supper was a sober affair, a kind of heavy silence of defeat hung over them. Brian was sitting on Jerry's lap, he was a fair haired bouncy boy of five. Mairead, he called her Mairead the magnificent, was tugging at his sleeve with some secret that she wanted to impart and didn't want the others to hear. Brendan, the eldest, a tall athletic boy like his dad had been when of that age, had gone out to play with a hurly and ball. Jerry called him his Cuchullin, after the hero of the ancient sagas in the Irish language who supposedly could strike a ball a hundred yards and catch it again before it hit the ground. The area of Kerry the Lofties lived in was all hurling, not football. Michelle, he called her his beautiful shell upon the sea shore, was pushing a pram around with a naked baby in it that she was feeding with a toy bottle. Suddenly she chirped:

"Dad we've all agreed we want to climb the mountain tomorrow, Nelly says she'll go with us part of the way anyway. It'll be a great adventure and you Daddy will go with us wont you?"

She looked at him with large pleading irresistible eyes.

Nelly had been fussing around them as if they were her own grandchildren, getting special fish fingers and chips and cans of fizz for them, and chocolate bars, spoiling them rotten in fact, and they weren't adverse to being spoiled, lapping it up. Deirdre was in the corner with a computer buzzing busy with the composition of her lecture, and now she glanced up at her husband as if to say, a good way of getting them out of the way and keeping them busy while I'm in the city giving my lecture. They had reached the stage, which many happily married couples do, where they could communicate without words.

Jerry said, taking his cue, "of course, my beautiful shell on the sea shore, I'll go with you. We'll take packed lunches and go up early before the big rush, so you'd better get to bed if you want to be fit to rise early for that adventure".

A ruse to get them to bed, parents become adept at such ruses though more often than not children are more than adept at seeing through them. But they were tired after the journey anyway, and trotted off with Nelly, their adopted grandmother, a new novelty and source of good things, to put on warm night clothes and brush teeth and get ready for bed.

When they had gone up and Jerry had kissed each of them in turn and tucked them in, he went back down to the sitting room and looked at Deirdre's evolving lecture, leaning over her, his arms around her and his cheek against hers, a pose they often adopted for their discussions of her work; intimacy before a deeper bed intimacy. She was very much advanced now more mature, her fair hair tinged with grey, her bodily filled out in a more attractive womanly way, her face was more lined maybe from thinking too much and not living enough, maybe! But he loved her all the more for that; they were a sharing couple taking turns with caring for the children's growing needs; looking after their family Jerry knew was the greatest joy, even when things didn't go well; suffering faithfulness and integral behaviour, no matter how difficult, in any sphere of life was the key they both thought. And they had their own artistic and intellectual interests which they sometimes shared with their beloved children. They didn't believe children should be talked down to its amazing what children can think of and work out at a relatively young age.

Kissing her neck Jerry looked over Deirdre's head at some notes for her coming lecture in Galway University, gleaned from the internet and various learned tomes. They were glad the internet was the source of so much knowledge now, a knowledge available to all which in itself is post postmodernist. Knowledge in our modern age, once rooted in the universities and other seats of learning and so exclusive to the rich who could afford third-level education, has now shifted, from those who could publish or read books, to being available to everyone on the tube. He looked at her learned notes as she listed them and commented where appropriate: her title was "Post postmodernism the need for a new Departure".

She began (he read over her shoulder; her lecture material is in italics, his in normal type and not meant to be delivered as part of her lecture; she was the intellectual he was the poor poet and biased church deacon); *the root of postmodernism is in Saussure's structuralism which he said would undermine or force people to rethink all the arts and sciences. Basically Saussure said that there is no reality, only structures of reality created by man. We live within these without really adverting to them as artificial and arbitrary. For example the structure of a dinner, soup, main course desert, coffee, is a common structure we accept as natural. But in other cultures it is completely different. So our structuring of reality is arbitrary. Recent experts such as Derrida and Foucault carried this on into deconstruction. They said that structures are not fixed but are constantly changing. Once we realize the structures by which we are shaped, and that constitute our reality, we can "deconstruct" them; indeed their subconscious, the other they suppress, always rises to defeat them in the long run. For example postmodernism is a deconstruction of the tenets of modernism. And my Post Postmodernism is a radical deconstruction of postmodernism.*

Yes Jerry said, bringing this more down to earth. Pink Floyd in their composition The Wall compares the structures that control people in a school setting to bricks that build a wall that restricts and controls children. There is no doubt that the educational systems creates walls around us early on, structures of secret control that limit people's creativity and ability to think outside the box as it were. The box of the TV or the media in general is another such structuring and controlling wall or force in society conditioning people to a way of thinking and acting dictated by the dominant ideology. Most of the time this is concealed especially in the so-called free west; but in communism and fascism it was more blatant, enforced indoctrination, as in the re-education of dissidents in camps and gulags. Our re-educating media is more subtle today, hidden agendas.

I was told by a media expert recently that one had no chance of getting a job in a certain TV station he worked in if one's views were outside the station's left-wing views – in right wing stations the boot is on the other foot – In effect there is no such thing as total freedom or even real reality, all is just controlling structure after structure like the layers of an onion that has no centre. Most of the time structures control us even as they are cleverly concealed as freedom. In fact it is just freedom to act and speak within the parameters of social norms laid down by the dominant ideology; there is free speech for example now in the west only as long it is liberal free speech. Soon even the internet will soon have such controlling norms set by the dominant ideology, they are already being aired and prepared.

Where then is real freedom? In the unconscious and related to this the eternal truths of the highest faiths notably Christianity, which is proved by the fact that it has endured for 2000 years whereas in the same period purely human ideological structures have come and gone in multitudes, because they always contain the seeds of their own destruction in their 'them' and 'us' exclusivity; the other they exclude always rises up either openly or unconsciously, that's why purely human created ideologies are always limited, temporary and tyrannical because of their enforced exclusivity, that is especially true of the grand-sounding utopian ones of the totalitarian era. So many of these such as communism have come and gone while the more enduring wisdom structures of the Christian faith have endured; that's why Christ talks not about ideas but divine eternally valid divine truth; they must be so valid logically or they would have not endured while thousands of man-made ideologies have laid around them in ruins, even in our own day ideologies like fascism and communism for example, as the modern liberal or woke ideology will also logically fail in the long run, only fools follow such temporary power traps invented by clever ideologue masters".

Yes Deirdre said aside from her notes, but faith can also be turned into an ideology as in Northern Ireland, when its basic eternal truths are turned into passing human political and social systems of bigoted power contrary to the central eternal truth of the real Christianity they profess, love one another is sadly turned into kill one another. Christian eternal truths of love and unity are made a travesty of when turned into political systems, that is why Christ said to Pilate, the emblem of ruthless worldly Roman power, that his kingdom was not of this world, which is also why it is unfair as many atheistic gurus on YouTube do to condemn the faith because of particular basic travesties of its basic truths in certain world arenas; it's like setting up a false duck and then glibly shooting it down smugly".

"But surely", Jerry objected, "the multitudes of Christian sects and denominations must be accused of the same travesty of the truth, they are all different twisting of the age-old faith by individuals who create their own limited version of the truth like ideology. Logically then the only enduring truth I am commending as the antidote to limited ideological tyrannies is in the Catholic faith which had kept Christ's eternal wisdom doctrines the same since the time of the apostles to which they were entrusted. And the Catholic Church has systems set up to ensure these truths are maintained unsullied, notably the papacy and the councils. Even eastern orthodox churches are too tied to national structures to do that effectively, they are all nation churches and so inevitably share the limiting influences of the nations of which they are a part. But the greatest threat to the faith is the watering down of its eternally passed down truth today under the influence of modernist and post modernist woke ideologies. It is vital that woke postmodernism should be resisted in the church lest it sell-out its enduring truths for a populist 'mess of pottage' to use a biblical analogy".

But what was modernism in the first place, Deirdre wrote reverting to her strict lecture notes. It had literary and social and political dimensions. In literature the modernist mode of complex texts reigned in such as in Eliot or Joyce, with endless allusions from the larger discourses of western, or indeed world, art and civilization. This was seen as high art, in a sense an art for the elite to decipher in universities and place of higher tone. Modernism at the turn of the 20th century, in the social and political fields envisaged a new age of endless progress, of gleaming machines and shining architecture; it dreamed of 20th century utopias, a perfect progressive society without injustice or war. In fact this was an illusion. In fact especially at the political level it spawned various destructive utopian ideologies from fascism to communism to woke libertarianism today. All of these reacted against and undermined the traditional Christian bases of western civilization and produced modern libertarianism, secularism, Hitler's National Socialism, Soviet communism to name but a few of its cruel offshoots. Yet the object of all of these was a secular utopia, a so-called enlightenment that in fact turned out to be no enlightenment at all but destructive tyrannies, the factors I have outlines above, the them and us partiality came into play. Consequently in fact in that "light" the 20th century spawned the most savage wars in human history; modernism turned out to be the opposite of what it originally envisaged. Far from utopias it fuelled ruthless secularism, and produced genocides such as the holocaust or the Soviet mass collectivism which in the Ukraine led to the death of up to 12 million peasants many of whom starved to death. And modernism produced, despite its stated objective of utopia, far less just societies; the sort of horrible tyrannies and warring power blocks Orwell wrote about in his novel 1984. It had its successes also of course in the advance of science, notably medical science, gleaming modern architecture, and the rapid advance of technology and the advanced modern media of TV, radio, film, the mobile phone and the internet, though these have all had their dark sides also notably in the way in which technology threatens to produce the machine man, reducing his natural life and humanity, and the way in which machine industrialism and the car pollution is threatening the biosphere. Again we need a post postmodernism that brings the self sacrifice for the sake of the earth that foregoes all the cars and pollutants of our technological toys. I know many households today who have six cars in their yard, even for some in secondary school, and a mansion with masses of unnecessary lights; this wastefulness of resources must give way to a more responsible stewardship of the earth and a greener healthier environment such as Tolkien sketches in the Shire.

Postmodernism did not so much react against all that destructive industry and technology as continue it in more extreme contemporary forms. For example its literature deconstructed the established artistic order of modernism. It undermined the complex allusive styles and tenets of modernism by mixing genres, blurring the distinction between high and low literature, using parody and pastiche in relation to traditional forms, using inter-textuality to reveal how our presentation of history is riddled with prejudices that reflect the dominant ideological discourse in any moment in time. Hence postmodernism set to undermine all that; it stressed "creative experimentation..the real and the imaginary is absorbed into the symbolic liberated word which cannot be pinned down" (as the old Irish ashling poems subverted colonialism). This approach was soon not confined to literature. From the outset it filtered down into society and politics, in the deconstruction of a traditional world view and any eternal social and spiritual wisdom teaching. It deconstructed dominant discourses of western society some in a good way at first but ultimately in a destructive way in fascist's National Socialism, Communism, ultra-libertarian mores and woke radical left doctrinaire impositions now. Instead of utopia totalitarian hells emerged.

So we can come to the definition of postmodernism: a development within thinking and aesthetics today, either emerging from, in reaction to, or superseding modernism. Inventing new rules and changing the game, creating a new sense of justice as well as knowledge. This was accentuated when it was taken up by Marxists. Radicals set out to undermine all "unjust" structures in society real or imagined. But after everything was deconstructed, what is left now? Some would say a waste land of mindless nihilism, again no utopia but a spiritual waste land such as Eliot and Orwell exposed, it is no wonder that the latter also like Tolkien or Dostoevsky or Tolstoy turned back to the eternal truths of the faith which are not the passing limited and limiting constructs of man but the everlasting wisdom of God, which is not machine minded but soul nourishing for man's deeper natural happiness now and forever. The ultimate mistake of postmodernism was the neglect of man's spiritual and humane essentials. Sadly a new era of artificial intelligence is just accentuating the reign of the faceless machine mind, maybe that film The Terminator wasn't so way out after all, with its image of a ruling machine world replacing humans"?

At this reading and commenting was interrupted by a phone call. Terry and Sally and Billy and Molly wanted us to come to Billy's flat the following day; they were writing their philosophical theses on modernism and postmodernism belief and atheism and would we come to discuss this with them. Great we said, the input from that gang would greatly inform Deirdre's lecture series on this very topic, what she called post postmodernism, the need for a radical new ideology given the terrible violent legacy of the modern and postmodernism secular ideologies and anti-environmental industrialism and wasteful fossil fuel machine technology of the 20th and 21st centuries. But as Sam says in the Lord of the Rings how can things go back to the healthier spiritual, moral and environmentally friendly way things once were when so many bad things have happened, or who really is willing to give up a woke, hedonistic and fossil-fuel affluence they enjoy now. "That's the question we face today", Deirdre said, "it's that I try to answer".

CHAPTER 13

"No Life in the Void"

THE NEXT DAY JERRY AND DEIRDRE WENT TO BILLY'S FLAT ABOVE THE
pub for the promised philosophical discussion, the first of five which
the university would accept as summer school credits. The four
young budding scholars and philosophers unashamedly wanted to
pool their brains to get good grades for their papers. The meal and
drinks were so different from Jim's cottage fare. There were high
balls and low balls and cocktails of every description to oil their
thinking and finger picking fish and chips to fill their stomachs.
Jerry loved young people and the four were real fun; gone were
the boy-band bash outfits and they lolled about in casual clothes,
almost like night clothes all loose-fitting sexy and colourful like in
a pyjama party.

For the first time Jerry saw the real character of the each of the
young people. Sally was thin, thoughtful and very conscious of her
figure and her weigh; indeed her parents were worried about her
and wondered if she should go to see a psychiatrist because she
kept herself so ultra-thin. This had become an obsession; she looked
in the mirror and saw a fat chick when in fact she could be blown
away by a breath; this left her pale, with a continual malnourished
look, that is why her parents feared bulimia. This worried Jerry
and Deirdre also because they regarded her as their own since they
were so close to her parents. Molly by comparison with the slender
Sally was a roly-poly life-lover like her mother, but in a nice way.
She had a full figure, a gorgeous mass of blonde-dyed hair, and
full lips with bright red lipstick, long silver earrings a nose ring
and romantic rose tattoos all over her neck and arms and boobs.

She enjoyed and smiled at life and she took whatever it offered her without thought-tormented angst.

The two boys were also quite different. Jerry saw Terry for what he was for the first time a serious intellectual and spiritual chap. He was tall and sparse and almost looked austere like his father but where the father was practical Terry was dreamy, mystical tattoos decked his neck and arms. Maybe this spiritual bent was due to conviction or maybe it was an effort to be the opposite of his father, children do revolt and he was at the rebellious age. Billy by comparison was small and more like Terry's father in his attitudes and convictions, but Jerry was disturbed and worried by Billy's obsession with drugs. Jerry soon cottoned on to Billy's addiction to marijuana, he feared a deeper addiction might have followed.

During the discussion, the two boys would occasionally drift into the neighboring room and return with a slightly glazed look in their eyes; they had been smoking pot Jerry surmised and it worried him for he feared they might graduate to harder drugs later on. He said as much to them and Billy responded with a look that said mind your own damn business. What a stuck in the mud lot Terry also seemed to say, looking at Jerry and Deirdre, no wonder the church is in a backward mess if these are its representatives, no modern savvy at all.

When food and drinks had been consumed the four sat with Jerry and Deirdre for their purposed philosophical debate. Jerry said before they began that this was for life, for to get one's life right one first has get one's philosophy or faith right, no one can live with an inner void. So the topic was postmodern atheism and the role of faith in Ireland today. Billy set the ball rolling by citing Nietzsche and the irrelevance of traditional faith and morality in the enlightenment and post modernist world of today. Science he said had put all the airy-fairy stories of religion to bed. Terry and Sally took the opposite view. Billy and Molly, on the atheistic side were setting themselves against Terry and Sally on the faith side; it was to be a philosophical battle with Jerry and Deirdre as commentators and referees, though they were also on the faith side. The debate was a bit lop-sided as it was bound to be given the group's composition and the nature of truth.

Jerry rubbed his hands he was really looking forward to this debate, in his new deacon enthusiasm he wanted to convert them to the essential nature of faith in human life. For he knew this was not just an abstract debate but a life debate, for everyone has a philosophy behind their actions and it's important that that philosophy is the right one, so that the resultant life might also be the right one.

Responding to Billy, Dee said there was certainly a curiously alluring quality in the philosophy of Nietzsche. She remembered when a young student herself being bowled over by Thus Spoke Zarathustra. But when he dumped God and Christian morality as oppressive, and, though a finite man, set out in arrogance to write his own bible her ardour cooled; happily he went mad, she said, laughing, before completing that silly alternative bible project."Man wanting to be God is as old as the Genesis story and as sure an exile from paradise now too", she added.

"Good" said Terry, and Sally nodded, adding that "maybe Nietzsche was always a bit on the crazy side, he arrogantly saw himself as a kind of secular prophet, the idiot. There was no such thing, a prophet is one who listens to and speaks for God, at least that's how it was in the scriptures I learned in my religion classes, you can't speak for and try to be God if you don't believe there needs to be a God, so in a curious way Nietzsche believed in God, even in trying to kill him".

At this Molly frowned and said no and Billy got red in the face with aggravation, muttering that this was religious stuff and nonsense as usual, and someone like John Lennon in his song "Imagine" burst that bubble in our time. Though of course what Lennon imagined was very much a divine vision, what God also wants as that song "God is watching us" also expresses so succinctly. Lennon was attacking the distortion of faith in human ideological and political power games, using God to bolster one's own narrow position as in Northern Ireland or Islamic extremism.

To alleviate a tension that was now creeping in to the discussion Jerry added that some of postmodernism had good liberating aspects. For example it opposed the suppression of dissident voices in the sixties in the US, seen in works such as One Flew over the Cuckoo's Nest. Those who threatened an over-rigid established order were locked up. Eliminating this was a salutary change. So were aspects of the sexual revolution of the sixties which demolished restricting aspects of traditional sexuality. Hippy flower power was liberating though many thoughtful feminists now say it hasn't been good for women in the long term. Other vital revolutionary changes were accentuated by protest against the Vietnam War and feminism. Much of the latter again was salutary but it all became too extreme when it saw all males as oppressors. Similarly an intolerant ultra-radical left libertine "woke" ideology now unduly abolished every aspect of what it saw of oppressive traditional social and religious norms and morality, leaving a void in modern life and in the soul of men especially; "I read recently a study that said American men today are shell-shocked", he added.

"Yes" Terry said and Sally agreed, she was like a mindless echo, "that process of demolishing everything valuable of the western culture which led the world in so many ways resulted in a void of foundationless secularism and rabid mindless libertarianism. And it became a tyrannical new orthodoxy when it penetrated into structures such as the Democratic Party in the US, and the new bludgeoning western media. 'Token' women, and gay or black persons dominating in media does offset patriarchy, sexism, or racism, it just replaces one tyranny with another but kick out racism a new chant before and after football matches does help correct social imbalances in sport. Similarly total political correctness must characterize people selected to represent the public in government or media. This too is valuable in breaking down unjust stereotypes, but when it became too invasive and dictatorial it spawned a new tyranny. Tarantino the famous film director recently noted that in woke Hollywood now "ideology trumps art", if one doesn't toe the woke line one is shown the door".

"No" Billy said angrily, "this isn't tyranny it's just progress reflecting Nietzsche's deconstructive views, we must demolish the old before we can build the new and woke thinking is the new way whether we like it or not, we can't turn back the clock".

"Sure, but the dark side of such views soon emerged", Sally said and this time it was Terry supporting her. She cited the present revolt against woke impositions when the movement started to use undue coercion, compromising the larger good of human freedom. "The curse of the modern age is in its relentless tendency to turn well-meaning ideology into totalitarian tyranny", she said with emphasis.

"Yes", Jerry said adding his Christian point of view as usual. "As disturbing was the woke attack on age-old truths, basic common sense and timeless natural-law norms of morality rooted in the humane and sane Christian foundation of western society. In this climate the view arose that anything goes, all things are allowed. But this has led to alienation, nihilism and a morally and spiritually foundation-less society. And its weirder aspects are too way out to be healthy or even believable a void replaces the key age-old moral and spiritual bases of western civilization. And as the satanic Sauron says in *The Lord of the Rings*, 'there is no life in the void'".

At this Terry and Billy snuck off into the kitchen to smoke some weed, Jerry surmised, for they came back a little disorientated; some cuddling and kissing followed among the young couples that also halted things for a while. They all mixed new drinks and had some sandwiches and rich trifle desserts that Sally refrained from taking, looking at them in horror, she ate some blueberries instead.

"Look here", Jerry continued when the youngsters refocused on the debate, "a good example of the drift towards insane woke extremism is the explosion of a bizarre trans-gender ideology. It eroded the traditional sensible view of mainly two genders, male and female, as in the bible 'male and female he created them, in the image of God'. Thus a person on the You-tube recently said that she has three children, 2 boys and a girl. Though they had normal genitalia she refused to say what gender they were. About four they could make a decision and then be chopped up in hospitals to fit the gender they had chosen. That is normal gender, now another supposed universal structure of oppression must be abolished. In the meantime the You-tube woman called her children not he or she but genderless terms like 'theybe' and 'itbe'. This ideology is enforced craziness".

"Other like coercive and bizarre aspects of postmodernism", Sally added, "make up woke ideology, it is everywhere now and, like communism before it its becoming more oppressive than the ideologies it replaced. This is because postmodernism was hijacked by radical left-wing ideologues. Rigid political correctness originally a salutary force in universities began to be ruthlessly imposed. Exaggerated feminist efforts to bring down so-called oppressive patriarchal structures of western culture soon created unbalanced male-female divisions. It *also demoralized men, especially young men. We see that in our own university, a new kind of imposed orthodoxy that would be good if it wasn't way over the top, and eroded the greater good of human freedom and free expression and the rights of all people including men, all races including white, religious believers the backbone of society and those happy in traditional genders".*

"I saw that myself too when I was a lecturer", Jerry said; "Imagined structures of racism were read into innocent lectures though in fact we all supported the liberation of women, black people or other racial groups. We only became uneasy when this was unduly simplified into 'all light-skinned people are oppressors and all dark-skinned people are oppressed, or all men are oppressors and all women are oppressed'. What then of Obama, a black man, who was voted into the American presidency by white and well as black voters? The whole postmodern experiment degenerated into a mindless extremism. Thus in American universities mobs with bats harassed those often falsely accused of racism due to some innocent remark taken out of context; and administrative mobs began looking for people in the university community to 're-educate'".

Sally jumped on this, "In effect problems arose when postmodern ideology, like the progress of all utopian ideologies such as communism or fascism, became extreme and oppressively enforced tyrannies. The universities came to be controlled by woke postmodernist extreme ideologues, we haven't learned from history. As one university expert noted on the YouTube recently, 'Education was replaced by indoctrination'; normal teaching disappeared. In effect, in this imagined freeing of all from oppressive structures the greater good of freedom of expression and in-depth and proper varied education open to all views was trashed as you noted earlier. It was not true liberalism either which is Christian and summed up in the open and all-embracing heart, for true freedom is best seen in a world that develops heart and soul freely for a happy life here and hereafter".

"Yes I follow the YouTube too", Terry said, "and the new guru of the anti-woke platform is Jordan Petersen, a noted clinical psychologist and Ontario college professor, I love him. I'm sure if you were debating with him, Billy, he'd wipe the floor with you. The Canadian government passed a law that all teachers and university lecturers must use up to 20 pronouns so as to recognize a new bizarre range of gender types. The

law reflected a sudden explosion of trans-gender ideology in Canada out of proportion to actual cases of dysphoria in society.

At one time a person clearly in the wrong gender was a relatively rare phenomenon. But soon changing people from the gender they were born with became an ultra left heavily promoted norm, often for slender reasons. Huge numbers against all common sense had their gender changed by operations and drugs. And large numbers who later wanted to revert to their normal gender were trapped in chopped up and even chemically changed or physically castrated bodies monstrous examples of the crazy evolution of a monstrous ideology. As the great modern thinker G K Chesterton, the apostle of common sense said, when common sense goes out the window and is replaced by ideology so does human sanity".

"Are you saying", Billy said, "and this applies to Nietzsche, that leftist ideology triumphed over common sense and that it usually does. I don't agree, in that case there would be no progress in social justice structures. Liberating new ideas have to be strictly imposed or they will not make a real or lasting impact. That's why Lenin said that to safeguard the revolution the party must control the media".

"But" Sally responded, "undue gender bending was not so much necessary progress as ideological madness. Most are confused about gender in teen years, Petersen as a clinical psychologist pointed out, but studies showed that at about the age of 18 the vast majority revert to the biological gender they were born with. But in an over-ardent trans era such counsel was not given to very young people with gender concerns. At a very young age many were too easily subjected to gender-changing operations that made them neither man nor woman before they were 20, lost and confused in an no-man's land.

But Petersen refused to accept the pronoun law for a deeper reason it violated his right to free speech, a higher good that he felt the gender ideology impositions were undermining. He was cancelled and a committee was set up to 're-educate' him. This reminds one of Orwell's 1984 world of big brother tyranny and the 're-education' of innocent dissidents in gulags and concentration camps. Due to left-leaning biases in the west, such atrocities were not highlighted, so we haven't learned from history's mistakes, they are being repeated now in new forms?"

"*Sure, but these* aspects of new postmodernist oppression are also being subconsciously revolted against or healthily deconstructed at the populist level", Deirdre retorted as she sipped a cocktail of gin and Vermouth. "This is proved by the fact that Petersen's s opposition to the pronoun law made him a hugely popular figure. One of his books sold seven million copies".

"All this proves", Molly said, "is that reactionary conservatism is alive and well and trying to stop all progress as it usually does. I am a feminist and Petersen's books just give a weapon to a reactionary patriarchy, men don't like losing an unquestioned power they enjoyed for generations, seen even in the bible".

"That is not quite true", Terry said taking the side of young men of his own age, "Petersen's supporters were not just young men who felt demoralized by the constant attack on men as the source of all social oppression, a silly generalization. This doesn't compromise the larger objectives of moderately imposed feminism and moderate imposed racial equality processes which are still very valid. It just prevents an anti-men or anti-all-white-men tyranny from taking hold in society. People always go from one extreme to the other. We need the classical and Christian motto of the golden mean to be implemented, again the history of modern totalitarianism is the history of well-meaning ideologies carried to extremes and that seems to be happening now through woke fanaticism".

"I agree", Jerry added "but Petersen's You-tube lectures and published books offered a deeper critique of postmodernism than just opposing bizarre transgender ideology or feminist indiscriminate trashing of men. He criticized the wider postmodernist attack on the formative narratives of western civilization such as Christianity, which he argued was the force behind so many modern western advances: human rights, tolerant liberalism; feminist and racialist respect for every human life from conception to the grave; open science, art and literature. It was no coincidence that these civilizing forces flourished best in the Christian west. But as such foundations of civilization weaken the whole edifice must fall. There must be structures but it's important that they are structures that have stood the test of time and bring life in every age".

"Yes", Sally broke in, "I read somewhere that Woke ideology

also subverts the other classical side of western civilization, the rationalism of the enlightenment even though Foucault, a great postmodernist, had said that anything opposed to reason was madness. Much of woke ideology itself is contrary to reason and even common sense as noted in the Petersen case and efforts at his 're-education'. For Petersen woke postmodernism is becoming a madness of man against man and his transcendent inherited greatness, freedom and dignity; it continued the oppressive secular utopian madness seen in ideologies such as communism and fascism that subverted the sane values and religious discourses of western civilization, only to provide awful alternatives. Woke postmodernism threatens to go down a similar road, to follow a similar totalitarian path".

"*This identified the main question facing atheistic postmodernism that I try to answer in my post postmodernism*", Deirdre said, "*is postmodernism, in the extreme forms into which it has evolved, any longer a force for good in society? Is its 'progressive' agenda in fact creating a 'regressive' society, undermining all that made western society great and enabled it to lead to the world such as in democratic freedom of expression and openness to all views? Many say yes. It's tolling the death knell of the most redeeming features of western civilization without replacing them with anything of equal value or any real value at all? It's the killing not only of God, but also of all inherited civilized norms, as here in Ireland it threatens our great spiritual heritage since Patrick as represented by the Mountain above us that has nurtured peoples souls through every horror from the inequalities of colonialism to the terrors of the famine to imposed EU secularism*".

"*But this thinking you are thrashing is a new way*", Billy said, "*therefore it must be progress, things always have to be new no matter how painful that may be. We can't go backwards again, we must go with the tide of new ideas and trends or lapse into backward norms of thinking and behaviour, life must move on or stagnate forever in the stale religious forms of an increasingly stifling past*".

"*I agree*", Jerry said, "*we cannot roll back the clock, but neither should we see everything new as progress; the modern myth that everything new and modern is inevitable progress is not logical. New ways could just as easily take us backwards rather than forward, history shows many upward and downward curves in civilization. Indeed due to postmodernism's ravages many now talk of an imminent collapse of western civilization due to contemporary movements This may be an inevitable process of human history however. All civilizations go through a process of growth, development and decline like the seasons".*

"Are we now in the inevitable winter of our civilization?", Deirdre said, "a recent article by a noted sociologist I read, claimed that what postmodernists are producing now are 'technological savages'. Society is progressing technologically and scientifically but regressing in the areas that really make up a civilized society, faith, high moral values and a transcendent vision of human meaning, freedom, purpose and destiny. All is replaced by the vapid moral and spiritual relativism of Nietzsche and postmodernism that gives no real guidance to any one for a better and more integral life, what Petersen calls the highest value in the highest place, a grand motivational idealism rooted in the vital God hypothesis. As Jung noted even if God didn't exist we would have to invent him, for without him there would be no great human achievements or saintly examples to inspire us such as Patrick and his mountain here. Without such self-transcending guiding ideals we lapse into a regressive spiral of moral and spiritual decay for as Einstein said the greatness of man is in the degree to which he can transcend the self. For Nietzsche the self was everything, but as an absolute it leaves one mired in inward-looking narcissism and alienation from man's vital self-sacrificing community trust".

"I must acknowledge", Billy added, looking a little crestfallen, "that even the inventor of the catch phrase 'God is dead' admitted that his ideology would lead to moral and spiritual chaos, the collapse of all civilized values and a despair-filled nihilism. But he still felt we must push on to new horizons regardless, take the plunge rather than live by illusions no longer viable. Facing uncomfortable truths is painful but necessary though the very ground is taken from under us".

"Not a good idea" Deirdre said, "if the plunge entails cultural suicide. Let me go back to structuralist basics and say that even if all constructs are arbitrary, we must choose and maintain those that are life-giving and humanely nourishing, notably faith and a morality that transcends human finiteness and tendency to selfishness and inner corruption. For

example centuries-old proven Catholic morality based on the natural law is not an arbitrary social structure but provides a solid enduring basis for human vitality and soul development, the most important development of all. Nature based it can't be dispensed with anymore than nature can be dispensed with. And a culture whereby the west led the world in democracy, science and the rule of reason, which distinguished man from the purely instinctive animal state, must still be still validated and supported against the alterative void of nihilism at all costs. Again 'there is no life in the void'".

"But Nietzsche", Billy said clinging to his idol, "insisted all faith must go. The supreme modernist or postmodernist, it's hard to categorize him, he thought man must dump God and create his own values 'beyond good and evil' as defined by Christianity. He must take the power given to God into his own hands; this fully invested and amoral power-pursuing individual beyond theism and related social moral restraints is the way of progress. Without dumping of the past there is no way forward, no future and the individual is forever a slave to theistic nonsense, tyranny and non-scientific gobbly-gook, we have nothing to lose but our chains".

"Yes" said Molly, echoing Billy, "and Dawkins says the God we would leave behind is not so good or great. The God of the Old Testament is horrible at times, jealous, supporting Israel's horrible massacre of their enemies and so on. Even in the New Testament the God who would let his son die so horribly on the cross is hardly a good God, how can we be redeemed by such a horror, do we really need to be redeemed at all? As some such as Blake says maybe Satan is the real God and we should be following him, the rebel against a tyrannical patriarchal God that feminists also rightly reject today. And what about all the evil and suffering in the world this good God is supposed to have created. No, Nietzsche is right we must get rid of this vile tyrannical God and create our own god and our own perfect values without him; atheistic beliefs and systems of government are the way forward, a true enlightenment atheism is needed. That's my view and I stick to it, so there!", she said defiantly thumping the table.

"I support you", Billy said, "as Dawkins pointed out recently on the You-Tube, look at the bad effects of religion in the sectarianism it has produced in Northern Ireland and a host of other areas, where people use religion to kill and hate and blow up women and children, as the

Jihadists do. Religion gives a basis for all such evils, and so it must be abolished so people have no foundation on which to base their fanaticism and hatred of other human beings".

Terry responded, "You both offer a series of ignorant criticisms of Christian theism. The Old Testament is a mixture of human limitation and divine revelation and is perfected by Christ in the New in his own person which is totally peaceful and gentle and the ultimate perfect example for man. He died on the cross to show the only way to perfect the world is by self-giving love, God so loved us that he allowed himself to be crucified to give us this example of humble service rather than dominance of people. This is the opposite of Nietzschean and Satanic pride and power lust the cause of all the evils and wars of the world. To serve Satan is to serve these worst aspects of humanity. Similarly to blame God for the distortion of the faith in places like Northern Ireland ignores the complexity of the situations in such places where the roots of division and violence goes directly against the teachings of the religion they claim to profess, notably Christ's central and last command 'love one another'. The history in Northern Ireland cannot be used to discredit that. It is in fact an offshoot of the evil of power-based colonialism, where the Unionists who were planted in the country were mainly Presbyterian Scots, and the Irish they drove out and whose lands they took were Catholic; the violence is between Irish nationalists and pro-English unionists and religion is twisted to suit that division, it's real base is colonialism not religion so it's unfair to blame it on religion, it's roots are in history and power struggles among various groups not faith, and that is true of practically all other areas of conflict in the world where Christianity is unfairly blamed. I cannot speak for other religions such as Islam for I don't know enough about them except that the Dali Lama says that the central trust of all religions can be summed up by the term loving kindness".

"Moreover faith cannot be attacked under a general abstract heading of 'religion'", Jerry added, "that is an easy duck to set up and knock down, abstract all the worst aspects of all religions and use these to shoot down "religion" in general, what about the infinitely more abundant good aspects. In any case there is no such reality as religion in the abstract anymore than there is such as reality as the abstract term 'bird', there are only different types of birds. The fact is that all religions are not the same and Christianity which we are defending here as the best example of religion has produced millions of saints and progressive social movements and is fundamentally anti-violence; Christ perfects the old Testament in the new as in his supreme mandate, the Sermon on the Mount, 'blessed are the peacemakers' etc is the whole moral and spiritual basis of his teaching. Gandhi, the supreme peacemaker, in a correspondence with Tolstoy said it was the most beautiful thing he had ever read and he rebuked a Christian advisor for advocating violence in the Indian struggle saying doesn't your Christ say to turn the other cheek. So to say Christianity is violent or sectarian is nonsense, it is only so if misrepresented, one finds its authentic aspects in the saints. The fruits of real lived faith has produced untold good here in Ireland and throughout the world, look at all the workers for justice and equality such as Vincent De Paul that still fills in for lack in government social policies. Indeed true religion is the only thing that keeps at bay the worst aspect of human corruption, violence and decadence in my view; without it and a related sane morality all things 'fall apart, the center cannot hold' as Yeats says in that famous poem of his and is replaced by the rule of the "beast". In our faith as seen on this mountain we have a sure centre of belief and morality that has stood the test of time, the same can't be said for the totalitarian violence of all the modern secular systems from communism to Pol Pot to modern day North Korean enclosed madness. Like Dawkins they thought by getting rid of religion thay would produce an utopia but the opposite happened, they let loose the beast that religion had held at bay and showed the true utopian way. I think of that Prussian leader Metternich's anti-Christian mission statement that one 'cannot rule by the values of the Sermon on the Mount', yet the Sermon is the perfect blueprint for a perfect peaceful and happy communitarian world".

"Yes", Jerry added, "and does the history of secularism in our era in any way prove your or Dawkin's point that it is a better way? What about Hitler's Reich and its superman and super state ideology based on Nietzschean power atheism and the horrors that spawned when implemented; what about Stalin's gulags based on Marxist atheistic utopianism that killed up to 60 million Russians and brutalized as many more while turning churches into museums, or Pol Pots regime that killed a third of the Cambodian population including 1 million *intellectuals and monks seen as parasites on society; what about Mao who killed up to 100 million Chinese while demolishing the temples and sending monks and priests to re-education camps; what about the Mexican Marxist revolution when priest were hung from the lampposts; what about Saddam Hussein's Marxism with its little green book, it was the only system in recent times that used poison gas on its people, the Kurds; what about North Korea still, building nuclear bombs while its people starve and so on and on. Surely all this proves that atheistic systems are not an enlightened way forward. Indeed getting rid of God and the heaven his gospel makes possible history proves will produce the opposite, hell on earth as the atheistic systems I cited created; its logical once you get rid of the main force for good, self-giving faith then the opposite results, the unchecked reign of evil; as in physics when one system wanes the opposite rushes in to take its place".*

"But this is not just our biased view", Dee added, "the famous author Solsynitsyn proves that point. He spent many years in a Stalinist gulag for criticizing the system, and he retorted when asked why the soviet systems created such inconceivable horrors, that the reason they got it so wrong was 'they left out God'; modern history proves that when God goes so does even basic morality and humanity and man lapses into a hell of total power-hungry egotism and ruthless inhumane self-interest and power pursuit such as Nietzsche espouses, again there's no life in the void that comes when the floor or faith is taken away and we're trapped forever is a meaningless power gulf".

"Addressing your other point", Terry added, perking up, "one can also rail against evil or suffering in the world and blame God, but this again is a useless negative approach to existence; the positive approach is redemptive humility, goodness and love as Christ and millions of saintly people down the ages, such as our own Patrick here proves. Thereby man progresses and transcends the limited godless deterministic ideological lowlands of the purely individualist and self-centered soul who though finite and imperfect still thinks it is adequate in itself alone. Modern history proves it is not, on its own it's a road to hell".

"Yes", Sally piped in, "I was watching a debate between Petersen and an atheist on the You-Tube and the latter said Petersen was 'too religious' and this was not permitted today by the secular powers that be now and which are sadly creeping into Ireland. What do they want,

reversion to the savage? The sort of savagery that characterized the 20th century's secular ideological wars, as Deirdre noted. But violence and war the atheists try to argue is due to religion but this again is a secularist myth; it is disproved by the facts, a recent study showed that of all wars of history only 3% were in fact rooted in religion. Anyone with even half a brain could see that all the modern wars were in fact all fuelled by fanatical secular ideologies: Fascism, communism, Mao, Pol Pot etc etc. As Deirdre noted It is calculated that between them they killed not only the Jews of the holocaust, but killed or sent to gulags or concentration camps over 200 million people and brutalized as many more".

"Sure", Jerry added, "One can see why solzenityzen who spent many years in a gulag, when released and asked why the system he suffered under killed and brutalized so many, answered "they left out God". We are in danger of repeating these totalitarian disasters now, look at the war in Ukraine, nothing has changed, the old superpower conflicts drag on, and are renewed in every age by secular lords of men who in every age as Tolkien notes 'most of all desire power'. The one answer to that, Christianity, is shelved. But we can live by it and bring perfect peace if we want to as the truce between the Germans and British proved in 1916. The truce was in answer to Christian words that echoed across the lines, peace on earth good will among men, the message Christ came to inaugurate. But the will to war persists though as John Lennon's Christmas song says there is 'peace on earth if we want it'. True Christians want it, but our secular world doesn't. If the latter really wanted it, it would have come long ago in our increasingly secular era. But it came in 1916 in answer to a Christian song which proves we can do it if we will the way of God rather than that of power-hungry men. But secular systems of super power dominance persist today as in the west against Russia today in the Ukraine. And no one, especially a secular media, says that the emperor has no clothes. Instead a new film celebrates the dropping of the atom bomb, a true war crime that if it wasn't done by the west would be decried as the ultimate crime against innocent men, women and children, and now 'cluster bombs" the most evil of modern armaments, long decried by the west when used elsewhere, are now being supplied by the west to be used in the Ukraine war, if they help the west win they are no longer evil. This is the sort of travesty of truth we're asked to support in a so-called enlightened era!"

"As Petersen rightly pointed out similarly the secular totalitarian atrocities of the west in our era have in fact not only not been highlighted but have been played down, even hidden in western discourse because of radical left sympathies among intellectuals. So we need a radical revolution, we need a revealing of the truth behind endless self-justifying atheistic atrocities or we risk repeating them. Surely only the restoration of a faith and a transcendent truth-based love-based real Christian culture can offset the worst aspects of human tendencies to power and repression the perennial sins. I think of a scene in The Power and the Glory, Green's novel about the Mexican Marxist revolution, where all the priests have been killed, hung from lamp posts as in that famous picture of the period, and only a whiskey priest remains; they lure him to the communist headquarters by claiming a man there needs confession. As the communist commander shoots him he says "we will bring about the perfect system, now that these superstitious rulers of the peasants are eliminated". "Ah yes the priest replies but you forget about sin". The fact is that man is fallen and prone to evil and without the restraints of religion and the grace it provides man is bound to be lost in darkness and despair and violent power-seeking justified as progress, as the godless systems of out era proved. Indeed, as even Nietzsche admits, without God there is no foundation for morality, all things are permitted even the worst evils such as fascist cruelty, power is the only norm and the godless superman reigns, he will continue to reign unless we put a stop to his gallop by peaceful Christian hearts, as Our Lady of Medjugorje says 'there will be no peace until there is peace in each human heart from a relationship with the Prince of Peace'. This is proved by the fact that there is no violence or war in Christian convents and monasteries set up to promote peace within; there the key to everything is inner peace in God".

At this their discussion came to an end, for all were tired. Yet though their views often differed they were all the best of friend at the end and embraced each other fervently. After this Deirdre and Jerry headed home to the children that Nelly had been baby-sitting. Again Jerry reflected that without a good philosophy and faith, one that has passed the test of time, there is no good life.

CHAPTER 14

The Magic of the Storied Mountain

W*hen* D*eirdre and* J*erry reached home,* J*im's extended cottage,* their family eagerly awaited their return though Nelly had done her best to keep them amused. But suddenly their kisses and hugs and donning of night clothes in preparation for bed, were interrupted by a frantic hammering at the door. Jerry rushed to open it and halt the commotion, for already the house was in chaos, children trooping out in unsuitable night clothes, to see the cause of the uproar. Donie rushed to Jerry's side as he opened the door. Before them was the figure of Molly, all dishevelled and in tears, crying:

"Daddy it's horrible, Sally was brushed by a car on our way back from our philosophical discussions, she is in the hospital in Castlebar, come quick! I don't think it is serious, she seemed alright afterwards, but it could have been more serious, she is bruised and all that of course but come and see her and comfort her, it's been a huge shock to her and us all". A strange thought came into Jerry's mind that if might have been deliberate, trying to warn off Donie using the children as they tried to warn him off, but no it can't be so surely he said! Yet he remained uneasy. This whole excursion was getting too dangerous by far.

Immediately Donie took over as usual, the practical man of action.

"Nelly and I will go to the hospital, no need for you or Deirdre to come, you have to stay and care for the children"

"Yes, Jerry said, "and I hope everything will be OK, I'm sure it will, but keep us informed by mobile phone when you get to the hospital"

At this Donie and Nelly drove off and Molly and Deirdre and Jerry were left to clam the bedlam in the house and get everyone to bed.

Something Shell said echoed in Jerry's mind when Deirdre had finished writing the first part of her lecture and the children had all gone up to bed, "we've all agreed".

"Jim", he said, the latter was still in the corner downing a nightcap to help him sleep, "does the will of your late father state that all must agree before anyone can sell part of the farm? Wouldn't Davy need you and Biddy's consent before doing anything with his part?"

"I've been thinking about that myself", Jim replied, "The will does state that no one can sell their part without consulting the others, but we don't strictly own the mountain, we have just had the exclusive right to run our sheep on it from time immemorial, no one can put us off. I suppose he could take the sheep off and let the company in, but then again some of the sheep are mine and I have been running them there for a long time, I can claim squatters rights. I think there's a good chance we can block them there. We'll talk to Tim Thornton about it, he's studied the law on property disputes today, it's made him rich, so he'll advise us definitively on that. But I think you're right, we can't be pushed out so easily, even by Davy, though we are brothers and I don't want any rift with him. I can understand the huge money the company offered was tempting and he's always wanted to travel and see the world, not be cooped up here, so different from Biddy and me who wouldn't want to leave this place ever".

After that Jim drove off to his flat in the village.

Jerry called in to see the kids and kiss them goodnight. When he went into Brian's room he was already asleep, so he let him be. But as he lay there, innocent of the world's conniving, greed, violence and death around him, he envied him, and bemoaned the fact that children have to grow up so soon today. That like Sally, he should be bombarded every day with the world's harsh realities; sexual games and porn in the media and the internet. Modern technology, of course, was so exciting; he'd have so many opportunities, but it was so sad that something so good had to have its downside in slavery to mobile phones and violent war games. As Brian lay there Jerry was inspired to write a poem about him and for him, when he got to his own room. He'd always marvelled how children managed to take the world as it is and adapt, tomorrow for them was always a promise. He found that quiet time at night the perfect time for writing, with the experience of the day still rich in one's head, so he wrote a poem for his son that ended "sleep on my son, a new world of joy under Patrick's mountain has just begun". He thought of the wisdom of that popular song that he often quoted for them: "Don't worry be happy".

After that Jerry went into the girl's room and immediately they screamed for a story, so he told them an old children's story he'd composed that remarkably related to the dilemmas they were in.

Once upon a time there was a goblin in the west of Ireland, on one of its great storied mountains",

"What's a goblin?" Mairead interrupted,

"A little fellow like a fairy", he said, "there were lots of them in Ireland at one time".

They accepted this without a blink; children's imaginations are so free, though Brendan, who had risen and drifted in to hear the story, was already coming under the control of school conditioning and a related sceptical cynicism that was undermining the openness the others had; he was growing up.

"Well this goblin was called Watlin the Wisp, and his wife was called Caitlin the Wisp, and there was Rathlin the wisp, and Pathlin the Wisp, their children, and grandma Matlin Wisp and Grandpa Hatlin Wisp who always wore a huge hat as big as himself.

At this Jerry pushed a big hat down on Conor's head and he laughed in delight wriggling out from under it, and Donie, our next youngest, squealed and tapped a bowran Nelly had given him, and he was constantly playing it liking the resonance of sound no doubt, that echoed the music of the spheres.

Jerry continued the story:

All the wisps lived in a hole in the mountain called Wisp Cave which was full of their whispering voices night and day, for they had low soft voices and loved to play, riding on the mountain hares, and on the wings of eagles and dancing the night away with jigs and reels and hornpipes, as happy as the day was long.

"What did they eat", Shell said

"Don't be a fool", Brendan said, he had come out of sleep next door to listen to the story. "There's no such thing as goblins" he said. He wanted to seem to be a grown up man of the world, already his imagination being stunted into conformity with the world; he wanted to be worldly wise, Jerry wanted him to be just wise.

"Some say that they came from space and landed on the mountain, but they came from a planet where people were smaller and that explains their strange powers", Jerry said, Knowing Brendan, having reached the logical age would want some solider basis for their existence and powers. He reflected on that, it knocked the wind from his sails for a while. Strange how textbook science has no room for the imagination or creativity but in fact all the great leaps forward in science came from sudden moments of inspiration and usually went against all the staid science of the day.

"They ate honey given to them by the bees of the mountain, Jerry said in answer to Shell's query, "and milk from the mountain goats, which they also made into cheese, and bird's eggs gathered when there was more than enough because they were small they didn't need so much to eat, Ok baby. They also grew lots of crops on the fertile parts of the mountain, cabbage and carrots and special space plants unknown to us. They had one special plant which they called Mock berry, which if you ate it you floated up into the sky and was able to sing beautiful songs and imitate the soaring seagulls under the cliffs. Maybe the seagulls were wisps once.

Well the good wisps were not idle goblins, O no, they gathered gold and packed it into the mountain, and they loved to watch it, gleaming and shining before their eyes. They loved it for itself not for the money if brought, like they loved everything, and were able to see into the soul of nature put there by God.

But another bunch of evil goblins lived in the lowlands below them. They were called the Crackling Fingertips because they loved to go around cracking the flowers of the foxglove with their fingers; they didn't have any such things on their own planet (Jerry glanced at Brian planets it seems weren't out of bounds). They wanted the Wisp's gold, for they *loved gold, not to see it shine but to make them rich so that they could conquer the world. So one night they crept up onto the mountain and killed all the Wisps".*

"No they didn't", Mairead said, "you're making that up". Evidently her heart was with the Wisps and not the cruel Cracklings; she wanted a happy ended, as in any other fairy tale. So Jerry had to revise his story.

"No, he said, "I'm only joking, the Wisps saw the evil goblins coming and fled to another mountain far away, to be safe, but before they went they put a spell on the mountain so that no one could get the gold that they had been packing into the mountain. And St.Patrick when he came kept the spell and said that the mountain itself would be the shining gold for all the people, bringing them to God in pilgrimages on high and healing their souls as they climbed and said their prayers which became shafts of gold piercing into the very heavens themselves. So the gold is still there to this day, that's how it got into the mountain, and that's why the mountain is a holy mountain. St.Patrick spent forty days there fasting and praying for the people of Ireland so that when the end of the world came, the West of Ireland would sink softly beneath the waves and not be burned by fire like the rest of the world. And Patrick baptized the Wisps before he died".

"When will the end of the world come", Mairead said, getting a little worried, "I can hold my breath under water".

"Well", her father said ,"we don't know when the world will end, it will probably be a long time from now, but even scientists agree that because the world is finite, that's limited, it will grow old like you and me and die at some stage, break apart I suppose, like a machine that has run its course".

"In school", Brendan said "we were told the gold was formed way back after the ice age"; he was following another train of thought and thankfully probably hadn't heard what his father had said about the end of the world.

"Maybe it was formed then", Jerry said, "but it was packed into the mountain by the goblins", he said in jest, winking at the girls. Humour is perhaps the greatest deconstructive force of all.

At this they clustered around him, quiet and full of kisses; it's strange how stories soften the savage beast in our breast and makes us lovey dovey. That's why all civilizations have their mythic stories, even in the modern age with all our stress on science, everyone still accepts Superman and Batman and Spiderman and such like, without a blink. We think of ourselves as progressive and not ruled by myths but the modern myths are just more from children's comics than from folklore.

But the best myths and fairy tales of old contain deeper truths that nourish the soul beyond the mind's tyranny; and as the character in Joyce's The Dead says, we "live in a thought tormented age". We need thought, but that is not just what makes us human, what makes us even more human is the greater mystery of art and its perennial healing role, like the wondrous stories of faith that always awed people; the realms of the soul that include thought and yet thinks in the "marrow bone", just as true art turns thought into wisdom, and so is also always a greater door out of darkness. It's what makes us human and civilized, gives us a higher value and sustains our souls in a crying world of hard ruthless greed, cynicism and thought control for power and wealth.

At this, tired, they all went to sleep to dream of fantastic worlds beyond the realities of our machine world. Jerry lay holding Deirdre, like as if he would never let her go. He was fearful of what was to yet come, even in this fragile paradise. The accident to Sally made him worried, would they all be targeted or maybe even finished off like Danny Pat, he shivered. We are stupid he thought, what have we let ourselves and the children in for, would we be better off abandoning the whole project and going back to the peace of The Cottage? Should they let the local people resolve their own problems?

CHAPTER 15

A Serpent in the Garden

THE FOLLOWING MORNING WAS BEDLAM, FAMILY DECONSTRUCTION itself, children and adults rushing around in various stages of dress and undress, the chaos that is the world's strange creativity, Jerry often thought that world is not so much order, as a glorious swirls of ever new creative chaos and uninhibited glorious bursts of life and light; Murphy was a great philosopher. Certainly their house in the morning was like that, with its chaotic choruses of strident voices in various sharps and flats, and its patter of numerous feet was like the chaotic dance of life itself:

"I don't like porridge, aunt Nelly, I want my coco pops, no coco pops here I'm afraid just corn flakes, put on your top dear you look like a wild girl from Borneo..Brendan don't be hitting that ball against the wall..Shell stop whining and eat your toast..I hate tea, can't I have just milk, I don't want that boiled egg...Brian stop throwing wet cornflakes at Shell, you'll ruin her dress..". Life is a song Jerry thought, sung in a thousand different tunes of God's glory that defied logic.

Jerry was used to creative family bedlam, and so was Deirdre, who though dressed in her professional suit for the lecture tour, she still had to mediate many disputes and adroitly dodge missiles the children playfully threw at each other. Conscious of her appearance she had to avoid soiling her professional dark suit in her mediating motherly role.

When, happily, the breakfast was over everyone dressed appropriately for the mountain. It was wet and misty outside with "wispy" clouds sweeping over the peak. They put on long light coats with hoods over their shorts and tops, or trousers and t-shirts, and sturdy shoes on their feet for the climb. Jerry put various forms of grub and drink in a pack on his back and off they went like ancient explorers about to climb Everest, a motley crew, the children shrieking in delight, with little crooked staffs they had cut from the trees to help with the climb. They were like Patrick and his twelve followers tramping to meet and confront the Druids in the bleak high worship places of the misty Ireland of the past.

Jerry decided to write little poems on the way as a kind of journal of the journey, that he might be able to use in one of his books later. Nelly had Brian in tow, holding him by the hand and lifting him in her arms over the rougher rocks and stones. Dad had Mairead, a thin light little girl with long gold locks, lifting her onto his shoulders and carrying her when things got tough. She enjoyed slipping down out of his hands and then he would have to lift her up again, a happy game of family love touching.

Their first stop was the statue of the saint. He was standing there holding a shamrock to bless the throng; Jerry explained the legend of how Patrick had used the shamrock to explain the Trinity - it was one plant but it had three leaves - and how it became a richly symbolic emblem of Ireland during the struggle for our independence in Ireland and abroad, where the Irish went after the famine. Like the wearing of the green, it became a symbol of our proud identity and desire for freedom, for people were hanged once for the wearing of the green, a sad reflection on man's inhumanity to man and the terrors of colonialism all over the world; he thought of the old classical view that man is basically a wolf to his fellow man, as much of even our own Irish history shows. But Patrick and the shamrock were symbols of a transcendent victory over all that, as was the mountain.

"Sit down", he said when we reached the first plateau, "We'll take our first rest here. Immediately he took out his notebook and put the first part of the climb to verse ending: "They trek on high on this hill of gold, to seek the summit of the Irish soul".

With the children around him he thought this was a trek of innocence they were all of them going back to their youthful innocence on the sacred mountain of life, and the youthful innocence of the world that the saint challenged them to return to, beyond all the systems of control devised by perverted self-centred man. Here there was no internet addiction or construct of artificial intelligence.

But that innocence was soon challenged, the serpent was up here too in this fragile Garden of Eden, with the company menace. Where good is, evil always muscles in to ruin things; Genesis is the supreme wise work of literature. Indeed, when they were on the second part of the climb, someone brushed against Brendan so that he almost fell over the steep cliff into the valley.

"Let's rest", Jerry said, annoyed, "and have some refreshments".

The stranger who had brushed against Brendan also stopped and spoke to them. He was a stocky individual with a pale face and hard shifty eyes,

"You'd be the Lofties, I think", he said, "staying at the old home of the Sugrues. I'm Jasper O'Leary (hard as jasper too, Jerry thought; he heard later that all his family had been thugs and bullies). I work for your neighbor, Miley Ramsbottom", he went on, "great local financier and developer, brought us out of the dark ages. You like the mountain and the climb I see, but be careful, you saw what happened just now, it's not good to get too involved in local events and places such as this. They can be dangerous, especially for children. Lots of people who breeze in here don't realize that..Thought I'd just give you some friendly advice...I wouldn't go up all the way if I were you, it can be cold and misty and dark on top, you have to think of the children...don't put them in danger. Well, I'll move on, good day to you..take care..and watch out for the children", he said again.

Jerry noticed he went down, not up. Was this a warning to them, to butt out of the mountain dispute? Was he telling Jerry that it could affect the children adversely? Would he and his employers dare to harm the children? Jerry was worried, that's the last thing he wanted was to put them in danger. He'd never forgive himself if something he did was responsible for their injury.

Jasper had looked hard at him and said "watch out for the Children", to make sure that he got the coded message; if you want to protect the children stop meddling in what doesn't concern you. He as good as said get out of town before noon like thugs did as they threatened the hero in the old gun-fighting movies.

Very clever, Jerry thought, they knew that he and Deirdre cherished the children even more than their own lives. There was some strategist behind their campaign too, and he knew how to play dirty. What have I got myself into, Jerry thought? "Was I being a fool again, thinking I could solve all the world's problems on my own and without it rebounding on those I loved? Should we go home and forget about it all?" Maybe! But as usual, he hated being pushed around, the more people pushed against the Lofties the more they pushed back. My God if they thought they could intimidate him they have another thing coming, he thought. He looked around for O'Leary, rage rising in him, to say to him he'd be the one pushed over the edge, but he'd gone.

After a while he cooled down, it was all a bluff of course. They didn't want to break the law. Jasper's master wanted the whole thing clean and above board. But a bit of subtle intimidation, yes, they'd allow that. If there was even the slightest danger, he should ask Deirdre to take the children away again, down south. They'd talk about that when they got home. It was one thing Jerry pushing back but it was another thing altogether if it hurt the children. Deirdre could take them to the sick aunt, no one would know about that place, and she'd promised to help there, they'd work something out. One thing was sure, Donie and Jerry could take care of themselves, but the children had no part in this, they were up against men who'd stop at nothing to achieve their ends, short of lawless violence. It would be wise to get the children out.

Even though the day grew brighter and the rain cleared, all now felt as if a dark shadow had suddenly fallen over the mountain. A scream from the left alerted Jerry to a simpler crisis,

"Daddy Mairead is drinking the dirty brown mountain water".

He rushed over lifting her up, "stop baby, that water may be dirty, here have some of this mineral water", He took some from his backpack.

Yet despite such funny mini crises and complaints they continued onto the first plateau of the climb. It got colder and windier there and the children who had been throwing off their clothes and consigning them to dad's rucksack, now wanted them on again; for the sometimes cold high up was also something to be braved, as the saint knew, it was easier to find shelter in the lowlands.

As they circled the little stations on the plateau, saying the proscribed prayers, the children were also complaining about the endless circling, he told them it was part of a very old Celtic tradition, seen in our early spiral art, going back even before Patrick; a spiral towards the centre of all life and glory that was also seen in the spirals of the Book of Kells. They were happy with that, for they had learned about that magical book of early Irish sacred art in school. We are living that book, he told them, to make it all seem more significant.

Indeed, immediately they had finished their magic circles, and said their prayers for the whole world, they rested and had some hot tea from a flask, and Jerry wrote his second journal entry:

> Walking in mystic Celtic circles,
> Murmuring mantras as we go -
> We link with our ancestors who
> Climbed and prayed here long ago,
> And still in the last Sunday
> Of every warm or cold July
> Throng in hordes at sunrise
> To ascend to this bright sky
> In a grand and ancient custom,
> Of an Ireland that will not die.

He wondered, then, if they should go on. As the hard Jasper had suggested should they give up all this mountain adventure, and climb back down to reality; it was hard on the children but they didn't seem to mind; maybe it's the adults who impose limits on them. He remembered some observation on TV that because someone had been injured on the mountain ten years ago no one should ever climb it now. It was strange. In this so-called freer age how things are in fact often becoming more and more restricted and dictated, and we must find excuses for undermining anything deep and wise; but then again, Jerry thought, that's how the dominant ideology always worked, it seeks to control every aspect of our lives. Certainly, on the mountain the shrieks of the children told him that they felt free here and relished the challenge. Brendan especially was delighted; it would build up his endurance for the hurling games he played in school.

But should they go on, or take the easy way out as many around them were doing, only going part of the way and then packing it in. Certainly, the climb would task the younger children to the limit the final climb was steep and very stony and slippery from earlier rain. But then again there are mountains that challenge us at every stage in life and giving in would set a bad precedent for their future; he wanted them to feel that once they had started the climb towards their goal, they should carry it through no matter the obstacles put in their way. It would build character and teach them to reach for the highest peak of excellence their abilities would allow. Who was it said that most people only use ten per cent of their real potential.

But Brendan, not even winded, made up our minds for them; he bounded on ahead of them like a gazelle, and they followed reluctantly, picking their way carefully among the stones and slippery gravel, for at the side there was a great yawning cliff, a steep fall down to the valley. Thinking of Danny Pat Jerry made sure the children gave that a wide berth. He put Mairead on his shoulders and Nelly lifted Shell up for most of the way.

Thus we struggled on, slipping and sliding. Every so often they had to rest for a while, to recover their breath. It gave them an opportunity to admire the stunning view of Clew Bay, and watch the other climbers, of various languages and nationalities, their variety like a cross section of humanity, with every possible appearance, dress and accent for this mountain was a panorama of life; it seemed, as Jerry watched, the mountain of all human aspiration.

Every so often they stopped to sip some hot fluids and take some energy drinks and sweets; "sweets for the sweet" as he said to them, and they smiled and glowed at the compliment.

Eventually they trailed, weary and sore, onto the cold misty mountain top, with its further stations for circling and prayer, and its small white chapel, that seemed like a frail gateway to heaven. Here the view extended to glorious vistas of scenery on both sides of the mountain, like heaven indeed; the saint had been wise and had known that beauty is God, and God is beauty.

The children having reached their goal were tired out, like rag dolls, but they were also very excited again, they had done it, fought the good fight, run the race to the end, gained the crown as the good book said; though what crown he could offer them here other than another round of "sweets for the sweet", the reward was important. They stayed some time there, watching others straggle over the crest with varied cries of delight, or relief or surprise that they too had made it, run the course. People of various nations were doing it not for money but for the spiritual delight and value of the climb in itself, something to take back to their own countries from this remote spot the furthest point of the western world.

At length they decided, reluctantly, that they had to get back to terra firma, back to the world of "getting and spending", where men "lay waste our powers", as the great poet Wordsworth put it in another era. Jerry was reluctant to start back for he somewhat dreaded the way down, it was harder on the backs of the legs, and even more dangerous. Not like another less exalted poet had put it, "the road downhill is an easy road and that is the way we went".

They did the circles at the top, had some more grub to energize them, and then he sat down and wrote his final journal piece before facing the grim descent into the "valley of death". There were six of them, not six hundred and it was valleys to the right of them and valleys to the left of them, not cannon, but there was danger all the same in the slippery downhill slope: the verse ended with praise

> "For the saint of our pride
> Of Mayo, the whole world,
> And the mountain of the divine".

Going down, constantly bracing themselves lest they tumble head over heels into the abyss, wasn't as bad as they feared. Nelly and Jerry took the smaller children and Shell and Brendan romped along ahead of them like mountain rams, skipping over the stones and making light of every obstacle. What great children I have Jerry thought with pride and what great friends in Nelly and Donie. That was the real gold on the mountain. Our priceless family, the treasure of our heritage, and the enduring bright gold of continuing love, family, faith and art. That was truly living on the high mountain of misty wisdom and eternal youth.

But when they got down into the lowland and Jim's house, no reward awaited them but another shock to the cause. Deverly was waiting with the grim news. Biddy had also agreed to the sale of the mountain. In a way Jerry understood why. She and Bill were behind in their house payments, their youngest boy was in college with rising fees, the government offered no assistance, and the banks were threatening foreclosure and eviction. It was like the times before the famine, but the new landlords were the banks who had ruined the people, that the government had bailed out with the people's money, and that now were about to take everything from the very people who had come to their aid; that's the way of the world, he thought, a world that claims to represent reason. It's a wonder they weren't knocking the roofs in, accompanied by peelers as in the eviction period. In any case Biddy probably figured it was best to abandon the sinking ship while there was still time. But they were underestimating the resilience of Jim, Deverly and Jerry. They wouldn't give in without giving the cynical opposition at least a few bloody noses. Jerry's family had climbed one mountain, and run the course to the end; his larger family would do the same with this struggle for the future of the sacred reek, for if that went the West would have no mountain to climb for the soul-nurture of its people, the most important nurture of all.

CHAPTER 16

Preparing for the Great Village Meeting

THE CHILDREN AND THEIR MINDERS WERE SO EXHAUSTED THAT NIGHT they headed straight for the bed after a supper of local fish, peas and chips.

In the morning, in the quiet before the children storm, Jerry consulted with Deirdre and she agreed the children must be taken out of harm's way; they were their mountain and must be saved also. Then she came up to him and put her arms around him, and kissed him fervently, her eyes full of tears of anxiety:

"Jerry dear, maybe you should come with us. We'll be worrying all the time we're at auntie Kate's if you're safe or not. I'm so afraid of all this, afraid for you, come with us! People who kill once feel less compunction in killing again. There's no more you can do here anyway, Deverly and Thornton have it in hand anyway, it's not your business, and we need you, and your parish needs you more than this godforsaken place with its insane squabbles".

He felt like the character in the Bible who said "get behind me Satan", for he was sorely tempted by her pleading to give it all up, to admit defeat and crawl away with his tail between his legs, like a fallen angel. Indeed, only that morning he had sat on the old rock outside the cottage door and brooded on his situation; he had always tended to run away from his troubles in the past rather than face them, and these troubles were not really his.

He looked at himself reflected in a mountain pool of water. Here he was, a poor passing poet; in his fifties, putting on weight, haggard and pouched from his literary and spiritual labors, and now drawing more trouble on himself. He looked up the mountain and felt again the emptiness of existence and the suffering of being, the black anguish that occasionally assaulted his sanity, and made him seek solace in the bottle; the pain of the cold world he lived in and man's inhumanity to man, a constant selling out to the soul for dross, even here in this western idyll.

But then he said no! The mountain is worth fighting for, love is worth fighting for, beauty is worth fighting for, truth and integrity, culture, art and faith, the bases of civilization, are worth fighting for against the wolves of the world, the self-centered greed-merchants and iconoclasts of every age, though there was a place for those who modernized our heritage and faith without blotting it out.

"No, Deirdre dearest, my dream of love's delight", he said, kissing her back with all his heart, reluctant to let her go, "no, I have to do this, we'll face it and we'll win, don't worry, Deverly and I are a great team, and his ingenuity is great when put to the test; we'll come home bathed in another triumph of the intrepid soul. We'll come through and keep the mountain intact for our future kids, and I'll phone and text you every day to keep you up with what's happening and if things get too hot, I promise I'll join you, OK baby".

He watched her packing the kids into the car, everyone in tears.

"Mammy why do we have to go, I want to stay with Daddy..we love it here...can't we stay another day at least..why can't Daddy come with us...Daddy remember they (the Wisps) put a spell on the mountain.. and St.Patrick blessed it..no one can get at the gold..shut up that's just a story you ejits, Brendan said.

But children are amazingly perceptive, more aware of adults issues than they allow, they listen to what's going on and seek solutions too, though their solutions can be very imaginative and unusual but deep.

As he waved them goodbye with a heavy heart Deverly came out of the house,

"Jerry, he said, "a parley, one other thing we have to do to prepare for the meeting. We must see the PP, to get him on our side and Biddy and Davey to try to get them to change their mind. Nothing is set in stone yet. We might also see the leader of the local committee against the mining project, he's Tom Dook Delaney, a clerk in the church, very active, he's already orchestrated several big demonstrations in Westport. And we also have to continue exploring the issue of who killed Danny Pat, he might be able to help us there too. I better not forget that's the main reason I'm here, and paid for it, whatever Jim can raise, though I'm not sure I'll take anything. I'm a native and it's my issue too, I knew and loved Danny Pat when growing up and often rounded up sheep with him on the mountain with Lillie his gentle collie, a wonderful animal, like an old man himself. I loved him dearly. I spoke with the local sergeant and he agreed to bring everyone associated with the case in for a brief interview".

"Deverly, you old demon", Jerry said. "no doubt you have something up your sleeve in all this. But first let's go to the local hostelry for a bite of lunch and a jorum. I'll feeling really thirsty after all the exertions on the mountain yesterday".

He recounted O'Leary's intervention. Incensed, Donie vowed to have a word with the thug first chance he got and put the fear of God into him. Which Deverly was able to do, his vast bulk alone made even the toughest thugs shiver in their boots. When it came to dealing with thugs he was far from an angel of mercy.

CHAPTER 17

The Enigma of Davey

WHEN THEY ARRIVED THERE, AFTER SEEING OFF DEIRDRE AND THE kids with heavy hearts, Fleming's pub was fairly full with climbers seeking a bit of sustenance for the trek, or recovering from the ordeal with plenty of nourishing food and drink. Billy was in one corner polishing glasses and sorting our orders. But at the main bar there was a more salubrious sight, a gorgeous lassie, Billy's much older sister, apparently he had been the "shakings of the bag" as they say. Kate, that was the sister's name, leaned over the bar, her fine cleavage fully exposed. When she saw Jerry coming she had tripped over immediately to greet him with a cheery smile on her face. She said, with a glint in her eye (not yet engaged to her mountain boy, she was up for any sport and tease):

"Ah, how are you pet, the last day I didn't have a chance to chat with you, the famous Lofty boy, writer and poet we hear so much about. I spotted you coming in with Donie Deverly, son of the famous Sheamus Paddy Jack from Mullagharierk, fine old family here they are. By the way, I want a quiet word with you later, I have some information about Danny Pat that might be useful to you both; it's no secret in these parts that it's as how you're investigating his death. It's what we need, surely, sure the guards around here are useless; sitting in their squad cars watching the babes; since they closed the station here it's a case of a free run for the criminal gangs, not that they come from here, most of them are blow ins".

Yes, Jerry wondered, what information had she, maybe it was just a ploy to do a little further teasing and flirting no doubt, he thought ungraciously, the ten year itch reawakening. Even happily married men get that at times, and she was certainly a looker in a mature curvy way. Kate Fleming was like the Eve of old holding out the apple to the glamorous celebrity, as no doubt she saw Jerry; village life could be boring for a red-blooded girl like herself. Have to be careful there, he thought, restrain your thoughts and latent lusts, Lofty old son of a gun, after all you are a married man with four glorious kids. No harm looking in the shop window again though, he thought in a moment of weakness, deluding himself, it was always his weakness and his downfall of old and would bring him more pain, his inordinate love of women.

"I'll be in here tonight and maybe we could meet somewhere private then", Jerry said, and added, lest she misunderstand his intentions, "to discuss the information you mentioned of course, I mean. We need all the local help we can get in this case, and local advice on how to deal with the other sore issue, that of the greedy mining company encroaching on the mountain".

Having established this useful contact, she hurried away to serve another impatient customer, Jerry went to the food counter, where Billy presided over some giggling young girls, and ordered a light lunch for himself and a large one for Donie. A real ladies man, he thought, with his fair hair, big blue eyes and clear skin, but what was he like within? Look out Molly, he thought, marriage to him could be pure hell. He began to revise his view of him; he now saw him as the sort of person at a fair saying "step up here", a salesman who sold you something useless and when you asked him what it was made for would say, "just to sell", we bought many things today that we didn't need; and Billy was the sort who'd sell you a lame horse without blinking and eye and when you took him back would say, all innocence, "ah sure he wasn't lame this morning", and you'd believe him because of those blue innocent eyes; the reddest apple is often the one most rotten inside, or the canker is often deepest in the bud of the most blushing and pinkest rose.

Do people really do what they want, then, in our world, Jerry thought, or what they are conditioned to do and want; like the Irish forced to vote again and again on the EU Treaty until the ideologues got what they wanted, so much for real choice. If Billy told one to jump off a cliff would one do so? Or could he possibly have pushed an old man off a cliff, maybe!

After lunch, they set out first to see Davey, they told him they were coming, and Donie had been doing some research on him.

Apparently he wasn't so happy in the teaching and the parents didn't trust him, there was some doubt about his sexual orientation. Some said he had tried once to molest one of the small girls in the school, but it had been hushed up at the time, no one wanted the bad publicity. And without proof they couldn't remove him, he was set in the job, which he wasn't particularly good at. But any dismissal could mean him suing the board of management for thousands, which they could ill afford, given the strain on schools today and the cutting of subsidies.

He had got the job through Danny Pat putting in a word for him and his impressive array of qualifications, for in his own way he was bright and saw himself as a worldly intellectual lost in this hick village backwater.

He lived in a little condominium near the school, a glorified flat really that the developer, the wily Miley Ramsbottom, had glorified into "an apartment" to fool the rising middle class, to whom gloss was all. Davey had bought this miserable flat for much dough, after all it was a "condominium", but it was really the dimmest thing he could have done. He had bought it for a small fortune, during the boom. It was now virtually worthless. He lived above a ground floor "town house", a little balcony his only escape from his own apartment's close confinement; strange and hard perhaps for a man who had been born on the free spaces of the mountain; perhaps it had cramped his soul as well, turned it into a narrow reflection of ancient family grandeur. No wonder he wanted out, to spread his wings again in greener pastures.

They climbed the outside stair to his door which he opened, seeing them coming.

"Welcome, he said..won't you come..take a seat..beer perhaps", he said, going to a fridge and taking out some cold beer. He was a tall gaunt figure with thinning fair hair, and the air of a thinker rather than a doer. Jerry's first impression, because of his very thin appearance and haggard air, was of a man living too much on the edge of mental strain. There were lines under his eyes and he had a sick hangdog expression; maybe an addict of some kind, or a secret alcoholic, Jerry thought. He had seen the signs before, a man on the edge of a nervous breakdown. He could go over the side very easily, at any time. His voice was slightly halting, not exactly a stammer but close to it, and he had a weak mouth.

A weak man Jerry thought, but also a man who could be dangerous if his pent up frustrations were not given an outlet in violent action; even to the extent of pushing a frail old man over a cliff? Maybe!

He had never married which reinforced the sense of something lacking in him that was abroad among the natives. But it may be just rumor mongering, Jerry thought, judge no one until you know them inside out. He must have some of the nobility of his father, though they also said that the rumor had gone round that he was conceived before his mother met Danny Pat, conceived in her by a good for nothing sleazebag who fled to greener pastures abroad.

In every community there was a "they" who pronounced definitively on everything and especially on anything sleazy. But certainly he was as unlike the sturdy red-headed and swarthy Jim as chalk and cheese.

Nevertheless, it seems that he had loved Danny dearly. And "they" said, he had been loved dearly by the latter also. Jerry couldn't conceive of him planning to kill his father, and he was not sure he would be capable of it anyway, too weak, too much of a vacillator. But his mental instability could make him dangerous if he was pushed to the limit. Normally, there was no streak of violence in him, Jerry was sure, but there could be a lot beneath the surface that would explode in the right context. There were people like that. Even the Lofties were a little bit like that too, congenial most of the time, but liable to explode at any time into savage anger if crossed or harassed to the limit of endurance.

"Davey", Deverly said softly, "we won't beat around the bush. You know your brother Jim has hired me to help him with this mountain mine encroachment and to investigate the death of you father, we're hoping you might be able to help us in both instances".

"I understand Jim's concern..and anxiety to see justice done by my father, but don't you lot think you can turn me from my set course of selling my share of the mountain land", Davey replied in his halting speech style, "we all wish that the cause of Dad's fall was swiftly found out ...and I'll help you in whatever way I can of course in that..for his death broke my heart also...but, a separate issue, no doubt Jim was disappointed when I decided to sell my share of the mountain. We had more or less decided to stick together on that...but reflecting on it I changed my mind. Of course the money tempted me but it's not just that...I don't hold with this heritage thing, or keeping the land in the family...we can't hold up the march of progress, and the mine represents that..the new age...the modern Ireland of hard economic good sense..my father fed me that crap... about the holiness of the mountain...I loved and respected him..but didn't accept everything he said..we're in Europe now..the narrow Irish line cost us a lot..look at the north...our future is out there in the big world..that's where I want to be...I told my father what I'm telling you...before I'm old I want to explore the bigger world...to go with the flow Miley Ramsbottom helped me to see that...he's not the ogre many people think...just a sensible business man who can really help the area with his well thought out development plans".

Jerry thought of Shakespeare, "methinks the lady doth protest too much". He smacked too much of self-justification. Like the typical libertine, deciding first what he wanted to do, according to his own dark desires, and then afterwards inventing all the reasons in the world to justify his position. One can argue persuasively for anything, for every perversion of the good and of the environment. Billions cheered Hitler to the echo, but ultimately, as was pointed out at Nuremberg, there are higher and more permanent laws of right and wrong, natural laws all must obey, objective standards of right beyond cold self-justification or individual passion, the natural law such as the church upholds. The court had to appeal to this higher natural universal law because the war criminals had said that they were just obeying German law as it was then; even law then in any country is not the measure of right and wrong. The view that once a thing is law it's OK is very dangerous, law just deals with the minimum of conduct needed for social order but sets no higher bar for us to leap over.

Jerry also felt there was something bugging Davey, some furtive nervousness that betrayed a deeper angst. Perhaps they had some hold over him, he thought, due to his sexual proclivity or something else hidden in his life that he didn't want exposed. Though if he was wise he should know that it is always better to get things out in the open, then one is free. Yet, Jerry also reflected that a certain amount of hypocrisy is necessary for civilization. For not everyone can achieve man's high ideals, but yet the ideals must remain to challenge us, otherwise we have a lowest common denominator culture where the soul stagnates and man dies to his higher dignity. Jerry felt Davey was on the brink of selling his very soul for something of little lasting value, like many do in every age. Like Faust, that too is a story relevant to every age; for ideology is slavery but faith and culture are the bases of eternal wisdom.

They left Davey with more a sense of despair than optimism, another dead end.

Davey watched them go thinking "how would they react if they knew I had killed my father?".

CHAPTER 18

A Philosophical Interruption

BEFORE JERRY AND DONIE WERE ABLE TO CONTINUE THEIR SURVEY of the people likely to support or oppose the mine, Jerry and Deirdre were called by the four young people for the next of their summer school tutorials. Jerry was delighted for it would be a welcome break from the more serious issues of the mountain. Philosophical discussions were Jerry's main form of recreation, but more than that he saw them as a preparation for life, for everyone had a philosophy that underlay and informed their lives and it was important to get it right for a good life.

Leaving Donie to pore over the material on the mountain issues and the problem of finding Danny Pat's killer, Jerry went again to the flat over the Hillside Rest where the 4 students, now close friends had gathered with food and drink in abundance to loosen their tongues and thinking brains. As usual Billy began with a brief trip to an adjoining room for the smoking of some weed, which the girls frowned on. Terry began as they had ended the last discussion by showing the peaceful core of Christian belief, that if all practiced there would be no war; there is no war in the Christian convents and monasteries set up to build peace within in a relationship with the Prince of Peace. Deacon Jerry had also been pushing this view. Billy responded:

"But what about all the violence other religions cause, you can't isolate one religion and use that to exonerate the rest, all are tainted by the sins of any one religion. We see the Muslims blowing up innocent people nowadays and justifying it by their beliefs, is that what we want worldwide, all are not as gentle as Christ".

"As I said I don't know enough about other religions such as Islam to defend them, but even on a world-wide scale religion is only a very minor cause of war and violence, and pales into insignificance beside the atrocities of modern secular systems", Jerry responded". "A recent study showed that of all the wars in human history only 3% were caused by religion, religion as the source of war is a myth that secularist use to reinforce their own more pernicious ideologies. But in any case I am not here to defend religion defined by secularists in terms of its worst aspects, as I said Christ the Prince of Peace is my model and the great timeless wisdom content and mythic stories of the bible are my guide".

"Yes" Deirdre added. "That is why greater thinkers than Nietzsche such as Chesterton and Tolkien and Petersen argue we need to restore the higher God-given mythic (myth as deep-level eternal truth) spiritual and moral bases, enshrined in the Old and New Testament and the church's teaching passed down from Christ and the apostles for 2000 years. Without these saving sources which have made the west great, civilization dies and man freewheels into the abyss of savagery and relativism of the limited fallen self without God. 'If you don't believe in God you soon believe in anything' Chesterton said. We become a plaything of every inane fad and fashion and fanatical secular man-made ideologies of power and greed and delusory self-promotion without restraint; but with God we have enduring spiritual and moral peaks to aim at, as Petersen said, these heal a broken world, like climbing our western holy mountain here. Hence Chesterton saw the Catholic Church whose truths have stood for 2000 years as 'the only thing which saves man from the degrading slavery of being a child of his age'. Like Jung, the great psychologist, he thought quoting the latter that 'Catholicism is the sanest human beings can get'. It expands the inner as well as healing the outer world, making the healing grace of God available to all and raising all up to more that they can be on their own within a community of faith, worship and charity that alone reverses the fall, the timeless communal greatness that is the church".

"I agree", Deirdre said, "that a religious community where wisdom is imbibed and lived, is vital to bring the world to peace and goodness, for we cannot do it on our own, we need God and a supportive community that initiates us into and keeps us on the right path. In this the church also transcends arid rationalism. Another great modern thinker and psychologist Jung, was concerned with the inner world of the subconscious which links us with the wisdom world of religious man from time began, and that cannot be reached by rational conscious thought alone; as he said 'the task is to give birth to the ancient in a new time', and he had printed over his front door that God "whether called or not God is present". God is in the deeper visionary realms of the noble human mind and soul, the real source of civilized progress, not surface thought alone. Even so-called rational enlightenment without soul is not enough. Higher revelation is vital for society, for only true religion, Jung thought, could tame the violent power of the unconscious into spiritual health and inner peace. 2000 years of timeless Catholic sanity from Christ through his apostles until now is the key to a sane future for all".

"But", Billy responded, "The church has also been involved in war and violence throughout its history. I think of a scene from that film 'The Agony and the Ecstasy', about the life of Michelangelo. The Pope Julius the Terrible rides up to the artist dressed in armor having just returned from leading a horrendous battle in defense of church lands, he was no different from other warmongers of the day. And what about the Crusades, and the horrors they inflicted on innocent easterners, or the Spanish Inquisition that tortured and killed many for their beliefs or learning such as Galileo, if we had followed the church we would still be believing in the flat earth. And you exalt Catholicism but it needed the Reformation to bring it back to even basic rational and Christian beliefs, otherwise we would still be living in the middle ages, God help us", Billy ended with a laugh.

"Touché", Jerry said. "Because it is and was made up of human beings concerned with power and glory rather than Christ it has made many mistakes and committed many crimes in its history, one cannot deny that. But even in the era of the Borgias power-hungry Renaissance princes who took control of the church by force or intimidation of its leaders, the popes from that family never passed a single doctrine contrary to the deposit of the faith as passed down from Christ and the apostles, and the Crusades were more to do with the political expansion east of the Norman empire than Christianity in essence. And the church did see the error of its ways in relation to science and Galileo, and many of its leaders also became great advocates up to the modern era for science and rationalism, I think of someone like Thomas Aquinas and Teilhard De Chardin, and most of the great universities such as Oxford were founded by monks and the Irish monks after Patrick as a recent BBC program proved 'laid the basis of the modern world' by their libraries and technologies. Our mountain is part of a great tradition in that respect too. The church is not perfect because it is made up of fallen human beings. But the mystery of the church is the divine in the midst of human imperfection, yet there has to be that imperfection or the church is not human at all, incarnational theology. There is a story told of a priest in a hall talking about the church and a man stood up and started ranting and raving against the church, OK the priest said 'so go and find the perfect church and don't join it', for of course the perfect church would be up in the air somewhere not human. But in its deposit of truth from the apostles it is perfect in the midst of human imperfection and the church has constantly reformed itself for example in the two great modern councils, Trent and Vatican 11."

"Sure", Deirdre said, "and the Reformation was far from all light. For G K Chesterton, one of the great thinkers of the modern age as seen in his hugely influential work Orthodoxy, the undermining of Catholicism by the rationalism of the Reformation was the root of more negative passing constructs like Squirarchy and industrialism and a Puritanism that purified religion out of existence, the root of modern secularism and its evils. For Tolkien, another great Catholic thinker, this also spawned related secular modernist industrialism that destroyed the environment in which humans can thrive; power and profit replaced the true God, as in the Protestant Ethic, the root of capitalism, if you are rich it's a sign you are saved, Calvin's horrible doctrine. So people used industry and every other means to get rich. Hence the blackened world that surrounds Sauron's tower is set by Tolkien, a committed Catholic as against the environmental health and beauty of the shire in The Lord of the Rings. Indeed one can say that Postmodernism's effects today are related to this blackening of the world by human greed and secular pride, for these aspect and the reformation and classical rationalism arguably spawned the more negative aspects of the modern world today and are 5-fold: (1) the capitalist state at war with the family; (2) the capitalist globalist state at war with the local; (3) the totalitarian state at war with God and man; (4) eugenics to 'perfect' the ordinary man, and (5) contraceptive pills and abortion to control a natural 'swarming' of 'common' men and women who are in fact the real foundation of all societies. Creating an elitist power-hungry superman such as Sauron to replacing the ordinary man is a deadly fascist vision".

"But this again is backward thinking", Billy said, "Can we go back to a world of bucolic simplicity? The world has moved on, and modernism and postmodernism have moved us out of the world world of bucolic poverty and religious ignorance to a world of enlightenment and industrial progress, and a world of liberal freedom for all, black or white, gay or heterosexual, men or women, or any other once excluded minority, as in the Irish republican manifesto all the people of the land must have equal rights and have equal access to the means of prosperity. That's progress not going back but going forward in freedom and equality for all the people of the nation without any restricting creed or limitation".

"Sure, we too support the best of the modern, but certainly the view that everything modern in the fascist elitist power-hungry mode is progress isn't very logical", Sally said, "As Aristotle said the unexamined life is no life at all. We must submit modern theories of progress to the same rigorous examination as other philosophical theories, by their fruits you will know them as the bible says, and the fruits of modernism and post-modernism have not in fact been salutary; the great modernist and post modern era of the 20th century you are extolling for its secularism was the most violent in human history and that's why its norms must be changed modern life given saner post postmodern bases if we're to survive at all".

"Yes what some see as progress when examined can in fact be dangerous" Jerry said, "such as the Nietzschean view that unchecked power was the only absolute. His work 'the Will to Power' advocated the rise of a 'Superman'. The dangerous aspect of this was shown by its logical implementation in fascist cruelty and tyranny, the super Aryan race and its ruthless pursuit of unaccountable power as the supreme value, the elimination of 'inferior' races and groups. Tolkien in the Lord of the Rings illustrates where this leads to in the person of the tyrants Sauron and Saruman, like Nietzschean secularist fascists pursuing unchecked power they would create hells on earth. Is that the world you want Billy?"

"Yes", Sally said, "I am a great fan of the Lord of the Rings; it won 17 Oscars didn't it; like all good films I can watch it over and over again. And though its values are traditional and religious, Tolkien said it is a Catholic book in essence, the film is still vastly popular after 20 years. That people long for a return to more authentic values is proved by the work's enduring popularity".

"I agree, I love it too", Terry said, "and the youth seems to be its main fans, it shows as Petersen argues that there is a foundation of values that are eternally valid that once we dump leaves us in a nothing waste land of the soul; again as a character in the Lord of the Rings says 'There is no life in the void'".

"That seems all right", Molly said supporting Billy, "there is no life either in a church that here in Ireland produced the Tuam Babies and the Magdalena Sisters and the wholesale abuse of the young and innocent by predatory priests in recent times, is that a church we can trust or believe in, or the faith they apparently espoused something we can trust or believe in, I think not!"

"Sure mistakes were made Jerry" said, "but as I said the mystery of the church is the mystery of holiness in the midst of human imperfection, to expect all members of the church to be perfect is to expect them to be angels not men; even Christ's apostles betrayed him and yet he did not give up on them; similarly we should not give up on the church because of its human failures. In any case the scandals you mentioned were in the past and would be impossible given the safeguards put in place now. We can trust the church of today that has left all that behind it, and come down from its pedestal and become more democratic, because like my criticism of Nietzsche the root of all those evils you mention was in the fact that the church had become too powerful and unaccountable. But again you cannot blame Christ for this or the faith passed down; Christ was clear that the leaders in his kingdom "shall not lord it over them", but be humble servants of all and he gave the example by washing the feet of his disciples a role usually done by the lowest servant in household. The church of ruthless power is not a Christian church but a corrupt worldly one of unaccountable power and as the saying goes absolute power corrupts absolutely. Too much godless power leaves a void in human life. Here Jerry falling into his old voice of quoting his poems at every hands turn, said:"I wrote a poem about this once. It is part of my dialogue with my old man, my imagined wise other self, before he died".

"Let's hear the poem", Sally said, she had always been Jerry's main fan:

Jerry read as follows:

> I had one last dialogue with the old man
> Before he died.
> Suddenly as I sat by his bedside
> He opened his eyes and cried
> There is no life in the void.
> What void is that I replied.
> The void of unbelief and the dark tower
> Of greed and Satanic pride and power
> That leads to a vast emptiness inside.
> There is no life in the void
> He said again grasping my hand urgently:
> No flowers of hope
> Or blossoms of beauty and truth,
> No music or forever singing,
> In blessed heavenly choirs,
> There is no life in the void
> Only a hell forever beneath a great divide.

"Good" Sally said, "Turning to another theme, we must by faith re-assert the human soul and its eternal value and destiny that Nietzsche denies. Are we just like animals living and dying with destiny or meaning, of no more significance than a stone or a rat? Even the greatest of Greek philosophers Socrates believed in the immortality of the soul and every civilization that ever existed, that called itself civilized so believed. What about the Egyptian Book of the Dead or the Pyramids, perhaps the greatest products of the human mind. They were built on the premise of human immortality and our need for its achievement and ensuring of our eternal happiness in the next world, all passing worldly equality and freedom and prosperity is useless without that final soul freedom and happiness".

"Nonsense", Billy said, "that Egyptian book was written when people were more backward and un-enlightened by theories of evolution and science. Their system was just another fairy tale of religious superstition to keep the ordinary people under the thumb of the kings. There is no after life, only this one, and only by realizing that can we make the most of this world, as Marx pointed out, religion is opium for the masses and we no longer need that drug. We can stand on our own two feet without the useless religious delusions of the past."

"Nonsense yourself", Terry said, getting a little bit angry, "Marxism was the real opium of the people, but more a poison than an opium, look at the world it produced in the Soviet Union, and in Eastern Germany where one third of the population were spies on the rest, where up to sixty million were killed in the service of a totally failed godless socialism and enforced collectivism. Yet it didn't even produce the just and progressive society it set out to achieve, when Eastern Germany was liberated the people and society there were fifty years behind the rest of Europe, while the communist elite had their villas in the mountains. They made the most of this world but the mass of the people didn't stand on their own two feet they lived under the feet of atheistic tyrants that reduced them to subservient chattels that made them less than human. Even your Nietzsche despised the ordinary people, he was a haughty Prussian aristocrat and elitist, he was no atheistic or Marxist saint serving the common man, he wanted the latter obliterated; that's why he advocated contraceptives, abortions and eugenics to decimate the ignorant proletariat and leave only the enlightened elite to rule".

"Getting back to the Lord of the Rings", Terry added, "Sauron is such a supreme Nietzschean figure incarnate, he gave 'nine rings… to the lords of men who most of all desire power'. Surely the power lust that Nietzsche praises in his Will to Power was the cause of most wars from the year dot, Nietzsche's advocating of a total 'will to power' ethics is no way forward. Nor is his total moral relativism other than a recipe for total social chaos, and the destruction of the immortal human soul that alone proves its greatness in moral and spiritual integrity".

"If I may change the focus of our discussion another question we must address in our papers is this", Molly said, "have you really answered the objection to God that the fact of evil and suffering in the world seems to undermine the faith that he is a good God and so worth believing in and serving?"

"Tolkien answers this too", Sally said; "he does not deny evil and suffering in the world, even his characters are drawn to or succumb to the ring or power and evil. But the best and humblest of them may be weak at times but they struggle on and overcome evil with the help of Ghandalf a figure of the killed and resurrected Christ; in the shire they live simple good humanitarian lives close to nature and so close to God. There suffering and evil is a distant reality because ideology is replaced by healthy lived life one with God because one with nature.

Moreover, suffering and evil are not from God they are a consequence of the fall and man's choice of doing both good and evil, even nature fell with man at that time, though this is not a historical fact but an on-going choice, we are all Adam and Eve and by our choices are exiled from the garden every day. Evil and suffering are a consequence of human freedom; but if God waved his hand and cured all evil and suffering he would be a tyrant totally controlling our lives, a sugar daddy God over mindless molls as it were, which would be a greater evil. Jerry taught me all this when he used to call to our house in the old days".

"Spot on Sal, Jerry said, "I'm glad you remember our theological discussion of the old days. The evil character, Sauron, in the Lord of the Rings is evil precisely because he denies human freedom; he is an image of what God would be like if he was a Mafia-like sugar daddy controller of everything such as people like Dawkins advocate. Sauron is driven by a will to dominate all others which he thinks of as service but is really tyranny; 'one ring to rule them all', and his tower is surrounded by a blackened countryside. Sauron is almost a perfect embodiment of modernist and Nietzsche's godless philosophy that accentuates rather than heals evil and suffering while trying to blame God and his sinless Christ for it when he gave his life to show how to redeem it by simple service and self-sacrifice. Sauron's alternative Satanic black world images the modern rule of gleaming machines, industrial production on a large scale, it employs technological machines of power and war rather than human instruments of peace and natural humane living. It is modern machine man as against an older natural moral and spiritual man. It is also modern man as his own God and purveyor of post-Christian values, modern people's God is the mobile phone and the internet now to which they are willing slaves. I am mortified when young people come to visit me; no conversation only constant texting or looking up things on the phone and YouTube; I feel I'm trying to communicate with technology rather than human souls. With this goes a vast progress in war machines now and their use, Russia and the west are competing in the Ukraine for who can have the most effective war machines and now competing to see who has the best and most horribly effective faceless drones and cluster bombs, ignoring the vast hordes of refugees that they create and the environmental polluting of the earth they leave behind; so much for the enlightened secular west of today. It is continuing the 20th century power struggles of mainly atheistic power seekers for anyone with even half a brain can see that all the modern wars far from being religious were inspired by secular power ideologies such as Nietzsche espouses in his will to power ideology whose logical expression was the fascist war machine, a continuation of the philosophy of the famous Prussian leader Metternich who said, repudiating Christianity that 'one cannot rule by the values of the Sermon on the Mount'". One can and it's the right way to rule one's life and others if one is in charge of a group.

"Yes I am a great fan of the Lord of the Rings too" Sally said. "The area around Mordor is a black waste land, its tower seems like a modern steel skyscraper and its minions are like mechanical robots marching

to war at Sauron's will, machine men driven by a Nietzschean will to power as the supreme goal".

"Sure" Dee said, "the latter's machine world may at first seem good like modern technology does with its evolving artificial intelligence, to bring progress to middle earth, in fact it brings chaos and evil 'one ring' to rule them all and in the darkness bind them. This images the pursuit of power through supermen and super-state state war machines as progress. In fact it is evil, because it means suppressing the free natural earth and the 'free will' of the masses, especially those weaker than oneself. Nietzsche had no time for the weak. Similarly Saruman in Tolkien's story images modernist blackening technology and elitism, he sees himself as superior and enlightened and thought weaker people and nations expendable and must be depleted by eugenics or contraceptives, to create the perfect elite society such as other modernist atheists and socialist utopian elitists such as Shaw preached."

"I agree", Jerry said, "and this denies the sacred human dignity of all, high or low class alike. It also denies the free will, which serves others in a gentle green community of peace and natural fellowship such as the Shire represents in the Lord of the Rings and which the church represents in general as a community of the blest. That all should enjoy free will, natural free life and a spiritual and social community for the nourishment of the soul, in that the church does the greatest role of all in society. This is a timeless Catholic teaching once embraced by all as a key human right, whose suppression is the essence of corrupt power. As against Nietzsche's egotistic individualism Tolkien celebrates the communal Christian values of love, friendship and self-sacrifice, that eventually destroy the ring of sin and power. The real answer to evil and suffering is healing self-giving love".

"Yes", Terry said, "now that I think of it, it is interesting that Sam's story goes on, does he represent the Christian principle of simple meekness as real strength; Christ's view that the 'meek shall possess the earth'?"

"Sure", Jerry said "Tolkien as a deeply committed Catholic thought that the 'meek shall possess the earth' in Christ's words, the meek here being the gentle good ordinary believing people who are the real foundations of society and progress, not Nietzsche's supermen. The Lord of the Rings remains so popular because in the shire citizens, eating and drinking beer and living one with nature in their houses built into their *hillsides are the perfect antidote to the postmodernist excesses that have so devastated the world: industrial pollution, globalism, the proliferation of machines of war, the dehumanizing march of invasive technology, the glorification of greed, the general spiritual and moral nihilism of libertine woke individualism as against the communitarian moral and spiritual health made possible in a Christian community. Hence Tolkien's hobbits have no lust for power, wealth or self-glorification. His work celebrates the courage and dignity of those looked down on and belittled. Gandalf the resurrected lord, says 'even the smallest person can change the course of the future'. All are equally valuable in God's world and the smallest person is the most important in his eyes".*

"I agree", Terry said, "it is the small ordinary people of society who are its real foundation not the supermen. It was the masses of the small people who won the two world wars, who sacrificed themselves, or were sacrificed to achieve victory. That is the huge mistake of Nietzsche and of the modern contraceptive society, to weed out the very people that are the real basis and foundation of society; that elitism is the death of culture and society as Chesterton or Tolkien pointed out".

"It seem to me then", Sally said "that Tolkien like Chesterton and other modern prophets sought to restore true democracy in the rule of ordinary man and local autonomy rather than centralized big brother state tyranny which is the logical result of Nietzschean philosophy or Marxist or communist atheistic systems of vast foundationless and so unaccountable power".

"I feel Sure", Jerry said "that Tolkien and Chesterton held this view because they shared the Catholic bases of western society rooted in the natural law and conscience and an illuminating spirituality that lighted people's way from the cradle to the grave and shaped the eternal happiness of all not just the few. This Catholic vision is set against the modern secular evolution evolved mainly from reformation errors, once the unified structures of Christendom and its vision of the dignity of truth evolved from its beginning in Christ evaporated anything is believed and anything goes morally".

At this Molly seemed shocked. "Are you saying that one could see this evolution of the machine man in several modern developments accentuated by the Reformation. Certainly the faith alone doctrine, that you need only believe, and then you can do what you like may be an explanation of why the west spawned colonialism and most of the wars of the modern era; Luther stood by and sided with the princes when the peasants of the peasant revolt were being massacred. Again religion failed the people though claiming to be reformed".

"Yes", Billy said, "and now we have a host of indoctrinating denominations, each imposing their views on the gullible masses at their fanatical mass meetings where the speakers seem to think that shouting as loud as possible and mindless bible-thumping rather than reason is the order of the day. The bible is only a book, it is not God almighty, and hysterical hymn singing is the new opium of the people, turning them into hand-clapping zombies".

"Yes" Jerry said "I agree the denominational proliferation after the Reformation, where anyone could set up a church and call it what he will, too often it was just the basics of Christianity transformed into a church of a particular individual's prejudices though that said most denominations now are made up of excellent people and excellent Christians. And the hymn-singing Baptist churches in the southern US have had huge cultural impact on the nation's music. Your criticism of them as zombies is insulting and way over the top. However I do agree that Reformation rationalism based more on Renaissance Platonism than Christianity eventually may in my view have accentuated modernist no faith forms. This is because post-reformation Puritanism tended to purify religion out of existence, making it cerebral, taking away its crucial sense richness which was mainly kept by the Catholic and Orthodox churches, bells and smells. All knowledge comes through the senses and so does our sense of God, once incarnational theology goes religion becomes inhuman; I shiver when I enter some reform churches, they are so bare and cold. I believe these distortions or gradual dissipations of incarnational Christianity are one cause of many modern developments of dubious value, is it a coincidence that these developed in the west after the Reformation, though of course there are other causes such as classical rationalism. But the growth of certain postmodern excesses from whatever source is to be deplored and its various contemporary offshoots: capitalist imperialism, scientific and philosophical materialism, economic and social liberalism and moral relativism: big brother rule in centralized super states with their vast war machines, faceless globalist economics, the collapse of the spiritual and moral bases of society in a

moral libertarianism – no morality at all – an undermining of man's larger eternal divine dignity and destiny, a population implosion, and an almost irreversible devastation of the earth, setting of the machine over nature, even undermining of the natural man/woman gender norm, and superficial media rule and conditioning over deeper traditional visionary truths and mores. All these are in my view aspects of our world of today shaping our dubious future, God help us, and its apotheosis the population implosion".

"But surely this is how things are now and is the product of man who has evolved from primitive superstition to enlightened self-confidence", Billy said taking notes, he had just returned from the adjoining room and his eyes had a slightly glazed look. Indeed he had been unable to counter the theistic ideas of the others because he had been sunk in a drugged stupor. Molly had worked to bring him back from that with copious cups of black coffee and she had succeeded to a certain extent. Now Billy woke up further and added vehemently.

"Can all the aspects of modern progress be reversed without turning the clock back? We can't reverse the progress of humankind from primitive theistic explanations for everything to enlightened scientific rationalism, however much we may deplore the way it has gone in our era or is now going in the 21ˢᵗ century on a solider humanistic basis, man is the measure of all things not God. This is the way things are and there is no way it can be changed, it seems to me. We must accept reality not indulge in useless nostalgia; there is no way back from the enlightened thinking of today and the way it is leading us is inevitable; for the dominant ideology of the day always had its way; I'm sure even your views if the ideologues of today knew about them would be ignored or even suppressed".

"Doubtless you are right, since woke ways are so entrenched they may only with difficulty be changed or revoked", Dee said, "we are like a runaway train racing to destruction unless a divine intervention many predict comes to bring people to their senses, a healthy transformation for the individual and society in a new global politics, the restoration of humans over robots, true liberty over false destructive libertarianism and the unity of all peoples in a new healthy and flourishing spiritual, moral and culturally-rich world order. It is a dream but then the dream, as the poet said, is father of the man. We must dream beyond all corrupt *reality, the reality of the awful atheistic ideologies that turned humanity into the Killing Fields of Cambodia and many other countries now just awakening from a horrific nightmare of atheistic blood and gore. That awakening must accelerate".*

"Sure", Jerry said, "Humanity must be free to dream again beyond the iron fist and the little yellow book of lies. Nothing is set in stone and the human unconscious is always a center of revolt in the long run. So we can dream deep down and work towards escaping the worst horrors of modernism and postmodernism totalitarianism while keeping the positive aspects of modern life. This is what Deirdre's post postmodern is all about restoring life-giving norms while keeping the good aspects of modernism and postmodernism: advances in medical science and scientific knowledge in general; social justice systems, the liberation of women and oppressed racial groups, the use of new technology to make life better and so on. We are not arguing for an either/or choice, what's good must be kept in the eclipse of secular totalitarianism".

"The balance may come anyway", Sally said, "in the population implosion and the resultant coming rule of the third world whose riches are young people, but we must ensure that they will not repeat the mistakes of the collapsing first world, and its secularist wars and ideological genocides that made the era the most destructive and violent in the history of humankind".

"Yes", Jerry said "and of course all the 'advances' we are deploring, though claiming to be modern, postmodern and secularist 'progressive' ideology are not really so. They are as old as humanity. Nietzsche's philosophy is almost an exact replica of Satan's in the ancient Genesis fall story; Lucifer keeps repeating himself and imposing his values on foolish humanity. Adam and Eve must get rid of God he said in Genesis. They must become God themselves, and eat of the tree of evil as well as good, in effect create their own aberrant values beyond Divine laws. Yet when they implement these values arrogantly scorning God, the result is not utopia but exile from paradise. Sin, evil, death disease, mortality and even natural disasters entered the world. Some blame God for evil and suffering; we can't have it both ways; if we create the conditions for evil and suffering by our free will set contrary to God's will, we cannot then blame God if it all goes wrong. We must blame the evil one and those who follow his tenets in rejection of God. In that sense Nietzsche is the new Satan ruling modern-day culture. And the exile from paradise is the Nazis modern replication of his ideas, which logically led to the creation of Satan's alternative hellish world. But what Tolkien and all Christian seers say is that there is hope and it is all redeemable. Our mountain is an image of that opposite will to redemptive good, here we know good and as Socrates said 'to know the good is to do the good'. We reverse the fall, heal suffering evil within ourselves in a prayerful climb back to lost heavenly heights of holiness and goodness, in self-giving penance sacrifice and transcending godliness. This images an objective divine truth outside of ourselves that in each person can be perfected and the world is enriched if we so will, for as Dostoevsky says what we do affects everyone else. And here we climb in bare feet. In effect we replica the primitive state of our first parents, but make the opposite choice from their prideful lust to be their own god. Hence the mountain will still be here and climbed when all arrogant ideologies of limited prideful man have faded away, we must climb this mountain like our ancestors, free and unafraid".

"I think we can take your pro-religion thesis a bit further", Jerry said. "We must learn from recent history that all human ideologies are limited since man is finite, and so only fools follow them. They ditch the real divine way that is not finite, and that is the only real enlightenment. Modern woke ideology is drifting towards the totalitarian state opposite to this timeless truth. Indeed it seems, given modern history that secular utopian systems always become totalitarian which is why we should run a hundred miles from them despite all their atheistic mentors, with their carefully tailored insidious arguments on the internet and the You-Tube".

At this they paused their discussion, it seemed enough had been said for the time being; they would meet again soon for a further discussion. For the present it seemed as if the theistic arguments had the last word, maybe because it was four to two, but Billy and Molly were still unrepentant and held to their convictions and we praised them for that, and apologized for any unbalance in our debate. They bonded together arguments forgotten over a pizza and fizzy drinks which Sally partook of sparingly or not at all, which worried them a little, and Molly scoffed down with a smile. Deirdre and Jerry felt the boys and girls were now part of their extended family; Jerry had a new and more positive view of Terry in particular, he saw that he was a fine young man in potential and revered the mountain and the holy saint of our land with true devotion. In general the debate had cemented their regard even love for each other, and now Billy and Molly Terry and Sally seemed part of their extended family; they kissed them all goodbye and they said, Jerry's favourite quote from his favourite modern song: "don't worry, be happy".

CHAPTER 19

Know Your Enemy

The day after the philosophical discussion Jerry and Donie resumed their canvassing for the coming village meeting. Their next port of call, after Davey, was Bridie and Bill Sheehan. The lived in a large mansion outside the town, it had masses of lights and electronic gates, wasting untold precious energy, the whole paraphernalia of showy affluence. But inside it was a different story one of barely clinging on to solvency. Jerry had intense sympathy for them, as indeed he had for Davey, he understood their dilemma. For they had got themselves into a hole that they could not get out of; they had a large mortgage, and their income was very small at the moment, just Bill's dole and what she earned part-time in the Post Office. The danger was that they would soon be fodder for the new evictors, who indeed were on the verge of knocking at their door, like a ravenous wolf pack descending on the sheepfold. Men behind posh desks with posh bonuses who had never to look the person they evicted in the eye or share their pain.

Jerry saw Bridie as in the Post Office on his first visit to the mountain, and that work at least got her out of the house, she was still a beautiful woman in a full-figure mature way, and she had been a stunner once, he guessed. Also, by contrast to Davey she seemed a strong woman who knew her own mind and could act decisively and stand by her decision. By contrast Bill was a small dumpy man, with a florid face and a gentle diffident way of talking. He even looked a bit frail at the moment, almost as if there was something seriously ailing him; Jerry like all the Lofties could intuit such things; maybe it was just the worry of Bill's situation or the demoralizing effect of being unemployed which made him look unwell, unemployment eats away at a man's soul and pride.

There is no accounting for taste in the love game; Bridie could have married most anyone with her youthful looks, yet she chose this seemingly dull, ugly, paunchy, unattractive individual. Marriages are made in heaven they say, and this one was God's surprise surely. But there is someone special for each of us, and that someone is not always the handsome paragon of all virtues that we expect.

But it's often opposites that attract, and as they got to know Bill, they soon saw his attractive side. He was an extremely simple, innocent man, charming and totally self-effacing, someone she'd want to protect against the world, like a child. It is clear that he was uneasy about the selling of the land and very much wanted to shower hospitality on them in the old Irish style, but his wife restrained him with a dismissive wave of her hand. Very much under her thumb, he was one of those quiet innocent countrymen that are the salt of the earth, but who are out of their depth in the more ruthless world of business today. Jerry thought of Byron's poem: "A mind at peace with all below, a heart whose love is innocent". Is there any place for such in modern Ireland of our new foreign economic and cultural masters, he asked himself. In the new Ireland of an increasingly lost innocence, are you, Bill, a throwback to bygone days, he asked in his mind?

But they received the duo politely. Bill would have been effusive but Bridie quashed him with a glance which said, "fool do you want to encourage them, we have to get this deal through, I'll handle it dear, don't worry your head". Jerry could imagine his response, though he did not say it, "sure she's fine woman, too good for me really, and I can always trust in her judgment". No mind of his own or a mind too humane to exert itself and cause conflict

She wore the pants, and, like Davey, the lady was not for turning, yet in a way her husband was the dominant force because everything she did was for his welfare. Was she capable of killing her father? Yes, Jerry thought, if it meant saving her husband and family and their future. She was the sort who would resort to anything; she was the force behind the "big" house, and did not want to draw in her horns. And, though big in ambition, in her heart there was no bigness, no openness or generous hospitality, no offer of drinks or anything else. They sat in her cold posh sitting room, in the embarassed apologetic presence of her husband, and froze to death inside. But that's the way things were evolving perhaps, in our poor western planet. They left the grand electronic mansion of poor pretence much depressed. Later Jerry was to learn, however, that her motives were purer and more altruistic than he supposed. People are a mass of contradictions.

If the Sheehans were a surprise, the person of their main adversary in the company case was even more so. They came to his Georgian style mansion, that he had built at the height of his wealth and which now seemed a little bit run down and were shown into a large parlour with pseudo decorative plaster ceilings that could do with a repaint and plastic crystal chandeliers that could do with a good dusting. Jerry thought of that popular song: "will the timely crowd that has you laughing loud, help you dry your tears, when the new wears off of your crystal chandeliers". Miley came out accompanied by Terry and the ever-present Jasper, who seemed a cross between a faithful lap dog and a large growling German shepherd ready to pin one against the wall, slavering for blood.

Jerry had the image beforehand of Miley as a large fat, cigar-smoking gangster with a perpetual smile and a machine gun under the table. Instead what appeared before them was a small thin ascetic looking man who reminded the deacon more of a monk or a parish priest than the executive of a dubious company. Evil, if he could be so described, is seldom clear cut, it hides itself in every guise of freedom and progress and self-justification. We are all so good at fooling ourselves, indulging our dark desires and then justifying them, or blaming others like Adam. Jerry thought of an old western film he had seen once about the "Badlands", and a poem he had written about it, seeing badlands not just in the west but everywhere, the badlands created by human greed for wealth and lust for power over others, the badlands of injustice and inequality that plagued our world, the badlands that was largely created by man himself, by his desire for power, wealth and fame, the desire to ride to glory on the pain of his fellow man, the main and ultimately only real source of all war and conflict.

In the badlands,
The wind blows cold at night,
And there is no light,
Only a waste land,
Way out west,
A land that God
Had long since abandoned,

It was a very pessimistic poem, but it was exotic and compelling Jerry thought, and that's what he liked about it. For of course there was so much good also around us, in our wonderful young people, our wonderful country still, and many of the evils of the past had healed today, in the new liberal social awareness. But each age also had its drawbacks and there were arguably many of those now. But then maybe he was biased, maybe his heart was, one supposed, lost in an idealized view of the past. Indeed, lest you think he was an old stick in the mud, he had also written about the good lands he remembered from his youth, much of which was still there in another up to date form though fading:

The road I forever travel
In desire
Is the yellow winding road
To Cullen,
Where my father lies

Did he want to go back and lie with his father and forget all trouble? Maybe it was his vice, living in the past and not seeing all the good around him today; but he couldn't help feeling the kind of alienation now that other poets like Eliot had depicted; The Waste Land had always been one of his favourite poems. Of course all was not black in any age; there were people as fine and wise today in every town and village in our land, the silent people of faith, goodness, truth and beauty; often unheralded people who keep our world from lapsing into total chaos in each age, and whose prayers and good lives redeem its darkest elements, mountains of goodness amid all the world's lowlands of despair. But the numbers who climb that mountain seem fewer today.

Strangely all this was passing through Jerry's head, he was inclined to go off in poetic and spiritual tangents at a moment's notice his mind was apt to wander into strange paths of the wondering soul at the drop of a hat. While he was thus lost in his own world, sometimes a one-sided and sometimes a prejudiced world maybe, Donie and Miley were rambling on, reminiscing also about the old days.

The two visitors were sat down and showered with lavish hospitality, while the business guru sat like a charming Buddha, smiling, nodding at all human requests or like one of the high kings of old captured in stone on our ancient Irish monuments.

"Jerry, he said, "I've heard so much about you, it's a privilege to meet you, and Donie, sure you may not remember it but we were in the primary school in Knockrockery an Clochair together. We all looked up to you even then you were a terrier of a fighter if I remember. Do you remember that big bully, the Crusher Costello we called him. Thank god they have structures to deal with such bullies in our schools today. You put him in his place, we were so grateful, for I was the one picked on most of the time - I learned a lesson from that: "an te nach bhfuil laider, ni folair do bheith glic", as the old saying in Irish puts it, which roughly translated means the one who is not strong has to be clever; I haven't got where I am by mindless brawn, you can get others to do much for you if you are cute enough, let others climb the mountain and then sit on top looking down on them.

But we must get together and jaw about the old days sometime, Donie, you were my hero in those days. Great to see you again after all the years and I hear you're making a name for yourself among all those jackeens up there in Dublin, a light for the west, eh. Well how can I help you, I'm at your disposal as a poor developer now, trying to make ends meet in these difficult times for everyone, pulling the devil by the tail like everyone else".

Jerry now understood Miley, son of a poor labourer, brought up in a humble cottage, bullied all his growing up life, he was driven as an adult to take revenge on the world. He gloried in having people like O'Leary, the bullies of this sad world, as his subservient slaves. He wanted his son to have what he lacked when growing up. His wife, Ava, the daughter of the owner of the now ruined manor, a real beauty, was another trophy in that pursuit if a troublesome and tarnished trophy. Despite her health drawbacks she had certainly brightened up Miley's garden of trophies. He gloried in seeing the society that had looked down on him suddenly under his thumb, but fate and a few reckless bankers ruined his show. Now he had fixed on another way to fly his kite, and nothing would stop him; like Davey and Bridie Jerry felt a certain sympathy for him, his own inner demons were driving him to his higher fate, and maybe his destruction in this world too. He wanted to climb the mountain of success but was digging a grave in the lowlands.

But the strange thing was that otherwise he was a kindly and charming man, and there was no animosity in him, just ambitious ruthlessness, he was just doing what he had to do. Know your adversary they say, and now that they knew where Ramsbottom was coming from it would be easier to find a way round his opposition, if he could be included in some way as one of the top dogs in their little enterprise then they might succeed in bringing him on board. A vain hope?

"Well, Miley, "you've come a long way from the little scrawny kid I knew in school", Donie said, much mellowed by a glass of the best malt served in a fine crystal glass, gleaming and dazzling them like the light of the fading manor.

"Well I won't mince my words", he went on. "You know I have been employed by Jim Sugrue to look into the death of his father, we were hoping you could help us in this, you're a powerful man in the community. Also Jim wants to repulse this company who are anxious to devastate his mountain for gold. He wants to preserve it for the people and others who come here to benefit from the climb and the mountain's great history and heritage. I know you have some connections with the company, maybe you could persuade them to back off, help us in this crucial fight for the preservation of the unspoilt heritage of the mountain".

"Certainly Donie, He said, "I'll do what I can to look into Danny Pat's death, I knew and loved the man growing up, he gave me many a half crown for helping him round up the sheep for dipping and shearing. I assure you I want justice for him too. I'll also see what I can do to get the company to modify its plans, though the actual development will, I'm sure, be good for the community, give employment and bring a prosperity that's badly needed in these difficult economic times, but I'll do what I can and see what can be worked out..I want no lingering animosity on this, I assure you. We want to work with the community not against it."

He seemed so plausible Jerry was almost convinced, except that Terry who was young and less diplomatic and less used to wheeling and dealing, burst out:

"This mine may seem like progress, and I can see why some think that we shouldn't let a few fuddy duddys block the path of progress, why give a damn about that old medieval mountain anyway, get the gold whatever way is quickest, But I don't agree with this view, the mountain and its heritage is more valuable than any amount of gold I say, we must protect it at all costs, and oppose the foreign spoilers, and I say more, down with the feckers!", he said vehemently, standing up to make his point growing red in the face with passion. Miley was mortified and told him to shut up and go somewhere out of their way.

Was this passionate support on Terry's part real Jerry wondered or only an effort to cover up for his father or his own crimes. No! He knew the boy from their philosophical discussions as a spiritual person and couldn't see him as a dangerous adversary; he didn't seem the type to act on impulse and anger and push an old man off a cliff? But then again people often act out of character if under extreme pressure people are a mass of contradictions.

"Terry will calm down presently, take no notice of his outburst", Miley said indulgently, and added "youth sees only one way to everything I'm afraid, Donie, but you and I are men of the world, there is more than one way of catching the cat, I'm open to all reasonable proposals in this...it will all come out at the meeting anyway. Lets relax and enjoy ourselves". Obviously he wanted no more discussion, lest Terry leave everything out the bag and cut the ground from under all arguments in favour of the mine.

CHAPTER 20

The Simple Man

After finishing their drinks they figured that we could get little but platitudes from Miley, underneath he wouldn't budge in fact from his advocating of the mine. He would be their main adversary and muster every weapon he could against them, but in such a subtle way it would seem good and plausible action on behalf of the community while really it was on behalf of the smiling business man.

So hoping for a better result they set out for Pat Delaney's place, doing the rounds of all the suspects and feeling their way in the mining dispute, seeing where everyone stood. He was the parish clerk and president of the local save the mountain society. His house was a small cottage type that had been modernized and extended but was very quaint and appealing in its own way still. He was a stout balding man with a round genial face and pulling one leg after him, due to an accident he had when he was young. He fell off a tractor apparently on his father's farm; there was less concern for children's safety in those day. His wife, Philomena, was a big stout jovial woman with glasses, a smiling face, and a good heart. She was all over them with welcome, and brought out tea and cakes despite their protests. A squad of their children, Jerry counted five, were buzzing around, for schools were out for the holidays. It was real warm household and Jerry felt as if he was back in his own little cottage with Deirdre and the kids.

They sat down, after some delicious tea and scones, with butter and jam piled on, no stint there, to discuss the issues they were facing, and immediately they realized Pat was not dragging his feet when it came to protecting the mountain.

"We've had several demonstrations in Westport", he said, "well attended, with environmentalists from Dublin, and from all over Ireland, I tell you, and even from abroad..bang (he had a curious habit of banging the table to emphasize his points, his face growing redder with each vehement bang, for like Tim the environment was one of his great hobby horses). These demonstrations have put the issue before the public eye, it was in all the papers, though the TV program was negative, damn lot of philistines in Dublin, to them we might as well be on the dark side of the moon rather than true servants of Ireland..bang. But we are doing much more than demonstrating; we've challenged the planning permission. Jim was one of the main objectors, he said that his family had run sheep on that part of the mountain for generations and he had the right to continue that tradition..it's surely a right beyond dispute I say, bang". His wife told him angrily to stop banging the table it was making a bad impression on the visitors.

He paused, looked sheepish, and took out a bottle of Paddy, and poured them a generous portion; they now saw another reason for his red nose and punishment of the table. "Also the unsightly mine would loom over Jim's house and destroy his access to the mountain from that side", he went on.

"They applied for an injunction against the company coming on to the mountain until that planning appeal is heard (muted bang, looking at his wife, more a tap); we're very hopeful that it will be overturned. But even for that, it's important that we get this meeting right, for if it goes against the mining company the people will row in behind the planning objection. We have some strong speakers lined up, and all the objectors to the planning will be there..so that's where we are..We'll beat the bastards, feck them all..bang, bang, bang", he lost control again.

"Watch your language, dear", his wife said, frowning more than a little, "you're scandalizing the deacon, and don't batter my table to death, we might need it tomorrow, and you know getting all worked up is not good for your heart take it easier my dear, no need to shout, we're in pleasant company here speak easy and carry a big stick as the saying goes", she said with a smile.

"With your help, We'll beat the f..", he was about to say fuckers and bang the table, but the look his wife gave him stunted his normal rough irreverent style.

Jerry and Donie explained what they had done with the help of Thornton, and he was much heartened, though he had reservations about the alternative plan for a smaller mine; he wanted to leave the mountain totally untouched. But they explained that we had to give a sop to the local development committee who were leaning towards the mine. Ramsbottom was its chairperson.

They left, glad that Pat would be fully informed going into the meeting and they could work together; their biggest worry was that Bridie and Davey might speak against them, side with the mine. Divide and conquer, the oldest ploy in the world. It would leave Jim out on a limb, but there was nothing they could do there, they had tried and failed with both.

CHAPTER 21

A Discordant Priest

THEIR NEXT PORT OF CALL WAS THE PARISH PRIEST, MANUS Macgillicuddy, who had a huge influence in the area despite his advanced age and rambling mind. He had been the incumbent priest for ages and was well liked and respected as a man of the people. And the parish priest still was a very powerful figure in country areas, his word was seldom contradicted since the time he had inherited the leadership of the people from the landlords and their agents. Indeed, the presbytery had once been the residence of the local land agent, an imposing building that had housed three priests at one time, as well as two housekeeper and a farm manager, for there was a small farm attached. Indeed the PP was noted for being seen on the mountain herding sheep like any local, and knew as much about rams and yews and sheep diseases as anyone else.

They were greeted at the presbytery door by his housekeeper, Betty Hillacotty, a stout older woman, not blessed with good looks, for the priest housekeeper had above all to be plain, and past the age of child bearing, lest she tempt the poor priest to sin, one supposed. But in everything else she was a peach and some even claimed that it was she and Pat Delaney who really ran the parish, leaving the PP to his masses and prayers and pastoral duties among the sick and needy, which was as it should be.

"Come in my dears", Betty said, her broad plain face wreathed in her usual smiles, for her heart was as stout as her ample person, "the PP will be back in a short while, he had to go down the road to anoint a sick person, Tadgh Sean Og O'Casey. Maybe you knew his family, Donie, they were from Drom an Easpaig. Nearly ninety he is, but alas failing now..I remember when he was a tall imposing man, of handsome bearing, God bless him. All the girls around here, including myself, had an eye for him (she looked wistful), but he never had a mind to get married, too taken up with his mountain farm he was".

They were treated to another round of tea and cakes, which they dare not refuse lest she would be offended, though by now tea and cakes were nearly coming out their ears. Happily, the PP soon appeared to put them out of their misery, all the "ah have another of those nice scones and some of my best coffee cake, it's the PP's favorite surely".. and so on..

The PP was a medium size frail looking old man with more the air of a school teacher than a priest, grey haired, bent and academic looking and slightly deaf; over the retirement age of 75 Jerry guessed but kept on because of the shortage of priests and his own great popularity among the people. Sent to Maheragh because of he had none of the grandeur of the more aggressive glossy exponents of clerical politics. He welcomed Jerry as a fellow pastor with great effusiveness. Immediately he invited him to give the homily at next Sunday's mass. He agreed readily. In replying to the PP, they had to say everything twice of even three times and raise their voices, which when they did so he would say,

"Ah no need to shout boys, my hearing isn't that bad, I just have to adjust my hearing aid, blasted use the thing is, if you'll excuse my language, yes, excuse my language" (he had a habit of repeating himself for emphasis ad finitum, and he went on and on, like a wonderful if disjointed sermon). They explained the reason for their errant and he replied in his usual eccentric way.

"Well, this mining thing has us all addled, yes, all addled. Don't know what to make of it myself, don't know what to make of it. Of course I want to see the holy mountain left untouched, left untouched, but there is also the problem of employment and development for the area, development's important, yes"... he paused, pouring them more whiskey, despite their protests, and then went on:

"We've been going backward for so long, so many of our young people have left, and left the church, yes that's the worst, don't practice, don't practice any more, huge disappointment..I fear for their souls..what a loss to them and us. Faith the only thing we have in the long run, only thing we have in the long run, can't carry anything else worthwhile with us into the grave or into the next world where otherwise we are lost wandering souls forever.. yes lost wandering souls..and it gives our lives depth and happiness here..shows us the right way to live..the white light of the lord.. his love and beauty, yes.. and truth lost forever to young needy souls.. such a tragedy, such a tragedy.. His most beloved children, yes, and the right integral way to live...so sad, none of his wisdom in the soul...it breaks my heart, nothing to keep them here, or to protect them abroad in the world against the evil one, and save their young souls... sheep without a shepherd, yes..sheep without a shepherd.. lost lambs cast abroad in the cruel desert of today, yes, the cruel desert of today, the cruel desert of today" (in his style he reminded one of a forgetful professor, unsure whether he had made his point or not and so kept repeating it).

"Yes", Jerry agreed when he could get a word in edgeways "without the lord's light of love, we are but darkness dust and ashes here and hereaafter..but I suppose us ministers let them down too."

"Yes we let them down", he replied.."so sad all those scandals..we have much to answer for..but we should see beyond it to the Lord still there..I blame the boom..affluence is bad for the soul, yes, bad for the soul..how difficult it is for a rich man to enter the kingdom of heaven..we were too rich too in the church..I suppose with the boom even priests didn't think they needed God anymore". He went on and on, and didn't seem to hear what they said, so they had no choice but to let himself wear himself out like a tape coming to its end; like many deaf people he bluffed it out by speaking himself out; Jerry was reminded of Beckett's work, Krapp's Last Tape.

"Money was enough, yes the world was enough", he went on, "no need for God or to save souls..yes..their souls...can't carry it with us, so nothing at all at last and for eternity, and for eternity..such a waste, such stupidity, nothing at last, just empty souls, so sad, so sad..even in the church..power, yes, power was the drug...but here the people are wonderful, wonderful people ..yes..I bless my luck every day, bless my luck".

"But what do you think of the mine thing", Donie shouted, to halt his rambling flow of consciousness, now he was like Beckett's Lucky, a mouth rambling on and on until forcefully stopped.

They were interrupted, mercifully, by Betty coming in to say that supper was ready, and father had his supper at this time every day, without fail. She invited them but they were stuffed with tea and cakes. They did, however, go into the dining room and took some coffee to accompany him as he ate his frugal meal of rashers and scrambled eggs and homemade bread.

As well as everything else he was a bit of an ascetic, frugal in everything and simple in his tastes, a simple man to cater for though this was a trial for Betty who liked opulence in every way and would have him take better care of himself. They sat in silence, looking out at the mountain, that loomed above them like a monolith of infinite mystery more lasting than their frail ministries. We all had mountains to climb, Jerry thought and gold to find at the peak of our endeavors.

When supper had been taken care of, father came with them into the sitting room again. They felt they had to get in quick and try and pin him down to the practical issues they wanted to discuss.

"What do you really think of the mining company and the issue of the mine development", Jerry half shouted in his ear. "We are leading a fight against it and would like to get your views on the issue..where do you stand father", he seemed not to hear so Jerry spoke a little louder, leaning nearer to him and his good ear; Donie had given up and was sitting back, smiling :

"No need to shout, I hear you well enough", Father said, at last, lighting a pipe and sitting back by the fire, for the evenings were getting cooler.

"Trouble is, having gotten used to the higher expectations of the Celtic Tiger it's hard to argue against things such as the mine now... hard to argue against it..a lot of heritage concerns went down the drain with the Celtic Tiger..down the drain, yes..as the Pope says when the light of faith dims every other light dims as well, dims as well, so sad..that tiger devoured everything of value in this country, in my view..now we're neither fish nor flesh, yes neither fish nor flesh, yes, neither fish nor flesh..neither Irish and so neither anything else either except in a third class sense...all our ancestors suffered for, lived for gone, thrown away as if nothing, as if nothing, so sad, so tragic..I pray every day for a return to sanity, yes pray every day.. for all we can do is pray, hard hearts you know, what made the lord cry, hard hearts closed to God.. to light, closed to light, lost in darkness..fed by false prophets, so sad..the old Satanic temptation.. all the world I will give you if you bow down and worship me, worshipping sand..cruelty and death, so sad..I cry every day, but I feel so helpless..so helpless now..too old to change anything".

He was rambling again, perhaps a little "doting" as the old people used to call it. They felt as if they were listening to a kind of disjointed prophetic monologue, yet they waited until he was finished with great respect, for he struck them as kind of reflective holy man, no doubt that was why so many discerning people in his parish cherished him so much, despite his annoying mannerisms, but then again we all have mannerisms only others see, and which we forgive readily in those we love. Jerry made one last effort to get him to address the issue:

"Father", he said, "how do you really feel on the mining issue?"

"Well", he said speaking to the point at last,

"I suppose we can't hold back the tide of prosperity, I saw too many people leave here in the fifties, yes, too many fine people left, have to keep our fine young people here now, they need something that will give employment..yes, the mine will give employment.. give employment..badly needed in the recession..we must try to restore some of what was there at the height of the Tiger". "Well", Jerry said, moving closer so that he could hear, "many did prosper during the tiger era, people who had nothing growing up didn't know themselves, I suppose it's natural that it went to the heads of some, and they went in too deep with mortgages and big cars and so on; though they're still I suppose a lot better off materially than they were in the past; we had nothing when we were growing up, going out to slave labor with farmers at the age of 15. Tough, but on the other hand it built character, no time to think about suicide or the like, we were too busy surviving. Now we've the opposite problem, many depend on their parents until they're thirty, perpetual adolescents, housing unaffordable. It's healthy to leave the nest when adulthood comes and stand on one's own feet and face the world which as the poet says, which when we face its trials and sufferings bravely, is a vale of soul-making".

Moved, unconsciously and in spite of himself, by his style Jerry found himself beginning to ramble off the point also and he suddenly realized this and pulled himself together.

"Father, I see your point that we want to get things going again, do something for the area. Though I don't quite agree with this view that a rising tide lifts all ships. I was looking at some statistics and apparently the gap between the rich and the poor widened in a major way during the boom; only the richer third of the population benefitted. Now our youth will have to bear their debt for the rest of their lives and live in miserable flats with massive rents to pay".

"What we want is a more sustainable system than the tiger, and something that will benefit everyone equally and Donie and I think we have that, in our own plans for a community development of the mine. Even things like electricity production could use little local sources like little local rivers; overcenteralisation is the curse of today. I always thought the greatest development for rural Ireland was the local co-op system, now that's gone too, swallowed up by a few remote big companies ruled by shareholders from abroad, even going to the creamery is gone. But I'm straying from the point. Father, we have laid out our own plans for a benign development that will help all, and maybe in simple sharing those young people gone away will return and also recover the precious faith of our ancestors..please God. They need that riches most of all as you said."

At this, he as a kind of riposte he showed them a letter he had received from the mine company with a large donation of 2000 Euros for the renovation of the church, with a hint of more to come, funds badly needed for the parish account was in the red.

"Look at this, can I ignore the needs of the church", he said "yes ignore the needs of the church, those needs are my first priority, yes my first priority, to get us out of the red; we also need to restore some of the stained glass windows, expensive that would be, yes very expensive".

They countered that argument by pointing out that the spiritual value of the mountain pilgrimages surely outweighed any physical church building needs; his greater role as priest was to cater for those pilgrims. He agreed. Also when they showed him the photos and other negative material about the mine as well as their own plans for a minor development he came off the fence a little bit more, though he was at pains to point out that at the meeting, as the chairperson, his duty would be to give every speaker a fair crack of the whip and to remain as impartial himself as possible. He was too honest, but it was a better trait than deviousness. He didn't want to seem to be siding with one part of the community against the other, it would ruin the inclusiveness of his ministry, he said, but all the same we left feeling that his heart was with us, despite the lost revenue for church projects a rejection of the mine might entail.

Yet they left not exactly sure how he would fall when it came to the crunch.

By this time they were thoroughly worn out from their labors, so they retired to Flemings for a few sustaining pints before retiring. Jerry had forgotten about the redoubtable Kate Fleming, until she accosted him at the bar,

"Ah there you are Jerry, thought you'd jilted me", she said with a laugh, "and I expecting you all evening". Donie stood by looking bemused; and Jerry was somewhat embarrassed.

"What are you up to now, you old conniver", Donnie said, "the middle-aged itch, the male menopause is it, and Deirdre sent away too, very handy". He laughed and Jerry blushed bright red and hastened to explain that Kate had crucial information that she wanted to impart. He looked dubious, but said;

"Go on, she's beckoning you from the back of the bar, go on before she changes her mind..information me eye", he murmured under his breath trying to hide a guffaw, "when the cat's away the mice will play".

"Be careful, he said then, "the predator is waiting, claws and all, the old fault resurfacing", and he burst out laughing; Jerry was embarrassed, with all the bar looking at them, he was making a show of himself, though he was supposed to be setting a good example to win them over.

He went on into the back room out of the limelight, where Kate was waiting, a pint laid out for him and a glass of white wine for herself, grinning like a Cheshire cat. He had to admit she looked a picture with her provocative short skirt, partially exposed breasts and her slightly graying hair brushed back over a pleasant mature face tastefully made up; for a moment Jerry saw his former wife another Kate again, in a snug in Dun Laoghaire, the two of them snuggling together over hot toddies on a cold Christmas eve. It was like a vision from the grave, and he shivered.

"Not cold are you, darling," she said, "the day was fine and I hope it's warm enough in here for you", she laughed.

"No", he said, "it's just that I was thinking of something else, someone else now dead that you reminded me of".

"Sorry, if I stirred up bad memories, we want to make your stay here happy", she said with genuine good will, "it's not often we get a celebrity in our midst, diamond cottage Jerry himself, mark that, aren't we lucky, only dull mountain men usually here. But seriously, I want to help you in any way I can. I won't deny it, the moment you came into the bar the other day, I took a fancy to you, a breath of fresh air, I said. There's a noble and learned man I said, a man of real culture and taste, one well worth getting to know better", she smiled and brushed her hair back with her hand, as women are wont to do, to denote sexual interest maybe. "Come into the garden Maude, I am here at the gate alone", Jerry quoted Tennyson in his mind.

"Hush Kate and have sense", he said, "I'm a married man and a deacon to boot, you wouldn't have me running after the most gorgeous girl in Murrisc na Domhnda, would you want me ruined altogether?", he said, she blushed at the compliment, he had only made things worse, by meaning to make them better. To divert her attention to business he said,

"What's this information you claim to have, don't tell me you got me here under false pretences".

"Ah sure, I thought we'd enjoy ourselves first, but since you're in such a hurry, what if I told you that I saw someone unexpected on the mountain the day Danny Pat died, up that side of the mountain and around the time he fell to his death".

Jerry was agog, "Who! Who was it?" he said, leaning forward so that his chin nearly rested on her generous breasts.

"Who but the son of the monarch of the glen himself", she said.

"Terry Ramsbottom on the mountain, at the time of Danny Pat's death…you say you saw him, how?" Jerry was all ears now.

"Well I was doing my usual exercises to keep trim on that side, when he appeared out of nowhere. And that's not all Terry washed his hands after he came down here. And who do you think was with him when I saw him on the mountain, Jasper the Masher O'Leary himself. I think they did the dirty work, that's why I wanted to tell someone, but I didn't want to get mixed up with the guards here. Some say Miley put them up to it. Tell Donie, he'll do something about it, but don't mention my name for the time being, I want to stay out of it, I want no truck with the law or testifying in court or anything like that. So Jerry dear", she said, leaning over and putting her hand gently over his, "I tell you this in confidence, just between the two of us as friends".

"Yes, as friends", he said, leaning over and giving her a peck on the cheek, though she proffered her lips and luscious lips they were red and full of promise:

"We can't thank you enough", he said, blushing a little at the offer of intimacy.

"This is explosive information, although it confounds some of our suspicions, but don't tell anyone that, you're an angel surely".

He left her, smiling, and almost purring like a cat who had got the cream, and went out into the main bar again, his mind in a daze; his emotions in a tangle.

Had they enough on Terry to make it stick, he thought, when he was able to think straight again for what she said didn't fit the image of Terry he had from the philosophical debates, or what his father said of the boy. And what of Sally, would it break her heart. Just being on the mountain proved nothing after all, Terry could have been there for a hundred other reasons, and washing his hands proved nothing but it could be a nail in his coffin if they were able to find more incriminating evidence like there was blood on his hands when he came down from the mountain and that's why he washed them. But there was still the question of motive. Why did he do it? Jerry could see no motive, except maybe his father leaned on him in some way, forced him to do something that seemed against his nature. The fact that the slugger O'Leary was with him was interesting but again proved nothing, they could be together there for a hundred other reasons. So telling the guards about this information was far from a clear cut process. Indeed, given the involvement of Sally, and by proxy Donie and Nelly, did they really want to find out more, to land Terry in the dock before the whole world? But if he was involved they had to do that, to vindicate Danny Pat, to bring Terry to the justice he deserved if he was guilty but that was a big if, they needed more proof than him just being seen on the mountain at the times of the death of Danny Pat. Should they confront him with this information and see if he would respond in a guilty or not guilty way? It was a difficult conundrum, the first of many in which this affair would land Jerry and Donie.

CHAPTER 22

A Philosophical Debate with the Young

Before the village meeting Terry, Sally Molly and Billy called Deirdre and Jerry to the fourth of the philosophical "tutorials". It was a welcome escape from the worries related to the meeting and the murder of Danny Pat. They all really looked forward to it and met in the usual place over the pub with some grub this time provided by Deirdre and Jerry. This time the four had been set the topic of Dostoevsky's philosophy and writings.

"Before Dostoevsky died, like Orwell, he returned to the Christian faith, but that was already prefigured in his writings", Jerry said, "Though from another age his work contradicts all the central tenets of liberal modern and postmodernist atheistic philosophy still prevalent today. Dostoevsky outlines 6 contrary truths to these ideologies in his novels: (1) that secularism is a grave mistake, evil enters us and the world when we get rid of God (see also Solzhenitsyn's work in this regard) (2) that we need to be saved from the evil embedded in the human condition and only faith can do that; (3) that total moral freedom is no freedom at all, it just enslaves and corrupts; (4) that we cannot create our own absolute values because we are not absolute, we are finite beings; (5) that only Christian compassion and love can overcome the nihilism and alienation of man due to sin; and (6) that emotional intuitive and visionary knowledge is as insightful as rationalism. Indeed Dostoevsky says that the only thing one can say about the world is that it is not rational, that men are still men and not piano keys, that man will purposefully go mad in

"

order to be rid of cold reason to obey his deeper and greater spiritual and imaginative self. In effect, even rationalism can't reign in the world. It restricts man's spiritual, emotional and imaginative life too much, his true sources of greatness enriched only by inherited faith and literary wisdom".

"In this, after Tolkien and Chesterton, Dostoevsky is one of my literary heroes too", Terry added. "As part of our university course I have been reading his masterpiece The Brothers Karamazov. In this the second son Ivan's rationalist rejection of God is all right on the surface, but it is easily answered by the simple lived faith tenets of Alyosha, the youngest son. Even Ivan's extended "poema" of the Grand Inquisitor is so much hot air; the Christ he imprisons ends his tirade by lovingly kissing him, and the Inquisitor lets him go free in shock. And the evil of Ivan's atheism is proved by the fact that it was at the root of his father's murder. Though Dmitry, the eldest son, was convicted for that murder, in fact it was committed by his half-brother, the bastard Smerdyakov on Ivan's behalf, and the bastard felt no guilt for the murder because he had absorbed Ivan's philosophy that because God didn't exist all things were allowed. The death would greatly increase Ivan's wealth and his power over others so the bastard brother committed the murder on his behalf without the slightest qualm due to the atheistic philosophy he absorbed from Ivan".

"Yes", Sally said "and the good book shows that the lust for power and wealth is everywhere and is the cause of all the cruel oppression even of children as Ivan outlines in his indictment of God in his long 'poema'".

"I have also be reading the 'poema'", Billy said "and it seems to me that it indicts God for creating a world where the most frail and vulnerable are crucified daily and he does nothing about it; the world God created has so many crimes against the innocent he is not some deity I want to follow, nor do I think like the Inquisitor that he deserves to be even revered".

"Yes" Molly said, "and what about the evils and diseases of the natural world; if they are God's creation he must be called to account for them, I side with Billy".

"Yes", Billy said, "but you haven't addressed the anomaly of natural evils and disasters in the work of a so-called good God, nature "red in tooth and claw" as Tennyson wrote in answer to the romantics' idealisation of nature. Then again what about horrors like bone cancer in young children or in Africa there is a parasite that burrows into the eyes of children and makes them blind. Is God not evil since he creates such horrors?"

"You are quite right in one sense and hopelessly wrong in another", Dee said. "When man fell and under the influence of the Evil One chose to eat from the tree of evil as well as good, man's counterpart, nature also fell; as St Paul says nature also "became subject to decay", just as man became subject to sin after the exile from the garden, but that was not God doing, it was due to "Satan's envy" and man's prideful sin in succumbing to the Evil One. For originally as the bible makes clear God created everything good and perfect, "God saw all that he had made and it was very good". But all that was subverted by man's choice of evil, and with his exile from the Garden of Eden; death, disease, suffering, cold and hardship came into the world. But the goodness of man and nature was not totally subverted; despite the imperfections the vision of the romantics was a deeper insight into the fact that nature in its deepest aspect is still predominantly the world of God's original creation. Billy, in picking out a few imperfections you are ignoring the still pervasive wonders and beauties of nature. As the poet Hopkins wrote "there lives the dearest freshness deep down things" and the world is still charged "with the grandeur of God" as all the wonderful nature programs on TV show. Moreover as with man's redemption so nature is also meant to be restored in Christ through those infused by his grace working to heal nature's imperfections, hence God's providential raising up of conservationists for example. Also by God's providence science and medicine provide us with chemicals and healing properties to kill harmful parasites, and medical advances limit cancers, and we also have early warning systems to warn of hurricanes and earthquakes and so on. As De Chardin says all this is part of the re-perfection of nature and man made possible by Christ's incarnation; it is no coincidence that all this is happening in the Christian west, and all this will come to fulfilment before the second coming of Christ to create "the new heaven and the new earth" redeemed in the image of the original perfect creation. This is now man's great task, and we have made so many advances there is no reason to believe it cannot be achieved with the help and grace of the all good God"..

"And one might answer" Terry said, "that God can't be blamed for the sinful cruelties of man that cause so much suffering in the world, it is man exercising his free will. He decided at the fall, the bible makes clear, to have the freedom to do good 'and evil'. Though the fall is a religious motif we are not bound to believe, yet even on the practical level, leaving out God, it is clear that evil exists in the world and is freely chosen by many. So it is part of man's free will. If we bring God into the debate we cannot blame him for it; if God rescinded that freedom to do evil man would become his manipulated slave. But its antidote is Christ's Sermon on the Mount, the gentleness and humility of God seen unto the cross; the irony is that Christ, the lord of the universe, the real Superman, is humble and gentle, the real antidote to evil. He went down among the poor healing people in soul and body and that is the mandate he gives us also. For because of free will God cannot wave his hand and cure all human evil and suffering, or even the evils of the natural world that also fell; we are free and the world is free and for God to eliminate all suffering and imperfection would be to make us puppets of an all-controlling God, molls of a sugar-daddy God as it were, a greater evil, but God is with us in our suffering on the cross and shows us how to heal the world's ills and turn it back into a paradise by following his son's teachings".

"Yes", Sally added, "if God has to allow evil and suffering because of our more vital gift of freedom, this does not mean he wills evil and suffering, indeed he gives the solution in the form of Christ who allowed all human evil to expend itself upon his innocent body. One can rail against evil and suffering and use that for a nihilistic atheism, but this leads nowhere; that bitterness only makes the suffering greater; the answer is to use suffering to deepen our souls and make us greater people like Christ on the cross. Moreover the embodiment of a gentleness and redemptive blueprint for the reformation of the world in God's image is Christ's Sermon on the Mount. It is a sure road to perfection and redemption of all evil and suffering but sadly it is not universally practiced. The amazing lesson of the Sermon is that the great lord of a billion stars is humble and gentle as his son was, not a power seeker like the hash Prussian ruler Bismarck, who once said 'one cannot rule by the values of the Sermon on the Mount'".

"But" Billy responded "the church itself which you say represents Christ has fallen into the trap of following an opposite ruthless will to power at periods in its history; the grandeur of St Peter's was built on a Renaissance will to grand art as evidence of overweening power in the Borgias who shaped the church to their corrupt will; the popes of the day went along with all this power and glory not the way of the gentle Christ who I agree reflected the humility and gentleness of God. I remember a scene in that film 'The Agony and the Ecstasy', where Pope Julius arrives from a bloody war dressed in armor to talk to Michelangelo".

"True", Jerry said, "the sad fact is that people, as the Grand Inquisitor in Dostoevsky's novel shows, can use even religion to achieve their cruel power ends; in Ivan's parable the Inquisitor would even have no qualms about burning Christ at the stake. But we cannot blame God for man's misuse of the religious systems geared for his perfection and that of the world, a return to the Eden that man by his free choice rejected initially and rejects over and over again in every age; Genesis is not religious history but a universal parable of human mistakes perennially repeated due to the main sin of humanity, arrogance. Even in Northern Ireland the so-called religious conflict there is really an effort by the majority to maintain the power over the native Irish that England gave that majority at the plantation of Ulster".

"Such twisting of religion to man's perverse power lust is the road of human perdition, it is not a reason to reject everything divine, Sally added, we cannot blame God for all the evils of man perpetrated in his name in pursuit of man's main evil desire the ruthless pursuit of power. As the Lord of the Rings says: "nine rings were given to the race of men who most of all desire power". The monk Zozimus, Alyosha's mentor and spiritual guide in the Brothers Kamarazov, shows even Ivan how his inner conflicts, sinful areas of his soul, if unresolved by higher grace will destroy him. By bowing before him Zosimus also shows Ivan his need for humility, recognition of his human limitations, for the perennial fall of the world into evil and suffering is due to recurrent human arrogant pride and misuse of power. It was recognition of his actual sinful limitations, though like Job he set himself up to judge God, that eventually causes Ivan's breakdown. When he argues with Aleksey about the uselessness of religion the latter has simpler but more effective Christian intellectual arguments, the ultimate ones being gentle peace humility and love. Ivan may have the better arguments but Alyosha is the better man, and that proves his point. Alyosha has the larger healing presence of God in his heart; 'blessed are the pure in heart for they shall see God'. One can rail against God but that only makes things worse within one and does nothing to change the world for good. The only thing that can do that is to make things better by active love and goodness fuelled by God's grace. It is in that light that everyone trusts and confides in Alyosha, they turn to him because of his faith and goodness; he is the main light in the grim atheistic world of the other brothers and the self-centered hedonism of the father that leaves them unloved".

"Yes", Jerry said, "after Ivan's great atheistic diatribe Alyosha's answer is to go and kiss him. Instinctively he knows that what Ivan needs is the love his self-centered father never gave him". At this Jerry kissed Deirdre. Love was their wisdom too. "The point", Jerry went on, "is that wisdom is needed as well as intellectualism and gentle selfless love as embodied in the Sermon is the Christian basis of redemptive wisdom in a suffering and evil-ridden world of the fall; "blessed are the pure in heart"; it is the heart of man that needs to be changed from power lust to gentle loving self-giving, once that is done universal peace will follow as day follows night. The love of Patrick for God led him up this mountain. There he gave Ireland a gentle divine sanity for all time. All the prideful human arguments in the world are no use if, failing to nourish the inner man, we end up in an asylum or in a hell of our own making as all the brothers but Alyosha do in the brothers novel. But this also applies to our own world and modern history where secular totalitarianism systems created hell after hell on earth, though in godless arrogance they promised utopias. Hence all the communist and fascist 'bibles' of hate and oppression as the opposite of God's healing word in the gentle Christ: Hitler's Mien Kamp, Mao's little yellow book, Khadafy's communist green book etc. Satan always negatively copies God? As Solzhenitsyn, the great Russian anti-communist dissident proves in his books atheist utopian totalitarian systems of man in our age notably communism didn't work because "they left out God".

"In all this the other central insight of Dostoevsky is that the 'inner man' must be fed as well as the body or the intellect" Deirdre said. "That is the church's key role. The faith, love and grace it channels to people are needed lest humankind end up in a desolate moral and spiritual wilderness, a desert of the abstract un-developed soul. Dostoevsky thought abstract philosophy without God can bring no happiness. Only integral spiritual and moral lived life can do that (see the ten main aspects of Dostoevsky's philosophy as expounded by the greatest experts on him in the You-tube). The Elder monk that inspires Aleksey in the Brothers Kamarazov identifies Ivan's inner conflicts seething underneath his secular intellectualism that needs to be healed for his soul and mind's peace when he bows to the ground before him. Dostoevsky by creating Zosimus showed that he was a great spiritual psychologist who saw into people's souls and saw where they most needed healing".

"Yes", Sally continued, "we should all take to heart the truth he reveals that healing wisdom from a higher source is needed to make the human being complete. Even a great scientist such as Pasteur realized this, we are not sufficient in ourselves we are limited and imperfect and above all we need prayer. Even abstract science leads to a dead end, because it only deals with material reality, and there is much more to man than a material mix of atoms and molecules, even animals have that. There is a true story told about a man going to a scientific conference by train. In the carriage with him is a little man in the corner saying The Rosary. The scientist berates the little man saying, we don't need superstition any more, we have science. When they come to the conference town the scientist gets out, so does the little man. The scientist says to him are you going to the conference as well, what's your name?' 'My name' the little man said 'is Louis Pasteur'. Pasteur was of course perhaps the greatest scientist of our age".

"Yes", Jerry added "but this story is not to disprove the value of intellectualism or science, the opposite. In those faculties God is also served and humanity is vastly enriched, but more is needed. Indeed Teilhard De Chardin, the Jesuit theologian, said that scientific advances particularly in medicine are a preparation for the perfect world that Christ will usher in at the end of time it is part of the redemption he brought. What Sally's story says is that even scientists need spiritual wisdom and prayer to develop their immortal souls as well as their minds, Pasteur was even greater in realizing this fact. So was Shakespeare; he says of King Lear in the play of that name: "thou should'st not be old before thou had'st been wise". Wisdom, especially visionary wisdom in the Lord, is infinitely more valuable than mere worldly knowledge and is a greater key to happiness. Ivan has all the grand arguments in The Brothers Kamarazov but the less-intellectual believer the wise Alyosha wins their arguments in the long run because he is a wise man that everyone trusts and confides in, he exhibits both intellectualism and the faith that makes life complete in the long run, and influences the life of everyone for their good in this world and their eternal destiny beside which this life is passing dust".

"Yes", Deirdre said, "in this Dostoevsky is greater than Nietzsche, as Petersen notes, because he fleshes out arguments in his living characters contrary to Nietzsche's atheistic ideas, though he didn't know Nietzsche or live in the modern era. His most believable characters, not abstract entities to be shaped by argument, prove their Christian values by the authenticity of their lives".

"And in this the other clinching argument of Dostoevsky against Nietzsche and atheistic wokism is the fact of conscience", Jerry added. "It is Kant's moral imperative, 'conscience or nothing'. That's why the Catholic Church says its morality is not just Catholic. It is a universally valid because based on natural law and conscience and so it is valid for all people and all time, and it's why it has stood the test of time. It is a universal inner reality, the divine within all people recognize, and not just a passing social or one-nation or one-person or one-religion construct. All people know what is right and wrong, and the vast majority of people have a sense of a divine source for this sense. I see atheists arguing for their 'faith' on the YouTube, and they all, almost to a man say that they would also know and do what is right. They are in effect arguing for the very transcendent moral conscience that Christians argue is a divine attribute implanted in all people by a transcendent deity, otherwise it is an enigma that cannot be explained in naturalistic terms".

"But like all human attributes", Jerry added "conscience can be distorted and even destroyed. In this context one identifies the why of Christianity and the why of the church? They are necessary because of human limitation. We need revelation and a supportive community of truth to know the full perfect truth and God and what he asks of us, for no one person knows it all, no person is God. Christians and notably Catholicism as the church from the beginning stemming from Christ and his apostles have preserved the highest truth of God and his morality as an unbroken tradition coming from the Son of God, Christ, as the key perfecting and fully informing completion of conscience. That is why the church that also came from this source is needed; because again man is finite and liable to err even in matters of conscience we need a community of faith and worship not only to lead us in the truth but give us the higher graces and helps towards our perfection that we cannot attain on our own. That why all nations should promote the church because it does the most important role of all in society, the nourishment of people's immortal souls, all else is passing dust and ashes".

All of this can't be constructed by reason. Because of conscience we can't create our own values like Nietzsche claimed. The values of nature and of God are already deep in us in the reality of our consciences; maybe that is what Jung had in mind when he posted over his house entrance 'whether called upon or not God is present'; hence also God cannot be killed as Nietzsche claimed. There is a divine in each person through conscience that nothing can destroy. Though as noted this needs to be perfected and clarified and made complete in the one true church from the beginning, where conscience and ageless truth reigns supreme.

Dostoevsky illustrated this in his novel Crime and Punishment. Raskolnikov's torments in prison after killing an old woman he thought a parasite on society, come not from his prison conditions but his conscience. Though he was not particularly religious it would not let him be at peace. In effect the inner pain that comes from denying inbuilt natural and irrefutable dictates of conscience are undeniable in anyone even half human. That's why modern extreme libertarians are sentencing people to lives of pain and inner torment; that's why Dostoevsky says total moral freedom is in fact no freedom at all. We cannot be free of the divine in our inner selves which makes us human and truly free of extraneous forces. That's so true today too. I remember the universal condemnation of a notorious child abuser recently. He was described universally, not just by Catholics, as an 'inhuman monster' because he showed no remorse, no sign of suffering from the pangs of conscience. So everyone knows that our conscience is what makes us human and causes us to feel guilt when we do wrong. The greatest evil of communism and fascism was a killing of conscience by amoral indoctrination".

"In effect neither we nor the state can create our own values as Nietzsche claims", Deirdre re-asserted. "Don't just believe Dostoevsky or me in this, she added. It was proved by the international War Crimes tribunal after the 2nd world war. That tribunal set aside the plea of the prisoners that they were only obeying state law. The court said that there is a deeper timeless humane law that all must obey regardless of state or any other extraneous dictates. In effect the tribunal was stating the assertion of Dostoevsky and ultimately of the Catholic Church. It says that we must obey the law of God contained in the natural law embedded in our consciences or endure inner torment in this world and the next and wreck untold damage on others during our earthly journey, for conscience is there not just for us but for the good of all those we live with and influence. As Dostoevsky says everything we do has an influence on others for good or evil.

Yes here was an international court, made up of all faiths or none, asserting the position of religion and the church and Dostoevsky and proving its universal validity, Terry said, Hurray you are scuppered Billy, we win! And in writing this book Jerry you are following Dostoevsky's novelistic model of combining a murder mystery with deep philosophical discussions, resolving all human issues.

Yes, Sally added, that is also why I admire Jordan Petersen for he shows that the wisdom literature of the bible is the basis of all western civilization and to abandon this is the leave us with no basis for civilization at all.

Yes that is why Nietzsche got it very wrong, Deirdre continued. There is an objective truth and morality within us that contradicts the absolute subjective will to power and to being our own arbitrar of moral laws. Ignoring this more objective fact of a good godly conscience produces inhuman monsters like the Nazis. So did the hells of the communist gulags based on a similar suppression of a normal sense of right and wrong, notably respect for human life and human freedom. All such human utopian atheistic ideologies are dangerous; they've justified horror after horror in our era against basic laws of God and man, and oppressed or killed billions.

The conscience argument, Deirdre went on, is also a decisive argument against the no-God discourse. Conscience is a godly spiritual force within each soul which can scarcely have come from processes of blind atoms and molecules. Totalitarianism by over-riding a God-given conscience produced monstrous human beings and systems. True liberalism is Christian which is why it emerged in the Christian west; the only real freedom is the freedom to do what our conscience tells us is right regardless of the consequences; Christian martyrs are the true images of human freedom".

Yet, Jerry said, Nietzschean and Nazi thinking of purely subjective morality, lives on today. Much of modern western society's values are pseudo-fascist in that sense. Besides largely amoral atheistic mores – the west now sees itself as post-Christian – they embody an elitist despising of the over-fertile masses. They must be perfected by eugenics or thinned out by birth control. The Christian pandering to the weak ordinary man or inferior race deprived man of his full power Nietzsche claimed. He was an elitist aristocrat who despised the masses. The abortion and birth-control impositions of woke postmodernism continue that vision today. Yet what is it producing? A population implosion, an aging top-heavy society without the vitality that youth provides. We must import young people from the third world to provide the workforce we lack. What is the lesson? We should not deconstruct profound Christian discourses based on the natural law, in this case the law even animals obey of increase and multiply lest we deconstruct ourselves and our societies in doing so. In Japan now they are trying to reverse the results of the abortion and contraception generation. They seek to restore higher fertility to prevent society's total collapse. Again the timeless Catholic teaching of 'generous fertility' based on the natural law is vindicated as universally true. There is a conservationist balance in the human area too that short-sighted man ignores at his peril. The Catholic position derived from a natural and divine law of 'increase and multiply' is immutable conservationist wisdom that we ignore at our peril, it is universally applicable not just catholic".

At this our debate ended and our meeting broke up. We resolved to meet again and discuss these issues further at a later date.

CHAPTER 23

The Village Meets and Decides

"Sweet Auburn loveliest village of the plain
Where health and plenty cheers the labouring swain".
— Oliver Goldsmith

IT WAS REASONABLY EARLY WHEN THE PHILOSOPHICAL DISCUSSION broke up for next day, Jerry, Jim and Donie had to face the crucial village meeting and needed a good night's sleep. Curiously next day lines from Goldsmith's "The Deserted Village", echoed in Jerry's mind as he walked down the village lane in the twilight of a soft summer's evening to what was to be a fraught meeting in the parish hall. That old Irish poet, and similar defender of country life and country people, had deplored the land grabbers and money grubbers of his day who evicted a noble people to make way for more profitable livestock; people replaced by sheep to make the rich landlords richer and their foreign masters happier; history repeats itself. Jerry remembered another line of Goldsmith's, his wise old aunt in Cork, his second surrogate mother, now sick, was fond of quoting: "Ill fares the land to hastening ills a prey, where wealth accumulates and men decay". How it applied to their situation.

They arrived at the village hall, a small old stone building with ancient latted ceilings, a tiny stage, and an old maple dance floor lined with seats. Here the expectant villagers had quickly gathered, a hundred or more they judged. There was a sense of tension in the air, they could feel it. The main protagonists were all there, lined up for the big fight, like heavyweight boxers warming up for a bruising contest, with Fr. O'Donnell as the uncomfortable presiding referee; his gentle nature abhorring any conflict or unpleasantness, for unpleasantness all knew there was going to be; this was no Sunday parish meeting in the sacristy.

On one row of seats in front were Jerry, Jim and Donie, with Thornton and Pat Delaney behind them preparing their charts and illustrations with frantic industry, and making sure they had everything. On another row of seats sat the suave and persuasive Miley Ramsbottom, by his side his son Terry, his minder Jasper O'Leary, Christie the cynical TD, and several beautifully suited company representatives who had busily flashed money around the village all day. Behind them sat Biddy and Davey to add local weight to their case. Immediately Jim whispered to Jerry,

"Jerry, we're scuttled, I see many strange faces here. I fear Miley has packed the meeting with hired supporters; if it comes to a vote I don't know how we'll fare, it could be touch and go".

Father called the meeting to order and gave the stage first to Miley who cleverly stressed the fact that the anti-mine lot were outsiders, with some imported environmentalist nonsense, without regard for the prosperity and employment of the area, which should be the main focus in these difficult times.

He then stressed the vast amount of money the mine would bring to the area, both in terms of initial construction and later fruits of the mine, quoting impressive statistics, backed up by a representative of the company whom he referred to every now and then to back up his claims. He used a slide presentation to show all the money the company had brought to a community in Venezuela. He made no reference to the environmental aspect, other than the fact that the place was left just as they found it now, after the mine had run its course. He finished:

"People of Croagh, my people, You see my son here, I want him to stay here, to have good gainful employment, to live in a village, which can become a town, with all the modern amenities, to live in a growing prosperous place..he paused to let his point sink home, and took a drink of water..

"Outsiders who oppose us can go back to their fine mansions in

Wesport or Dublin, but we have to live here, and we want to keep our children here and see them enjoy a better way of life which they have come to expect in modern Ireland, rather than living on the scraps from passing pilgrims who come for a few months and then forget about us. We can still have that, but we offer much more as well, a bright future for you and your children, a bright modern future of peace and prosperity unheard of, just waiting around the corner. Don't reject that, even the son and daughter of Danny Pat you see sitting here, recognize that this would fulfill his wishes for a prosperous community. Give us your support and ensure your bright future, it's what everyone wants".

He went on and on in the same vein, and got a huge clap at the end from his gathered backers, we now knew what we were up against. There followed statements by the company representatives from various countries: Lars Willander, Sven Haaland, Sir Herbert Makepiece Grout, Samuel Lichenberg and Hamish Mackie McMackey. All stressed the environmental requirements the company had met in Ireland and internationally, even the UN heritage organization had given their mines the thumbs up. These contributions were very impressive and made a big impact, as was clear to Jim and his backers.

Then Father handed the stage to Tim Thornton who, to contradict the previous speakers, produced charts that showed the mining company's terrible developments in other countries; there were murmurs of horror from the locals, and one burly farmer stood up and said:

"Send them packing, I say, we don't want land grabbers and destroyers around here, send the fat cats packing", and he sat down, heavy with the effort of even these few words.

Tim went on then about their smash and grab methods, the importation of specialized labor which would not benefit the locals, the use of machinery which would devastate the mountain, and leave residues that would the pollute the area and the water table for generations. He finished and Pat Delaney replaced him on the podium putting the case for leaving the mountain untouched even more strongly: his simplicity impressed people as he said:

"I'm no orator just a plain man who loves his area. I am no

fanatical outsider environmentalist, I am a local man with the real interests of the locality at heart (he glared at Ramsbottom and banged the table twice, which woke up some in the audience who were nodding off, though his wife urged restraint on him).

"I want to preserve intact what has been handed down to us for generations", he went on, "to pass it on to our children as their great inheritance..bang". He paused and observed the effects of his words, he had had a few pints before the event and it had loosened his tongue. Growing ever redder in the face, he went on even more loudly, having supped some sustenance from a bottle of whiskey:

"And we can do that and provide prosperity and employment also, real prosperity that will benefit us and the whole community, not just rich fat cats abroad, prosperity that will be more real and long-term, without destroying our great heritage here..bang, bang (his wife grabbed his hand to stop further punishment of the table which was in danger of collapsing). "But to illustrate our plans in this respect I hand you back to a local man you all know, Tim Thornton, who represented the community before and with honor in disputes such as this. Tim tell the people about the more environmentally friendly smaller development we have in mind, it would see the best of both worlds. He was about to bang the table even more fiercely but his wife stopped him saying".

"Don't bang the table, I tell you", she whispered to him, stopping his arm and getting angry, "it doesn't look good, Pat dear, and it frightens the children"; one of the youngsters looked startled and was pulling a long face.

Tim outlined the alternative plan of the smaller more environmentally friendly development, employing only locals, and benefitting the tourist trade, the profits going to all the people in a little locally run co-op. It was most impressive and brought great applause. When he sat down a hush fell on the audience. But they were unprepared for the contribution of Miley's mine engineer. To counteract Tim's points he pointed out that the company had submitted their plans to government and environmental overseers, and they had received the approval of all the relevant agencies; the examples Tim cited, he said, were outdated, the company had moved on from a previous irresponsible era. In any case the checks on such developments could not be circumvented nowadays; their plans met every objection possible and were totally responsible and environmentally friendly, and would bring more comprehensive wealth and employment.

After this further attacks on Tim's points were addressed by hecklers the company had placed in the audience with their series of pointed one sentence attacks:

> You talk of heritage but our children can't eat heritage.
> An environment is no good if its people are all gone.
> We want the proper amenities and housing the mine will provide.
> You may bang the table all you like but it won't bring us employment.
> We need a way out of this present recession and the mine is the way.
> We can modify this planning, put in amendments to protect the pilgrims.
> We want real big money in here, not the Mickey Mouse stuff you propose..
> This was debated on TV, the people there supported the company and they knew far more than Pat or Tim here, good men though they are.

But the telling blow to the anti-mine case came when they claimed that the man that owned the land in proposed alternative plan site wouldn't let them onto his land, he was there to say so.

Jim replied that there were alternative entrance areas.

So men of Jim's people in the audience also responded with heckles.

"We can have both our heritage and prosperity, we don't need outsiders hiving off the profits...there are no real way of stopping this company, in other countries they promised all sorts of things but did not deliver, they can't be trusted..

"The TV debate was rigged, we did not get a fair crack of the whip...this area is famous all over Ireland, indeed all over the world, for its pilgrimage climb, do we want to turn our back on that and on our forefathers who revered this holy mountain as sacred, will we allow it to be desecrated and stand idly by?"

After this Jerry spoke briefly saying as an outsider he could see the problem more clearly, and the mine development was an illusion, it would bring no long-term benefits. Donie also spoke as the son of a local man who wanted to preserve what his parents and grandparents had slaved to preserve.

But the best intervention on their side was by Jim's girlfriend, with big sparkling eyes and a soft pleasant way of talking; Noreen was one of the Mackie-Donoghues from the other side of the mountain and all respected her as a native of the mountain who wanted the best for its people.

"I don't know much about all this technical stuff", she said, "but I speak as one who had come back from abroad when my parents passed away, God rest them, one who has come to a greater appreciation of what we have here. Weighing everything in the balance, I say thread carefully with this mine thing. As you know my parents died and left me some land and mountain grazing rights. I'm not a farmer, but I don't want our free and open range on the mountain destroyed. Like Danny Pat, my parents, Tadgh and Grace, revered this mountain and taught me to revere it as something precious to be protected at all costs. I want to be faithful to their memory, and I agree with Jim here, we went to school together and I know him as an honest man like his father with the interests of the community at heart (Pat was about to bang the table with delight at this unexpected support but his wife stopped him with a restraining hand; he just said "here, here",and Jim glowed with pride; apparently he and Noreen were shortly to be married).

"We can have it both ways", she went on, "it seems to me that both ways is in the smaller community plan that Tim proposes. Why should we take the chance with a company whose record is at best dubious, will we be able to live with the devastation they will wreck on our land? They won't wreck my land, I tell you, I won't let them, I'd rather die first".

At this she sat down, and Jim looked at her with even more shining eyes and squeezed her hand; then he in turn took the floor with an impassioned speech, with some emotional tearful moments, stressing how his father would turn in his grave if this development went ahead. Most of the local people present were moved and impressed by his contribution for they had revered Danny Pat and were still mourning his passing.

Jim sat down and held Noreen's hand as they sat together. Jerry knew that there was something deep there that would soon mean the end of Jim's bachelor days; good, Jerry thought, another budding romance on the mountain. But, he asked himself, the old codger, how had he managed to conceal this secret romance from them up to now, and spring this softly softly attractive speaker on the meeting out of the blue, it was a real coup.

But it was a temporary victory they had far from won the war.

For after this the debate swung backwards and forwards again, with the Miley crew often gaining the upper hand. And his final ploy was to bring forward some planted agitators, claiming to be environmentalists, who tried to stir up trouble to blacken the anti-mine contingent. They tried to start a fight with the locals as the debate became heated. A punch was thrown, so that the meeting threatened to disintegrate into chaos, the two factions squaring up to each other, the last thing Jim's contingent wanted was to seem like troublemakers so they gestured to the chairperson to do something.

Father Macgillicuddy then stood up and called for order and calm. To bring things to a head and defer useless conflict, he suggested a vote, but he said that only locally recognized people would be allowed to vote, for Jim had whispered to him, and pointed out the many strangers in the audience and their ineligibility, for they wouldn't have to live with the consequences of any decision.

"Each person voting must state where they came from in the area, in the area, yes, and be accepted by the local representative present, be accepted as local, yes..accepted as local, as local yes ", "play it again Sam", some locals shouted in jest and this relieved the tension. Ignoring this he handed out specially prepared stamped papers to avoid rigging.

The vote proceeded on this premise, Jerry and Donie and their crew were on tender-hooks to see how it would turn out, for they knew it would be close, Miley's men had spread much company money around earlier in the day.

Indeed when Father counted the papers, he stated that there was a hopeless tie. The votes for and against allowing the company planning were 46 each. He was a clever old codger. Jerry suspected he may have hidden a few votes for the company under the seat, but he did it very surreptitiously. We have it now Jerry thought, Father has the casting vote, but he reverted to his hurler on the ditch stance:

"Well it seems to me", he said, dissolving the meeting, "that we are a divided community on this issue..yes, divided on this issue.. divided on this issue (play it again Sam, some local wit again shouted, and there was general laughter that relieved the tension again). I don't want to decide it by my one vote, decide it by my one vote. I say let's consider this issue further, and meet again in three weeks time to make a final decision, meet again, yes. I propose also that cards be delivered to each household in the area, cards for each area, yes, and only presentation of these cards will allow people in to the meeting, we want this to be above board, to be totally above board, yes, no undue influence..no undue influence from outside.. and we want as many local people as possible to present, as many as possible, yes, this is a serious issue for our future. So think on it, think on it well, the meeting is dismissed, dismissed, yes go home!"

Like a diffident professor he sat down and the hall erupted into a general hub- bub of dissenting voices. Jerry saw Jim in close conversation with Noreen, his arm around her shoulder arm, and he went over to them.

"Ah Jerry", Jim said, "meet my friend, Noreen, we were in school together, she's just come back from abroad and we've got together again, She's one the Mackie-Donoghues from the townland of Port na Farraige na Gabhra, you know the townland south of Sliabh a Mhadra, where we live".

As they chatted Jerry thought, with the mention of the townlands, of what wonderful rich place names we have inherited and how the Irish poets of the past were so enamored of place names. They had a sense that places took on the soul of the people who inhabited them, and that that soul lived on after their demise. Certainly Croagh Patrick had accumulated a rich soul made up of those who had lived on and climbed it from St. Patrick to Danny Pat; like Knock, it exuded an ageless spirituality that was hard to pin down but was all beauty and truth.

Did countries generally have a soul, Jerry wondered, as he ate a sandwitch and drank some beer. Certainly entering each country one had a sense immediately of entering each one's unique atmosphere. Was the Ireland of today evolving a harder less uniquely Irish soul, a cold hard cynical and skeptical spirit that was alien to our famed soft hospitality and native richness of welcome, our poetry, music and fiercely extravagant Celtic imagination and spirituality since Patrick. Was the intrusion of the mine a sign of this harder Ireland; no longer a gentle holy isle spirit, but a cold unholy spirit creeping in from elsewhere through the media Jerry wondered. Was Yeats right that we needed to rebuild the Irish soul lost through years of occupation, but had we in fact until recently any need to rebuild that spirit? It was there, if one only looked for it, in quiet places like Croagh, indeed throughout the island where the best yet thrived which was in many secret places, from Duneen's fiddlers to the slopes of Mount Brandon from where St. Brendan sailed to the Americas in times long past, in the greatest feat of endurance of all; he sailed from another mountain now called after him. And our mountain here was the most beautiful of all towering into the clouds, a great monument to the creator of all the great beauty and glory of our green and shining earth now threatened by the greed of selfish and thoughtless men of clay.

Jerry left Jim and Noreen to their intimate tete-de-tete and drifted towards Donie's group. They were of the opinion that night's result was like a draw at a heated local GAA match and the sides continued the dispute after the final whistle, and the referee seemed to get the most criticism. Pat was fuming,

"I can't see why he didn't use his casting vote, the bloody ejit, a disgrace to the cloth he is", he said, about to bang the table in rage, but a look from his wife stopped him, and she whispered again, "watch your language Pat, we don't want you to make a show of yourself in front of the deacon and come straight home, no more drink".

They left somewhat disappointed, but at least they had lived to fight another day.

Deverly, however was quite confident leaving:

"Father was clever really, they won't be able to pack the next meeting and we have a great chance of winning the next vote, and it should be decisive..though of course we don't know what they might have up their sleeve. This question of the ownership of the land on which our alternative plan hinges must be explored, we must find another way to develop the alternative mine. We have lived to fight another day".

That day came more quickly than they had planned.

CHAPTER 24

A Homily and a Lunch with the Devil

TRUE TO FATHER'S REQUEST JERRY ATTENDED THE NEXT COMMUNITY mass. He was there with Deirdre and the children who had returned from the south for the occasion. Indeed, the whole community was gathered to hear the stranger speak, the poet, the famous Diamond Cottage man, though some thought that book was a bit one-sided on faith issues, a bit unfair on non-believers, though Jerry explained that was not what I had intended, they had every right to their beliefs too; the conscience of no one should be forced, the faith to have any credibility must be freely accepted or rejected; he'd just pointed out the importance of faith, how vital a role it has and should play in our civilized society and had done so in Ireland since Patrick. Without it he thought life was an empty sham, an impossible void, the death of man in his true greatness. But others had every right to think otherwise and indeed increasingly did so, he added, and more luck to them.

Miley was in the church with his family; they had not neglected that tradition of mass as part of rural life, appearance there gave them more credibility. And Kate of the pub was regaled in all her splendor in the front seat, the opposite side from Deirdre and the kids, casting surreptitious eyes at Jerry. The church was packed and as he went into sacristy to robe, there was a good deal of whispering and pointing in his direction. He began to feel a bit nervous and self-conscious, especially since the Gospel theme, on which he had to speak was about the injunction, "let your light shine before men so that seeing your good works they might give glory to their father in heaven". It was so apt for their situation and the mining dispute, he thought and that was why the shrewd old parish priest had given him the forum.

Father would preside at the mass since as a deacon Jerry could not say mass as such, or say the words of consecration. A deacon, however, could do most of the other functions of a priest, baptisms, weddings, funerals and preaching the word. As a poet Jerry felt the latter was his special calling, and he had a captive audience in the church, more than any writer could hope for. He always thought of each homily as the greatest poem of all, to be so carefully composed, and rewritten until perfect, without a word wasted, for its theme was of the greatest one of all, God and the good and happiness of our immortal souls for here and for forever more. Sadly, so little literature today addressed this key theme, he felt a calling to redress that balance, to be a necessary prophet for the religious dimension today.

Indeed, he reflected, the books of the prophets of old were pure poetry, as indeed were all the works of scripture and why shouldn't there be prophets now too, recalling people to what's true and best. He felt like a commentator on a perfect enduring literature of supreme beauty and wisdom which contained and had passed down the best aspirations and beliefs of man, and had inspired and made so many saints to enrich the world beyond measure unto the glory of God.

Father intoned the opening prayers and Jerry gave the introduction.

"Scripture this Sunday is a mixture of hope and warning. Christ tells us not to be afraid, we're part of his holy kingdom. Yet on the other hand he warns us not to be complacent, the Son of Man will come in Judgment; we must be ready for his coming, stay spiritually awake walk in his light through life and by good works make a contribution for good in the world and for our fellow man as we pass along, make a difference by integral lives. Lets confess any ways we fail to do so.."

When the time for the homily came he was extremely nervous. Would his words be accepted or rejected; one never knows in the modern world where there are so many wonderful believers, but many also with very closed minds, even hostile to faith. Father introduced Jerry and there was a general hush in the church, which was near full for the word had spread. He decided that the gospel theme of light should be his theme, walking in the light of God by faith and good works for without living charity faith is dim light. So he began:

"Light is vital to us humans. Even our distant ancestors knew this. At Newgrange, at the heart of winter, the 21st of December, they'd a system rigged up so that the light came in and flooded the graves of those buried there. Faith was their centre too. It was a sign of hope for the new year, of the return of light-filled summer days, a sign to those lost in the darkness of death of light to come. The flood of natural light signified saving spiritual illumination that would light the dead home to the spring and summer of heavenly delight.

We've had a good summer, but from now on days will get shorter again, there is no eternal summer, darkness always threatens to blot out the light. But total unrelieved darkness is unthinkable. In the dark we're often afraid. We sense I suppose the link between darkness and evil. And no one wants to live in darkness forever. When there is an electricity blackout there is a major crisis until the lights are restored to our houses and streets. Nowadays houses and driveways tend to be radically lit up as if to fend off all darkness by artificial means.

Our Gospel today is about keeping the light blazing in our souls so that we will live in light here and so enjoy it forever. We're told not to let our inner light go out, for the master may come at any time to require our soul of us. God forbid that any of us should lapse into a pagan darkness without Christ, though that's an increasing risk today, to let our lamp of faith and practice go out, to lapse into darkness, and so at last choose, as we have in life, to exclude ourselves from the Lord's love and the banquet of eternal life he has prepared for all his beloved children in light and peace and happiness forever".

He paused, looking at all the rapt faces gazing up at him.

"Let your light shine before men, that seeing your good works they may give glory to your Father in Heaven", he went on. "so Christ says in his central Sermon on the Mount, the peak of his ministry. In that sense light has special meaning in Christian life. Christ is described as the light of the world. When we're baptized, we get a candle lit from the paschal candle. Were told to keep the light burning in us, the light of faith and good works, for faith must be lived in loving action to have credibility, until we go out with all the saints to meet Christ at last having been a light of goodness, truth and faith to our world while alive, having made a difference by our good works on behalf of the world and all around us.

This wise gospel is so needed today when we're so tempted to go asleep spiritually, to forget our spiritual duties in the hustle and bustle of modern life, to let the ruthless pursuit of pleasure, wealth and self blot out the larger vision of our soul's purpose and mission of goodness here in God. To find no time for God or prayer or the sacraments, or the humble service of our fellow human beings as we rush around frantically making money and enjoying ourselves as if the self-centered self-serving life were all there is. But all that fades, it is shadow and dust at last. Only the mountain of faith remains like our sacred mountain here, we must all climb that mountain and come to a peak of life and happiness thereby".

He paused again, looking around for effect.

"'Make us know the shortness of our life that we may gain wisdom of heart'", our psalm today tells us. Lack of care for the inner man or woman, the true source of our lasting peace and salvation can lead us to lose our souls. The light of salvation in us can all too easily flicker and grow dim. There's even the danger that the lamp of saving faith, through lack of the oil of practice and good works, will go out altogether, amid the distractions and scrabble for money and power which can become our whole focus today and blot out all our saving inner light. So that when the lord comes at the end of time he won't even recognize us. Our relationship with him will have gone out like the watchmen who fell asleep in our gospel while waiting for their master to return from the wedding feast.

Jesus tells the disciples and us to stand ready for the son of man will come at a time we least expect. That's true of death or on the last day, we know not the day nor the hour and as Jesus says we do not want to choose then the fate of the unfaithful; as we risk doing if we are unfaithful in life. We are given much, much will be expected of us, lets never become complacent about our salvation, or make our whole focus the passing things of this world in total greed without regard to justice or the care of others or the beautiful fragile world in which we have been placed (he glanced at Miley who was squirming a little).

This is an apt warning for our times when fewer people seem concerned to carry out their charitable and religious duties as part of their living legacy to the world. Many are falling back into that sleep of total pagan self-centred materialism and spiritual darkness which Christ labored and died to deliver us from, the darkness of sin and inner death, the soul sickness today, when godlessness is rampant; when false empty gods are becoming the idols we serve in total slavery even unto soul destruction; for as a man lives so will he die; and hell is not God's punishment, it's our own free choice. Let's not fall into that trap. For in today's gospel were told that at any time our souls may be required of us.

I think in this regard of that fine book Pincher Martin by the Nobel laureate William Golding. It's about a man whose ship is blown up in the war and he is in the water and swims and swims until he comes to an island, where he tries to survive on water from rock pools, and shellfish, while all the time he is reliving his life, which has been a very bad one. He had even connived at the death of his friend so that he could get the man's wife. All the while on the rock he is resisting and rejecting a great force of love that is trying to reach him and save him, in the form of a great giant crab. Then the book ends with the people gathering the bodies from the water and they say of this man, Pincher Martin, whose body they find: 'poor fellow he hadn't even time to kick off his boots'. All the swimming, and the island illusion is his soul trying to cling to an empty evil life and the hell it involves, to resist the salvation offered him even then, despite all, he cannot let go the darkness that has been his life. He chooses the hellish darkness that has been his life, rather than the saving light offered of another higher way of love forever.

It's vital for us Christians not to fall into that trap of making worldly darkness our light; of letting the pure light we received at baptism go out. It's vital that like the wise saints we'll be ready for Christ when he comes, so that we'll freely go in with the just and believing and loving host of saints into the banquet of eternal life. It's not about fear but building wisdom of soul and making a real difference by our lives here. For surely that's why we're here, so that God will say to us at last in the words of Christ: "well done good and faithful servant inherit the kingdom prepared for you since the foundation of the world". And we will be spiritually rich and free enough within to accept a place in that kingdom; for God cannot force it on us; the real enduring mystery is our freedom to choose darkness or light here and forever. But let's be wise and see that all the passing things of this world of which Satan is Lord fade to dust at last and leave us empty here and before eternity, but Christ is the glorious lord of light, truth, goodness and happiness both for our deep life and light in this world and forever and ever, amen". A hush fell on the church as he finished.

He paused and looked around, at least he had got attention; even the little altar girls in their white robes, like little angels, their faces glowing in the light, looked up at him with shining eyes; this is what makes my life really worthwhile, he thought, while father intoned the prayers, enriching their souls, giving them ideals that will raise them up to glory even here. He thought of a seminary student interviewed on TV. He said he had been a rich engineer and had experienced it all, sex, pleasure, good salaries, and so on, but he had felt empty inside. Then he discovered the joy of serving the Lord and others selflessly, where he could make a real and more lasting difference by his life, work and example. For the first time he felt whole.

Father was going on with the prayers while Jerry was reflecting on these things; he had composed the prayers to link with the gospel theme and the sermon:

"So as God's servants, keeping the light of faith alive through all phases and trials of life's night watch, which is a vale of testing, a challenge to grow within, lets profess our faith and live it in good works of charity, so that we can make a difference during our short life in this vale of tears".

There was a general recital of the creed, and then he proceeded with the prayers of the faithful. What a wonderful word that is "the faithful", Jerry said, lets pray to remain faithful through all the trials of difficulties of life sent to try us, so as to inherit at last the reward of eternal life, for as the poet had said its life's trials that make it essentially a "vale of soul making": Father went on with the rest of the prayers: he had linked the prayers with the homily, and the same was true at the end of the mass when Jerry gave a short reflection.

"A great example of failure to watch with Christ is the apostles. In Gethsemane when Christ wanted their support in his agony they slept. Three times he came to them for help and found them asleep. Let's not be like that, so worn out by the cares of the world as to neglect our service of the Lord and his Holy Church, especially our call to rise every Sunday and come to listen to his word and receive and be his holy body of light to the world. For the Eucharist is the greatest and most necessary light; Christ say he who eats my flesh and drinks my blood has eternal life already and I will raise him up on the last day. Imagine that we're already part of eternal life through regular Sunday Eucharist, so nourished within that we are sure to flower into glory with Christ when he comes. This banquet of light prepares us for the final banquet. Let's ask Mary to keep as part of the Eucharistic faithful walking in light to the end of time.. Hail Mary..

CHAPTER 25

A Confession shakes the Self–Righteus Deacon

WITH THIS THE MASS ENDED, WITH PEOPLE MILLING ABOUT AND praying at the various altars and lighting candles for loved ones. Many came up and congratulated Jerry on the homily; others murmured a few objections and hurried away, saying it was too long winded and self-righteus. But one could never please everyone, and the Gospel was always very challenging; it was seldom a sop to the easy morality of some today; but then again that's why it was so great and enduring, it was no straw in the wind, blown wherever the world blew. But the objectors had a right to their views too and could reject or accept it, that was their great freedom. So even the objections were something Jerry wanted, for it meant he had made people think and the questioning faith or lack of it was always the deepest in the long run; maybe he had stirred their consciences to new heights of Endeavour to find their souls. For the soul needs a little jolt into life every so often.

It was in this spirit that after the mass father and Jerry stood outside and received various comments about the homily, mostly positive but also a few negative. Even Miley came up to Jerry and said,

"Fine homily Jerry, but surely someone has to care for the things of this world too?"

"Of course" Jerry replied and went on:

"As I said we're here in this world to enjoy its good things and try and make them possible for all. Christ himself says we will be judged at last by not just faith but the degree to which we have practiced basic humanity and service of others, especially the poor and needy, our faith must be more than just faith it must "have practical fruits - feeding the hunger, clothing the naked etc".

Father chipped in:

"Sure, Miley, but don't be put off by Jerry's zeal and dogmatism; we need questioning faithful like yourself...yes like yourself..but Jerry is right too..faith to be real must be lived in real charity for the material welfare of the world..real charity..yes. Christ didn't just have faith he spent his life in healing and helping the rejects of society..yes, reaching out to rejects, fullness of life in every way".

"But surely capitalists and developers serve the people by developing the means of wealth and providing employment", Miley replied, again addressing me, and adding:

"I see that as important for the good of all, and we must first care for people's bodies before we can care for their souls".

"Of course", Jerry replied, "and the church teaches that there is nothing wrong with working for riches per se. The problem is when it is irresponsible, self-centered, ruthlessly soulless, and benefits only a few, not the community as a whole. A recent example is the taking from old age pensioners to give to rich bondholders, mainly living abroad; or the modern cult of economics which mainly serves big banks and financiers. That said we badly need all the dynamic and more responsible entrepreneurs we can get".

"Come to the house for lunch", Miley said, still eager to continue the debate, and unsatisfied with Jerry's answers, maybe eager too like the rich scribe in the Gospel to justify himself.

"Yes, Jerry", Miley said, "come to the house and we'll discuss this further. You must be hungry after all that preaching, takes a lot out of one, they say", he said with a twinkle in his eye. Jerry was seeing the humane part of the man.

But before he could accompany him he was accosted by Bridie Sugrue who asked if she could have a word with him in private in the sacristy. He hastened there with her, a tenseness about her made him worried. He sat her down and all the strength and hardness drained out of her, she broke down and began to cry.

"It's all right", Bridie, Jerry said, "I understand the financial pressures that you are under; I am sorry if we put more pressure on you. Do what you think is best for you and your family".

"You blow in here", she said between sobs, "and you start preaching to us and twisting our arms..you know nothing..".

"I understand and I'm sorry..

"Understand", she said, "you understand nothing..do you know why I need money..why we really are at wits end..".

"I presume it's because of your mortgages and the children...

"You understand nothing..its Bill..I tell you this in confidence.. Bill is very ill..he is dying of cancer..I tell you this in confidence.. pray for us..and pray we'll get the money for some special treatment that they say can help him in the States..but it is very expensive.. now do you understand?"

You could have knocked Jerry down with a feather. Suddenly the cold wind of reality blew upon him, and he realized how petty his little worries were in comparison with what she had to face, and all the while to put a brave face before the world. Her husband, her child man, dying in front of her eyes and nothing she could do about it. It shook Jerry as nothing up to now had. He had been so full of himself and by self-righteousness and his artful homily that he had forgotten he was dealing with real people, every one before him with perhaps some grief or trouble like Bridie of starkling implications. Struggling to make ends meet or save for such a crisis as she was now encountering, or in over their heads to give all to a loved one to give them some vital opportunity in life. Like glib politicians it was not all a public relations exercise, a question of looking well, or speaking the right words, it was often a matter of life and death, the decisions they made so glibly and even easily it seemed, echoed in people's lives and perhaps tipped the balance for their families.

He took Bridie by the hand and knelt before her,

"Bridie", he said, "I'm sorry you must be really suffering, going through hell".

"Hell is not a word for it", she said, "and Bill is so undemanding, so unselfcentered even in this..it breaks my heart..not a word of blame for anyone...not even blaming God but saying it is His will. But Jerry, know this, I'd blow up the mountain, precious and all as it is, if it would make him even a little bit better..He is my whole life, now that my children are gone..pray for us.. pray we'll get the money somehow".

"I'm sure", Jerry said, "that if we put this before the community they will organize fund-raising events to get the money you need, we'll see to it".

"No", she replied fiercely. "One thing Bill won't hear of is charity, he's a proud man who has always stood on his own two feet..pray for him, for us, it's also hard on the boys..and I hope this will make you understand...we have our own more pressing trouble..even in the Post Office I find it hard to concentrate thinking about..I can't lose Bill".

At this her sobbing was renewed; such a show of emotion made him realize his own inhumanity at times, everything was mind and nothing of heart.

He had thought of her as a hard unyielding woman but he had been very wrong. She was a strong woman but had to be so for she had to be strong for both herself, her husband and her boys. We'd find the money for her one way of another, Jerry vowed that then and there even if it meant giving up the campaign.

CHAPTER 26

The Challenge of Miley

After Bridie had left, drying her eyes and trying to look as if nothing had happened, Jerry took up Miley's offer of lunching with him and Ava. But he went up to the big house with a heavy heart, thinking all the time of Bill and Bridie's dilemma; the terrible thing was that he could tell no one, she had sworn him to secrecy and it was like the seal of confession. It was a burden Jerry would have to carry too, to keep him humble.

He went up to the manor house not because it was a big house but because he hoped he could reach Miley at some deeper level, for he sensed that, despite his show of having a thick skin, he was a troubled soul at heart, looking for answers. His wife Ava, it was one of her good days, was trying to be a charming warm and welcoming hostess. She was a tall impressive looking woman with a pleasant sociable way of talking when at her best and kind grey eyes.

She had got Louise to lay out a simple lunch for them in the garden; cooked meats and some salad and bread and tea. When they had eaten Jerry and Miley retired to the living room for their tete de tete.

"Reflecting on what you said", Miley said, pouring some fine whiskey into Jerry's glass; "I just thought there that the church doesn't always live up to its ideals. It's easy for you people to preach", he said bitterly, "but when we were growing up and had nothing, I was the son of a cottage laborer, the priests were living in a big house like this, and dining well I'd sure. Sure, they cared for our souls, but I had to make my way in life by the use of my own wits and hard work, no one gave me anything least of all the church".

Jerry nodded, and said, "my life was much the same, with the death of my mother and being sent to my aunt in the country to be reared. But I did find the church a comfort, despite its sometimes worldliness, that's why I joined it; it gave me something more than just bread, deeper food for the soul".

"Of course", Miley said, "I must admit, to be fair, the free education I received from the sisters and brothers did help me get on, but they were sometimes cruel and snobbish too. All about the rich too at times, although of course they did provide most social services in Ireland when the state could ill afford them. But all this living of bishops in palaces and such like was hardly living what they preached. They were hypocrites too. I had to do it my way, and by my own sweat and blood. Surely the men who rise to riches that way are to be admired, not criticized?".

"Of course", Jerry said, "and like the song says God wants us all to do it our way, and I admire you for that. We are all unique and should make use of our talents to achieve all that we can in our short life here on earth; that's what makes the world tick; we have things to do in this world to develop it, we must all make our best contribution to the development of the earth. On the other hand soulless capitalism just benefits one third even of the first world, and the rest of the world starves, and even in that process it produces so much waste through consumerism, its fruits now are global warming and pollution on a huge scale; I don't see that as praiseworthy development", he paused as Miley refilled his glass, though he began to feel uneasy, was he being too intellectual again, not really answering Miley's deep needs as with Bridie. He didn't want to seem to be a kill joy.

"You are obviously an intelligent man", Jerry went on, "who has made the most of all that was given to you, and good for you. But just beware it doesn't make you hard, destroy you in the long run; remember you have higher responsibly too, to all your fellow men and to your God who gave you those talents to do right by everyone not climb all over them on your way to the top".

"But what about the church's hypocrisy in judging such as I and then doing the same themselves in their palaces", he said, "you haven't really answered me".

"Again, I agree, I'm sorry if I'm up on my high horse all the time", Jerry said, "sure, the church was wrong too, and it needs to get rid of all the trappings of power and wealth, and I think they are beginning to do so now; I hope it's not too late. The French revolution should have woken the church up, as should the rise of socialism, which in its essence is very Christian; the early church had everything in common; it was really a communist commune but without tyranny.

But to answer your question, yes, you had to do it your way and no churchman helped and now they try spike your guns; it's hard for you, and the church is a hypocrite in this. I suppose my intellectual training makes me a poor listener, I'm sorry. Go on and say what you like and I'll try to really listen for a change, not try to preach, or go off in tangents, or judge you harshly".

"I'm glad", he said, "and happy that the abuse scandals have brought the Irish church down off its rich and hard institutional pedestal. I say hurrah! And thankfully the people aren't accepting its rule without question anymore; that's good. All that old secretive monolithic system of harsh clerical power and self service of the institution rather than the gentle humble Christ is being brought down and its God's work, I think. Lets tumble it all down, I say, let the people rule, I say, and people like me who will make a difference by creating wealth".

"Certainly", Jerry replied, "that's what it's all about, being with people in distress, there for them where they are, not hierarchical pontificating (Jerry thought of his encounter with Bridie). In this new awareness, I admire the present Pope, his going out among ordinary people and to help the poor like his namesake, Francis, who also so tried to revive a corrupt and self-serving church in his day. Once the church is with the people, then the people will be with the church, as they were in times of persecution here in Ireland, the mass rocks and all that..".

"Sure", Miley said, "I wish the Pope would get rid of that horrible monstrosity of St.Peter's and witness to a lord who had nowhere to lay his head. That's what will make the church credible again; even our own bishop, I hear, is living now with the priests as one of them and not apart in the palace. We are moving forward, and back to our real roots. A lot of the church's structures, as we knew them, came from the worldly lord and serf model of the middle ages as I learned from the Jesuits who taught me; the church must become more democratic, humble, modern and open in its treatment of its own priests as well as the people, in its financial dealings and so on. They say Bishop Casey used two thousand of the money collected from the people to pay off the girl who bore his son. The church must be forced to come down from its pedestal, and not like a very reluctant mule, kicking against the goad. But the church always moves too slowly in my view.

I know the church is different now, the people won't take crap from it anymore, but why must you still lecture people like myself who do it my way and make something of their lives?".

"I'm sorry if I seem to be lecturing you", Jerry said, "I was just reflecting on the gospel this morning, not targeting anyone in particular, indeed I was criticizing myself as much as anyone else. But with this mining thing I think you are making a huge mistake, and I hope you don't mind me saying so; it could destroy you in body and soul, that's all I'm worried about, if it hasn't done so already. Draw back and think of the community and what's right, not just what serves your own power, wealth and ambition. Is that all you will leave as your legacy, the world around you ruined to serve you, as I said no removal van accompanies the coffin, all we have at last is faith and whatever good we have done in life to carry before the Lord as our passport to an eternal paradise".

Yet even as he said this, Jerry cringed, for he knew he was maybe preaching too much again, but he couldn't help himself.

"Sure, I know at last all our worldly goods, as you said, fade to dust and ashes, and we are all but shadows and dust", Miley said, "but our developments can help present and future generations, that's a good legacy too? They say greed is bad, but I say it's good, it helps people to drive on and get things done for the future".

"Yes", Jerry said, "developers like you can help shape a better future and we need that badly. But naked people-trampling greed just eats one away inside, it can take over one's soul and makes it hard; I think that's what the Lord meant when he said: 'how difficult it is for a rich man to enter the kingdom of heaven'. Yet he also says that nothing is impossible with God. They can do their thing in a responsible way for the good of all and in accord with higher laws of right; ambition and doing it your way doesn't give one the right to trample on all that's holy and crush all that stand in your way; then you serve only the evil one, and risk having only him and your own lost soul for all eternity. I don't apologies for saying that, though I'm sorry if I offended you. I was just doing my duty".

"I know that, Jerry", he said, "but maybe I am too far down the road now to draw back. What play was it that said, 'returning were as tedious as go oer'. I suppose I am too set in my ways to convert to total philanthropy or try putting community good and noble righteousness before myself", he said with a smile, "but then again preachy condemnation solves nothing, it just gets people's backs up; I am, I suppose the free thinker and free doer you church people fear most".

"Free thinking holds no fears for the wise man", Jerry said "but self-serving ideology is froth compared to the wisdom that is at the heart of all things in God. In that sense I have no fear of your free thinking, but I was worried about your soul and where it is going at a deeper personal level where the heart is".

As Jerry said this he looked into his eyes his eyes and thought he saw something hard and incorrigible there. There was a hardness and coldness there that frightened him, a refusal to open to anything other than a cold worldly way. Was he like the little crooked man who lived in the crooked little house or just a victim of his circumstances in a kind of tragedy of evil heroism? Jerry didn't know and didn't want to judge him harshly. He knew now that he was what he was and to him the end justified the use of any means, however perverted those means might be seen from a faith perspective. Miley was a long way from the ideal of the integral just man who lived his life in peace with God and man, intent only on doing good; the wise man whose dignity was beyond all ideology".

Yet they ate and drank without animosity, and Jerry left with a kind of mutual understanding between them that he hoped might bear fruit at some time in the future. As he left he gave Miley a parting bit of advice.

"Miley", he said, "did you ever see that film, About Smith. Jack

Nicolson is wonderful in the main part. It's about an aging rich man at the final stage in his life. His wife has just died and he is all alone in a big house. Even his daughter to whom he sends regular checks to keep her, and for whose big wedding he is paying, rejects him and doesn't want him to live with her; he hates the nincompoop of a boyfriend she is marrying and his awful dysfunctional family. He feels lost and alone, even his beloved deceased wife, he finds out, had been cheating on him most of his life. He has a sense that his life, as it draws to a close, has been useless, he had never really done any good for anyone or really been deeply loved by anyone, just made money; all he had left was his riches and big empty house and a sad empty soul.

But he has been sending letters and checks to help a little African boy. Right at the end, the religious Sister who is running this charity, sends him a letter and a little drawing the boy has made, of himself and Smith hand in hand. Tears falls down his cheeks, he has at least done some little bit of good, and someone does love him, someone is better off by his life.

That's what it all boils down to in the end, as the song says 'if I help somebody as I pass along, then my living will not be in vain'. Its love and faith and depth of soul that matters when the chips are down and we look at ourselves in the cold light of day before we die, before night descends forever. Have you ever looked at yourself in that way, Miley? Have you ever thought that we are but dust and shadows, fading away every minute to shades whose material accumulations can in fact become insurmountable loads weighing us down from the freedom and richness of soul that are our wings of light for the next world. I speak to you as a person now, not as an abstraction. Are you happy inside?"

Off he was going again in his grand sermonizing, yet it came from his heart from a region of glory he could not explain; He was afraid that knowledge was more than he could ever be. Did he reach the humane part of Miley or failed him, just fed him clichés? Maybe, maybe not? He felt his final words had made some impact; like Smith was his soul empty, was that empty self-centered soul all he would have for all eternity. Knowing the devil was in that inner death Jerry shivered at the thought.

"Did I help him see that", Jerry thought on the way home? "Did I reach his soul? Did I help his floundering spirit? I don't know!"

When Jerry looked into his eyes, they had been cold and unblinking, was there anything there that could be saved? Had everything in him that was gentle and soft and kind been stripped away and all that remained was a hard ruling lust for gold and power. "Had I done nothing to wean him from that", Jerry asked himself "though unconsciously he wanted me to do so. I know that if I was judging him I would take into account all he came from, all the circumstance that had shaped his life and I would not judge him harshly, and I'm sure God would not either. I wished that like Scrooge, he would change and become more human at last, give and not just accumulate, but I feared it was too late, for crime had also now got a grip on him and that was much more serious than even unfettered greed".

CHAPTER 27

Another Shock
to the System

WHEN JERRY GOT HOME HOME ANOTHER SHOCK AWAITED HIM, DEE said that there was some incident at Pat Delaney's place, and they should go there immediately. When they reached the site chaos faced them. Delaney's house was in flames and sparks were shooting up into the sky. Suddenly with a crash the roof caved in and showered red hot sparks in all directions. Pat and the children were huddled in the garden with blankets around them and people giving them hot drinks. Pat and his brothers were crying because the house had been in the Delaney family for generations and it was like the death of one of their own children; also Pat's five children were in deep shock and there was sense that they were lucky to be alive. A group of local men were busy with buckets of water dousing down the fire at the back of the house lest it spread to the outhouses or the barn. Jerry and Dee immediately went to the Delaney family and tried to comfort them as best they could while they were waiting for the fire brigade to arrive which it did fairly speedily. Everyone remarked at how miraculous the fact was that none of the family had been killed though Pat and the eldest son Tim had been fairly badly burned trying to bring out some family heirlooms.

Luckily Pat as sacristian had been helping the priest at a funeral, the children were in school and his wife had been working in the garden when the fire broke out and so there had been no more severe casualties. But then they arrived at the scene, Tim had rashly rushed into the burning house to rescue some heirlooms and his pet canary that was trapped in his cage; Pat ran after Tim and both had been burned by pieces of falling ceiling. Now Jerry and Dee ushered the family into a nearby house out of the cold and to attend to their burns for doctor Moriarty had arrived to bandage their wounds. It was important to get them in out of the night air for Pat and his wife with the five children around them had been shivering in the cool air, shivering also no doubt from shock and the burns; indeed Pat had been beating the ground and crying piteously, he had inherited that house from his parents and they in turn had inherited it from their ancestors and there were things in it that couldn't be replaced. The loss of the house was an even huger loss for him for Pat had added on to the house and modernized it incurring much debt in the process which they had been struggling to pay off or even pay the interest on a mortgage that they had taken out. He had done much of the renovation with his own hands in more difficult times. His wife was trying to console him both in terms of his loss and his injuries. The doctor was hopeful as with Tim that these injuries would not leave permanent scars, though only some time in the hospital would clear up that worry.

Once the family had been secure and warm in the nearby house and wrapped in blankets and plied with sweet hot tea and sandwitches some neighbors came to form a line of buckets of water to prevent the fire from reaching the barn behind the house and the hay and grain that was stored there to provide forage for Pat's animals for the winter. As he saw the people rallying round one of their own in his need, Jerry reflected on how important community was or had been in country areas; was all that now gone too in the name of "progress", the progress of every man for himself behind electronic gates, how sad. Jerry was reminded of his old home in Crossmagnier when he was young when all the neighbors rallied round for the "meithel" a gathering to help at crucial times such as the hay-making season or the corn havest, as the old Irish proverb went "ni neart le cur le cheile" (there is no strength except in togetherness or community solidarity). That community support for Pat was later proved when the community gathered a large sum from local donations for him, they also provided furniture and bedding and other necessities for their new provisional home while the old one was being rebuilt on the site, as close as possible to the orginal.

Now in answer to their immediate needs Pat's neighbors offered to put the family up for the night, but the priest pointed out that the presbytery was empty, though it would need some renovations, furniture and clothes to cater for a large family. Fr Manus had moved to a smaller house already a house more suitable for a single person. But the large presbytery could with some work be made ideal for Pat's large family. But the family had to have some suitable shelter for the night so Jerry and Dee went with Pat and the family and some other kindly neighbors to tidy up the presbytery for them as best they could; Dee got some fresh linen and duvets to furnish the rooms fit for a night's rest which the family badly needed and she provided provisions for the morning breakfast and midday dinner from her own provisions at home. Bridie also brought some provisions from the post office shop.

Once all the practicalities had been seen to by Jerry Dee and the neighbors Donie came and nosed around to try and ascertain the cause of the fire; he said he suspected arson for there was a smell of petrol among the smouldering ruins. He also saw and empty petrol can in the bushes where it had been tossed obviously by someone in a hurry to make his or her getaway; here was another crime we must solve Donie said, another crime probably at Miley Ramsbottom's and the mine's door. He with all his police experience would ensure that they would pay for their crimes in the long run.

The next day the police also came to the burnt house to investigate and they came to the same conclusion as Donie though they had no hard evidence for the theory. Some neighbors said they saw Jasper O'Leary near the house in the hours before the fire and that he was acting suspiciously. Apparently he had also bought a container of petrol from the post office shop which also had petrol pumps. But when questioned he claimed the petrol was for his lawnmover and they could prove nothing against him, but many nodded their heads and said they could readily guess who the culprit behind the burning was and who put him up to it. It hardened their suspicion of the mine and their opposition to it, indeed it also achieved the opposite effect to what had been intended, to turn Pat Delaney from his opposition to the mine, to frighten him into submission and warn others against embarking on an anti-mine campaign.

Next day a meeting was held and the process begun of raising as much money as possible to support the Delaney family in their loss and put them back on their feet. The fund had soon swelled to a substantial sum of money. The family used the money to set the presbytery in order and pay the nominal rent that the priest had asked for; the presbytery was diocesan property. But soon the house was given to the Delaneys it was a white elephant anyway.

Looking further into the future indeed everything turned out very well in the long run. Pat also got the running of and the income from the farm that was part of the presbytery grounds. He and his family set up an organic farm and sold the produce in all the nearby towns; it provided much needed income for up to then he had only the income he got from his sacristan work and that was meager enough. The farm money was useful for the education the children and it was supplemented by Pat's role on the community development committee and his later leadership in the community mine that was set up. As the saying goes it's and ill wind that does not blow good to someone.

But the incident hardened Jerry and Donie's resolve to clear up the mine and the murder of Danny Pat issues.

While the drama of the burning had been unfolding, on the other side of the bay Miley Ramsbottom was raging with his stupid subordinate Jasper O'Leary.

"You total idiot", he screamed, "I thought I told you to keep all your actions to discourage the locals from opposing the mine legal and above board, we are very lucky no one was killed or seriously maimed by your irresponsible act; I have a mind to dismiss you at once from my service, one more stupid act like this burning and I will do just that".

"I take the criticism", Jasper answered, "It was a foolish and dangerous thing to do and I should have known bêtter, but beware of dismissing me. I know too much about you crooked dealings to make such a move sensible, you need me but I do promise to work more cautiously in future, I can swear to being more cautious in future boss".

CHAPTER 28

Deirdre's Wisdom

AFTER LEAVING THE SITE OF THE BURNING JERRY RETIRED BACK TO Jim's house and Deirdre and the children. They were in bed. Dee was up finishing a draft of her coming lecture. Jerry as usual leaned over her shoulder to assess her work and offer comments. She had got as far as the work of G K Chesterton, also one of Jerry's heroes. Jerry knew that if everyone had followed his philosophy of "common sense" as against outrageous ideologies and totalitarian utopianism there would be a much better world today.

"Another and perhaps greatest voice against dangerous postmodernist insanity", Deirdre wrote in advocating her post postmodernism "was the great G K Chesterton. His 'Orthodoxy' is one of greatest and most influential work of the century. In it he demolished all atheistic elitism and moral relativism as deeply dangerous long before those concepts spawned the Nazis. He said everyone, not just the superman but also and especially the common man is sacred. That's why he advocated democracy. The ordinary man must be free to do what he knows is right, that's the essence of democracy, not having everything done for him like a child and dictated to and talked down to by Big Brother governments; the local is the real center of sanity. Chesterton debated with Shaw and Yeats on this issue. Far from giving the ordinary man his democratic rights Shaw had advocated weeding him out by birth control or eugenics or even extermination. Yet curiously Shaw advocated a socialism that aimed to free and bring justice to the very proletariat he wanted to phase out.

But Chesterton, a great modern prophet foresaw that such elitist postmodernism would spawn totalitarianism and genocide. And it would ultimately negate the dignity and value of each human life regardless of class or social status. A convert to Catholicism he thought that that church upheld the natural laws that protected that dignity. For Chesterton the elitist intellectuals were even seen as inferior to the ordinary man. The latter's natural wisdom from being close to nature made him instinctively moral and believing though because of human imperfection he needed higher guidance, an informed conscience based on God's revealed law and a holy church community that embodied that law. Chesterton thought man needed an overarching faith to guide the whole world as in a noble eternal truth-bearing institution such as the Catholic Church. It must have lasting truth and value for it has seen off thousands of passing secular ideologies and persecutions from the year dot. For Chesterton the Catholic Church was bigger than he was – he was a man of enormous girth – and it was also bigger than the world, bigger even than the cosmos because it contained the very presence of the God of the cosmos in its Eucharist. And Chesterton thought the seemingly restrictive timeless dogmas and doctrines of the church are in fact infinitely freeing as God is (Chesterton loved such truth-bearing paradoxes). The church's teachings are road maps to a higher destination and liberation rooted in conscience and the sane natural law, whereas the elitist self-exaltation and narcissism of the super man is a form of madness. By contrast Chesterton advocated humility and realization of our limitations before God, the wonders of the world and every ordinary person's unique value.

Jerry noted that Chesterton was also one of his heroes for he had taken up the cause of the ordinary man over the vain philosophy of the superman, and Jerry pointed out that this was very much in keeping with the Christian environment of the mountain and Patrick who straddled it like a colossus. He noted the amazing fact that the influence of Patrick had survived for 1500 years, when billions of worldly leaders and their philosophies had faded away and disappeared into dust and ashes. It was because Patrick reflected the holiness of God and the humility of seeing himself as simply a product of God's grace and support; indeed in his Confessions he wrote that any good he had done must be attributed to God, not to Patrick his feeble servant.

"Yes", Dee wrote in her lecture "Patrick was imitating Christ, though the latter was God he was also humble even to the extent of casting off his golden clothes and accepting the worst ignominy possible, death on a cross. Why did he do that? Obviously because he saw each person had infinite worth; like Pope Paul 11 he saw each person, regardless of class, as a "logos of divine value" that even God himself was willing to die for. The world languishes if any person is not allowed to be all they can be. This is also the theme of Chesterton's novel The Emperor of Notting Hill. It celebrates an ordinary city man's wisdom. Chesterton argued that without a concomitant supernatural vision man descends to the unnatural. He even sinks below the state of the beast, for all animals follow their created natural states of being, a natural inbuilt law that is their guiding light".

Science is another postmodern false god that can be used to distract us from the deeper truths of our divine origin and destiny. Science keeps us stuck in the lowlands of the soul when it becomes a totally materialistic atheistic ideology. It is often put forward by postmodernism as the only source of truth; but because of the way the scientific method itself works it cannot really address metaphysical issues, to it realities like that of the mountain and its presiding genius Patrick would be irrelevant superstitions. Postmodernists who unduly deify science fall at this hurdle. But they ignore the stark fact that no amount of science can give our life its deepest meaning or give us the eternal life we crave".

"And science cannot even explain the origin and purpose of human life on earth" Jerry added. As Chesterton noted 'the world is not only made up of matter it is made up of what matters". What matters Chesterton added is the deep truths and beauties and joys and wonders of existence that faith lays bare in mythic stories that enable us to more deeply appreciate life and nature's everlasting depth and beauty.

"Moreover", Dee said "the purely material explanation for the world's origin and development is now denied by much of modern science itself. Most scientists now believe again in the

'God hypothesis' as the noted Cambridge scientist Steven Meyer, puts it in his book 'The Return of the God Hypothesis'. The chance atom and molecule claim for the origin and development of life just makes no sense in the face of the complexity and ordered design and exact replication in the atom, the cell, and especially the DNA's programmed code. And quantum physics defies all logistics. As one modern scientist put it, to say blind chance molecules and atoms created life is like saying a monkey with a computer can type all the works of Shakespeare in a relatively short time by blindly tapping keys; it's statistically impossible. And if there is a design in everything as there obiously is, then as in computers there can be no program without a programmer. Or as the operatic artist and ardent believer Andrea Bocelli puts it, "I can't believe in the clock without the clockmaker".

"Yes", Jerry said, "and most scientists also now debunk Darwinism, another vain construct of postmodern atheism; we are just the chance products of blind evolving material forces and of no more value than a mite. But now this too is seen by most noted contemporary scientists and mathematicians as an inadequate hypothesis for the origin and development of life (though there is no reason why if there is a creator God that he couldn't have used the evolutionary method). There is so much in the origin and development of life and the fossil records that show not Darwin's gradual development from inferior to higher forms, but huge gaps and sudden inexplicable leaps to higher forms that again point to the intervention of a cosmic 'designer'".

"And from where came the soul?" Dee exclaimed, "That can hardly have come from purely blind material processes, it is not material. The Christian view is that it was inserted by God at the apt stage of man's bodily development. And it's man's soul that makes him unique and it's so above all it's what we should be nourishing today for it is much neglected and narrow scientific materialism has contributed to this. Pervasive secularist constructs in society prevent the soul nourishment that man as a spiritual as well as a physical being needs. Hence states are subsidizing everything else except the crucial soul-nourishing aspect of human life the church provides; in not aiding or opposing that states are creating a future hell of soul emptiness unknowingly. And a person or society without spiritual depth cannot be a healthy or successful person or society in long run as all the 20th century secular totalitarian societies prove.

And it's only in light of faith that the evil and suffering of an imperfect world, imperfect due to man's own on-going choices of evil as well as good, can be faced and overcome. As Goethe noted the devil is the best servant of God. Satan-inspired evil challenges man to his greatest triumphs, those won over the darkness within and around us. We need such challenges to grow within. As the great poet Keats said 'life is a vale of soul-making'. In effect, meeting and overcoming the challenges of the suffering and evil now deeply embedded in the human condition builds our souls. Hence Dostoevsky says to 'hate suffering is to hate life'. Bravely faced it can change the world. Hence in the Brothers Kamazorov the words of the devil to Ivan during his sickness and delirium: "…suffering is also life. Without suffering what pleasure would there be in it? Everything would turn into one, single church service: much holy soaring but rather boring". In effect if God cured all suffering and disease he would not only be a controlling tyrant negating our free will, but also a creator of a boring world that would have nothing to challenge the human spirit. Moreover, though suffering is hard to bear at times – such as a parent watching a six year old die of cancer – it is not the will of God, he merely permits it due to our freedom but he is not indifferent to our suffering, Christ spent his life healing the sicknesses of the day and that is our call also by the power and help of God to bear suffering and turn it to gold, and work to alleviate it in whatever way we can. But suffering is not always an evil it can also be a revolutionary weapon for change and betterment of the world. I think for example of the martyrs in every age. I think of the words of Terence McSweeney, the lord major of Cork who died on hunger strike to help win Irish Independence (his sacrifice made international headlines and hastened the birth of an Irish Republic): "It is not those who inflict the most but those that can suffer the most who will prevail".

"Moreover", Jerry added "without suffering we can't appreciate or enjoy happiness. Proust observes that 'suffering makes us think' and like the Marxist view that if all had riches there would be a utopia, the view that lack of trials would lead to perfect human life is illusory. As scripture says we need to be 'tested and refined like gold in a furnace'. Suffering in that sense can be looked at in two ways. The negative way that only makes it worse and solves nothing. Or the positive way that makes it a gateway to higher good if bravely faced and overcome like Christ on the cross. I remember old Irish relatives saying about suffering, 'we'll offer it up'. That attitude made them wise gentle people. Like on the cross God suffered with us and for us to make all suffering infinitely valuable if faced in the right spirit and 'offered up'. A perfect painless disease-less world, like us being puppets of a sugar-daddy God who solves our ills with a wave of his hand, would be very dull indeed; we would have nothing to challenge us to heroic deeds, or scientific or medical advances; by these we are gradually being given the means to alleviate human suffering by a providential God, look how many diseases have been wiped out in our time.

But the worst cause of suffering, war, is less easily solved. It's a fatal instance of man's wrong exercise of his free will. Yet God had to tolerate even the horrible warmongers of the 20th century because he dare not negate our free will, to do so would be a greater evil. Indeed respecting our freedom he even allowed us to crucify him in a supreme act of humility. Nietzsche wanted us to kill God but didn't we do enough in killing him once horribly, on a cross when he dared to come down among us to show and tell us how to create healing and redemption and turn suffering into wisdom and light? With his help peace can also enter the world. All it needs is the human will at one with God's will to peace the only antidote to war. I once wrote a poem about this, about the Ukraine war. The angels sang at Christ's birth "peace on earth, good will among men". Good will is the key. John Lennon says in his famous Christmas song; 'peace on earth, if we want it'. We mustn't want it or it would have come long ago; for man has the knack of always finding a way, for good or ill, if he wants something badly enough. We must want peace enough to bring it into being within and without and so negate a huge source of human suffering, war.

CHAPTER 29

New Information and Some Home Truths

When Dee had finished her Chesterton paper we went to bed with the children. The next day Jerry met with Donie to resume discussion on the issue of the killing of Danny Pat. After the parish meeting, the issue of the mountain mine was now on the back burner. Jerry and Donie let Pat Delaney and Tim Thornton sort out the negative issues raised against our plans. Indeed, Deverly was of the opinion that there must be an informer in their midst. How did they know about the alternative plan? They had to know before they could have bribed the owner of the land, and Jim's group had kept their cards very tight to our chests. The people that knew about it other than Donie and Jerry were Thornton, Delaney and Fr.Manus. They would have to ferret out the mole that had nearly ruined their strategy, before the next meeting, lest he scupper that too.

But the mine problem now on the back burner Jerry and Donie could devote all their energies into finding of the murderer of Danny Pat. Jerry had now reached a decision at last and told Donie about the sighting of Terry Ramsbottom and Jasper O'Leary on the mountain that day.

"Maybe we could smoke Terry out by letting him know that we know", Donie said, "lets also see if the guards have got any useful information from their interviews after Danny's death. We'll go to Westport to see Sergeant Colm Dinnity who is in charge of the investigation to see if anything has turned up. He was a colleague of mine when I was a young guard in Dublin, and he's as straight as they come. I have something else planned there, and am waiting to see how it turns out". He would say no more, no matter how hard they pressed him.

They drove to the garda station in Westport, the station in Croagh had long since been closed down, another victim of austerity. Dinnity received them in his office and was effusive in welcome for his old buddy. He was a burly grey-haired man with the broad red face of a west of Ireland farmer. He was reluctant to reveal anything about how the case was progressing, but his friendship with Deverly at last persuaded him to devulge some very important information:

"Donie, I tell you both this in confidence, if you tell anyone else about it I promise I'll crucify you, I'll come looking for you myself and God help your skins, you cynical bastards". He leaned over the desk and said in a quiet voice:

"You told me Peter Ramsbottom and Jasper O'Leary were seen on the mountain that day, around the time of the murder, or accident, we still can't rule that out. I am grateful for your information so I want to pay you back in kind. What if I were to tell you that Davey Sugrue was also seen on the mountain at the same time, and in an agitated state. We think he may have been the one who secretly called in the ambulance, the deliberately muffled voice on the phone, but why would he leave the scene and disguise his voice unless he had something to hide; why didn't he stay with his father and try and help him? Its worrying me, his covering up of his presence there, it seems to be the actions of a guilty man, but at the same time I just can't imagine him killing anyone, he seems too weak a person, and it seems he did love and respect his father. It makes no sense. What do you make of it, old buddy, I remember you were the best analyst of evidence I ever came across, a real whiz kid in those early days when both of us were raw country lads abroad in the big city, ah, what good, and bad times, we had in the big smoke which is still such a wonderful city; I often go there still".

"This is big news surely", Donie replied, "I agree it puts Davey in a bad light and he does want to leave the village, and live in comfort elsewhere, and if he bumped off the old man, it would be his passport to paradise. They say the company will pay big to gain access to that rich vein of gold, that stretches deep into the mountain and is of very high quality. But to kill his own father, that's a hard to believe and like you I don't think he has it in him. No, the other pair of Jasper and Terry seems to be much more likely suspects. Though Terry is less likely Jasper would kill, urged on by his ruthless employer, who maybe sent him up the mountain that day and Davey saw the murder but is too scared of Miley to come forward; or maybe they've some hold over; he's the sort that's easy to manipulate. Have you heard anything yet about that other thing I asked you to do".

"No", he replied, "but they should have the results any day now".

We could get no more out him, so we popped across to see Thornton, and to get some lunch in his usual haunt. But as we went in the door of the Painted Cow we were amazed to see none other than Miley Ramsbottom leaving Thornton's table. What was he doing with his arch enemy? Could Thornton be the informant against them? Jerry was shocked. Could they trust anyone in this affair? Where big money was involved anyone could be turned? As they came up to his table Thornton started and looked a little askance, the look of a guilty man? Maybe! Every man has his price.

"Oh, Donie and Jerry, welcome, sit down and have a bite, there's very good Peking Duck on the menu today".

"Tim", Donie said, "what was Miley doing here? We saw him leaving and it seems he had been at your table?"

"Oh that", he replied, "tried to offer me money to abandon the campaign, I turned him down flat, you know how much this means to me, I told him where to put his money, I tell you. You don't really think I'd betray you, Donie. Why only today I was with that group in Sligo fighting the fracking about to begin there, could contaminate the water table they say, and I'm inclined to agree with them. These campaigns are what I live for. But sit down and have a bite. I just found out, by the way that that man who owns the area of land that we want to access, never really wanted to shut us out. Sure they offered him money and he said he'd think about it, but only today he rang me to say that he had changed his mind, he wouldn't sell his soul for money".

Despite his protestations, they left with a new worry assailing them and no longer with an appetite for lunch. They would have to keep their cards even closer to their chests if Thornton had gone over to the other side.

When he reached the farmhouse, Jerry went for a long walk up the mountain to clear his head, while Donie, who could cook well when he had to, prepared some dinner, his special lasagne and salad with French fries and Croagh black pudding.

The mountain was bathed in a gorgeous red sunset, the last of the day's pilgrims were trailing down, tired and sore, as Jerry went up and sat on a rock looking out over the glory of the bay. Somehow here he thought is a place for love, not squabbles and he thought of Kate, her masses of dark hair and red lips, the unconscious rising to the surface. Then he thought, what nonsense, this stupid temptation, what a fool you are. Your life is Deirdre and the kids. Yes, how he wanted to be with them now, away from all trouble and worry and temptation and fear, down in Cork again with aunt Kate among the lovely lonely hills of home. Yes, I'd go, tomorrow, he thought get away from it all, join them; what was keeping me here anyway?"

He rose to go and then suddenly, out of the blue something hit him in the side of the face with the force of a battering ram. He went down and almost over the side. Recovering he looked up at a brawny face, with outstretched fists, and an angry voice saying:

"Leave our Kate alone, you lot come in here and think you can hijack our mountain and our fight and our women, with your grand words and fine ways. Go back to where you came from, crawl back under your stone you worm. Leave us alone, I say. I'll kill you that I will, you sick bastard, and think nothing of it, Kate means too much to me to let her become your plaything".

Jerry remembered then someone telling him that Kate had a man from the mountain before he came, here he was in the flesh and here Jerry was threatened again, a strong young man, younger than Kate, and handsome in a rugged way, with longish brown hair going bald at the temples. But Jerry wasn't nicknamed the Scrapper Lofty for nothing, known for his temper and hard fists he rose and struck out at the stranger. Catching him off guard, he knocked him backward against a large boulder, where he hit his head and lay slightly dazed but still angry and defiant, gathering himself to continue the battle.

"No one is anyone's property around here", Jerry said, "she can do what she like".

"Yes", he said, "and you a married man and a man of the cloth, talking like that, you should be ashamed of yourself, or do you just pick up girls like toys and then throw them away. Leave her alone, I say, she's mine and we intend to wed, or did, until you the sleazy Diamond Cottage hero came along".

Jerry's temper left him then, and he realized the mountain man was right.

"I'm sorry, he said, "you're right. I'm a thorough hypocrite. I'll leave you and Kate alone and I'm sorry if I came between you, I never knew you even existed. There's no need to fight, I see your point and I accept it. I'm going home anyway to my wife and children tomorrow, I'm sick of this place and all its troubles. You can tell whoever sent you that I'm going".

"No one sent me, I'm not that sod Miley's or anyone else's slave", he replied; "I'm my own man and Kate is my girl and I'll do anything to protect her from predators such as you".

"Listen, now", Jerry said, "if there was anything between us, and there wasn't really, it was she who initiated it, or imagined it; I've been fending off her attentions since I came here. Ok I was tempted like any man would, she's a beautiful girl, you're lucky and I'm glad she has someone like you to love her and be prepared to fight for her, I wish you both good luck".

After this things cooled down, a crowd had gathered and they felt ashamed of themselves. They shook hands and were the best of friends. Later Jerry actually officiated at his wedding with Kate, they invited him; "maybe she had only been playing me along to get his attention and get him to propose, which he did that very night", Jerry speculated.

But this encounter made up his mind, he'd go home to Deirdre and the children, for his heart was heavy from the separation, even for a short while. He would go down to Cork and forget all about the mountain. It was not his fight anyway, he would go away to peace like he did before, on the farm where he first found faith and healing, in the country that was his real home, and the people that were his heart's life blood.

He went down the mountain then with wild Matt Moriarty, that was Kate's man's name. Donie was at the door of the farmhouse and he snorted, "what happened to you, you look like you were in a heavyweight brawl".

When Jerry told him he burst out laughing, "Serves you right you old conniver, your conniving will get you killed some day, if Deirdre don't kill you first. By the way she rang and asked me to tell you to ring her back, something urgent I think"

Jerry hastened to the phone and was so happy to hear her voice, but not the news, his aunt Kate had died. He told Donie and that he was going down for the funeral, his heart heavy for he loved her, and fondly remembered all the joy they had in the walled garden of her house and the quiet walks in the wood, and the apples and cherries they stole from her orchard, as wily boys.

"Go of course, Donie said, "you have to, but come back, we need you here to help finish off this business".

"I don't know if I'll ever come back", Jerry said, sore and thoroughly sick of everything.

CHAPTER 30

Home Again

The drive south was soothing, going back to his first love, and his second love and his four best loves. Forget about the mountain, the real mountain is within, he thought, all that we have climbed up to in life and all of the clear visions that we have seen, that lodge in our souls and enable them to grow.

What was really bugging him with Kate really was time, a sense of his time running out, of his life ebbing away, in dullest everyday chores and fixed ways of being, a kind of death in life that he always dreaded. He immediately stopped at a roadside cafe and wrote a little poem about where he was going in life, for he felt he had reached a new crossroads: "Will I walk on until I'm washed clean to the bone, polished like a river stone deep down reflecting light safe from the storm"?

Certainly where he was going out of now, out of darkness into light, back to his old farmhouse home was where he had gradually emerged out of a dark night of the soul and found his vocation, in a gentle environment where faith and simple goodness was nurtured as a natural part of life; the Christian way of the old people that was built into their bones. Kate had been the sister of the woman who had succored Jerry as young boy, coming from Dublin after the death of his mother. She had lived in the original Lofty farmhouse, and must have been well over ninety now when she died. She was a fine mature woman when he knew her as a little boy. She also befriended him and turned a blind eye to the pranks of him and the full-blooded boys the O'Keeffe gang of which he became a part. Having never married Kate had lavished all her motherly affection on

Jerry and other children, giving them sweets and tea and chocolate cake and the most gorgeous buns, topped with rich icing.

Jerry used to help her in the garden and there got his first love of gardening, of flowers and vegetable marrows and even grapes and tomatoes in the greenhouse. There in the garden he wrote his first published poem about the joys of nature and the first awakening of sexuality, "Dreaming of a maiden among the tall grass waiting, her golden tresses wound round a white body, her liquid looks inviting love?"

I suppose he was half in love with his lady Kate, though she was three times his age. Human sexuality is a curious thing, full of twists and turn and strange byways where people linger awhile or for life. But that was forty years ago and long forgotten, and now he was going back to where his more enduring love was, and the seeds of that love, the lovely boys and girls of the garden of his heart.

First he would have to call to Betsy and Derry and the children in their own original farm. Of course most of the children were now grown up, in college or secondary school. Derry and Betsy came out to greet him with shrieks of delight, it had been so long since he had actually visited them, though they had played a big part in the diamond cottage adventure. The usual squad of dogs came to greet him with them, but the little gathering of wondering children was missing, those he had told stories to and amused in the old days.

Derry was older, the fair hair faded into grey, as was Betsy, become more matronly, grey-haired and round as a tub.

They went in together to their usual meal where they sat and discussed Derry's new situation. Apparently, he had given up the farming, too many overheads, he had to sell the cows and some fields to pay off his loans. He now only kept a few dry cattle on the rest of the land. His main work was as a school bus driver. Betsy did some check-out work in the local supermarket; this was the fate of the home farm that Jerry had loved and that at one time had been a hive of activity, with many employed all the year round. It filled him with sadness to see all that gone in so called progress, the modernist dream become a nightmare, narrowing human life more and more every day. But despite the disappointing nature of their news, the time with Derry and Betsy was a wonderful one.

Later he travelled on where Deirdre and the kids were staying in Kate's old grand farmhouse. But when he arrived there was no sign of them. The house was dark and silent as a grave. Fear began to rise in him, could something have happened to them, could Ramsbottom's gang have got to them, even down here.

Thankfully, his fears were groundless. Soon their car drove into the yard and they swarmed out of it and swarmed all around him, with kisses and hugs and general screams of delight. The reunion did his soul so much good.

The following day was the funeral and as they stood in the old graveyard where Kitty and Tom were also buried, a sense of the weight of time again came to him; it was as if all the past that he had held dear had been blotted out, just as the Ireland he loved had been destroyed and sold out, it's very soul sold into slavery; things move on of course he thought but not always for the better. Time, he thought is our real enemy, it defeats us all in the end and only faith and art defies it, or our on-going memory of the departed, they remain green in our memory and in our continuing honoring of what they meant to us; indeed these are some of the main products of man's efforts to transcend time. Jerry thought of an old poem he wrote about that in the quiet graveyard in Crossmagnier where his father and mother were also buried and the sense of mortality it awoke: "The clock is ticking away the hours, the sand is trickling away our powers. Today, tomorrow, every cursed day we stumble towards a leaden tomb of clay".

Feeling all the old griefs again Jerry drifted with the children to the graves of all the dead he had known as living gentle breathing beings, beings he thought, as boy, would live forever. He prayed with Dee especially at his father and mother's graves, they had come from Dublin to be buried here side by side. He thought of the old song that said life was "a river of no return". As a character in the Lord of the Rings says, "all we have to do is decide what to do with the time given to us".

We must make the most of our brief time, help others and make a difference by our lives and work out our salvation for our whole eternity is at stake. Why are we here? He thought of the old catechism answer: "to know, love and serve God and others in this world and so be happy with Him forever in heaven". So sad then that some spend their lives in the byways of the river of life, in stagnant selfishness and greed, and that's all they have for eternity. He shivered, a sense of death in life, and life in death, creeping over him for he was a poet philosopher.

When they went back to the house, which he learned with great surprise had been left to him, the land went to Derry who already had a house, the mood lightened. He told stories of their youth here and how different things were then to enthralled children, who became less inhibited as the other relations gradually drifted away.

"Goodbye Kate", Jerry said at the graveside, "I loved you in every way and we will meet again in the land where the tyranny of time is forgotten forever, and we like you have made our mark in faith, love and service of our fellow man, in graceful living and so gracefully dying surrounded by all the angels of God".

CHAPTER 31

Of Heroes and Their Destruction

That night they were in no humor for stories or high jinks; the children were sent early to bed, with much tears and protestations, and Deirdre and Jerry sat in each other's arms, as if we were meeting for the first time; conscious of the Kate episode he had left behind in Maheragh he wanted to woo her all over again, producing chocolates and roses and a carefully worded poem written specially for her, and using his pet name for her, Dee and comparing her to an eternal rose: "More than a flower of fancy that withers as soon as it grows".

Love is the one other enduring grace of life, he thought as they renewed their vows, true gracious and faithful love. That night in bed was like their first honeymoon, which they had spent in the highlands of Scotland, climbing and hiking. That world was real for them now again, the world of Burn's poem: "My heart's in the highlands, wherever I go".

Jerry thought of Danny Pat and Jim, and himself, and even Donnie. Their hearts were in the highlands too, the highlands that are the free places of the soul, and the Ireland of dreams and beauty that their forefathers had fought and lived for.

To escape from recent grief, Jerry and Dee decided to take the children to another one of their high sacred places, where real Irish gold was, the Cliffs of Moher, now listed among the wonders of the world by the UN yet often not appreciated, like so many aspects of Ireland, by our own people. He remembered his nephew telling him that when he went to Australia, they were all saying to him, "have you been to the Cliffs of Moher", "what cliffs?" he said. They knew all about these, he didn't, had never visited them, had never even been told about them; Jerry blamed the education system which teaches modern children everything except their own island's glories.

They headed on up to the cliffs, another highland of soul gold if properly seen, God present in the soul of nature. They went across on the Shannon Ferry, in a scorching summer day of 2013, when there had been Mediterranean temperatures. The children were delighted as they climbed up to O'Brien's tower and looked out over the panorama of the cliffs stretching away to Hag's head.

As they sat admiring the cliffs, Jerry told the children the story of Brian Boru, after which the tower was called, Brian the great visionary lion of Thomond as he was called, for as his nephew also told him, "we never learned about that in school". He was amazed for this "emperor of the Irish", as he was called in the annals of Armagh was a figure of greatness equal in many ways, on an Irish scale, to the great emperors like Caesar or Alexander on which he modeled himself.

But he was more a man of peace, whose dream was to unite the warring clans of the island, bring peace and neutralize the threat from the Vikings who were spreading terror everywhere. They were even worse terrorists then than those abroad now.

Brian was born to a king of Thomond, bordering Limerick and Clare, Jerry explained to the kids as they sat atop one of the little grassy knolls above the deep down sea, with seagulls like butterflies among the cliffs far below them.

When he was young Brian's family were massacred by the Vikings, and he vowed to fight them when he grew up. He was educated by the monks in the great monastic city of Conmacnoise where people from all over Europe flocked for learning during the dark ages and where the Irish, in a sense, saved European civilization.

In Clonmacnoise, Brian's great quick mind was appreciated and developed. From the great manuscript books they had there he learned the military tactics of Caesar and the great leaders of the past. After he finished his education, he used these new tactics in his role as clan leader in battle. The Irish tended to rush into battle, but Brian soon outwitted his enemies with clever new classical strategies. He also persuaded his doubtful followers to adopt the new sophisticated ways of living, for he was a visionary as well as a great leader of men and a learned sage. He also learned the Viking way of making boats, and took the control of the Shannon from them, sailing his boatloads of warriors up and down the waterway to keep the peace. And he copied the Vikings great battleaxes, which the Irish dreaded most of all. He forged them for use by his own men.

But he was outlawed by his father who had made a pact with the Vikings of Limerick and for many years he led a band of outlaws fighting to combat the savage raiding foreigners, very often winning battles when completely outnumbered. Eventually his father accepted him back because his fame was growing and more and more warriors were flocking to him, shouting his slogan "Boru, Boru", for his family came from Beal Boru. He persuaded his father to take the kingship of Munster, and helped him secure this prize by clever stratagems.

When his father died he became king. He married the daughter of a king of Galway. She was called Mor and she bore him a strong son Murchu to fight by his side, and a daughter Slaine whom he married to the Viking king of Dublin as part of a series of strategic alliances he built up. He also went among the people, copying the great Anglo-Saxon king Alfred, finding out his people's needs and mediating in their disputes, using the great Irish code, the Brehon Laws. Indeed he kept many lawyers and employed many scribes, poets and musicians to build up a cultured kingdom. Indeed he himself played the harp well and wrote music for the harp.

At Kincora he built a fortress to rival that of the high king of all Ireland in Meath, winning back many of the church treasures and learned manuscripts stolen by the Viking and restoring them to the monasteries. His own brother was abbot of one of these monasteries.

The O'Neills of the North held the high kingship but they made no effort to unite the Irish clans who were easily defeated by the Norsemen because they were constantly fighting each other. Brian with the help of the Danes of Limerick and other disparate allies, who were proud to fight under his lion banner, marched north and without fighting a single battle, just by a show of force, won over Malachy of Armagh. He then marched south and claimed the high Kingship without shedding a single drop of blood. For ten years under his protection there was peace all over Ireland, for his vision was of a united and peaceful Ireland and his power kept all factions at peace; and he had the scribes write out the great histories, listing his failures as well as his successes for he wanted the truth to be told, and he loved learning as well as wise and just rule based on the rule of great leaders such as Charlemagne. There in the great Annals of Armagh, Brian himself was described as such a great and wise ruler, as the great and wise "Emperor of the Irish".

Fearing his immense and ever growing power however, and because he had destroyed their lucrative raidings throughout the island, the Viking conspired with the king of Leinster and Dublin to challenge his rule, sending for help to the Vikings in the Isle of Man, Orkney and Britain. They gathered in a huge horde in Dublin to challenge his rule and Brian marched to meet them aided, ironically by many Danish foreigners who were proud to fight under his banner. He was then an old man and weary from his great works and battles for a just, united and peaceful Ireland.

But he set out the successful plan of battle, and despite being outnumbered, he won the fight, though he himself had to oversee it from his tent. This was due to his old age and infirmity. He was then 73, a great age for that time, when most people died relatively young, at about the age of 40. Sadly, on the day of his greatest triumph, the final victory over the Vikings that he had always sought, he was killed in his tent by a fleeing Norseman; his son Murchu and grandson Turlough were also killed in that battle.

Yet his fame lived on after his death and to this day. All the O'Briens are called after him and since his father was Kennedy, or O'Cinneide in Irish, many famous people such as John F.Kennedy and Ronald Reagan claimed kinship with Brian. Indeed the "lion of Thomond" left a lasting monument to his greatness in the Deise and the Dalcassians who were his followers. This greatest and wisest of Irish rulers died in 1014 at the famous battle of Clontarf, his greatest and final triumph and remains perhaps the greatest of all the high kings of Ireland and a figure of great international fame in his day we can still emulate. For his great achievement was to unite foreigners and Irish in new fresh and integrated Ireland, at peace with all its peoples.

They listened mesmerized to the story, even Brendan saying, "sure we never learned all that in school, I want to be like him", swishing his hurley stick around like a sword, it was his type of macho story, not like sloppy fairy tales. Jerry thought how little attention we pay to such inspiring heroes. Why don't our TV stations make series about such Irish themes instead of silly canned imported series that has so little relation to our Irish life. In this way we might educate and inspire our new generations to a new appreciation of our ancient history and the great lessons of peace and wise rule and cultural depth of soul we can gain from them.

After walking the whole length of the Cliffs, from O'Brien's tower to hags head, and after a good meal in the cafe at the heritage centre they travelled home again to Cork, all the troubles of Croagh, and the sorrows of Kate's death washed from their minds. They were all so weary from this great adventure, that they fell into bed, the children not even crying out for a bedtime story.

But later in the night Jerry dreamed one of his strange Lofty dreams. He saw Brian Boru crying in his tent over the holy mountain being slowly demolished by huge caterpillar excavators, and helicopters from the air with demolition balls. And Donie was standing by, holding Jerry back and saying, "there is nothing we can do Jerry, it must all come down and you must be charged with causing its demolition, sent to the county jail". And then they too were crushed by the demolishing machines, and their blood mingled with its stones in a great mound of devastation, over which Jerry saw St.Patrick himself hovering and crying bitter tears. And Miley was standing by with some fat company men smiling and laughing rubbing their hands at the prospect of coming loot.

It was partially prophetic. For all that day's ecstasy and night agony was soon to come to an end. Early next morning, Dee, who had risen with the children, early, came to Jerry's side saying that there was an urgent call from Maheragh.

"No, I will not go back", he said, "I'm done with it all, even my dream was a warning to let it be".

But the news shocked him out of this escapism. The voice at the other end of the line was that of Donie, a voice quivering with emotion and near despair, and he could hear Nelly sobbing in the background.

Apparently Donie's trap to catch Danny's killer had been sprung but it had rebounded on himself. He had had the people of the village interviewed, not so much for information, but to get samples of their voices. The muffled voice on the ambulance call to tend to Danny Pat that fatal day was then sent by Donie to compare with the voices on tape from the interviews. With modern technology they could separate out the interference and get a clear map of the voice. And there was no doubt whatever, the voice was that of Terry Ramsbottom. With that and his sighting by Kate on the mountain, a warrant was issued for his arrest.

But like in the former case against him, he had got wind of the development and fled. Not only that but Sally had fled with him, or he had forcibly taken her with him for insurance. No wonder Donie and Nelly were in tears, their baby at the mercy of a murderer, and God only knows where he was taking her, maybe she too was already dead, that was their greatest fear, that he had dumped her body somewhere along the way.

Jerry hurried back to support Donie and Nelly in this crisis. He felt depressed again as he travelled north and he thought of O'Casey's words, "the whole world is in a state of chassis", dark humor. What is happening to our fair island of saints and scholars he asked. Maybe this small place's horrors was a microcosm of a wider chaos in our world, even the collapse of our western civilization.

He thought again of Splengler's theory that each civilization goes through a spring summer and final winter of decay. Were we in the winter now and could it be returned to spring; others had hoped for that before. The poets in the Thirties had taken that up between two terrible wars, "waiting for the end, boys waiting for the end". They tried to warn and offset the coming holocaust, but people never listen to prophets, they just plunge ahead to their doom. But certainly those poets' fears had come to pass, in terrible wars and genocides. But the underlying modern western system had not changed. It was still in place, only the further destroying of any redeeming features, such as the wisdom and moral bases, seems to be going on. Maybe we need a total clearing of the ground before a new world order can arise, the old apocalyptic dream come true, Jerry dreamed.

CHAPTER 32

A New Crisis and a New Shock

EARLY IN THE MORNING HE HEADED STRAIGHT FOR THE REEK, DRIVING without stop. When he reached the farmhouse the mood there was funereal. Nelly, her eyes red with tears was like a Zombie in the corner. Donie was ashen pale sitting staring into space, the girls had been his life. Even Molly was there with the Fleming boy, in a perilous nervous state. They greeted Jerry numbly, saying they were glad he could come but hoped they hadn't upset him too. Jerry answered,

"Donie, Nelly", he said, "How could I stay away, what affects you affects me too. We have gone through too many hard times together, but up to now it was always you supporting me. Now I am here for you. Deirdre and the kids will follow later".

All he could add by way of comfort was:

"I think she might have gone with him freely, she does love him deeply warts and all; I think he loves her too and would do nothing to harm her, I'm convinced of that; they'll just try and hide out somewhere with some money supplied by Miley, he has connections. I'm sure all this will be solved amicably, and we don't know that he is really guilty yet it's just a few circumstantial pieces of evidence. He may be innocent as a new born babe and just panicked when he saw the cards stacked against him, the father had always mollycoddled him and I suppose he just couldn't face arrest and jail. That Sally went with him seems to prove that she believes in him and she was always a girl with good sense. Don't worry, it will turn out OK (He

218

knew how feeble and cliché that sounded, but it was all he could think of at the time)".

"Thanks for the kind words, Jerry, and we're so glad you could come to have a clear-headed person to take charge of things", Donie said. "But I know the world and I know criminals. Having committed one crime they will not baulk at committing another, it gets easier they say I might as well be hanged for a sheep as a lamb. But you're right, nothing is proved, there is hope, and Sal has always done the right thing, maybe she will be able to persuade him to give himself up peacefully and face the music; I have faith in her, that she'll find her way out of this, that's my hope".

Nelly could say nothing but come over and sob in Jerry's arms,

"My baby, my baby, with that animal, what will we do?" He comforted her as best he could, his heart breaking too.

"By the way", Donie said, "the inquest is on today. Maybe you could go down to the courthouse and see what the verdict is, though I don't expect any surprises there, they may adjourn it, given the new circumstances. I'm in no fit state to go, so I'd appreciate if you would represent me. It starts at 1 o'clock so you had better get down there straight away, something might turn up to help us", grasping at straws, Jerry thought.

But he did drive to the courthouse in Westport, glad to have something useful to do, the farmhouse was like a morgue.

The proceedings were just beginning and the garda in charge immediately asked for an adjournment given the new development, but the coroner surprised everyone by refusing this request.

"I think we should proceed, he said, "for there may be some evidence emerging that throws light on the case, some new developments".

At this Jerry cocked his ear, new developments? He thought it would just be a formality. And the early evidence given was just a series of formalities. The call, the finding of the body, dead at the time of finding. But then the coroner surprised everyone by calling an unexpected forensic expert.

"Mr Flinchley", he said, addressing a tall distinguished looking expert in the witness stand, "are you of the opinion that the victim,

Daniel Patrick Sugrue, died as a result of a fall from a cliff face on the mountain called the Reek?".

"No, your honor", the expert said, "it is clear from our findings that Daniel Patrick Sugrue died from injuries inflicted about a half hour, to an hour, after the fall".

There was a huge hub bub in the courtroom.

He went on to show by means of technical evidence that Danny Pat was clearly hit by a blunt instrument, probably a rock of some kind, and this is what caused his death and it happened between the phone call made and the arrival of the ambulance, about half an hour or so. There were further gasps of amazement from the audience and press present.

Immediately Jerry put two and two together, and it was now clear that this completely exonerated Terry Ramsbottom from the murder. For after finding the body he had run down to Fleming's pub to make the call, it would have been impossible for him to get back up and commit the murder, and in any case some would have been already on the scene before him, notably Bridie and her husband and Jim and Davey, who had all hurried up there before him. This put a new complexion on everything and the case was wide open again.

Jerry couldn't wait to get back and tell Donie, for if Terry was off the hook then he could come home safely and so could Sally, if he could be traced, but doubtless Miley had some idea of their whereabouts and how to contact them, since it was most likely that he had engineered their flight.

The verdict came in of willful homicide by person or person unknown. By the time Jerry got back to the farmhouse the news had already filtered through to Donie and Nelly and the atmosphere had completely changed, they were hugging each other with delight. Terry had been contacted by Miley in some safe house in Dublin used by drug gangs, and he and Sally were on their way home. What a turn of events.

For the first time Donie and Nelly were able to sit down and have a bite to eat, up to now they had been too worried to do anything except worry and fret.

"The first thing we will have to do", Donie said his appetite and clarity of mind restored, "is to get her away from that thug. Sure he may not be a murderer but he had no right to take her away from her family like that, it was almost akin to kidnapping in my view, and perhaps bodily endangerment".

"Leave it be for the moment", Jerry said, "if you start tearing into him, you'll only hurt her more for obviously she cares about him deeply. Let things be for the time being and be grateful you have her back safe and sound, be grateful for small mercies. But this means the case is wide open again, and I have a feeling that if we solve the question of who the murderer is we may also solve the problem of the mine and saving the mountain, for the two are closely connected".

Deirdre and the kids came that evening and they were all reunited in happier circumstances. Even Sally arrived late that evening from Dublin, falling into the arms of her parents with many tears. When they gently remonstrated with her there were just further floods of tears,

"Mammy, Daddy, I love him, I never believed he could have killed or touched a hair of Danny Pat's head. You don't know him as I do, he's a gentle much misunderstood person. They say he ran away before but it was his father who forced him to do that, he wanted to give himself up, as he did this time but the father was insistent. I went with him freely for support, for I love him and saw how much he was suffering. He told me what happened. He came onto the mountain and found Danny Pat fallen and unconscious. He tried the mobile phone to ring the ambulance but the reception was poor, he rushed down to the pub and used the public phone there. By the time he got back up some people were already there, Davey, Bridie and big Bill, Jim and some people who had been doing the climb from that side. So he couldn't have been responsible, I believe him, I believe in him even if you don't. You're all against him unfairly", another flood of tears on Nelly's shoulder followed.

"Hush, darling", she said, "we believe you now, and we'll stand by you and him, no matter what, darling hush, we're with you now, all will be well, you'll both be OK now. What you need is rest and recuperation from your ordeal and you can go to see Terry tomorrow if you wish, we won't stand in your way, hush now and rest and get a bite to eat, and you'll feel much better, we all feel much better now that Terry is exonerated and you are home".

A real mother talking, Jerry thought, she had learned. Sally had believed and now we were all beginning to reassess Terry. How easy it is to condemn someone without really knowing them, he thought. She had kept the faith and won us over, like faith itself, or those flags football followers hold up when their team isn't doing so well, "keep the faith", the real test of faith and love is when we keep it through every storm and suffering and pain, that's what's meant by the "faithful", the saints of God are no straws in the winds of the world, blown this way and that with every new fashion or ideology, their reward is their steadfastness. Real love is like that too, a solid rock amid all the storms of life. Sally had proved her love was more than a passing infatuation.

CHAPTER 33

An Assault on Kate

Molly came later and cuddled her sister. Even Jim, who had been sitting in the corner, came and patted her on the back. He would have his own troubles shortly, and very serious ones at that. In the middle of all this a note arrived for me from Kate

Jerry come and see me, I have some further news for you of vital importance about Danny Pat's murder that I want to impart to you in private. Come as soon as you can.

Love,
Kate
XXX

He hastened to the pub to seek her out. Billy was behind the bar and when he asked for Kate he said she was in the back sorting out some bills and business invoices, the tax audit for the bar was due shortly.

Jerry went in there and opened the door, but she was not there. He went back to Billy and explained that there was no sign of her. "Look upstairs", he said impatiently, "She sometimes goes up to her room for a rest".

He went up the stairs, with a strange foreboding in his heart, the Lofties have that facility of foreseeing the future. When he got to her room the door was shut. He knocked but there was no reply. Even more worried he shouted to Billy for the key of the door. He came up the stairs with it, a little sulky at this invasion of privacy. When they opened the door they got the second great shock of that day. She was lying at the base of her bed, blood on her head and all over the floor. Someone had tried to ensure that she wouldn't pass on the information to Jerry; but who could have known of her intent? Apparently informants were everywhere.

How many more victims must the mining company have before its thirst for gold is assuaged? Jerry thought enraged. This was the latest frail and beautiful victim, Kate the fair of the full breasts and bubbly ways.

He lifted her up in his arms, and felt her pulse,

"Thank God she is still alive", he shouted to Billy, making her as comfortable as possible, "please ring for the the doctor the ambulance and the guards, she needs immediate help".

After putting a blanket over her to keep her warm, he whispered reassuring words in her ear in case she could hear. He was angry, someone would have to pay for this, he felt, for all these innocent victims of a cruel world manned by cruel faceless people who sought only that muck called gold, and would do anything to acquire it, people didn't matter anymore.

It seemed like an eternity as they waited for the ambulance. Dr. Moriarty came and gave her some injections to help with the pain and the shock, but he could do no more. Fr.Manus came and anointed her, mumbling, "shocking, most shocking, what's the world coming to, knocked down in plain daylight, shocking".

Eventually Billy came up the stairs with the ambulance paramedics and the stretcher. Billy and Jerry accompanied her in the journey to the hospital. Jerry held her hand, a little guiltily for he was conscious that Deirdre might view this unfavourably. But he wished he had been kinder to Kate during their short acquaintance, he hadn't seen her as person only, perhaps unfairly, but as a sexual predator and temptress. His focus had been on himself not on her and how she was feeling, her life running out and nothing achieved, just slavery behind a sordid bar she didn't even fully own, and doubtless the unwanted attentions of all sorts of sleazy drunken patrons; she was a beautiful desirable woman.

She had the sturdy Matt of course and Jerry hoped he would now whisk her away to the mountain and a more pleasant domestic existence, with beauty at her back door and sleazebags of the world far away. But maybe they were just his wishes not hers. Maybe she liked living on the edge maybe that was her downfall, being too much hand in hand with the world and its ways.

In the hospital while they waited for news of her condition, Donie had joined them they speculated about the information she might have and if she would ever be able to impart it now. He showed Deverly the letter, and the detective began to reflect:

"Who could have known she was about to divulge this information. Billy maybe, apparently he was her half brother and they had never been close, but he had no connections that we know of with Miley or the mining company, he seemed such an innocent boy. Maybe someone in the bar had heard her discussing it with Billy, or she had confided in someone else, the wrong person. What is clear is that we are dealing with a ruthless murderer, who having committed one crime is not adverse to committing another, who perhaps enjoys inflicting pain, one of those rare psychopaths who roam the world, and can be found even in the mystic west".

At this Matt the Thrasher, as he was known locally, his father had had a threshing machine in the old days, came in and cast a malevolent look in their direction which plainly said, another mess you've landed her in, why didn't you fellows stay away; he came up to them and said as much, his grey eyes full of pain and worry.

"Why didn't you lot leave us alone, we've had nothing but trouble since you came, now you've killed Kate with all your meddling, I hate you slimy lot".

"Well the trouble was already here", Donie said soothingly, "they had already killed Danny Pat. Kate was only trying to help us; she loved The Mountain and was willing to do her part in finding Danny's murderer, whatever the cost and danger it might entail, she was a brave woman and you're lucky to have her".

At this he calmed down and said a little shamefacedly:

"How is she anyway..is she Ok? Will she get out of it..I'm sick with worry since I heard it..I never thought they'd touch my Kate..I'll get whoever did this if it's the last thing I do..I'll tear the bastard limb from limb..will they let us in at all to see her? I want to just hold her hand and comfort her?"

"No, Jerry said, "but I think she'll be OK, she'll get out of this all right, she's a strong girl and a fighter", he said to ease Matt's torment, though he was not so sure she would survive this cruel assault.

CHAPTER 34

A further Shock to the System

After leaving the hospital, with a better report on Kate having been issued by the doctors, they were confident she would recover, knowing he could do no more and leaving her in the care of Matt who refused to leave her bedside, Jerry went home. The children were being packed off to bed. Like the night before they screamed for a story, so he continued the story of the Wisps and Fisps.

After the Wisps left the mountain, he said, the Fisps took it over. The dug and dug into the mountain, trying to get at the gold, but the deeper they dug the more the gold faded away even deeper into the mountain. So that they worked day and night, trying to get it, forgetting to even eat, they were so obsessed by the gold, so that they got thinner and thinner, until you could hardly see them at all, they got so thin.

"I suppose if we didn't eat we'd die", Mairead said.

"I learned in school", Brendan interrupted, "that we can last up to 40 days without food, but only about ten without water. Did they drink water at all".

"Well they did drink a little water", Jerry said, "but soon they died, and faded away into shadows you can still see if you go up the mountain, when the sun is shining and throwing the shadows of rocks onto the valleys..

As for the Wisps they went across Ireland to Glendalough, near Dublin, another sacred mountain where there is also gold still that they packed into it; people even go up there panning for gold as a pleasant pastime. St. Kevin, a holy monk, built seven churches there and it is a famous place now too. The monks could live anywhere their life was so simple, they even lived on a rock down off the Kerry coast, on a bare rock in the middle of the ocean".

"I don't think I'd be able to live on a rock", Mairead said, "sure they'd be no food or anything, or TV, or radio or internet, or electricity..or anything like that".

"This was before any of those things existed when people lived a simpler life", Jerry said. "I suppose they ate bird's eggs, there were lots of birds on the rock, and there were little sheltered areas on it where they could grow things. And they kept goats and sheep who lived on the grass there and gave them milk and meat, and wool to make their clothes. I must take you some day down to Portmagee. Scelig Micheal it's called, the rock, they prayed there for the whole world, they said, to keep it happy and safe and close to God, and safe from the evil one. But the Vikings landed even there and starved the abbot, the head of the monks to death. The Vikings, who were fierce warriors, thought there was gold on the rock and starved the abbot to death, because he wouldn't tell them where the gold was, but of course there was no gold there; it's hard to escape the world".

A this they were silent, for they had come a long way from mythical Wisps and Fisps to monks on a rock in the middle of the ocean but that's the nature of the free mind and free imagination, which is best seen in the unfettered souls of children; until schools make them think on rigid worldly lines. Jerry had much sympathy with that Pink Floyd song: "we don't need no education, we don't need no false control..teacher leave them kids alone..all in all you're just another brick in the wall".

Yes, we build walls around children's minds, he thought, making them sit silent under tyrannical control, killing all their spontaneity and vision. A friend of his had fled all this modern control for a kind of "good life" existence, where they taught the children themselves, though of course social intercourse with other children was important. In the church they should not be taught faith in school but as part of a free living community of faith in the parish, for faith must be lived not taught like another swathe of useless information. Conscious of this, Jerry finished with a little poem about the monks on the rock, which he turned into a repetitive song to lull them to sleep;

> Monks at peace in stormy seas,
> My little babies be like these
> Far from worldly cares and tears.

Jerry left the children sound asleep and tip-toed down to where Donie was having a night cap of malt whiskey and water; Jerry joined him for he wanted to discuss the strange twist in the case, now that they had a quiet house to themselves.

"What do you make of this latest development?" He asked Donie, "it's a boon for you and Sally but it lands us back where we were before, in a sea of unexplainable chaos. The attack on Kate makes an even stranger conundrum of the whole affair; Terry can't have done it, he was still in Dublin. What could she have seen on the mountain that day that only later became significant, after the inquest and her reflection on its findings?"

"Yes", Donie replied, "it's even harder now to make sense of it all. Kate's evidence must have something to do with the main suspects in the affair. But let's revert to my old technique of analysis. Let's look at each of the suspects in turn, starting with the three that were actually seen on the mountain at the time of the crime, Terry, Davey and Jasper. Terry seems to be out of it, but not completely, he could not have struck the final murder blow but he could have pushed the old man off the cliff before ruing his actions and rushing for help. If so he must have had the collusion of the others for the three seemed to have been up there together at the right time; anything one did most likely was seen by one or all of the others. The fact that Terry muffled his voice means there must have been something that he wanted covered up, he wanted to conceal his own presence and involvement in the event for some reason. Over to you".

"Well it seems to me we have two crimes here, the pushing of the old man over the cliff and the administering of final murder blows. I agree that the first seems to boil down to three, and it also seems to leave those three out of the murder part. Take Davey, he was on the mountain, he could have pushed his father and then the other two came up and he made a pact with them to conceal his involvement. If so what was the pact, obviously to conceal his crime in return for his giving his mountain land to Miley and the company, this would explain his subsequent giving in to their demands, they had him over a barrel. Maybe they phoned to Miley and he suggested that arrangement, it sounds more like his idea, and the mobile phones could call locally though the range didn't extend as far as the ambulance in Westport. He could have suggested that Terry call from the pub, he could have called from his house but that could have implicated him. Over to you".

"Well analyzed, Jerry", "you'll soon be as good as myself, you're catching on quick. The final piece in this first part of the jigsaw is the thug himself, Jasper O'Leary. He could have gone up first, sent by his master to talk the old man into selling the mountain, when Danny Pat refused he could have fallen back on the alternative plan, get rid of the old man and make it look like an accident. When the other two came up he said it was an accident, Terry runs off for help and he and Davey stay to watch over the old man. In that case Davey's selling out on the mountain would be simply out of weakness and a desire for escape and a leisurely life, nothing to do with the crimes, which is very possible. This leaves us no further on in pinpointing either the pusher or the killer, and there's always the possibility that the initial fall was an accident, though there is no doubt that he was killed by the subsequent blow, that couldn't have been an accident. Over to you..".

"Well", Jerry said, "this is certainly like a crossword puzzle of the most cryptic kind. The more so when we come to the second crime. Here the number of suspects expands. We know that shortly after the fall and the discovery of Danny Pat unconscious, three others were alerted to the fact, and went up to him, before the ambulance arrived or Terry returned to the scene, Bridie and Bill Sheehan and Red Jim Sugrue. True, Davey and Jasper were there, but it appears from the interviews that both Davey and Jasper left Danny Pat unattended for a time, Davey to ring Jim, and Jasper to contact Miley, the latter had gone to the other side of the mountain to get better reception for this so he would have been out of sight of the scene of the crime for some time. Ample time for the Sheehan duo to do the deed, the pressure of their financial problems egging them on, and another more serious issue that I can't divulge. Perhaps they reasoned that the old man would probably be a vegetable anyway as a result of the fall and it was an act of mercy".

"Finally we have Jim, unlikely as it seems", Donie said, "He would have been the first up since his house is nearest to the scene. Seeing his father like that he may have reasoned that it were better that he was dead, though I admit, that is the least likely of all the scenario's we've outlined, it doesn't match with his character or subsequent actions, though they may have been compensatory. The whole thing leaves us in an impossible dilemma, that gets more so every time we examine it..it's one of the hardest cases I've faced, I must admit..".

"Let's go over the time frame", Jerry said. "Danny Pat went up the mountain as usual at 1.30 after having his dinner at one. He went to the highest point of the north slope, and watched his sheep with binoculars for any sign of an animal who might have strayed or might have got sick.

Davey came to him about 2 0'clock and claims to have found him fallen and injured, and Terry and Jasper joined him about 2.30, but had been seen on the mountain earlier. At 2.30 Terry ran down to mountain to phone for an ambulance. Jasper left the scene about 2.35 to phone Miley and Davey went to phone the rest of the family a little later. Jim arrived about 3.15. So the murder must have taken place between 2.35 and 3.15. When Bill and Bridie came at about 3.15 they found Billy there, he had come from the pub with a first-aid box to see what he could do for Danny while they were waiting for the doctor and the ambulance. So unlikely as it seems Billy Fleming was there during the period of the murder and that makes him the main suspect. At 3.45 Jim left to go down to show the ambulance crew, who had arrived at the road below, where the body was. When they arrived to take the old man to hospital about 3.45 they found Danny Pat was already dead.

From this it's clear that the fall happened sometime between 1.30 and 2 0'clock which implicates only Davey, Terry and Jasper in that part of the crime. And the actual murder happened between 2.35 and 3.15. I will ask the guards, my friend Inspector Dinnity,to bring Billy in and ask him what he was doing during that time of the murder and if he saw anyone else there".

He was interrupted by a barrage of banging at the door.

"Hell", he said, "what could this be at this hour of the night", they both rushed to the door and hauled it open.

Bridie stood outside, her face white and agitated, trying to speak but failing. Not another murder, Jerry thought, this is too much.

"Its Davey", she said, "I fear he has killed himself, come quickly with me to his flat".

CHAPTER 35

The Delimma of Davey

"We'll come immediately Jerry said, "but first ring for an ambulance". Deirdre came down the stairs behind Donie with the kids who had been disturbed, and Nelly in her nightdress also came swarming down the stairs.

At length when they had sat Bridie down, and plied her with a glass of brandy, some color came back into her cheeks:

"Oh Davey, why did you do it?", she said, crying, "I called in to see him a while ago and he was laid out on the bed, senseless..he took something..drugs...he's not responding..Please come and help him. I rang the guards and asked them to contact the emergency ambulance.".

"Donie", Jerry said, "ring the local doctor, Moriarty, we must get to him fast, there may be a chance to save him".

Jerry, Donie and Jim drove to his flat and stormed in the door. He was lying as Bridie said, stretched out on the bed, an empty white packet that they surmised had contained drugs was on the floor. He was foaming at the mouth.

"At least he's alive", Donie said, after feeling his pulse.

At this Dr Moriarty, the local GP came up the stairs, post haste, he lived close by, and he examined Davy and administered some injections to counteract the drugs,

"This should help stabilize him until the ambulance comes", he said. He examined the empty drug container, "looks like some form of heroine", he said, "They'll give him a more targeted antidote when he gets to the hospital, fluids and proper counter medicines on drip. I just hope it will be enough to save him, it may be touch and go, but..he said, looking at Bridie, "I'm very confident, I think we got him in time..", proper soothing words for the next of kin.

Bedlam followed, ambulance and police sirens, people hustling Davey down the stairs in a stretcher after the paramedics had consulted the doctor and providing their own immediate medication.

As he was whisked away they followed with Bridie and Jim in the back of the car. At the hospital in Wesport he was rushed into the emergency room, surrounded by a sudden barrage of nurses and the residing doctor.

Jerry and Donie came in with Jim and sat in the waiting room to await some news of his progress, Bridie in tears, almost hysterical, and Jim somber faced. She calmed down after a while, They gave her a cup of warm sweet tea to stem the shock, and they waited around for what seemed an eternity, Jim pacing up and down and Bridie sitting with hand on her mouth, her head bent and her body very still. Now, Jerry thought, we know what hold Miley had over him, a drug supply. No wonder they said he was so peculiar at times in the school, and often absent, and so severe with the pupils, irrational behavior, drug dependence, strange that those close to him hadn't spotted it as such, but then again they had no experience in such matters, and Donie had never served in the drug squad at the raw end of everyday occurrences, more after the big fish. Will all these shocks never end, Jerry thought, this is too much, its one tragedy after another.

They waited for what seemed like an eternity for news of Davey's condition. People were around them with various emergencies also waiting endlessly, strained expression on their face and their relatives fuming. Understaffed and over pressurized doctors and nurses were doing the best they could cut backs had hit them hard. Many people were on trolleys waiting for a bed.

There seemed to be more sickness now, that's what baffled Jerry, with all the progress in medicine, half the people he knew were on one medication or another, and cancer seemed to be exploding everywhere. Maybe we didn't notice it in the past but that's a cop out too, a recent study in Britain said that most of the cancers now are due to changed diet and life style, it was a factor of modern life, and that had been proved beyond question, just as the graph of suicides in Ireland had been steadily and inexorably going up, and it was young healthy people who were most of the victims; yet we're told every day that we are making marvelous progress in every way, the more we toe the line of the new ideologies the closer we are getting to paradise, who do they think they are fooling? These thoughts went through Jerry's mind, maybe because of the endless waiting with the suffering of humanity, his frustrations boiled over; he got more and more pissed off, as everyone around him did.

After a long long time, a junior doctor, with lines of tiredness under his eyes, not his fault, came out to talk to them.

Apparently, they had just got Davey in time, he would survive but it would take time and he had to be weaned off whatever he had been taking, and that would be a much longer and more difficult process, like the alcoholic he would have to accept and want to change his dependence first and that would be a difficult thing to persuade him; also he would have to have the will to live and many now didn't have that, except older wiser people such as Danny Pat who had nothing all their lives and clung to life like a barnacle. Hardship and a settled way of life and culture and faith and a busy outdoor life had built not only physical health but also mental and spiritual health, the last in Jerry's view being the most important of all, people had to care for the inner man first and build inner depth and strength and grace to face the problems of life. Jerry felt no shame at beating this hobbyhorse of his; art must serve the people as well as entertain and delight, it must stir our consciences in the pursuit of what is eternally right, not just cow tow to modern superficialities.

After hearing good news they all headed in to see the patient, though only from a distance, he was not to be disturbed. He lay there in a white gown, looking pale and gaunt and frail, in a white hospital bib, his slightly bald head and wispy fair hair making him look somehow much more vulnerable than they had ever imagined. We never know what is going on within the person, Jerry thought, we had seen him more in terms of our own environmental cause not as a hurting person and, as with Bridie and Bill, now Jerry cursed himself for making that mistake. He noticed a pretty fair-haired nurse coming and looking at him and holding his hand for a moment.

Maybe he had some future there, for apparently he had paid a few day time visits here for therapy unknown to anyone. She obviously knew him well and he obviously had one friend in this impersonal place. Jerry thought these are the real healers, those who treat the whole person, body, mind and spirit, those who cared at every level and saw beyond the ailment to be tended to the suffering soul of which it might be a symptom.

After going to the chapel and saying a prayer for Davey, they headed on home; Jerry wanted to see how Deirdre and the children were doing after the disturbance, if they had been able to settle down again, but they were still up and full of excitement, it was a new game, the middle of the night game and Nelly was plying them with drinks and yogurts and all sorts of things to further hype them up, she was great, her heart was bigger than her head, God bless her, Jerry thought.

Then he and Donie went on to Davey's place to lock up and make sure all was secure. In his room they searched for more drugs, they wanted to clear all away before his coming home, make him exist without them. As they were locking up someone came and knocked at the door. He had something in his hand, and Jerry recognized him as a henchman of Miley's. Is Davey around he said, I have something for him, drugs Jerry thought, was this man one of his suppliers. As if reading Jerry's thoughts, Donie grabbed the intruder and using his policeman head-lock trapped him against the wall and pried the package out of his hand. Donie handed it to Jerry, "look in there and tell me if it's what I suspect", he said, Jerry did so and sure enough it was white powder of some sort, most probably cocaine. "Ah", he said, "we have you now Miley, if this can be traced back to you".

Donie drove the druggie to Wesport barracks where they had night staff and a lock-up. He showed the evidence to the guard on duty:

"We'll lock him up", he said, "and Inspector Dinnity will interrogate him in the morning, this could be an important breakthrough in our anti-drug campaign".

They went home exhausted after all the excitement of the night. The house was quiet by now, and Jerry crept up the stairs and into

Deirdre's room and slid into bed alongside her. She woke up and slid her arms around him comfortingly.

"By the way", she said, "Bridie found a letter in Davey's room addressed to Jim. it may be an old letter or it may have something to do with his drug coma, maybe a suicide note. Jim said he'd look at it in the morning and if it had any significance he bring it to you and Donie, it may have some bearing on the case".

Jerry slept fitfully, and dreamed of Miley holding a letter with a big D marked on it, and saying to Danny Pat, catch the letter, throwing it to him but it hit Danny and went right into his head, and Jasper O'Leary went to retrieve it for his master, but he turned into a great black hound and started to eat the body. Then Bridie came up with a little poodle trailing along behind her and suddenly the poodle attacked the hound and drove him away, holding Danny Pat's heart in his mouth. Jerry woke bathed in sweat, filled with foreboding. He knew this dream had some significance for the dreams of the Lofties always had deep meanings, signifying the terrors that had happened and the untold terrors yet to be.

But it was morning before they could peruse the contents of the letter and expose there the testimony of Davey, it turned out to be an explosive testimony that shook up all their theories about the case, it opened up a new can of worms.

CHAPTER 36

Davey's Letter

Jerry slept soundly later that night for Deirdre's wound her arms around him and soothed him like his surrogate mother used to lull him to sleep in moonlit nights when his dreams were worst. In Crossmagnier, when as a boy he would sob his heart out after the death of his mother and his separation from his father. He needed that succoring now also in this new crisis time in his life. He had always felt the pain of others as if it were his own pain, especially the pain of friends and relatives; for pain was a mystery that affected everyone that one came into contact with it, it was part of the human condition.

In the morning Jerry composed a little homily on the problem of suffering, as a man of the clothe he felt compelled to help people deal with the reality of suffering. He wrote that suffering in the world is something we were inclined to blame God for; but pain and suffering remained a mystery, though they are partly explained by the Fall narrative in Genesis; pain and suffering in the world and the related depredations of nature, storms, volcanoes etc came with the original sin and its destruction of the perfect paradise of the original Eden world and man. It was also explained by the resultant freedom given to man to do good and evil; and much suffering comes from man's inhumanity to man and his abuse of nature. Finally man's freedom presupposes that God cannot interfere to solve these sufferings for they have come from man's choice to be free; if God solved all our problems we'd be robots of a controlling God; so he cannot interfere with the ordinary functioning of nature, disease, death etc. So it follows that we cannot blame him for these or see them as Him punishing us. An old poem Jerry had written about this mystery he included in the homily:

> Too late beneath a naked sky,
> You seek for comfort from on high,
> Nor find it,
> And walking in the aged rain,
> You build the mystery of pain
> Around it,.
> You build the mystery of pain
> Around it.

There was only one thing sure in the world, Jerry's homily for next Sunday went on, that we would die, and that all of us would experience pain, suffering and trouble of every kind at various stages of our life. It was part of the free fallen condition of man as his own free choice. Where did prayer and asking for God's help come in? Well by asking we leave our freedom aside and show our dependence on him; he can't help unless we ask. And when we ask he always helps; though not by working miracles all the time, that would interfere with the normal free functioning of the world, but by giving us the inner strength and grace to help heal ourselves and make us strong to overcome all evil and trial; that's why evolution favors those of faith and those in hospitals who have faith and pray are more likely to recover and studies show they have tended to recover more quickly; faith provides the inner light to guide us out of darkness, and the soul evolves through suffering so borne and overcome. This was the best Jerry could do in explaining the mystery of suffering though an element of mystery always remained; the mystery was of man not God but an imperfect human being in a beautiful but also imperfect world in many ways, imperfect in not being heaven, though Christ came to show us the way to a heaven on earth as well as hereafter, how to redeem our fallen suffering state, and destroy the reign of sin and evil in the world, one of the main sources of suffering on earth. After finishing this suddenly inspired homily, Jerry went back to bed.

They all slept late that morning, even Donie didn't rise at six as normal, it was nearer to nine when he joined Jerry on the wicker seats in the garden, with cups of steaming coffee and sweet sticky buns laid out on the wicker table with a big dish of scrambled eggs, and rashers he had prepared on the grill; Jerry had at least persuaded him to stay off the sausages and grill the bacon to get rid of the extra fat, though he had added some grilled liver to the menu. Unsurprisingly Jerry was ravenous, for with all the shemozzle the night before they had eaten very little, and their bodies by now was protesting. The old body got more demanding as one got older and the waistline began to expand; the belly is a great tyrant at that age. Jerry felt like Conan Maol MacMoirne of the Fianna, constantly filling an expanding belly and slowing down physically as a result.

They ate in quiet meditation on events and Nelly sat down with them, being served for a change, her ministry to the children not yet begun, though Jerry could hear a few stirrings and stifled voices from above and splashing of water from the bathroom that signaled their early ablutions, and protests about what they were to wear for the day..Mammy I don't want that old sweater, it makes me too hot..that top is too tight for me..I don't like that old brown dress... One had to be a mentor of fashion as well as everything else as a parent, for children above all knew what was right for their age group, and what would make them look silly before their fellows.

Secret structures again, Jerry thought, we can't escape them, we can't escape the slaveries of our ideological conditioning, the more so today when we are bombarded by such conditioning through the media.

The children came piling down the stairs, in a whirl of youthful energy they needed to release, and another round of cooking began, with all pitching in. So that it was quite late when they got around to visiting Jim in his house in the village, to inquire about the letter; happily Nelly was taking the children to the zoo in Westport, and they were agog with excitement; she would spoil them rotten again there and more luck to them, it was their holiday time after all.

But before they could visit Jim they had to go to Westport to see how Davey was progressing and to call in to Dinnity at the barracks to see how their prisoner of the night before had fared and whether or not he had spilled the beans on Miley. When they arrived Dinnity came out to meet them a large smile on his face:

"Well done boys", he said, "we have been trying to get a foothold against the drug dealers in Mayo for ages and you have given us a partial foothold with this arrest, though he is very much small fry, a little university student making a few bob for his year's expenses, fees are up with all the cutbacks. I interrogated him this morning and I tell you this is confidence, he knew nothing about the big guys in the trade but he did finger one we never suspected, Billy Fleming of the pub the Hillside Rest. Again I think Billy is just small fry, just a middle-man, for the small trade in Maheragh, a handy distribution point, the pub, he seems to have no idea who supplied Fleming and I am inclined to believe him; that's how they work, keep the chain small, then if someone croaks they implicate as few as possible".

"Well, Jerry said, "I can't believe it, the blue-eyed boy, the one we all thought was whiter than white, who turned out to be the dirtiest of the lot, not only a druggie but a distributor as well, who would think it, is anything sacred any more". One never knows about people and first impressions can be very wrong.

Again Donie was a bit shook up. And Jerry too thought of Molly, and how she would take it, the publicity and the disgrace when Billy was arrested. Of the two girls in some way she felt things most. She was more extrovert and bubblier than Sally but she would still feel it deeply, though it would not be a major blow, he'd probably get off lightly, just small fry, and maybe it was just what he needed to straighten him out before he got in deeper. Jerry tried to console Donie with this, but he just shook his head, as if to say what is the world coming to, who can one trust today?

Both of us went on to the hospital to see Davey, in a very somber mood indeed, they'd have to tell Nelly and Molly, and they didn't relish that. When they went into Davey's room the little fair-haired nurse was there again fussing around him. She introduced herself as Maire Casey from Croagh, and apparently she had known Davey for a long time, they went to primary and secondary school together and she evidently had a deep crush on him then and still had, Jerry thought, some feelings never change. She, he thought, would do him more good than anyone else. As he later explained, he had never been comfortable with women, they had intimidated him somehow and that's when he leaned towards younger girls, they did not intimidate him, he was the master. Now it was different, Maire was the first girl whom he felt totally comfortable with, whom he wanted to be around, who loved him for himself and took no notice of the rumors or innuendos that haunted him. Before, Jerry thought, he just hadn't met the right woman, found the right person for him and now he had. She had been there all the time but now he was seeing her for the first time, appreciating her for the first time. For in a way the drug overdose had cleared up his thinking; and he realized the fact that he hadn't taken enough to kill himself meant he wanted to live, it was a cry for help, the help he was now finding in Maire. Davey was in deep, and he was a weak man, but she would be strong for both of them; here, Jerry had the feeling that there could be a happy ending in store, a light at the end of the tunnel.

Their next port of call, however, made them rethink that whole premise. They had gone on to Maheragh with plenty to think about. But first they decided to call to Jim about the letter, something private perhaps, they thought, maybe a will leaving his few possessions to Jim. They were little prepared for what emerged.

Jim's flat was at the end of the village in a little cul-de-sac. It was part of a modern set of apartments, plenty big enough for his needs and nothing showy about it. And the area in front was well kept and with a fine garden of flowers and shrubs and large potted plants, a garden that Jerry envied. Bridie came out to greet them accompanied by her son, Paul, a pudgy boy like his father.

"Welcome", she said, " Jim isn't in a good mood today, but I know he'd be lost without you. I'm not sure he'll like to see you now though", she said with a slightly formal and embarrassed manner. "I think maybe he'd like to be left alone at the present, he has received quite a shock. Not just about Davey but also a further shock today. But he'll tell you himself when he's ready, now is maybe too soon, I'm sorry not to be more welcoming. I know you have been very helpful to him and he's mad about you..".

At this Jim appeared behind her, looking haggard and drawn and pale, as if he had had a bad night, worse than they had.

"It's all right, Bridie", he said, "tell them to come in. I'll be with them in a minute", he disappeared into the house and she showed them into a simple little parlor with bright lace curtains and simple but quality oak furniture.

She brought in some cold beer which they said they would like, the day was hot, and they waited and waited, thinking what was going on, where was Jim?

At length he appeared a letter in his hand,

"Excuse me for keeping you, but I was not sure whether I should show you this or not, for it looks bad for Davey. Will you promise me that it won't go beyond this house, I know that's a lot to ask but I ask it of you as friends and this is a very private letter, and I don't want to bear the burden of its contents alone".

"You know us", Donie said, "we are not police, anything you want to keep private and confidential we will respect".

"Well in that case maybe you should read this", he said proffering the letter, "but in the name of heaven don't let its contents go outside this room..with the new developments it's not as damning as it seems". I leaned over Donie's shoulder to read it, and was shocked by its stark opening lines:

"Jim, I can't go on, forgive me, I was the one who killed Dad".

CHAPTER 37

The Confession of Davey

Obviously Davey had written the letter before the Inquest details had reached him, which in fact exonerated him from the actual murder. He thought the fall had killed Danny Pat, and he had been responsible for the fall.

Despite its stark opening lines the letter was quite a long one, a baring of his soul as it were as he felt he was about to die. It was the confession of a quite tormented soul and they felt a little uncomfortable reading it, as if they were privy to something that was so private it should be for certain eyes only, notably family members. Davey went on.

I didn't mean to kill him, I just went up the mountain to try and persuade him to sell the mountain to the mining company. Miley Ramsbottom leaned on me to do so. I had been taking drugs, and he threatened to withdraw my supply if I didn't do what he told me; I had got to the point where I needed them badly, my whole body was shaking and I was getting cramps; I realized I was becoming a hopeless addict but there was nothing I could do about it.

I had got them from Billy Fleming in the pub as a lark at first, also I suppose to ease my pain over my failure as a teacher, and all the gossip and innuendo that was going around about me; it was sick but there was nothing I could do about that either. I have never been comfortable with women, that's why I never married, and I suppose that's why I turned to younger girls, but I never touched them or abused them, that was a lie; I had pets I suppose in the school, and that's a teacher's worst fault, we should treat all the children equally, and so the other children started to despise me; I dealt with them severely but that only made matters worse, several parents came and confronted me and even threatened me with violence and to withdraw their children from the school.

It was an impossible situation, I dreaded going to school, I suppose it was never my calling anyway and I took more drugs to ease my pain, and that led to more sloppy teaching and missing classes, it was in a terrible spiral of self-destruction but I dared not tell anyone. And because of the drugs I began to disintegrate in every way, not eating and taking more and more drugs, I was like a zombie.

I knew my father would be on the mountain on that fatal day, at the north cliff. I had to go on the mountain and face him about my wish to sell my part of the mountain, my inheritance, though I dreaded it, I have never been very good at confrontation, always tried to take the easy way out, but Miley had me trapped, I was in a bad state, I needed those drugs and that's all I could think of, and I needed the money that would come from the sale of the mountain land. Then I could resign from the school and do what I liked, not dragging myself out of bed in the morning and into a classroom I hated, children looking at me and playing on me, I couldn't take it any longer.

Danny, dad, was there with his binoculars, looking at his sheep all around, they were like his babies, I often thought he cared for them more than his children, more than me. Certainly he never really cared for me and that hurt, they said I was a bastard, I never believed it but it also hung over me and ate me away inside, I never had any self-confidence, I always felt not wanted, especially after mother died, I had no one to turn to. Even you Jim, I felt had turned your back on me, never fully accepting me. Everything was piling up on top of my head and that day it all burst out in a flood.

I said, "dad you must also sell your mountain area to the mine, the area you have reserved for me, and give me the money, I need some money, I have to get away, sell the rocky land, useless anyway, and give me the money and I won't bother you anymore. What's this stupid mountain anyway, just a few rocks and we're more important than those stupid sheep of yours".

He looked at me for a long time, he knew what a bad state I was in, I was shaking like a leaf. "What's the matter DV, he said, that was his nickname for me, what have you been doing, abusing the girls in school, drinking, drugs, what is it?"

Then he started to get really angry: "sell the mountain, sell the life from under my feet, all I worked for all my life, would you have me sell my soul. I suppose you can't wait until I'm in the grave, to get yer hands on this mountain, on whatever few bob I have in the bank. Why can't you wait, I won't last long anyway. No! You'd like to see me with nothing, a traitor to my noble mountain ancestors, you can't wait to see me in the grave..you useless slob..You're no son of mine, just a bastard and a weakling and pervert, letting the family down and blackening our name in the village, where we Sugrues always held our heads up high". He paused and wiped his brow for he was sweating with the effort of his anger, red in the face: calming down a little he said:

"I won't sell, I tell you, this mountain we stand on is my life, I won't give you the satisfaction, I won't sell I tell you no matter what the mine crew do, I won't let them in to blacken and destroy what has been the joy of our family. You don't understand anything. When my father was dying he said to me, look after the mountain, Danny, don't let anyone take it from you, look after it and it will look after you. And now you want me to go back on my oath to my father, to sell out on my birthright. Get away from me you weakling, get away from me before I use this stick on you, I'm still a match for you despite my years".

I suppose I saw red then. All my pent up frustrations just boiled over.

"Don't call me those names, you've no right to call me those names, I loved you always as my own father, I never touched that girl, maybe I'm not as weak as you think".

God help me, all my frustrations boiled over and I aimed a blow at him and we struggled. Then suddenly, he slipped on the loose gravel and went over the side; I tried to hold on to his old tattered coat but it gave way in my hands and he went over, and hit his head on the rocks below.

I suddenly became cold sober, realizing what I had done. I went down and tried to help him, there was blood everywhere and he was unconscious but alive. I tried to help, I shouted out for help, I kept saying, I remember,

"I'm sorry, Dad, I'm so sorry..I didn't mean to do it, please say you'll be all right, please, please forgive me.."

Then he opened his eyes and said in a weak voice, "it's all right DV, I'll be all right, its just a blow in the head...go and get the doctor as quick as you can."

He lapsed back into unconsciousness, I took a hankerchief out of my pocket and wiped away the blood and wrapped it around the wound, then I took out my mobile phone and rang for the ambulance but there was no reception for that. Maybe I was too frantic to press the buttons right, my hands were shaking, my whole body was shaking.

Then Terry Ramsbottom and Jasper O'Leary came up, I don't know what they were doing on the mountain, maybe on the same errand as me. I said that it was an accident, I didn't mean to push him over. Terry was great, he tried his mobile phone to get through to the ambulance but failed. Then he said he'd run down to the pub and get through from there and also ring the local doctor.

I was left alone with Jasper. He said that I was in bad position, he had somehow got through to Miley after going to the other side of the mountain. Miley had special communication helps for his business, and that they would offer me a deal, they would conceal my part in the fall, if I agreed to sell my part of the mountain after Danny's demise, for there was no way a man so old could survive this fall, if he did survive he's probably just be a vegetable. They had another hold on me now and I had no choice so I agreed, I knew if this deed of mine got out it would finish me once and for all.

Then I told Jasper to stay with Danny and I went over to the other side of the mountain, where reception was better, for local calls anyway, and rang Bridie and Jim to say Danny had had an accident and they should come up, he might not last long. When I came back, Danny looked no worse, no better. I said I'd go down home, I didn't want to face Bridie and Jim, I was in no state, and they might suspect. I went down and Jasper left to ring Miley. On the way down I saw Billy Fleming coming up with a first-aid box in his hand and I was glad, he'd help Dad.

But I couldn't live with what I done, or Miley's forcing of me to cover it up. I couldn't go to school, or eat or do anything. I was living in a living hell, you saw that maybe when you came to visit me. I was glad when the summer holidays came; I knew I could never go back to the school or ever kick this drug thing; I had no one to turn to I was all alone; only a black void yawning at my feet. it was then I decided there was nothing to live for any longer, I was no good to myself or anyone, I'd be much better off dead, an overdose and die quietly and happily without any pain. It seemed the perfect way out of all my troubles and the deep guilt I felt at what I'd done; I couldn't look at myself in the mirror. Everything in my life had been a failure, it was better to finish it altogether. I leave this letter for you Jim, for you were the only one that even partially understood me, and to a lesser extent Bridie. I beg your forgiveness and God's forgiveness for what I did and for now taking my life. I know we were told in the old catechism that suicide was a mortal sin, like murder, only of self, but I felt there was no alternative though it might cause pain to all around me for a long time; again I throw myself on God's mercy and ask your and Bridie's forgiveness for any pain I caused you. Pray for my soul, have masses said, lest this act plunge me in darkness forever. When you find this letter I'll be dead and I hope at peace at last, though I doubt it; down there is the blackness of hell too from which one can never escape...

CHAPTER 38

Light at the End
of the Tunnel

AFTER READING THE LETTER THEY ALL SAT FOR A LONG TIME IN shocked disbelief, without speaking. At last Donie spoke,

"I'm sorry Jim, the one good thing that has come out of this is that his effort to die did not succeed, I have a feeling he has been given a second chance, his way wouldn't have solved anything, but at least it has cleared up one thing, how Danny Pat came to fall from that cliff; Davey is not really culpable in any serious way though; it's not murder, we now know that; the most he can be charged with is grievous bodily harm, maybe, and covering up the committing of a felony.

But the great thing about this is that he can now get help for his various problems, psychiatric help and counseling and he has found some hope to cling to in that nurse in the hospital who loves him, I feel she can give him a reason to live again. He should leave the school of course, there's no future for him there. As regards our investigation we are still faced with finding the person who administered the final fatal blows.

But out suspicions of Miley's involvement in all this are confirmed, and his key role in the drug trade has been confirmed, the one negative is that Billy Fleming's intermediate involvement, and possible arrest will affect Molly. Though I think her romantic entanglement there isn't as serious as Sally's with Terry, just a passing crush, I'd say, that she'll get over quickly, at least that's what I hope.

Billy, when arrested, may get off lightly if he spills the beans on Miley and the other fat cats of the drug trade around here; although his knowledge is probably limited, they know how to cover their tracks. No need to bring in the letter there, if you don't want to, we already have the testimony of our man behind bars in Westport. This could work against the mining company also, once people become aware of its main front, Miley, as a drug dealer and criminal, the whole thing should collapse. In a curious way, in all this Danny Pat has won".

"Yes, Jerry said, "but I think he would still demand justice for that final cowardly blow that laid him low. We must bend all our efforts towards solving that problem, we know the time it happened but not the murderer."

They left Jim in peace, to deal with all these shocks and called in to Fleming's pub for a drink and a spot of lunch. Amazingly Kate was behind the bar, she had been released, luckily her attacker had just left her with a bad concussion. She had made a remarkable recovery and was even back behind the bar; the only sign of the injury was a bandage on the side of her head where she had received 20 stitches; though she did look a bit pale, the aftermath of the concussion, and looked a bit groggy on her feet.

The secret that they didn't want her to divulge, she told us, was basically the same as that contained in Davey's letter; that Davey had pushed his father over the cliff; after her original divulging to us, she had heard the deeper revelation from Billy, who had heard it from Terry Ramsbottom; secrets are curious things; where human intercourse is involved they have a way of emerging; people very seldom know how to keep their mouths shut.

Apparently Terry and Billy had been drinking and snorting some weed, and Terry blurted out what really happened on that day in a drug daze; Kate had been in the adjoining room and had heard them discussing it; it preyed on her conscience until she could divulge it to someone, and Jerry had been chosen as the father confessor. But somehow Billy came to know that she knew and when he contacted Miley, they decided to silence her. Luckily the plastic night cap she was wearing deflected the blow but already then they had aggravated assault against the Miley outfit, that and the drug dealing would be enough to put them out of business for some time, but the issue of the murder was still unresolved.

There was no sign of Billy, so that's why Kate had to come out to tend to the bar, there were only a few there, though by right she should be resting even from such light work.

Jerry went up the counter to order, and spoke to Kate:

"Kate, it's great to see you back on your feet, you were brave to do what you did, we were worried about you", he said, detecting a kind of sadness in her eye, and wishing to cheer her up after her trauma.

"I met you boyfriend Matt yesterday", he went on, to give her a further fillip, "quite a reception I got from him, you've a real fiery young man there".

"He's a dote, all right", she said, cheering up, "we're to be married next year, the date has been set, sorry to let you down, I should have told you", even a faint smile lit up her pretty face in spite of her recent trauma, she was a strong girl. Jerry had the feeling again, and the smile seemed to confirm it, that she had used him very cleverly. But her satisfied smile quickly turned to a frown when Jerry said,

"Is Billy not here, anything the matter with him?".

"As if you didn't know, you old hypocrite", she said bitterly, "He's about to be arrested they say over a rumor that he traded drugs here", she said, "I had my suspicions of that but I'll stand by him, I'll say it's all nonsense of course. No truth at all in it, gossip mongers, with a good lawyer Billy will sort all that out. My one fear is that these false accusations may affect our trade, with the locals anyway, they may migrate to Tim Corney's a few miles down the road, but we're nearer the mountain and should keep the tourist trade. How are you yourself, Jerry, and the wife and the kids, I've missed your face here the last few nights, and the bould Donie, what would you like to eat or drink now, it's on the house today; I suppose I owe my life to you"

"One other important thing", Jerry said, "did you see the person who struck you?"

"No, she said, "I was sitting at the desk with my back to the door, he came in every quietly and struck me from behind and I knew no more until I woke up in the hospital".

"We'll have the best steak you have so to celebrate your recovery and engagement", Jerry said with a smile, she had retained the cook, "with all the trimmings and 2 pints of the black stuff".

"All that entanglement with Kate cleared up then is it", Donie said as we tucked into a fine meal.

"Yes, Jerry said, "just female cunning, though it nearly caught me on the hop, brought her man to the altar as a result, and more luck to her, she's no longer in the flower of her youth, but all the same I think Matt is getting a fine deal there, a fine mature woman who knows on which side her bread is buttered; honest as the day is long and as straight as a whistle; not so bad between the sheets either I'd say, that fine buxom barmaid of ours".

Donie looked a bit shocked so Jerry hastened to change the subject, "and she'll be a good catch financially for any man also. She'll have this place to herself once Billy is out of the way. Maybe I should ditch Deirdre and shack up with her", Jerry said in jest to further aggravate Donie; then he laughed and Donie got the joke.

They were tucking in to a fine dessert when two plain clothes detectives, you could tell their calling anywhere, came into the bar. There was stir among the locals who had come here for lunch,

"Is Billy here?", they said, "We want a word with him".

"No, he left this morning early and I don't know where he went, I hope he's OK and you don't want him for anything serious", Kate said, her face turning even paler, she looked really worried for the first time.

"Miley will probably be next to be arrested", Donie said, "I can't imagine the bould Billy not spilling the beans. He's the sort who crumble easily under questioning, the do gooder found out, no spine no backbone. Our mountain cause is looking more rosy every minute. The local People won't be impressed when all this comes out, a slur on the area's good name, and Miley behind it; the veneer of the benign business man will have dropped and for the first time they'll see him for what he is, just another bent developer and small time crook"

When they got back to the house Nelly and Deirdre were in the kitchen.

"Well babies", Jerry said, kissing them in turn, "how was the zoo?", "See anyone there like yourselves", Jerry said to the children and laughed.

"The monkeys were there", Mairead said, "they were funny, one of them grabbed a banana out of Brendan's hand".

"You are like a monkey yourself", Brendan said, and she grabbed the hurley stick to clobber him, dad had to come between them and make the peace,

"I liked the giraffes best", Conor said. Just then there was the sound of loud sobbing upstairs, Molly had heard the bad news, a text from her boyfriend. Jerry explained to Nelly and she hurried upstairs to console her.

"It will pass", I said to Donie, "at her age there are many more fish in the sea, people very seldom settle for their first crush. As we mature so does our love discernment".

"Children", Jerry said, eager to get away from things again, it was his way of coping, "How would you like a trip to Achill Island, to the golden strand there?

We'll go tomorrow, there's real gold sand there and silver seas more than any wealth we can win by work. But for today let's head for Knock, the other great pilgrim site in the West. It's only a short drive and we can say our prayers there, and then strike for a film in Castlebar".

The film tempted them, but they were more dubious about the trip to Knock, but when they got there they were enchanted, they prayed for everyone, circling anti-clockwise in the old Celtic manner as they intoned the prayers.

"Especially lets pray for Davey who is sick", Jerry said, "and Danny Pat and Molly who has had a disappointment".

He told them that in some mysterious way, prayer heals the world.

"Like the monks in the rock in the middle of the sea you told us about", Mairead said.

"Yes", Jerry said, "and here too is an island of peace, away from the violence and terror of the world. And there is real gold here".

"What gold is that", they said, "show us!"

Deirdre showed them the golden rose presented to the Shrine by the great John Paul 11, when he came to Ireland.

Afterwards, they went to the film and stayed in a Castlebar hotel, after the dreary tale of Davey and the intrigues of Miley and the mine company, it was escape into a more tranquil past of our Island's spiritual depths of peace.

CHAPTER 39

Achill's Golden Strand

Staying in the hotel and swimming in its swimming pool was a great treat for them all, cleansing their minds of the world of greed and intrigue they had left behind.

"Wait", Jerry said, "I have more magic in store for you, on the island, do you know that that the old Irish seers talked of Hy Brassil, an island out at sea that was the land of the blessed.

Like mountains he explained to the children that he always associated islands with peace and escape.

Deirdre had her island of philosophy and Jerry had his islands of poetic flight and the mystic Ireland of his heart's delight, which was still there if one just searched for it, in places where the hard world hadn't crept in and destroyed everything. For some reason people seem to hate to see people happy and happy just to be, they have to impose some hard ideology that weighs on the soul like lead. Immediately, Jerry wrote about this, surrounded by the innocent children in a happy place, inspired and filled with grace after their visit to Knock: "We are all grand designs of God, with a glory within more than anyone have understood".

"Achill", he said, "children that's our new destination, after we've climbed the Reek and prayed in Knock; they clustered around with kisses and hugs, in their frilly dresses and t-shirts smelling of the youth and freshness of the untainted world of the original paradise we can each recreate again, at least occasionally in far holy places, or in the imagination of the poet and artist; there the worlds available are unending and there are no rules really, as in the world, to tie us down. Like the free minds of children all was a sea of play and tranquility.

As they travelled towards the furthest point of the world, of Europe and of inner space, Jerry held Deirdre close and they felt like a king and a queen of the west like Grace O'Malley of old, the pirate queen of the western isles in ancient lore, who defied the foreign tyranny and sailed in and out of these bays with gay abandon in rich clothes given to her by raiders of sunny Spain.

The drive to Achill was trying enough, however, with the children fractious, fighting in the back seats and complaining about each other - Daddy, Brian is poking me with his hurley stick..Conor has put a sticky sweet down my neck..I want to stop to pee.. and such like etc

When they drove across the bridge however and on to the golden strand in Achill, it was a different matter; they poured out of the car like golden sand pouring out of the hand, to frolic among the waves and torture crabs, and build sand castles, and generally just play without inhibition. This strand is another aspect of the real gold of our great land, Jerry thought, all that cannot be bought or sold, or dismissed by ideology or hype, all that was the enduring gold of our immortal shores that will be there when all our vain pride is no more.

After lunch, a packed lunch, they went up onto the higher rocky part of the island. Where the children had great sport watching an eagle among the rocks, a strange thing to see at the seaside, but maybe that's how he lived, among the nests of the seagulls and their frail young, eating them, or taking them up high as easy food for his own brood.

"Anything is possible when you're living with Lofty", Jerry said, to them, when they wondered where the bird came from or why he strutted his stuff for them.

That night in the hotel they had an evening meal and up to their rooms where as usual the children screamed for kisses and a story. He told them the story he had made up of the original eagle in God's creation and how he was punished for his pride and vanity as against the small wren who was rewarded; it was in the form of a poem but they didn't seem to mind that, there was a story in it and that's all that mattered, stories to them were like sweets or sugary drinks for the soul: "The wren, hearing of the exploits of the eagle and his boasting, thought it extremely arrogant of him, and so he stayed small, in bush and furze, God blessed him for his humility, and proclaimed him the king of the birds".

They asked Dad if I had any other stories about birds and he told them about the robin and why he had a red breast. He pulled out the thorns from Christ's head to ease his pain, but in doing so stained his own breast red; so ever since the robin has had a red breast and is the happiest of birds, put on Christmas cards, and on holly, and on our Christmas trees, as the sign of being jolly and happy.

After this, since he had run out of bird stories, they snuggled up to Jerry and Dee to receive goodnight kisses. And Dee and Jerry retired to their own beds, which was nearby to keep an eye on them, and make them feel safe in a strange place. They all slept well that night, for their day had been long and arduous, but again Jerry dreamed a strange dream.

He thought he saw Deverly sitting in the dock as a judge, with the face of a fierce eagle, and Davey, Miley, Jasper O'Leary and Billy Fleming standing before him for sentence. Danny Pat with Jim and Deverly alongside him, stood smiling broadly at their conviction, and Terry was writing was down the sentence. Donie donned a black cap and said, "My sentence is that you will be hanged by the neck until you are dead, and may God have mercy on your souls". There was a huge clap from the audience and they shouted, "Hang them high", and a man brought a noose to hang them but instead of putting it around their necks he put it around Jerry's neck. He realized then that in judging them harshly he was judging himself. The unconscious tells us truth in dreams we won't face in our waking hours.

Jerry woke with a scream and Deirdre got worried and said, "What's the matter, dear, bad dream?" He told her and she said "you must stop all this gadding around solving crimes, it's not good for your mental health, if you keep this up you may end up a raving lunatic, and the children fatherless as result", not a very comforting thought.

The dream however had a strange prophetic quality, the Lofties were noted for their second sight, and being able to see the future in their dreams, it was some strange power built into their genes.

Jerry managed to get off to sleep again, but suddenly he woke up again in the early morning, his mobile phone ringing, no rest even in paradise he thought. It was Donie, "Come home he said, I think we've got our man". He would say no more until Jerry got back to the mountain and consulted with him. They were coming down anyway today Jerry said, as soon as they could get themselves organized, which was again a chaotic affair but at last they were on their way.

Jerry was agog with excitement all the way home. What new plan had Deverly concocted now to trap the vicious murderer of Danny Pat, maybe his dream was right, whoever he was deserved to be hanged for bashing in the skull of a poor injured man, a man who had harmed no one, and was respected and loved by all. In this Donie was an avenging angel, for he was a source of endless ingenuity when it came to catching criminals who were a menace to society. When they seemed most at ease and sure of themselves, he pounced. Jerry wondered what rat trap he had invented now to catch his most recent slimy prey.

CHAPTER 40

Donie Gets His Man

When they arrived back home to Jim's cottage the village was buzzing with the amazing news. Billy Fleming had been arrested for the murder of Danny Pat, and Miley had been arrested as an accomplice before the event. Apparently with Dinnity's help Donie had got hold of the phone record for the calls on the mountain that day. One of those calls was one from Billy to Miley, stating that he had found Davey with the body, but Danny Pat was still alive. The record had Miley advising him to finish off the old man, he would probably die anyway. If he recovered they were back where they started but if he died, then Davey would be held for his murder, and they would kill two birds with one stone. Jim would be forced to sell, he would hardly let Bridie go bankrupt and lose all she and Bill had worked for. So Billy went up the mountain under the pretence of first aid before the others arrived he struck the old man with a rock and when Jim and Bridie came he said that Danny Pat had passed away due to severe injuries from the fall. Donie also alerted the guards to the timetable of events and Billy was the only one present between 2.30 and 3.15, the period when the murder was committed. Also Kate testified that she saw Billy going up at that time and coming down afterwards with blood on his hands and clothes, she had not told of this evidence before now because she thought the blood on him was due to his first-aid work with Danny Pat.

When Billy was confronted with the evidence he confessed and implicated Miley even more by saying that the latter had forced him into the crime, he had threatened to withdraw Billy's supply of drugs unless he did the deed. Jim was delighted for now the company's campaign was in tatters; with their main man implicated in a murder, and inferences that it was pressure from the company that made Billy act as he did, their whole chance of getting the people behind the mine was gone; the crime caused outrage. There were also investigations into the TV program and Christie's motives in pushing through the initial planning; he resigned his party whip until the whole thing was cleared up.

When Jerry met Donie a large smile was on his face. He was perched on his familiar wicker chair in the garden scoffing beer and a barbeque smoking in the background loaded down with burgers, sausages, streaks and other good things; beer and soft drinks were lodged in a large box nearby, loaded with ice from the fridge; for the weather had turned into an unusually hot spell, Ireland was sweltering in Mediterranean temperatures. It reminded Jerry of the summers that he had often enjoyed when he was young, things were getting back to normal Irish summers a famous predictor in Australia had said, one cycle of bad weather had ended and we were entering a new one of warm summers again, also the global warming was ensuring that Ireland would have warmer dryer summers.

They had all decided to celebrate in with the barbeque to thank all those who had helped in the Save the Mountain campaign.

Fr Manus was there, Pat Delaney, and Tim Thornton, talking vehemently about the new campaign in Sligo against the fracking process there; his face aglow with the new challenge he subjected them to a long lecture on the dangers of that mining technique, mining for gas and oil trapped in shale underground, hinting that it might even cause earthquakes in the long run by disturbing the underlying layers of the earth core. He had been cleared of any involvement in the leaks of information to Miley. Apparently Billy Fleming had been the culprit, he had heard it from Molly who had divulged the information in all innocence having heard us discussing it around the table in the farmhouse. Billy had passed it on to Miley in return for fresh supplies of free drugs for the bar.

Sally and Terry were also there, he had left his father and moved into a little flat in the village; he had been cleared of all involvement in the crimes of his father, indeed his actions on the mountain had been commended. His involvement in the company's campaign still rankled with some. But inviting him, they thought, would be a good way of burying the hatchet in the whole acrimonious affair; some of the village development committee were also present and Kate Fleming with Matt Moriarty, she showing off a large diamond ring and purring like a cat.

Davey was also present, in a wheelchair, being wheeled around by his "minder", the lovely Maire, Jerry saw a bright future also there, maybe the end of Davey's long purgatory in life, his acceptance back into the Surgue family and back into the community. He would resign his teaching post of course, but Maire hoped to get him a job as a porter in the hospital; that's just what he wanted, Jerry thought, a non stressful job, away from children and near to the adoring Maire who would supervise his recuperation. He would not be arrested until he got better, and the charges would probably not lead to a long imprisonment, if any; after all he had not intended the accident that occurred.

Bill and Bridie were there also. She was looking brighter for a lot of the burden of their situation was lifted off her shoulders, a new community development committee had promised her compensation for any encroachment onto the land, once they had been able to raise the money from various fund-raising activities; it would keep the wolf from the door for the time being at least. And the committee had begun a campaign to raise money to send Bill for special treatment abroad.

As we ate and enjoyed the glorious day in the bright flower garden, they gathered round Donie to hear his final summary of the case.

CHAPTER 41

Donie explains it all

"CHILDREN", HE SAID, "LADIES AND GENTLEMEN, I CAN REST NOW AND outline the main aspects of the case. I suspected Billy from the beginning, because of all the people involved in the case he was the only one capable of bashing in the head of a helpless old man, excuse the crude terms I use. His amoral philosophy from Nietzsche and others had made him think that all things were allowed. I have had a lot of experience discerning criminals and under his innocent veneer I discerned a secret psychopath. But I also knew that he could not have done it off his own bat, he was essentially an instrument not an initiator. Miley on the other hand fitted the psychological profile perfectly, and I have learned from experience the key to solving a crime is knowing the psychology of the suspect. Miley was not by nature a killer but he was a driven man. We knew from researching his affairs that he was on the verge of bankruptcy, and could lose even his house and whatever land went with it, and there was his worry about his wife and her psychological state, he wanted money to send her abroad for treatment; but if the mine fell through he could lose everything. And for a man who had prided himself in rising above all who had once looked down on him that was a no go. The son of a laborer, picked on in primary school, despised in secondary school as a wimp, he was determined to get his revenge on society by beating it at what it loved most, wealth as power. He reveled in seeing those who had despised him now working for him, jumping at his every command. It was inconceivable that he should go back among the pack, reviled and scorned again. He was a driven man and that drive, on the verge of ruin, led him to baulk at nothing, not even murder to maintain his wealth, power and status. They say that victims can never see themselves as oppressors, even when they are so, for they see their oppressing as just part of the liberation from victimhood".

"Yes", Jerry added in the spirit of a man of the cloth, "He was part of a vast structure of sin as it were, that is the real evil in society. In that sense I pity him, he is a victim as much as a perpetrator of evil, a failing modern western capitalist and amoral society made him what he is. I recall the Jesuit concepts my father had instilled in me; he was a product of their exclusive schools for the intelligentsia. I was proud that my father was one of these. He told me that the moral problem always was not individual sins, but the structures of sin that society erect, in this case the worship of self-centered pride, desire, money and power as gods everything else must be sacrificed to, even one's soul. Even the discourses of radical individualism and human rights, always my rights, no mention of the necessary sacrificing of some of these for the common good, finding a balance there. As Marx said the modern western discourse of human rights is, without a self-giving social vision, no more than another narcissistic outcome of capitalist self-centeredness and selfish individualism; it was all "my" rights and "my" freedom, often without regard to the common good or any higher sense of social responsibility. But then again communist Marxism sought to destroy all individualism, the other extreme, to make people complete pawns of the party.

I know the younger generation such as Terry were not so driven, because they grew up with everything and had no need to be so driven. But with the recession and the failure of our leaders to take radical measures to stem it, such as default, get rid of this mountain of debt and start again, they are starting to become driven too now, doomed to endless unemployment, emigration and menial low paid jobs for that's all they can get here, and abroad most must start at the bottom of the ladder. And they are becoming more and more acculturated into the structures of sin that western society in the pursuit of self-centered power and wealth and uninhibited personal desire, regardless of the common good. For structures perpetuate themselves and form a vicious circle or spiral; we create structures of sin, and people get caught up in them, such as the cult of abortion. And then we say we must create even more radical ones to accommodate that, we dump procreation altogether, so that we become a top-heavy society and the people of the slave nations we once dominated, and still try to dominate culturally, will one day take us over, are already taking us over for they are producing real wealth for the future, young people. But we are unable to see beyond the culture of death we have created; the ideology has become so proscriptive it can no longer offer or allow a critique of itself. The whole forms a structure of downward spiral that threatens more and more to plunge our societies into a moral and spiritual chaos beyond redemption. We push out the boat further and further from the shore of what made us great, the foundations of our culture until as Yeats put it "the falconer cannot hear the falconer", the centre crumbles, the best lack all conviction and the worst are full of passionate intensity, all falls apart in the long run, only man reduced to the level of the beast remains to reign over a world of chaos. That was the worst scenario, but the great thing about western culture was that it was constantly able to reinvent itself; its demise had been predicted before; it had come through two world wars and was still going strong, and the love of liberty at its heart was a timeless truth, that redeemed all its excesses again and again and made it so attractive to other cultures and migrants. For without liberty no one could pursue their goals towards a better way of life".

Such was how Jerry drew the larger implications of our little crisis in the west, using his skill as a lecturer and boring his listeners. But Donie went on with his more prosaic analysis of the dynamics of murder.

"I knew that Davey was not a murderer, more a victim also, a weak man who allowed himself to be swallowed up by his own lack of a sense of self-worth; the fact of the early death of love in the form of his mother, and the failure of a man who was not his real father to fill that gap. His lack of self-confidence spilled into his relations with women and in his performance in the classroom. He could only be the victim, never the master. That's why I was surprised when he confessed, it just didn't sound right and the inquest's finding bore me out, as I guessed it would, and that's why I sent you, Jerry, to observe it, I already had an inkling of what it would find out. Just as I knew Terry didn't fit the psychological profile of a murderer, despite the identification of his voice on the tape. My one worry when he ran off with Sally was that his impulsive nature would make him do something rash, against his own deeper nature, that is another profile not of murderers, more usually that of those who commit involuntary manslaughter.

So it all narrowed down to Billy and Miley. But it was one thing to know the murderers and another thing to have the proof to smoke them out into the open. I wasn't really able to get the transcripts of Billy's talks with Miley on phone on the day of the murder I just pretended we had these transcripts to smoke them out. Here we worked also on Jasper, he knew all and if he felt the game was up he would crumble and try to place all the blame on Miley to save his own skin, just as Billy implicated Miley in the drug ring to save his skin. Billy was initially not an arch criminal, more like a petty thief, dipping his hand in the till, a young seizer of his opportunity, so I hope and feel sure a long spell in prison will teach him a lesson and wean him away from a life of crime, which he could in the long run have been lured into even more deeply. And he was obviously the one who hit Kate over the head; he thought he was killing two birds with one stone, he would have sole control of the pub to pursue his drug trading without interference and he would stop her from divulging the information she had about the murder in which he was implicated".

At this Deverly sat back and devoted himself to the drink and grub with a satisfied sigh. There was a general clap for Donie's wonderful perspicacity as usual in solving the case at both levels. But he pushed some of the praise over on Jerry, which caused him much embarrassment.

"It's not all my doing", he said, "it's also the doing of Dr.Watson here, my intellectual and creative helper. He always, as a poet and prose writer has that extra imaginative spark that constantly inspires me. I'm just a run of the mill detective who had gained his experience at the coal face of crime. Jerry is a master of philosophy and deeper thinking that turns it all into gold, as indeed are all of you, the great people of our western wonderland".

He got another thunderous round of applause for this; people will always respond with love to genuine praise. Our barbeque celebrations gained apace after this and Maire surprised us all by producing a violin and playing many Irish trad dance tunes and slow airs. The whole quickly turned into a joyous Ceili, with feet battering the grass, and the voice of rich old Irish songs, those that endure because they are timeless, rang through the twilight air. Maire even sang a song she had composed herself, with Jim substituting on the banjo, it had been one of Danny Pat's passions and he had passed on the skill to Jim. Maire Sang the following which he later wrote down to the tune of "My Sweet Wildwood Flower". It has the usual plaintive folk love theme of death for love, like Romeo and Juliet, though whether anyone would ever really die for love was doubtful in his view:

> I promised to leave you,
> You promised to die.
> The world spins around us,
> Let everyone cry.
> I promised to leave you,
> You promised to die.

Other songs were sung and music played until the night faded into dawn everyone's head was drooping with sleep and heavy with drink.

CHAPTER 42

Interviewing the Culprits

THE ARREST OF MILEY AND BILLY ENDED THE CASE OF THE MOUNTAIN, but not the effects it had on its main protagonists. The two culprits were sentenced to life for premeditated murder, for they had planned the final attack on Danny Pat in a cold and calculating manner, as the judge at the trial pointed out; Jasper was sentenced to 10 years as an accessory for he had been with Billy when the deed was done, and his arson attack on Delaney's home was even more culpable. The Judge noted after they were found guilty by a jury of their peers, that this was a premeditated killing of a helpless innocent old man, and there were few mitigating circumstances, except that maybe Billy was the pawn of an older man, an easily manipulated cats paw.

Jerry went to the trial and as he watched Miley being taken away, his face lined and worn, all his swagger and illusions of grandeur gone, Jerry had a certain amount of sympathy for him. He had been a driven man, until his inner demon took over completely, rendering him incapable of seeing the moral implications of his action. Circumstances drove him to the wall where he struck out blindly at the forces that trapped him. Yet in other circumstances he might have been a great captain of industry and leader of his community in prosperity. Billy in other circumstances could also have been a light to his community.

That's why Jerry went to see both of them in prison as their pastor not their judge, Billy first. He had grown close to the boy during their philosophical debates, despite being the opposite of him and his beliefs. He was pale and haggard looking when Jerry entered his cell, yet also defiant in a curious way, a shelf in the cell loaded down with atheistic tomes, and he was reading Nietzsche's work Beyond Good and Evil . After the preliminary greetings they sat down and Jerry asked him the question that had been bugging him for months,

"Why did you do it Billy, attacking the old man and Kate, it made no sense?"

"Well you know from our discussions", he answered, "and don't be shocked when I say this, that I am not a moral man in the Christian mode. You see this Nietzschean book, I also believe that there are no absolute values, only what we make up ourselves, and we should follow our desires no matter where they lead us. The only crime was in being caught. We, Miley and I, thought there was no way we could be brought to book for the crime; Davey had pushed him and we were sure that would be put down as the cause of his death, the inquest finding scuppered us, but I feel no remorse for what I did, again as the philosopher said, remorse is for the weak. I'll get out of here in maybe 15 years, given good conduct and I intend to play the game. I'll sell my half of the pub and that money will be waiting for me when I get out. Here I'll have plenty of time to further my philosophical reading; I have much more to learn of the way of living beyond good and evil. I know that shocks you as a Christian believer but our modern world has more in common with my beliefs than yours".

"Billy", Jerry replied urgently, "I don't believe what you say. I say this to you as a friend from our philosophical debates, I beg you please repent and change your outlook. You are being influenced by the wrong people and the way of life you are pursuing is a dead end both for this life and the next. Do you realize what the world would be like if everyone followed your philosophy, evil without restraint and crime without remorse would make the world into a living hell. Is that what you really want? I can't believe that is so for it makes you an inhuman monster. I can't believe you are justifying the beating to death of a helpless old man, and the effort to kill your own half sister; she was lucky to get off so lightly but the blow could have killed her or left her a vegetable for life. Also my heartfelt advice to you is to lay off the drugs, that's another dead end and as a result you may never live to get out of here; drugs are endemic in our prisons. Would you like to confess to me and start to shape a new life for your future happiness, and dump all those books which have led you into an abyss of evil?"

When he answered no, Jerry added: "Please listen to me for I am concerned about you and your mental and spiritual health".

"No", Billy said defiantly, "I don't need your pity or your shitty advise, I'll go my own way without preachy people like you ruling my life. I feel no remorse, I will not repent, I will not confess, so there! Go back to your dead end job and leave me to live my own life, I don't need you, I don't need anyone, I am my own man".

Jerry shook his head, he couldn't believe what he was hearing from a youth everyone thought innocent and good it was all an illusion. Jerry shook hands with him for it was obvious their talk was over and he was set in his ways. But he said as he was leaving, "Remember Billy people love you and you are not alone".

He reflected as he left that people's philosophy of life was crucial, for out of their beliefs they act for good or ill. He realized also that their seeming irrelevant abstract philosophical debates with the four young people were not irrelevant to this book. The debates were really part of life, for people lived out of their deep ideology as was evident with Billy. Getting one's philosophy of life right was vital then and for Jerry that was the Christian way he had given his life to, for it had been proven as the best way to live by all the saints it had produced. Moreover many of these continued to inspire for all time because their theology was timeless and divine, notably Patrick, his heritage lives on here in the mountain and the peak of grace and perfection that Patrick embodied enabled untold numbers to live it for 1500 years. That is a philosophy and theology worth having more than any other set of beliefs, it might have saved Billy as it saved Terry, if only the former had opened his mind and heart and soul to it but other more transitory philosophies had closed his mind to that enduring beauty and truth towering above him in the form of the sacred mountain, so sad!

After leaving Billy, his heart heavy and discouraged, Jerry went on the visit Miley in his cell, He received him with his usual geniality but Jerry sensed behind this veneer that he was a broken man. But at least, unlike Billy, he now accepted that his punishment was just, and that his actions were beyond all civilized norms. For that reason Jerry felt he was capable of rehabilitation; he sensed he would be out also in about 15 years and he would be a changed individual, though by then he would be an old and harmless man. His wife had been left in the house without the debts, for they had been Miley's, not hers, and Miley had shrewdly put the house and some money in her name; whether this would stand up in court was another matter, but she did have a quite substantial amount of money of her own, enough to keep herself and Terry, and allow him to finish his schooling, and her to get the advanced psychiatric help she needed.

By contrast to Miley, Jerry had little sympathy for Jasper O'Leary, his next port of call. He would be out in about 10 years, for he was only an accessory to Miley's crimes. But Jerry felt no optimism for his future. He made a show of remorse but Jerry knew it was a facade. He was a psychopath thug through and through, and would be best kept away from civilized society for a substantial number of years, for he was incapable of any sort of moral behavior. Jerry had no doubt he would after release enter the employ of come other gangster like Miley.

CHAPTER 43

The Death of Donie

When we thought everything was hoky dory another totally unexpected tragedy descended on our little group of friends. Donie died suddenly from a heart attack. He had been celebrating the success of the western case, celebrating maybe too well, he was never one for moderation in food and drink. When he came home, just after coming in the door he suddenly grasped his chest and got blue in the face, then he fell heavily, doctors said he was dead shortly after he hit the floor, his heart splintered and it shattered our hearts too, especially Nelly's. We found her inconsolable, her face and eyes red and swelled from crying. The two girls were also there sitting like zombies in total shock. The house was like a grave. We got some warm sweet tea and some sandwitches and forced them to eat and drink as obviously they were incapable of providing for themselves; it was then ten o'clock and they hadn't eaten all day.

After putting Nelly and the girls to bed they went to the funeral home to view the body and say a few prayers to help Donie on his way to the shore of the blest, where we had no doubt he was bound.

The next day was the funeral and Jerry was asked to preside at the mass in his honor and to say the prayers at the graveside, all of which he considered a great honor for Donie had been like a brother to him, a friend of friends and a colleague in their crime solving collaboration. He could hardly believe it when he got the news of Donie's untimely death; it can't be true he said, only a few days ago he was detailing the solution of the Danny Pat case and seemed his usual more than alive self. As Jerry saw him resting in the coffin that had been opened specially for the southern visitors, he thought of the old policeman's great sense of vital presence, it was still there in death. He lay there in his best suit and collar and tie, a rosary draped around his fingers and candles burning around the coffin, and masses of flowers from all his colleagues and friends still benignly smiling at the world it seemed to Jerry still telling one of his jokes, this time about death. Guards from Dublin and all over formed a grand guard of honor as the coffin was taken to the church near his house in Dublin.

When he got back to the hotel where he and Dee were staying in Dublin, Jerry sat down to compose the homily for the following day's mass. It was a hard thing to do for he didn't know what he could say that would be adequate to his friend's life and great character. And the theme he struck on was common sense that as a wise man said is sadly not so common. He remembered Donie as a man with his feet on the ground, very much in the world but on another level not of the world, a man of constant good humor and yet one with a great analytic brain who as Kipling said could walk with kings and not lose the common touch, but part of this especially was his jokes and refusal to take life and himself too seriously. He could laugh at the world and yet baffle it with wisdom out of the blue. But his main aspect was his larger than life personality, he was a big man is so many ways. Jerry would say goodbye to him with a heavy heart not only for him but for his family which for so long has been part of his family. There will be a great void there now but their consolation is that as one holy man said the dead go more further from us than God and he is very near or as another holy man said life is not an end but a beginning of a greater life. Ar dheis dei to raibh a anam uasal go deo, as the saying in Irish goes ni bheidh a letheid ann aris, his likes will not be seen again. One can say that of every person for each person born is unique, but some like Donie are more unique than others.

EPILOGUE

Tying up the Loose Ends

ONCE THE SADDEST ASPECT OF OUR TALE HAD BEEN CONCLUDED, THE funeral for Donie shortly after the scene of one of his greatest triumphs, all the loose ends of the case were tied up, Jerry and Deirdre and the kids headed back down south, where Dee continued her lecturing on Post Postmodernism and Jerry composed a new book on his Reek adventure with a special postscript tribute to Donie Deverly.

Nelly went back to the house in Dublin. Terry and Sally are still together and there were talks of marriage when they are both a little more mature; "we'll be married long enough so why rush into it until we are sure it will last", a wiser attitude than marry in haste and rue it at your ease.

By contrast Molly had of course to break with Billy who had come out of the whole affair in a bad light there was no future for her there. They still hoped against hope that jail would be a lesson to Billy and steer him back onto the right path. All his assets were seized, except his share in the pub which Kate redeemed, in lieu of money gained by his drug activities.

Davey was let off reasonably lightly for his part in his father's death, involuntary serious body harm, concealing a felony, possession of drugs for personal use. He got a reasonably light sentence, and Maire stood by him. After his release Jerry and Dee attended their wedding, they were making up for lost time. Davey resigned his teaching job of course. Maire got him a job as porter in the hospital after his release, and he was happier in a job of reduced responsibility. Of course he had a hard time drying out from his drug habit; that took place in the famous treatment centre run by Sr.Annunciata, and the support of Maire and his family pulled him through, that and a recovery of his faith and self-affirmation and self-confidence. But his new found love was the greatest healer of all. And every summer he fulfilled his dream of foreign travel, exploring the world with his faithful fair-haired bride.

Jim, by contrast being a home bird, settled down with Noreen, and they kept their sheep, and she kept a neat house - they moved back into the homestead, and soon they had a little flock of children to roam the mountain also, on fine summer days, and chase the imaginary wisps of cloud into the dark caves of the cliff face. Jim had got a lovely sleek new collie that soon became as much part of the new family as Lilly had been for the old family. Where Danny Pat died Jim erected a little cross memorial, where he often paused to watch his sheep also, and say a prayer for the soul of his gentle father.

Nelly returned to Dublin where Molly lived with her until she met another more amenable heart throb. Sally and Terry had shacked up together in a village flat; he took over what could be salvaged on his father's legitimate business, after the creditors had been paid. His mother sold the seaside mansion, which was developed into a small hotel, and moved into a more Spartan little house in the village where she was much happier; but tired of notoriety she soon moved abroad to a treatment clinic; where she went after that treatment finished no one knows, and that's the way she wants it to be.

Fr. Manus was forced to retire but he stayed in retirement in the village and Betty stayed to look after him, stoically putting up with his increasing eccentricities and absent-minded professor habits accentuated by a touch of Altziemers. Sometimes she could be seen shepherding him home from the pub where he regularly went "to say mass", and embarrass the patrons no end; yet all still loved and respected him as a real man of God. The presbytery continued to house the Delaneys. The parish was administered from the nearby town.

A host of local people, led by Pat Delaney, who had dinted more than a few tables with banging them, began the process of sorting out the mine; indeed he got much better off due to being appointed its vice president for development. At first, however, the development committee he led found it much harder to get planning permission than the mining company had; they didn't have the same political clout. But by persevering they eventually won through, they had to camp for days in front of the planning office at one stage. They also worked manfully to raise enough money locally to get the small mine started; all the locals were given shares in it in return for some cash advances, an admirable scheme that Tim Thornton had devised. The mine, without any loss to the mountain, it was so hidden and low key, brought employment and prosperity to the village of a sustainable nature; Terry even sold some of Miley's half-finished houses to local workers who had moved to be near their work in the mine. Indeed up there recently Jerry on pilgrimage with Dee and the kids bought some nice gold-plated replicas of the pyramid mountain, tasteful replicas embossed with bold little gold shamrocks and crosses and figure of St.Patrick holding a sprig of shamrock in his hand. Indeed Pat Delaney's wife opened a little souvenir shop for selling such trinkets and some of the children helped her after school.

As for Tim Thornton, he could be seen on the TV regularly, as leader of various environmental causes from Galway to Letterkenny and the Glenties of Donegal where some company tried to introduce a fracking mine to extract gas from shale; he gave them hell until they scurried away with their tail between their legs. Indeed Jerry met him at a later date in the Painted Cow, a large Lobster before him, for he loved the local fare fresh from the sea, and his children around him putting posters for some new cause into envelopes to be posted. He had married a stout and equally enthusiastic environmentalist from Dublin 4 and the two of them were like two peas in a pod, carrying their children around in a Rambler van to every demonstration imaginable.

Kate had married her mountain man and he helped in the bar, where his honesty and good cheer made the place popular with locals and blow-ins alike. They had a lovely boy and girl, the boy with his ruddy face the spitting image of the mountain man, and the girl as pretty a picture as her mother. Billy eventually came back on parole from his prison spell a soberer but not totally reformed man. At first he worked well in the bar and kept his head down, but Kate eventually had to expel him because he was caught promoting some brothel that had been opened in a nearby town; he said brothels were the coming thing in Ireland given the present sexual climate, but Kate would have none of that and told him to promote that trade elsewhere, they didn't want the good name of the pub sullied in that way. Billy told everyone that Miley was practically running the prison that he was in, living like a lord through trading every sort or smuggled merchandise to the prisoners, including drugs; he would probably come out richer than ever. This made Jerry rethink his view that prison would in fact sober Miley up and rehabilitate him, all his remorse was obviously just a show.

As for Jerry and Dee and the kids, they went back to the peace and quiet of Ballymac a sadder and wiser family. Jerry had to re-organize his life for he had a new house also in Crossmagnier, the one left to him by his wise aunt. Their expanding family used it as a holiday home, where Jerry could take them and recreate for them the natural ideal that had healed him, a way of life that was natural, noble and free for "God is a circle whose center is everywhere and whose circumference is nowhere".

As the children grew up they took their anointed roles in life. Mairead who had always had a perceptive mind followed her mother and took her doctorate and became a third-level teacher. Conor took over the running of the farm in Crossmagnier and eventually he married and settled down in the house there with his wife Nelly Moriarty the daughter of the local doctor. What most surprised the family was Brendan. He seemed to have a practical bent as he grew up, advocating science and modern postmodern progress as the way forward. But then out of the blue, after his leaving cert, he announced to an astonished family that he wanted to follow in his father's footsteps, indeed go one step further and become a priest. He is now in that active ministry and thoroughly happy. So the whole lofty clan is alive under the mountain of all their hopes and dreams.

AUTHOR'S EPILOGUE

Indeed the day the Lofties went back to Ballymac, marked the end of their and my vain dreaming. The day they went home, when Deirdre and Jerry and the kids pulled into the little cottage in the fading twilight, I, their creator, looked around me and they had suddenly disappeared as the phantoms they always were. I found myself alone, not in front of a cottage but a large modern mansion. Then I realised, like the Diamond cottage case it had all been a dream; there was no such thing as Deirdre or the kids or Deverly. One thing is real however, there is a sacred mountain and it needs to be preserved from the ravages of modern "progress".

But this was where I live in reality, alone in a large empty house, a celibate priest, not a married deacon. Yet in an Irish twilight I see Deirdre and the kids waving to me; I created them, and I love them and they love me still; they will grow up with me as I grow old and be buried with me when I die. I see all my other characters coming and taking a bow, both the baddies and the goodies and all in between, for in the modern state of civilization in the west, or indeed in any age, this is all we can do, dream. Or by sheer power of intellect, create a totally new way of being such as Deirdre envisaged in her post postmodern lectures that she never really gave, maybe some brave soul will give them in her stead.

But it is not total goodbye to the noble and lofty Lofties. My model for the novel was Dostoevsky, with a similar mix of murder mystery, philosophy and cultural reflections as in The Brothers Kazmasarov, but I spoke of Irish not Russian culture. But if I write again it will be to create a totally new world, but the ideals will just be loftier, the dream dreamier, the Lord closer and closer to my dying heart. For to be an artist is to set out life like a starship into

the vast reams of space where true freedom of the heart and intellect
and imagination is, and where dwells the end of all our dreaming
in inexcessible light. So I end my quest with a poetic aspiration:

> Space is the only place left
> Where we're still free,
> The infinite inner space of you and me,
> The free and precious man within,
> That is our torment
> And our great and joyful being.
>
> The space of imagination without end,
> The space beyond the world's chains,
> The space of life's great immortal gains.